James Rodill

Sink by James W. Rodill
Cover, Book Design and Illustrations by James W. Rodill

The material presented in this book is strictly a fabricated and fictitious story contrived by the author displayed for entertainment only. Any views, situations, sequences, hypothesis or opinions herein are mere substance to intensify the storyline. While some of this book discusses actual places, products and environmental conditions, the plot however is not fact or based on any truth.

Cobra & Cobra LLC
ISBN-13: 978-0615929095

United States of America

Dedication

I extend boundless appreciation and gratitude to my wife, Bozena, who provided the majority of our monetary needs during my writing stint. I am aware that it took great courage to both believe in me and endure that burden. Furthermore, she persisted with patience and provided an inspirational demeanor for instilling in me that my journey had merit, that it was not a wild dream…and if it were that is where all good things begin anyway. I am forever indebted, but then, I was from the start of our marriage now twenty-eight years strong. To her I say, 'Thank you', and 'I love you,' as I did yesterday, as I will tomorrow, since the beginning and until the end. Now, to the next book we go.

Preface

Cataclysm often receives no introduction. Habitually lacking a foreboding sign, a disastrous incident can strike without warning catching everyone in its path off-guard. Although people are aware of countless life-ending threats that occur with vicious intent and devoid of notice, folks live their lives expecting bliss, and why not, widespread annihilation is rare? Moreover, a free society cannot thrive if too many people live in fear of a premature and unnatural death, imagining demise at every turn. For this reason, people ignore that potential and our country's leadership expects such, otherwise quality life would cease long before an episode of physical downfall. On the other hand, should an indication of pending tragedy present itself, do you shout it out? Well, if it's an unconfirmed hunch maybe not... but a series of tangible and chronic hazards would reasonably present a different reaction. Then, another deterrent arises. People have cried wolf so many times that our rationale has become sedate, often to the point of insensitivity. In addition, honest complainers may be branded crazy and for little reason. This plight is tough to deal with, especially for an educated mind because this trend makes it difficult for a sane individual to illuminate problems. People simply do not want to expose looming tragedy at their own expense. Nevertheless, a professional in a comprehensive field can explain tricky situations—the task is standard procedure. Of course, how does a wife react when she thinks her husband may be the one to fear? Perhaps he is the principal adversary and the source of endangering humanity. With too little time to contemplate...the genuine danger is exposed—an event more catastrophic than the United States has ever seen. Truthfully, what does one do now? There is not time to defend it...no possible way to deter it, and it is not feasible to manage millions to safety. Anyone would be confused. When you know catastrophe is coming, but others are telling you to conceal it, how do you respond? Do you secure your family and flee escaping with your lives leaving the rest to perish, even your closest friends. Do you tell everyone, though few will believe you? If they did, no doubt the pandemonium will cause deaths too. So, do you embrace the last few moments of life? It does not matter. Terrorism is alive and adapting... but will the right people believe you.

Prologue

As an ecosystems director for the Department of Environmental Protection, an ecologist and green naturalist prodigy, Sheryl is eager to protect people and their surroundings from destructive manmade progress. She is strong willed, aggressive, argumentative and to avoid being shoved aside. Typically, her personality does not cower to powerful and influential individuals. However, being married to the VP of the most deep-seated development corporation in the state of Florida presents a few challenges. Richard, in his own right is forceful and persevering, and fond of getting his way. His firm is determined to rapidly construct and advance civilization, although her job is to slow them down. This would put a strain on any marriage but when Sheryl discovers inexplicable activity endangering the State's ecological composition, and analytical data points toward Richard's company as the cause, she becomes more inquisitive which only rouses greater concerns and additional suspicions. Unexpected incidents create doubt, probable dangers produce fear, betrayal looms, contradictions raise fidelity issues, children complicate matters and when forced to engage behavior and methods never anticipated the wedded duo are cast into an abrupt sequence of events spawning larger problems. While some anxieties get resolution, facts that are more significant remain murky as vital confrontation transforms their character beyond unimaginable realms. Uncovering information becomes a requirement, but a particular discovery leads to a horrific realization, more wicked than her worst fears could have envisioned and many will feel the wrath. Is the husband responsible? What will she do? Is there time to resolve it? Is love lost? Will life and family persevere? Is running an option? When all existence nears the end, is any issue a concern? Sometimes, there is no way solve the impossible?

One

Six a.m. is a peaceful time, like many June mornings in Harmony, Florida—a city destined for recognition. Dampness from waning night remains on plant life, merging on the rims of leaves before dripping from the tip. One by one, droplets disappear into either grass or mulch soaked up by soil, or splash onto a dense plane to gather with the bulk of moisture. Atop automobiles and decks, tiny puddles await intensifying rays of sunshine to whisk them away. Their essence will gradually vaporize, only a faint stain will remain to mark their brief existence. The cycle is a mysterious process but an enduring one understood well. They will return.

In front of first light, the atmosphere is warm and a distinct mugginess sates the air. This is the beginning of a tropical paradise day in the making. Morning calmness assists the tranquil vibe, not a peep from the natural world to disrupt. Then something starts resonating. It is the gurgling of coffee brewing escaping an indoor environment—but that plays a part for constructing a great day too. Those last few drops of water siphoning through the grind is such a pleasant rumble to a java lover's ear. For many, that's the sophistication of nature beckoning sunup to accelerate. It's the lone wakeup call getting frequent attention, obedient and measurable respect. The alarm clock echoing its painful reminder not far in the distance only receives a slap every few minutes like a pestering fly.

However, perking awakens the senses, inherently without persecution and is forever welcoming. Visions of robust nutty flavor comfort the soul and provoke pleasant temperament, long before savoring the first sip. In the kitchen, the brew waits, enticing its follower's presence with addictive aroma. Neither a connoisseur nor novice has a chance against the fragrance, facilitated by a mild breeze. It enters the nook's opened window, sheer curtains gently swaying. What lies beyond that screen-protected aperture? Sunrise will reveal it.

Across the way, a stove light gleams on maple floors and marble counters, dimly illuminating the notably organized surroundings. Only the niche has an array of clutter—a briefcase, leather satchel and items flopping out of a backpack scatter it. Though this time of day is quiet in the Olson household, it will not remain so very long.

From the main entry of the house, shuffling footsteps advance. Then a hand extends around the edge of a walkway obscured by shadowy dawn—toward a switch it reaches and flips it up. In a flash, the setting shows elegant home decor, and a man stands clutching a newspaper in one hand while placing his eyeglasses on with the other. He's wearing nicely creased slacks but undone they droop, and a well-pressed business shirt though that too is open with tails and cuffs draping. He scoffs at an article on the front page and continues toward

1

the entrancing brew, tossing the disappointing read on the counter. With a mild smirk, he grabs a hanging mug, pours to fill and adds a portion of milk from the neighboring fridge. As he leans against the counter's edge sipping and sniffing the hot roast, he releases an 'ahhh' of delight. His eyes relax and apparent frustration begins fading. At least until that bedroom buzzer sounds for a third time. Perturbed with it he turns toward the bothersome noise.

"Are you getting up or did you quit your job?" he preaches.
There is no reply but he could hear covers scrunching and a thump into a pillow.

Taking another swallow he again secures the paper, makes way to the niche, slides jumble out of the way and sits—and before flipping one page he blathers once more.

"Coffee's ready, do you want me to drink yours too? Come and get your survival," he nurtures a quirky smile while listening to the movement of a body thrashing…tossing within sheets. In addition, his wacky satisfaction of urging this someone to wake only intensifies when he hears a hand slap the mattress.

Within moments, feet are striding the floor. One after another, they draggle, nearing the room with the pleasant smell. He continues grinning as a sleepy female voice unveils itself from a connecting hallway.

"I'm up, okay, are you happy?"

Then, through the entry, a petite and drowsy figure emerges with puffy eyes and messy blonde hair. Wearing a knee-length sleep shirt covered with red hearts, and displaying a childlike look of aggravation, she utters once more while avoiding eye contact with the cynical man.

"Damn Rick, could you try being nicer. Just once, is that too much to ask?" she implores with negative attitude while staggering to the last cup dangling on the mahogany stand, and commences to prepare a mixture the same as he.

"Good morning to you too Peaches," with sarcasm he flips a page in smooth style to maintain stealthy view of her movements—peeking above his read. "But I've tried that," he pokes fun. "It doesn't work. I've discovered that irritation gets better results. That's what I do; find ways to achieve objectives with the least amount of effort. You should know me by now."

"I understand you're an ass," with her back turned she mumbles under her breath, bringing the caffeinated treat to her lips…sipping gently.

"And I thought I was being cute," he answers the barely audible mockery.

"Oh you heard that," she giggles.

"Yeah I did, and I'm pretty sure that was you're intention," he exclaims while folding the paper in a manner to highlight a specific article.

"So you can hear?" she turns standing relaxed, backside rested against the counter. With one hand tucked under the opposite armpit, she holds the delightful concoction near her mouth, displaying an amused smile.

"Just fine and I can read too," he replies with sass while altogether ignoring her jovial spirit, and continues his assertive agenda. Directing the tabloid toward her vision, he taps on an editorial.

However, she remains serene, calmly enjoying her coffee.

He pays no mind to her empty posture and paraphrases aloud. "It seems you spoke to a reporter yesterday. Right here on the front of the Ocala Star-Banner, 43,000 people are waking up to ODG being accused of rapid and irresponsible installation of gas line infrastructure," piercing above the rim of lowered spectacles he states with stern expression—still she endures quiet behavior. Therefore, he brandishes a disbelieving hand gesture and grills, "Can you see this? I'm trying to show you something."

He removes his frames to show a deeper disgust.

"I can hear you. I don't need to see it," she snaps with a sudden loss of playfulness. "I don't think you're making it up and I'm pretty sure you know how to read," she thwarts his desire of discussing it, and proceeds to top off her cup during which time he keeps scowling.

Altering position to rest his cheek on the back of his hand, he dangles eyeglasses between thumb and forefinger and pauses while his blunt demeanor insists she give a particular response. Once again, she only retains a cozy stance as she sips and scans his way. So he escalates his impatient fixation, intensely staring at the carefree woman. They glare upon one another, her shifting focus on the clock, he anticipating some kind of a reaction.

"Alright, what has got you so worked up?" unable to hold back she complains and sits across from him.

He sneers, feeling that her response was inadequate. "You seem to be biting your tongue. What are you covering up? Your name isn't attached to it," he persists with an offensive, "but I get the tricky suspicion you had everything to do with this commentary. Come on Sheryl, when are you going to let up?"

Her eyes widen as his closing judgment absorbs her self-control. "Ease off," she hisses, and continues with brash conduct, becoming confrontational using wild hand gestures. "Surrender you mean. You want me to give up. Stop doing what I've been trained to do, what I'm good at and what I believe in. Are you going to stop building—discontinue sucking up the environment and what about me and the kids? Are we going to get five minutes with the noble developer, the prize of forward movement? Is there a place for us within a thousand miles of your big dream?"

Pointing at him with disrespect, she persists, "and I can tell you, there are at least a dozen environmentalists contacting the paper every day, complaining about Olson Development Group. What makes you so sure it was me"?

Richard is temporarily shocked, but counters. "Right," he lashes, "and all of them have the inside information that you do."

Sheryl returns an astonished expression. "Privileged? You're saying I somehow get something special from you. Everything I learn comes from the same sources that everyone else accesses. I'm lucky if you tell me when you'll be home for dinner."

"Like you cook—microwavable trays aren't exactly family-time meals and you're gone as much as I am," he waves a hand.

"Don't start with the… 'I'm not a good mother crap again'."

"You know what I mean."

"No…no I don't Rick, what do you mean? Are you telling me you don't like coming home because there isn't a four course meal waiting for you, or that you can't because of…?" she hesitates and looks away.

"Because of what, Sheryl," he reacts with a touchy insulted arrogance. "Go ahead, finish?"

"It doesn't matter," she pines and backs away from the quip, but displays a perturbed head shake while doing so. Lifting arms off the table she adjusts thought and downgrades character. "We're getting off track. I'm just concerned that your company is causing irreversible damage, and I think it's happening faster than projected."

"So, it was you," Rick's hands raise and eyebrows flare. "You are behind this crap."

"No, it wasn't me. I had nothing to do with it," she returns fire, slapping a hand on the table. "But I would if I had the chance…so you can be pissed anyway. Does that make you feel better? We both know you're not going to believe a word I say."

Inside a few minutes, the two were exchanging verbal strikes like foes, volatile and loud. Solid glares wavered and snide remarks flew like misdirected darts. He's acting like a recipient of deception, pointing his fingertip like a stern father scolding children and she swings an arm with every shaped remark. Engaged in a battle of wit and words, neither retracts from their opinions.

They exchange off topic views, side-step sensitive matters, bring up old news and dance around underlying issues until she had enough. She's never one to give in, but with Rick, usually the first to let go of the internal struggle stemming from the endless wrath that their professional and personal disagreements trigger.

Releasing a mild sigh of defeated hope, she looks away with disappointment and wants to clash no more.

Sensing her weakened state and dislike for turmoil, Rick as well lessens intolerance. He has experience with this part of the argument—the grief he has caused. He lowers his hand to the table only inches from hers and prepares for gentle contact, apparently with a complete change of heart. Now admiring her beauty, he moves toward her but with caution, first touching the wedding ring upon her finger. He's skilled in commencing emotional repair.

She's avoiding his interest, eyes closed with head resting in hand, elbow propped. Taking a necessary break, she soothes her mental state before reengaging conflict.

He lets out a quieting breath as well, reducing his posture several steps from the hard-hitting complainer he was moments earlier. His intimidating gaze replaced with love while grazing a touch along the top of her hand. His mouth starts to whisper, moving yet closer he enriches affectionate sentiment. With an intense series of rebuttals and confutation now out of mind, he nears to embrace the disgruntled woman. Reaching for the caressing clinch, surely to turn ambiance from argumentative to contrite he initiates.

"Seriously…!" a young girl's voice shrieks. Wearing short-shorts and a sleeveless tee, a long brown-haired person enters the kitchen, streaming with contempt. She continues ranting while grabbing a fix of caffeine in a jiff, but making it like mocha and with extra sugar and cream. "This is why I don't want to be around you guys. The bickering is bad enough at home but totally embarrassing anywhere else. Just kill yourselves and end the tragic romance already. Has it been like this the entire eighteen years? Every conversation you have goes the same way. 'Fight, argue, make up. Do it all again.' Why did you even have kids?" She takes a sip with hand on hip.

"You're not to talk to us that way, what have I told you?

"Yes mom, respect your parents, but you don't have to do that with each other, is that right?" the feisty girl mouths back.

"See what you've done to her."

"Me!" Rick exclaims.

"Don't blame dad, mom. I grew up with both of you. Unfortunately, I had two depressing role models," she taunts with teenage flair. "Did you guys ever love each other or do you only act this way to make my life miserable?" Flipping a hand behind her, she departs with the mug of Joe.

"Jenny!" Rick shouts, "Come back here!"

"Let her go. She's right you know—we are letting our kids down."

"No," he counters while heading to the cupboards, opening and closing doors in search of something. "We're like every parent, working and doing the best we can. Who's going to pay for their toys? Do they think about that? College, cars, marriage—it all adds up to a huge cost. Someone has to provide it!" he squawks.

"She's talking about us Rick," Sheryl petitions, following him to the counter trying to get close. "Jenny's upset by the way we relate to each other. We're constantly bickering these days," she lectures.

While reaching for a snack he glares with another stern expression. "And why is that Sheryl—because you're always attacking what I do? How am I supposed to react to that? " Opening a granola bar he pulls away from her lose grasp and returns to his coffee and paper.

She crosses her arms and assumes an annoyed stance, staring into nowhere and shaking her head.

"Have you lost something for us?" she murmurs. "Are we…am I important to you?" Returning to the table in a gruff, she places both palms on the table, firmly supporting her attitude. Slanting her head a bit to get that perfect position between him and the newspaper she continues, "I need to know—if you had to make a choice, what would it be? Us…? Your job…?" she heightens tone, "Me! The kids! Would you choose this house and your family or your career?"

Planted in front of him she demands answers, but has to wait. He needs to swallow a bite of snack to reply. She rolls her eyes in observation of his slow and methodical chew, an obvious attempt to focus on anything but her. Still she holds, not willing to move from his personal space until getting what she wants. This will not be their last stare down but it's a tense one. Grit and fury oozes from her pores but calm escape is on his mind. The outcome of this early battle is crucial for the ones certain to follow. In her mind, any response from the cold spouse will give her the argumentative edge. Grinning, she anticipates victory.

'Ring, ring, ring,' Rick's cell phone jangles.
"Great!" briskly backing away she bellows. "There's the world cutting in. Go get em', tiger. Build away." With the phone still humming, she too grabs her cup and walks away while brandishing a 'whatever' hand-flick high in the air. "I'll see you tonight. Maybe I'll even have real food," she disappears with her derisive remark fading.

Ignoring his wife, Rick opens his cell. "Yeah, what is it?"
He listens and quickly becomes concerned.
"I didn't need this," he rumbles, "not today. Have you read the paper?"
He heeds.
"You're sure?" he pauses. "You better be right," he warns to another break.
"Alright, alright, I'll be there as soon as I can."

The call ends with Rick lending a restrained sigh; he looks toward his wife's direction, and then lowers his head in frustration.

Two

Half-dressed and sloped at the kitchen alcove, Richard soaks in the beautiful countryside now visible. He is alone in thought when the bedroom TV turns on—hometown news engaged in topic. The volume is up and the gist carries easily, naturally, he listens to the commentary.

"In local news, another instance of sinkhole mystery continues to baffle residents," a female voice updates. "Lake Marsha completely dried up sometime last night. Environmental agencies, though worried, promise to get answers."

Sheryl shouts, "Here we go again Rick, turn on your TV!"

He grunts and motions a 'shoot me in the head' gesture, but grabs for the misplaced remote anyway. Once located amid tabletop clutter he proceeds to watch the kitchen set, suspended from the corner ceiling, angled perfectly to allow seamless viewing pleasure. He listens as the flat screen mirrors the same newsflash.

"The sudden large cavity, absent of liquid and marine life, sits in the center of Orange Tree community, Orlando, only a stone's throw from Universal Studios."

Richard moans.

"The Department of Environmental Protection is being sought for an explanation of the episode, the first to arise within a neighborhood."

Richard shakes his head.

"Disappearing water seems to be a new trend. Two remote lakes emptied last week—no cause issued so there's little belief the DEP will have a reason for this one. However, Sheryl Olson, one spokesperson for the ambiguous agency gave an informal statement several days ago. 'They're just relieved that the events were secluded and didn't cause injury,' further adding, 'According to their sources', ongoing construction may have a role."

Richard is stunned, but his negative reaction ceases as Sheryl leans through a doorway. He did not want her to see him.

"Do you see what you force me to deal with?" she quips.

The bulletin continues.

"But will they change their attitude, now that these incidents have moved into populated territory? Are we watching something more hazardous unfold or is Mother Nature simply expanding her reach?" the news anchor challenges.

Sheryl reenters the kitchen waving her hands in the air. "This is what my day will be like, thanks to you," she remarks. "Reporters hound me non-stop as it is," standing brazen in full-view trying to get his interest she squeaks.

"But I don't have anything to do with this," he defends and returns his sight to the tube.

It is apparent that his suspicious indifference is bothering her, but decides to continue watching from the kitchen where she stood.

"Our reporter is on the scene with one local man who saw it first," the broadcaster continues, "Rhonda, good morning. I see the sun is helping to shed light on conditions. Who is with you?"

"Thank you, Katie. I'm here with Mr. Robinson, standing in his backyard, who is quite beside himself. He woke to something he never thought would happen and yes, daybreak allows us to see the fuss first hand. Tell us sir, what did you do this morning?" The attractive young woman asks, extending a microphone toward him.

"Well," an unsteady elder voice replies. "I got up like I always do, for the past forty years anyway, before the sun comes up. I go outside with my coffee to watch it rise over the lake. That is a wonderful sight you know—one of nature's marvels, but it just wasn't there. The lake I mean…it was gone and stuff was cluttered up in one spot at the bottom, like a bathtub drain would do," he explains in soft words.

"I should point out," Rhonda looks at the camera and then back at the elder man, placing a hand atop his feeble shoulder. "Mr. Robinson has lived at Lake Marsha most of his life, which is now a vast open pit. Our cameraman will pan around," she indicates while walking closer to the hollow.

She instructs the crew to get visual of the spectacle for the viewers at home. "Clearly, you can see there just isn't any water left," she explains. "Only a few dead fish remain, and this neighborhood is shocked."

Returning to the homeowner, she questions further, "Do you have anything else to say about this or to the officials investigating these strange occurrences?"

The man thinks for a second. "I hope they can get the water back," he responds. "I love to fish. That's why I moved here and bought my boat. My wife and I enjoy it. If it doesn't return, how will that affect the value of my home? And what if someone was swimming in the water? Would they get sucked away too?"

"All good questions," the reporter says.

"Katie, Mr. Robinson and I suspect every Orange Tree resident will be anticipating answers. Will they get them, and when? This is Rhonda Smith reporting live in Orange County. Katie back to you?"

As the daily report wraps up, Richard shuts the TV off while his wife stares at him with crossed arms, again waiting for some type of closure. He knows that look all too well. 'What do you have to say for yourself, huh?'

Once more, she sits to face him with her eyes fixated.

"What do you want me to say?" he lobbies with cordial hands. "I've told you, ODG isn't causing this. We're not behind it—probably nothing is. These things happen all the time, 'nature lashing out' like you've said so many times," he points at her. "How many sinkholes occur each year?" he reminds in euphoric tone and jabbers theatrically, pretending to be her. "Oh, about two-hundred or so and oh yeah—how common they are. They're a geological feature really—so unpredictable—a true phenomenon. Is that about right Sheryl? Water is always shifting land around or something like that." He taunts her by repeating her past statements.

Instead of agreeing, she merely evolves. "This is different," she attunes. "I feel there is a discrepancy—a variance from usual environmental evolution."

"What the hell does that even mean?" he refutes. "This is your field of expertise. You've been saying that since we met. Why are you so hell-bent on blaming someone now? Does there have to be personal fault or some anomalous reason for it?"

A rare moment of silence transpires between them as the two think.

Sheryl takes a deep breath.

Richard looks away.

She begins again but he interrupts.

"Again we didn't have breakfast," Richard notes. "I would have made it."

"I know. I'm sorry," she inhales. "But there's something going on. I can't put my finger on it and the confusion is driving me crazy. Is it you? I can't say," she waves a right hand. "Are we simply in a period of greater activity?" she extends both hands, palms up. "Is general construction becoming too aggressive?" the left hand goes. "Is the earth just repairing itself?" she shrugs, as her temper builds, "NO! I'm not sure, but I do know it will get worse. I can't prove that yet but…" she pauses with angst. "The media just won't stop pushing for an answer. They want explanations, and I don't have one." After directing a stream of aimless frustration, she stops.

Richard observes her for an interval, and then rises to button his shirt.

"I don't know if you're crazy or bold," he leads in, "but you'll get through this, you always do."

"That's your comforting advice," she develops a discerning frown.

"Where's Jake? He's usually 'up and at 'em,'" Richard changes the subject and begins working on his tie knot.

"There's no school today, remember," she answers without having an issue with his deflection from the topic.

"Oh yeah, it's the first day of summer recess. I did forget. That means Jake is probably at that boy's house, his friend…uh…working on the, the," he stutters so she interjects.

"The raft for Harmony's first annual contest, is that what you're trying to think of? He's been talking about it non-stop for months and his friend's name is 'Junior,'" she heckles his lack of memory. "He's probably at Buck Lake, the one in our community."

"Right, of course…that floating gismo," he pretends to recall while straightening his attire.

She gets up from the table and proceeds to the boudoir. "It appears you don't listen to your son either." Her dejected spirit projects attitude. Disrobing from her sleep shirt, she turns the corner and is out of sight.

Richard glances, void of expression, and puts on his suit jacket. However, before leaving, he takes one last gander at the newspaper and whispers. "How do these stories get out so fast?"

Meanwhile, Jake is fast at work, building his project near the water's edge at the north end of Harmony. He spent the night at Junior's since he lives right on that loch and he'll do whatever he can to get a jump on finishing that flatboat. Bringing materials to that location is easy and being on the water will enable testing their build whenever they want. Both kids desire to win the challenge and are prepared to stop at nothing to ensure they do just that—come in first. They know the main ingredient of success is having a seaworthy craft, but design and image need consideration as well. The boys have been planning and assembling for months, but now that school has let out and neither have homework to contend with, the time has come to bring their dream to fruition.

First, they review their master list and read aloud.
"Two by fours—check! Two by sixes—check. Rope, sailcloth, rudder, screws—got em."
Continuing to inspect their notes while discussing vivid strategies, the two sit amongst a pile of materials with the excitement of children waking up on Christmas morning. There is no shortage of enthusiasm between them.

Three

Richard views his Rolex, glimmering upon his wrist. The time is five till nine as he veers off I-4 taking exit 74-A to Universal Studios. Straightaway he turns once more onto a dirt road labeled, 'ODG Entry, Authorized Personnel Only, Check Point Ahead.' A short drive brings him to a wooden shack at the threshold of a construction project where a guard on the lookout recognizes the exec and waves him through immediately. In a customized brand-new Cadillac Escalade he enters, bumping along a coarse path until he approaches a group of workers huddled around an absorbing situation. At an area adequate for visual but far enough away for safety he places the vehicle in park and examines the commotion unfold.

Backhoes, bulldozers and hoisting equipment idle near the crowd with drivers anticipating instruction. In the ground, lengths of wide trenches branch-off and are filled with water. Away from the activity, muddy pickup trucks align the face of work trailers, one labeled 'Office.' A few workers are loitering in front of it wearing ODG hard hats with work gloves in hand. Near the outward tree line, held together with thick steel bands, multiple stacks of conduits lay, rugged connecting ends exposed—the large diameter of each is eye-catching. Next to them are piles of uprooted foliage, set aside to accommodate storage of materials and supplies.

While Richard is taking note of the surroundings, the crowd divides and a view of the affair opens. The crane had cables lowered into a small body of water and the operator was attentive to the foreman's hand signal. Several workers wearing rubber boots and wet-gear are head-to-toe covered in muck while kneeling to feel the inside edge. However, it was the man in a safety harness, suspended by the rig, which elevated Richard's frustration. The worker, lowered into the pool, was dipping and disappearing for periods apparently searching, and the attached crane lines ensured he did not drown. Closer observation revealed that the lagoon was widening and portions of excavated channel were collapsing too. His dissatisfaction grew watching employees point and glare at the disturbance without care, stepping back as the sides gave way. Others chattered unclear suggestions aloud, over one another and out of turn, heightening the overall tumult. The unsafe condition is causing confusion and the remedy is obviously unclear. Richard also perceives unauthorized individuals moseying in for a better look. The squabble was drawing greater attention and he became more displeased with each shake of his head. After a final snuffle, he rolls the driver window down to better eyeball the mob.

"Carl! What in the hell is going on? " he shouts, causing several to turn but the intended recipient began separating from the pack. Richard could hear faint comments emanating.

"Better watch out, the sheriff's in town."

"Don't get any dirt on the boss's shiny new ride."

Numerous chuckles circulated as the supervisor wearing tan work boots, blue jeans and a black polo shirt with the company name embroidered above the left breast pocket removed his hard hat, placing it under his port arm. He runs a hand through his hair and turns to rejoinder. "Don't stop till you find it, or I'll have all your asses."

He continues to the truck. "Hey boss, I'm glad you finally joined the show," in Southern drawl and mild sarcasm, he addresses Richard. "Why don't you step out for a better look?"

"No way you mudfish," Richard larks with a silly smile. "That's your job. I'm not getting filthy."

They both laugh and shake hands through the opened window.

Richard is quick to speak his mind, "Carl, you said this one would be easy to contain."

"Yeah, well about that," the nervy chap stammers and bends to rest hands atop the car door. "It seems this one is bigger, faster—definitely not a seven or an eight like I thought."

"Like what then?" Richard presses."

Carl hesitates, "Maybe a five or a four."

Richard gasps, "What?"

"Well, probably closer to five," he quickly refines. "Low five anyway. I mean—this isn't easy to classify. They don't have flow meters for these things you know," he picks up momentum. "Right now I'm dealing with finding the hole so I can get pictures, evidence of what blew it out. Then I can seal it up."

Suddenly Carl changes gears. "Can you get John out here with his plaything?" he asks.

"That ain't a toy," Richard disputes. "Besides, he'll take too long to get here. Half of the site will be washed away by the time that task is completed." Then his annoyance bolsters, "Dude, are you freaking nuts? You guys are working in an expanding sinkhole."

"Boss, you remember what this is like."

"Yeah, I do, but Carl things are different now. The damn media jumps all over these mishaps. Every one of them makes front-page news. And then the EPA, DEP and every other three letter organization protects their butts and guess how they do that?"

Carl jokes, "By crapin' on us."

"Go ahead, laugh it off," Richard lashes. "But you'll be the first to get the boot if this doesn't get fixed…and another thing, everyone at that hole is in danger. The equipment too—by the way is adding ten tons of weight above unstable—what if the ground gives way?"

"Yeah, I'm aware." Carl confesses.

"You're supposed to be in charge, leading by example," Richard reminds in harsh tone, pressing a stern grip to the glum man's forearm. "Get non-essential personnel away. Give them something else to do and for God's sake get that person out of there. You know what I'm saying," Richard thumps him on the hand.

"I do, but it's not gushing too much yet."

"Carl, you could be in a four about to become a three, maybe it hasn't completely blown through yet. You said yourself you don't know. Heaven forbid somebody gets drawn-in and killed. What if you're sitting on an aquifer flowing like a 'one' and it takes out the entire crew. Just plug it up okay. Don't make me ask again. This is already an order."

"Ten-four boss," Carl concedes.

"Get a few dump trucks down here—rocks, gravel, sand, fast setting concrete—and keep pouring it in until it's filled. Get it done. Block off the area, don't let anyone else in and get it done, in an hour!" Richard further instructs.

"But we'll have to reroute the pipeline."

"Then that's what you do. The lost time isn't as bad as staying the course if this blunder reaches the airwaves."

Carl stands up, nods his head with understanding, but has difficulty with the notion as he waves a hand at nothing, "Rick, there ain't no one down here."

"Eyes are everywhere," Richard corrects while looking beyond the car windows, and then back at Carl. "I know it seems like we're out of sight. Sure, there hasn't been much activity in this park's south end and since I've been dealing with Disney, only containers and equipment have resided here. That's why the organization requested we put a hub in it…but guess what? On the other side of Turkey Lake Road," Richard indicates toward his left with a quick point, "is a subdivision and over there is Universal Studios, the actual theme park— just up Adventure Way," he emphasizes to the right. "Anyone can happen along and trust me, they will if a story is to be had. My neighbors are even paying attention to the work we're doing here, closely I might add," Richard touts but Carl still seems unconvinced.

"Did you catch the news this morning?" Richard lowers his voice.

Carl shakes his head no, lacking a verbal reply.

"In that very housing community, right over there," again designating the same neighborhood, "is Lake Marsha, or should I say, 'used to be'," Richard raises his voice. "The thing dried up last night Carl! The water is gone, all of it—only a few rotting fish are left. Worse than that, a cute TV journalist flaunted a sweet old man complaining that he can't catch them any longer. He and his wife are miserable along with every other resident, and their property values are going to plunge."

Carl, surprised by the unexpected comment assumes an impulsive posture holding both hands up, "Whoa, whoa Richard, just hold on a minute," he begins with a defensive.

However, Richard suppresses him. "Relax. I know you guys had nothing to do with it," he eases the man's mind. "I just want you to know what reporters are saying. This debacle happened much later but can you see how it will look if this mess gets out? We'll be held accountable for the distress and financial woes of an entire community, and there's no way our deep pockets can avoid it."

"I'll get it filled in," Carl exhales.

"Carl, we're about to store the largest quantity of natural gas ever attempted, right here. Friggin lines stem from this spot in fifty directions. If there's a leak, another sinkhole, or any other negative event bringing the wrong attention to this site—I'll be making excuses and changing personnel for the duration of the project. Do you know what that means?"

"I see your point. I always do. Just get the hell out of here and let me get to fixin it. Go do your VP crud, project manager stuff or whatever nonsense office people do."

"I work Carl. It keeps you getting paid," Richard sneers with a burdened smile.

"Sure you do," he grumbles. "Now unless you're gonna get dirty; go on out of here before we drag your ass in," Carl laughs. "Remember 08'."

"You don't need to remind me," Richard reddens. "The pictures are on the office wall."

"We've been friends along time, huh."

"Yeah, too long..."

For a few moments, they share a chuckle about an old memory. Then the affair at hand regains focus. Carl puts on his hardhat and begins back to calamity and Richard starts pulling away.

Just then, Carl turns. "Hey boss," he calls out.

Richard stops the vehicle. "Yeah... What?" he pops his head out of the window?

"If we didn't cause that lake to dry up, what did?"

Richard didn't answer right away. Instead, he contemplated the idea and then shrugged shoulders. Finally, with raised brows, he forms a dazed look and in one unsure exhale, he offers, "I don't know." Then waves and drives away.

Carl salutes too as his boss and friend departs.

Carl wonders for a moment, but then turns his gaze upon the ongoing tragedy, and then to the lake of mystery. He has worried thoughts on his mind and his external stance seems suspect, but the transformed leader returns to the incident furnishing a mild head shake with hands extended from his sides.

"Why do I always get myself into these things?" he mumbles stepping up to his crew who were impatiently waiting for an update.

"Get out! Let's go," he and issues a loud directive. "Change of plans."

As with any new order, there are always groans of disapproval and this command produced no exception.

"What now?"

"We almost got it figured out."

"Oh, come on!"

In the distance a few wandering complaints are voiced over one another but to no avail. The team disbands and regroups for new instructions.

Four

Richard, absorbed by thick and tense driving conditions, rubs his forehead and notes the time as if another thought is gnawing at him.

Sheryl however, had arrived to her workplace.

Walking to a building resembling a strip mall with purse and satchel held awkwardly in one hand and a clutter of documents flopping out of the other, she displays a confident and professional posture nonetheless. With a quick yank, she swings the main door open, pushes it further with a foot and then bounces it off her backside to enter, move past and march on. Sporting an average pair of department store slacks and an outdoorsy short-sleeved blouse, she isn't the fashionable executive that her husband portrays. Her hair is pinned up too as if in a hurry, because she was.

Straightaway, a man donning worn loafers and wrinkly clothes under a loose fitting lab coat greets her—in need of grooming too. Pushing overgrown bangs from his eyeglasses to gain a clearer view, he holds up a clipboard teeming with papers while jostling them much too close to her face. Sheryl has to back away to avoid bumping in to them, but she proceeds walking nonetheless.

Matching her brisk pace he launches the nutty professor ambush, "Where have you been?" he blurts. "I've been staring at these reports for the last hour and the phone hasn't stopped ringing since the news broke."

Then he goes into ranting messages as they walk, 'What are we doing about the lake? Where did the water go? Is it coming back? What causes that to happen? Are there going to be more? Who's in charge? Why haven't we issued a formal statement? Who's running this investigation?' "And that's not the half of it," he yelps. "I don't know how long I can hold them off," he concludes to a pause while noticing her lack of attention. "Are you listening to me? What am I to tell them?"

"Jeff, haven't I told you to get a life," she stops striding to deliver a stoic look. "That's the way the media is, deal with it. You're acting crazy. You know," she breaks for an energizing inhale, "most of my days begin way too fast, but right now I feel like a racehorse being slapped out of the start gate."

Shifting papers to her overburdened hand, she snatches his report with the empty one. Then, turning her vision forward, she kicks open another door and treads into a test center where a few startled employees look up from their work.

With Jeff trailing, she conveys further judgment.

"You really need to go home once in a while. Shave, change your clothes and for Chrissakes take a shower. Get a cat, something to give you reason to forget that I'm the only thing you have to live for."

"I'm clean," he replies while smelling himself. "And this is what it looks like when someone," he heightens tone to blast her, "grows a beard!"

He trots to catch up. "It's just taking longer than expected—and I don't like animals," he confirms with absolute conviction. "They eat incessantly, leave hair everywhere and are much too clingy."

Astonished with his remark she comes to an abrupt halt, half cocks her head like a confused dog and squints at him with the corner of her lip raised, "Really! Did you just say that?" she jabs. "Do you see a resemblance here?" she mocks while motioning the clipboard back and forth between them.

"No, why, should I?" with a puzzled appearance he retorts, unaware of the similar dependency that he has developed with her?

Charmed by his toddler like mentality, she simply returns a reverent smile.

"Hey. Jeff!" a man's voice rebounds, entering from the other end of the room.

Sheryl plops her stuff on a desk while keeping a sneaky eye on the joining party.

"Sheryl this is Arnold," Jeff announces. "Arnold this is Sheryl," Jeff smiles making the introduction complete.

In an aloof manner she asks, "Do I know you?"

"This is the new guy," Jeff explains while placing a hand atop his shoulder. "He's the geologist Wynyard hired. You know, to help, with...recent events," he stammers for the right words, but recovers. "He was here before I opened up."

"Ah, an early riser," Sheryl notes while positioning a leather chair. However, her attitude suddenly shifts. She places a hand on hip and displays a curious aura.

"Events!" she states with pessimism. "That's what we're calling them now?" she continues with deliberate hesitation, "not disasters...tragedies...or...I don't know...corporate blunders."

Jeff, stunned by her tone in the presence of a new hire, can only express confusion.

Arnold gives Jeff a similar look.

"Whatever!" she blurts, changes mood and extends for a shake. "What did you say's your name is? And for the record...no one gets here before nine, except Jeff?" she tosses in valuable information.

"Uh, I didn't... but it's... Arnold," he greets though faltering words—but does provide a firm grip.

As they release cordial formality, she continues jesting, but perhaps a bit too much. "Is that Arnold as in the pig from 'Green Acres' or like the cheating swine 'Schwarzenegger?'" she glares for an answer.

Caught off guard he could not speak.

"Personally I think the first one is more adorable and a much better listener but who am I to judge," she persists.

At this point the new guy is perplexed by her calculated sarcasm and isn't sure what to say. He's searching his brain for the right response while looking to Jeff for help.

"Don't mind her," Jeff steps in to save the overwhelmed chap. "She's having a few issues with her husband and instead of taking it up with him, she lashes out on the most vulnerable male she can find."

"Lucky me—like every woman I dated," Arnold comes back with a cynical shot of his own. He's beginning to blend in with their mentality.

Sheryl is amused with his retort and smiles, releasing a pleasant chortle.

"I'm sorry, let's start over," she exhales and sits to ruffle through Jeff's report. Arnold and Jeff remain at attention to the front of her desk.

"I'm not usually like this but as much as I hate to admit it, Jeff's right. I do have a few concerns, but I'll get over them." Taking a pause from the research data, she glances up. "Stop standing there like that," she references their sturdy stance with a flick. "You're making me nervous. This isn't the principal's office. Pull some chairs up…we're not in high school," she imparts an order and naturally, they quickly grab an empty seat from a nearby cubicle.

Over the next few minutes, she and Jeff opened up, entertaining warm discussion, spontaneous storytelling, genuine dialog, good-humored debate, cute 'off-the-cuff' observation and each other's craziest experiences. Once social interaction kicked in, the awkward start was history. The well-groomed man seemed to fit in just fine. Of course, Sheryl had to end with the 'Do's and Don'ts' within the department and cover her expectations along with pertinent information such as, 'who to evade,' 'what to sidestep' and 'how to properly face the actual work.' However, once the employment details were covered, the spirit changed.

"Okay guys, time for business," Sheryl moves into topic. "Specifically…to dissect today's agenda, and it's an amplified one. Arnold, I'm throwing you in rather quickly, but there isn't time to back up and replay every scandalous media episode. Are you ready to jump in?" Sheryl dramatizes the invitation by jiggling Jeff's clipboard.

Eyes wait for Arnold to confirm, and he does with a positive nod.

Jeff gives him an encouraging pat on the back as they lean over Sheryl's desk.

Across from them, she rolls up her sleeves by assuming a more authoritative bearing. "Great!" she accepts and reels into action, "Jeff has information which I obviously haven't read or had time to analyze but in a nut shell, we've been experiencing increased natural activities throughout central Florida.

"What does that mean?" Arnold asks. "Natural sounds like normal."

Sheryl skirts a shifty look toward Jeff and illuminates, "sinkholes have occurred more than usual, 'sinks' as we say."

Jeff points out, "typical land erosion, busted water mains and construction are the most common cause… usual environmental behavior."

"Except…they're happening at an alarming rate," Sheryl tweaks Jeff's impression with careful objection, while giving him a concealed dirty look.

"And some lakes have disappeared…more frequently than we like and that is very curious too," She adds.

"What do you mean?" Arnold digs.

"Well, the water that was in them…just isn't there anymore," Jeff interjects with sass, drawing both of them to glimpse at him. "We'll…that's what it means," he bolsters, and directs Sheryl to continue with a gesture.

"Worse yet…" she resumes. "Hazardous chemicals and carcinogenic compounds have been found in neighborhood lakes which threatens wildlife."

"Humans too…" Jeff squeezes in. "My water samples reveal that something more than fishy is going on…if you know what I mean."

He receives another inquisitive stare.

"Right…" Sheryl stumbles. "And for the ones that dried up, we still don't know where the water went."

"Where it has been re-routed," Jeff cuts in again. "There have been breaches in the aquitard, an impermeable…,"

However, before he can finish explaining, Arnold interrupts him.

"I'm familiar with the term. My career hasn't dealt with the water aspect like yours, but I know your speaking of a barrier between two bodies of water. A zone comprised of layers of either clay or non-porous rock with low hydraulic conductivity that restricts the drift of groundwater…basically preventing the two from flowing into each other."

"Right…!" Jeff bursts with surprise. "You got the right guy," he happily confesses while eyeing Sheryl.

Immediately, Arnold forms a perplexed guise in observance of Jeff's remark, but refocuses on the subject—Jeff stutters back into explanation.

"But…in this case…we're talking about tunnels of water," he taps Arnold on the arm to get his complete attention, "flooding from one aquifer into another instead of water that's just sitting there—more dangerous when it's is gushing," he emphasizes. "Which brings me to their magnitude, a scale used to identify the volume of water they carry, some aquifers have very rapid currents. The problem is, sometimes the walls weaken and collapse, or disintegrate from manmade activity like drilling or excavating and then…" he pauses to let Sheryl speak.

"You see," she resumes. "There are many of these fresh water corridors beneath Florida's sandy surface—as with other areas across the U.S…but this State, by far, has the most abundant aquifer arrangement in the world. As such, many sinks have formed and then kept full with active springs—hence most of our ponds and lakes. Unfortunately, once inside them, toxic substances have nowhere else to go, but to and fro via these underwater shafts. Like traveling through a garden hose, they can be carried great distances without diversion. Where they originate or go to is virtually impossible to know. Then, there's another problem. A reservoir can disappear when a supply line blows out."

"Because the water exiting a pond is flowing faster than what's filling it," Arnold injects.

"Right, it siphons off," Jeff concludes.

Then Arnold changes dynamics. "I understand," he acknowledges with a raised hand, "I really do. Water is the constant force that shifts landmass and stuff happens, but erosion has been ongoing forever. The Indians gave changing land features names long before we arrived. Most have some great significance…at least they once meant something," he jokes and receives a slight chuckle, and then continues. "I know hundreds of sinkholes occur each year and they make Florida what it is, but what I don't get is why this agency needs a geologist from the Midwest. As I said, 'water is not my thing.' That's your gig," he finishes with a loose toss of the hand.

For a moment, silence permeates the air.

Arnold glances at them and notices, they are only fixed on each other.

Jeff lends a slight shoulder shrug.

Sheryl gives shifty eyes and smirks.

Arnold reclines further in his chair, observing a period longer.

Jeff gives a slight nod. Then, he follows with a subtle hand gesture and another peculiar head bob, as if compelling her to respond.

"Alright, what's going on?" Arnold requests in stern tone while eyeing both of them. "You both look like you ate a canary," he flares, planting both forearms upon the desk—his face consumed with dramatic expression.

A few more quiet moments pass. Then, Sheryl takes a deep breath.

Five

"Your fascination is with earthquakes, right?" Sheryl probes Arnold's background. "Studying what encourages them, what influences their strength, increases their frequency, what brings them on and what makes them tick so to speak. I mean...that's what your good at, am I correct?" she leans over her desk to look at him more closely.

He only stares back without giving a reply—his expression is lifeless.

"Your experience is in seismic activity, isn't it?" Jeff adds. "Is that your line of work or not?" he persists, his face nearing closer to Arnold's.

Both Sheryl and Jeff lean to hear his answer.

Arnold eases away and issues a hectored chuckle.

"What's so funny?" Jeff throws up hands.

Then, with sincere expression, Arnold responds. "Earthquakes don't happen here."

Promptly, Jeff puts his head in hands and exhales, dismayed with Arnold.

However, Sheryl rises to the occasion, as if seizing an opportunity. "Oh contraire," she is quick to respond while brandishing a finger pointed north. "There have been about thirty-three such episodes in this State over the last two hundred and fifty years, some of the worst in the eighteen century. Seismic activities reached six or so magnitude, and a similar quake happened about thirty-five years ago. Yes, they are rare but they do happen. Usually in northern regions like St. Augustine for example," she reclines with a triumphant smile.

Arnold appears shocked. "I stand corrected," he admits.

"I thought you knew this stuff," Jeff jabs.

"Yeah...in Utah," he declares.

Jeff shakes his head.

Sheryl sits back. "Listen...you're a quakes dude. You understand terrain, the ground, the earth. That's why I requested you."

"So you already knew who I was?" Arnold ogles at both of them.

They both seem quite guilty, looking down as if ashamed.

Arnold melts into his chair with disbelief.

"Yeah, we we're messing with you," Jeff divulges as he and Sheryl have an in-house giggle.

"I was going to tell you earlier," Sheryl explains, "but we were having such a great talk. But hey," she subdues tone, "we joke all the time...sorry about the frat house indoctrination, but you're the guy I need."

Still offended, Arnold shakes his head but does change his demeanor. "Go ahead...tell me what I need to know."

"Okay good," Jeff grins. "I recorded tremors, mostly of minimal intensity...but a lot of them. I don't know where they originate or what's triggering them. But this is right up your alley."

"Okay, I'm paying attention."

"Well, they are sporadic, but sometimes strengthening…highly unusual."

"And like Jeff alluded…they're getting worse."

"Okay, I get it…but what can I do?"

"Research, investigate…and if at all possible, determine the cause," she suggests.

Jeff gets ready to go a little deeper into the subject and Sheryl can sense it. She becomes noticeably reserved.

"We have reason to believe a construction company is causing most of it," Jeff states, "but they possess a lot of money and power…needless to say—they have teams of ambitious attorneys too and they're linked-up in the political structure. ODG is popular and integrated into corporate structures everywhere.

"Who…?"

"Olson Development Group…thee foremost developer in Florida's history," Jeff informs with dramatic tone. "They own everyone." Then he begins prattling again, "but we really don't know if they have any involvement or not and…since Sheryl is hitched to the main guy well, that makes investigating them even more difficult. We have to be…careful, you know how we… go about uncovering the facts and then…disclosing that information isn't any easier."

"Whoa…wait a minute," Arnold retorts.

By this time, Sheryl is edgy. With her eyes rolled back, lips drawn into her mouth and clamped together, she winces while veering away. She feels a dreadful moment approaching—one that she knew would come…eventually.

"Let me guess," Arnold now inclines toward her. "Not only do you not have proof that this magnificent company is doing anything wrong…but your husband also works for them, which places you in an awkward situation…rather, it puts you in a compromising position. Oh yeah!" his voice escalates, "and you two argue constantly."

She delivers him a scrutinizing gaze, as he persists with words that strike more nerve.

"He won't listen to you… you don't understand him. So asking in-depth questions about his company's practices is no longer an option, especially ones regarding comprehensive destruction of the environment. Am I getting warm?" he rhetorically blasts.

Her eyebrows rise, but she doesn't stop him as he continues raving. "So his actual wife…named Sheryl, with the DEP who is merely trying to protect the environment…but is on opposing sides of this construction leader…'SIMPLY' needs me to fill in the small but dangerous gaps. Is that about right?" he exhales with bold character.

Jeff is hinging on his next word.

A couple moments pass. She begins to respond, but gets cuts off.

"No, no, no…don't tell me," Arnold carries on. "I get it. You need an unbiased source to prod, pry and probe for the evidence needed to bring down a corporate giant…who I might add, has connections at every significant level. Oh…somebody on the outside that can be, I dare say…'thrown to the wolves' if the investigation falls apart or causes irreprehensible damage to the firm's integrity."

"Wowww," Jeff utters slowly, astonishment. "This guy is good. I can see why you wanted him. He's got you nailed and he hasn't spent two hours with you.

Sheryl delivers a fickle grin.

Jeff humorously asks, "Are you using some kind of telepathy?"

"Shut up Jeff!" Sheryl comes alive. "It's not like that…" she stumbles, "well, somewhat it is but…"

"What she's trying to say is that her husband actually owns the whole darn company," Jeff blurts.

Sheryl rolls her eyes.

"Oh great," Arnold scoffs. "That relieves so much tension."

Sheryl quickly tries to put a Band-Aid on this situation, "No, it doesn't help. I know that," she places a hand on his forearm and continues with a thoughtful tone. "But yes, on most counts. You got me figured out, except… I'll be eaten by the press not you. I take full responsibility for whatever happens. You're not a fall guy," she expresses in earnest character. "If everything blows, the department will come down on me, and probably pretty hard too…along with the media and whoever else can jump on board. In any case, my husband won't doubt that I was behind it. I assure you, you need not worry. Truthfully…honestly, you're not here to be my scapegoat."

"That's true. She wouldn't do that," Jeff corroborates with negative head gyrations.

Arnold is not yet convinced.

"Trust me. I need expert help, an individual sanctioned to make certain calls…and that's you. Being that I'm the vice president's wife and daughter-in-law to the president, I can't issue any of my own findings for obvious reasons."

"His father is the other half of the company," Jeff throws in a half-choked blurt just to clarify.

"Yeah, I picked up on that," Arnold lets Jeff know he already figured that out. "Sure, why not?" he fakes a laugh and shakes his head. "When does the family judge come into the picture, or the brother-in-law prosecutor? Are you related to the Sheriff too?"

Jeff stands, "hey let me tell you about this lady. All joking aside, she has never thrown anyone under the bus. And believe me there were times when I deserved it," he delivers complete candor. "She takes on more aggravation than anyone I've ever met. Oh sure…" he develops a crass demeanor, "she complains about each and everything that happens, constantly bitches about the enormous barrage of information that she has to handle, whines that deciphering unspecified facts is a huge burden…and she's appalled at working in harsh conditions with archaic equipment, hates bullshit company parameters…" his tone worsens. "Argues that my help is never good enough, verbally trashes me if I..."

"Whoa!" Sheryl steps in waving a hand. "I thought you were on my side. That's enough of the wonderful assessment...please! Just pull me aside the next time your feelings get hurt," her raspy voice gets a few pitches higher.

Arnold is in wonder and changes tone. "Okay, some of that was me spouting off," he raises his voice to impart impact. "BUT THE POINT IS...she always gets through everything. She doesn't even know how she does it, but calamity is always resolved. No one gets let down and as long as she is in control, never will. Let you take blame?" he scoffs. "Not a chance. That's not how she is. I've never seen anyone like her," Jeff graciously concludes placing his hand on her shoulder.

"Thanks Jeff, that was a little better," she smirks. "Moving on though, either I am a scorned wife looking for revenge..."

"Isn't that the case?" Jeff chuckles

"Sit down Jeffrey," she snickers.

He moves quickly gesturing a 'zip my mouth.'

"As I was saying..." Sheryl persists. "The media will portray me as either a disparaged spouse out to get her husband or a wife using her influence to protect him. I'm either enabling environmental destruction or simply going after a corporate conglomerate because I'm upset. In my position, I can't win," she pauses. "Truthfully... I'm not able to give him a fair shake. I'm too close to it and besides, I'm not convinced that they are responsible. Maybe I don't want them to be guilty. Perhaps I am not using my professional judgment because I feel devotion...attachment. Anyway, he assures me that he conducts operations with care, but that's where you come in. I need you to review and research, investigate through your own means and determine the source of the vibrations and...help us with these sink disturbances."

Arnold, still on the fence, is showing intrigue.

"Also, there's something else," Jeff brings up. "I haven't identified all of the contaminants in the samples from Lake Sheen or Big Sand Lake. They're strange, some type of bio waste, hazardous malarkey beyond the usual rotting automobile engines and washing machines," he shakes his head. "You wouldn't believe the crap people throw into sinkholes. Anyway, it could be a derivative of natural gas, which is what ODG is pushing through those pipes.

The procedure is huge," Jeff sidetracks. "A lot of dirt and rock has to be displaced to get them in the ground, which may be the culprit of the tremors. Anyhow, typical petroleum and corrosive metal tests aren't matching up to what I found. So if that's not it...then what is it? Then again, it could be nothing. So many substances resemble similar analysis. My readings could be erroneous...I can't be sure without proper equipment—molecular deciphering is a bitch. I need help on that too," he concludes.

"Okay, keep working on that," Sheryl gives sound instruction. "But one way or another we either prove ODG is causing harm...or validate their methods.

There needs to be a final report... supported and documented. There, that's it. That's why you're here," she faces Arnold with sincere appearance. "Those are the facts. Are you in?" she asks with genuine, almost desperate tendency and patiently waits.

Arnold contemplates.
Jeff gives a piecing stare.

Arnold understands the overwhelming complexities should he agree to take the assignment. His decisions could have lasting consequences. For starters, either Sheryl's dilemmas will receive attention, or her plans will be defenseless. Then, there is the challenging battle with the environment and powerful corporate men.

Arnold rubs his chin while contemplating.

Sheryl slowly taps a pencil on the clipboard.

Jeff merely shifts eye contact back and forth between the two with a quirky expression, waiting for an answer with optimism.

For Sheryl, the tension appears great.

However, Arnold seems calm.

Jeff, of course, is yet different altogether as he blurts an unrelated remark, "Does anyone want to eat, I'm starved?"

Sheryl glances to the heavens, seeking help with Jeff from a higher power.

Then, in the distance, a door swings open and a man's hard-soled shoes start resonating. "Where is everyone? Hello people!" a confident male voice calls out, trekking toward them.

"Great!" Sheryl turns to Jeff. "Take Arnold to get a bite. We'll continue this later."

"Wynyard's here," in a low voice Jeff nudges Arnold, impelling him toward the door.

Six

"Hello Mr. Wynyard," Jeff greets while delivering a laid-back salutation and a blasé smile. "How was your flight?" he asks with indifference as he crosses path with the Department Secretary, nearing the lab exit.

"A bit bumpy uh..." the man stops to acknowledge. "Um, I'm sorry..." he stutters, not extending for a handshake.

"I'm Jeff sir," Jeff reminds him, slowing down to explain. "I'm Sheryl's EP specialist...the milieu geek. And this is Arnold, the new guy from Utah," he makes Arnold known but resumes his stride without formalities, as Wynyard did not seem interested.

"Right, of course," he remains perplexed as the two depart.

"Is that the guy who hired me?" Arnold asks.

"Well, let's say he signed the papers."

"He seems a little dim."

"You've got no idea," Jeff swanks on. "But, we'll talk about him later."

Arnold looks back for a glimpse at the prominently strutting dude, but Jeff presses him along.

"Milieu...really, did you actually say that?"

"It's French," Jeff notes as they hit the parking lot, doors closing behind.

Yeah, I know what it means, but I'm surprised you do," Arnold jabs.

Their voices begin dissipating... "You're going to love the hash browns at this place, they're fantastic...crispy, chewy with loads of flavor. Pepper and onions I think..."

As predicted, the incoming personality reaches Sheryl's office. Dressed like an aspiring 'GQ' hopeful and acting much like one. He poses against the doorjamb as if taking pictures for the upcoming July issue, hands in pocket with a brilliant smile.

"Mr. Wynyard, what brings you here?" she greets him with a frosty undertone while rising from her seat. Staying behind the desk, she ignores his dreamy entrance.

"I told you, call me Scotty," he urges with over-the-top sentiment. "I'm not just your boss, I'm a friend. Can't I be here to visit you?" he appeases to her emotion.

She ignores him. "You run the DEP. You're the secretary...and..." she stammers, "you can do whatever you like." Mentioning the obvious, she continues, "but you and I are colleagues, yeah—career associates. I'm merely an employee. Um, that doesn't make us friends. And I'm pretty sure you didn't come all this way just to see me, especially unannounced," she simplifies the reception while lingering in the same spot.

He enters the office, and struts yet closer.

She begins fumbling with paperwork, paying little attention to his swagger.

"Don't I deserve a better welcoming than that?" he asks, standing at her desk.

25

"No, I don't think so," she remains focused on business matters, keeping her head down.

"You know…" he breathes with inspiration, taking a delicate seat on the corner of her desk, and then leans toward her. "I seem to recall you had a different attitude at last months 'Memorial Day' festivities."

"No. Oh no—I didn't," she replies with a nervous tick—pretending to carefully inspect a document. "That's your take on it," she looks up, gaining certainty, "Now; I have a lot of work to do so…"

However, he ignores the diversion and leans to smell the scent of her drifting perfume. "You and I shared a moment. I'm sure of it," he exhales, gazing with tender eyes while enjoying the fragrance.

She becomes wide-eyed. "No, no…there was no 'thing'…I don't think so," she mumbles showing an edgy behavior. She takes another shaky breath while withdrawing from his nearness.

He grins.

She lends a fleeting peek while feeling for safer ground.

"I remember you have soft hands," he accentuates while reaching for one.

Suddenly, she moves to the opposite end of the desk, searching for yet another file to scrutinize, within an old stray stack. "These things…no…they're callous—dry and rough…see," she brandishes one for less than a brief second and promptly returns to the paper quest. "Rough, rough, rough," she rattles with incoherent indifference, and then giggles a little bit, "I work outdoors too much…you know."

"That's funny," he cites, rubbing his chin. "I recall a gentle grasp; your palms were the right kind of moist. There was sincere conversation, a couple of dances, a lot of laughing and even a bit of babbling under a moonlit sky…and your skin was supple…it smelled of lilac. Like right now," he eloquently explains.

Finally, she looks up and for the first time makes lasting eye contact with the persuasive sort, but she isn't the confident, outspoken woman before his arrival. She takes a step back with uncertain posture. "That was the alcohol talking. It doesn't take much and suddenly…me can't stop blabbing," she chatters illogically. "Gossiping…drinking…and, crazy happens," chuckling insecurely, she appears to have become somewhat naïve, like a much younger girl.

He moves around the desk to encounter her. "And the perfume…how did you know it's my favorite?"

"Bathroom soap!" she blurts, "that stuff is amazing…but it dried me out…ha."

Sheryl takes another step away and breathes erratically.

He inches yet closer. "So the kiss…that was the whiskey too?" he whispers, still drawing nearer.

She backs again…now at the front of the desk. "It was Gin," she corrects with terse punctuation. "And that was…nothing. I've done that with relatives, shhh," In a panicky tone she explains. "I mean…ugh. It's like greeting them at the door. You know how you give a really welcoming hug because you haven't seen them in a long time."

"Well you're obviously really close with family. I think that's disturbing but hey, there are intimate cousins like that. I could get used to it," he swerves her denial again, and reaches for a hug.

She pulls away, just in time, and begins kneading her hands together.

Yet he presses forward.

"Listen, Scott," abruptly she stands firm, holding a hand up like a police officer stopping traffic.

"Scotty," he requests once more, stepping into her raised palm.

"I'm not going to say that," she argues. "What happened was a mistake. I had a weak moment. I...you..." she stammers for the right words and again, steps away.

"People let vulnerability happen Sheryl," he rationalizes. "It doesn't just come about. There is a reason for it. You had intentions...and made a move but you mustn't regret it," he justifies, beseeching her passion.

He edges closer again.

"May—be I did...but," she hesitates.

"What?" he begs her to finish the thought?

"I'm married okay," she screeches. "I know I said some things... stupid jabber...and I disclosed a tad too much about my personal affairs, but I was disappointed...and venting," she tries wit as a defense, though mumbling with humor and vagueness hinders serious resistance.

He does not cease. "You're always aggravated with him. I see the unhappiness...you complain all the time."

"Yeah...I've been told I do that a lot?" she jokes while waving a pointed finger at herself.

"That should tell you something," he gestures there it is. "If you're always irritable, maybe it's not working."

"Or...I need a more positive attitude," she insists, again with humor.

"No, you're with the wrong guy," he argues. "Listen, sometimes relationships don't work out the way we hoped. Expectations let us down or people just turn out different. We transform...things change—feelings change. It's okay."

He is trying to speak honorably, while convincing her that her emotions at the company party must be justified since she has such troubles at home. Unaffected by her retreats, he simply moves his body to hers.

Ultimately, she can back away no more.

He closes in.

"Stop!" she asserts in the most assertive tone yet, forcefully pressing him away with both hands. "It's really not that bad, and this..." she implicates the current moment between them, "is not going to happen." Regaining confidence, she returns to her seat.

This time he understands—finally getting the drift.

"Anyway, it'll get better," she continues. "Family is a work in progress and occasionally it takes plenty of labor, more than just lazy effort. So I'm not giving up and…I…don't want to talk about this anymore." Declaring firm words and a stern look of sincerity, she sits.

He winces and sits at desk front with arms crossed, for once acting normal. Defeated, he inhales his first perceptive breath. "I get it," he proclaims and stands making way to the door. "You need more time."

She is stunned. Her mouth drops over his arrogance. "No…I don't need more time," she blurts.

"No, no, there is so much going on," he returns with sympathetic character. "I know you need space…so that's what I'll give you." He extends the pretense, "Just remember, I'm here if you need to talk. I can bring vodka."

He departs with a big smile and elated expression.

"It's gin," with a faint sigh she corrects a last time, but he can't hear.

While listening to his footsteps bounce off the lab walls, she stares into the vacant hall. Blank and empty she sits alone, again tapping a pencil on Jeff's clipboard. Then she nibbles at her lip and grins—an iffy gleam in her eye.

Seven

Mid-morning on a weekday in downtown Orlando is a hectic period. Stressed and frantic commuters are late to their destinations and travel in every direction is either bumper-to-bumper or moving at speeds far less than the limit allows. Roads are jam packed with personal vehicles, cargo vans and eighteen-wheelers in a hurry to meet timelines.

This city is a hotspot for businesses, but of course, theme parks are the biggest draw this time of year and there are numerous amusements, which shape the area's personality. Nothing can make the roadways as overcrowded as the relentless stream of tour buses and guide vehicles accessing these dream spots. Vacationers scurry in a gruff to see the next attraction or experience another perilous ride, and as a result, heavy traffic ensues.

While Orlando represents entertainment, trades still make it a hub for their purposes too, and Richard's corporation is no exception, but he must be wondering why. Though the drive from the Disney site to the office at the north end is short by distance, congestion makes the journey a long and frustrating one, sometimes intolerable. A simple errand within town can take hours. Like every day though, he attains the endpoint.

Upon parking his luxury truck alongside a Mercedes and other top-of-line cars, Richard gradually glides out while ending yet another phone conversation. Donning his jacket and briefcase, he admires his company logo atop the moderately sized but well-designed state-of-the-art building, and then closes the door. From the outside parking lot, he begins a stroll; first approaching the publicly acclaimed Garden of Eden vanguard. Large branchy trees, not native to Florida, provide an abundance of shade. Hardy foliage magnifies the background, plants with striking features intensify the landscape and luminous flowers overwhelm the eye. While entering, a calm breeze meets his face and he quite appreciates it after an intense drive, evident by the exhilarating breath he takes.

The center of attention is an Italian water fountain, made of fine marble. It stands within a circular pond made of the same stone containing exotic fish. Picturesque vegetation grows above, concealing the subterranean world within. From it, marine water thrusts up and then flumes down into a large bowl spewing over the sides into the pool below. Incessant trickling produces aeration and along with spraying, waves of hypnotic and mind-altering sounds permeate—wonderful waterfalls mimic nature producing a tranquil setting attracting birds, squirrels and people too. Often, they relax with a favorite book, sitting on the broad perimeter wall.

As Richard walks by, he flicks a coin in for good luck, some glimmer beneath vegetation, under the fish as they swim. Beyond he strides passing a limestone bench, then a Greek statue and an arched trellis with vines intertwined. Manicured grass and English cobblestone walkways complete the architecture, paving a way to each attribute and ultimately to the building's entrance.

The façade of his office structure is brilliant clear glass, ground to roof, allowing unblemished views from both sides. Inside the lobby, Richard treks over granite flooring, proceeding past rock infused columns while grazing a hand upon a glossy stone counter. He issues a cheerful 'good morning' to the pleasing receptionist standing behind it.

She smiles back with brief eye contact replying, "you too Mr. Olson, have a good day."

Past reception, the waiting areas are no less calming, plants abound. Natural allure of green intentions is coordinated from all corners to the focal center.

Onward, he enters a transparent elevator, crystal-clear, granting spectacular sight of atriums during flight. After a gentle climb to the fifth and final floor, Richard reaches the most superlative vantage point offering magnificent vistas, including the courtyard paradise outside. Stepping off the ride a balcony awaits—precisely situated to observe the beauty below should one desire more of the inspiration, or it also serves as a place to entertain a conversation with an ideal backdrop. Then, he continues a pleasant stint along a plush-carpeted corridor, still smelling new. Then, there it is…ODG's lair, the administrative nucleus of the construction behemoth—their motto on the wall prior to entering. 'Let's build it with care, to live in harmony.' Although the huge mahogany double doors are heavy, Richard opens them with ease and without a creaking hinge to annoy.

"Is my father here?" he asks a young girl seated inside, behind a tall and long reception desk.

"Yes sir," she replies with proper character. "He's in his office."

Richard proceeds down the hall to a door labeled, 'Eric Olson-President,' and upon grabbing the doorknob, an attractive, short-skirted woman peeking out of an office labeled, 'Richard Olson-VP,' notices his presence. Richard enters without knocking and finds a man at his desk, rather engaged on a laptop. He has short graying hair, appears established beyond his years—a well-groomed man. Clothed in a pinstriped vest, a Dior white shirt and red silk tie—his demeanor exudes success and emphasizes control.

"Come in son," he softly says in a raspy voice. "Don't let that door hold you back," he joshes. "Have a seat. Tell me, what is the matter? What's so important you had to rush in?" senior Olson closes the computer lid and reclines.

Richard sits to the front of his father's desk, leaning with elbows on knees. "Dad, maybe we should slow down."

"I see… go on."

"The media is swarming, attacking every mishap and Sheryl…"

"She's your wife… she's manageable. It will work out if you explain things to her. You'll see."

"She has a different agenda pops. She defends the environment from everything, like a momma bear with cubs."

"She's a mother…that's to be expected."

"Did you see the paper… or watch the news?"

"I read it. You think she's behind it?"

"She says no, but the media reveals details that haven't been disclosed. I can only imagine where they get it. I wouldn't put it past her."

"Richard…once this project is complete, journalists will be badgering for your interview. You'll be so busy with investors and government officials wanting their name in the spotlight, these reports won't sum up to the potential of an abysmal blog."

Then the old man stands, augments character and reels off his vision. "Imagine…the most abundant and inexpensive energy source in the world available at every turn of a steering wheel or a flick of a switch. No transporting it, immediate access—natural gas at every fuel station, in each community, all across the State," he vividly details walking toward a window, "and not a single truck needed to deliver it. Modernized cars will roll off production lines in mindboggling numbers. 'New everything' will come to pass, and not just that," he gestures excitement, staring out the window with dreamy foresight. "Automobiles, appliances—you name it will need retrofitting. Factories and industrial plants, homes and business, government and private institutions, and hospitals for Chrissakes will all require upgrade. Millions will need training to keep up with modifications alone—jobs will flourish in every sector and ODG will be at the heart of it—all of it," he turns and points with a confident finger.

"The best news… Florida's economy will soar," he shifts focus again. "Truck drivers won't lose their jobs, distribution haulers can move up—promoted to repair, maintenance, sales or whatever division they want. There will be plenty of work to go around. Let the media pounce on that," he chuckles, moving back to the open room. "And once they're on board, other States will jump on the crusade so fast we'll have trouble keeping up with demand. Planning and setting up new offices will require several full-time departments dedicated to just that. Our presence will be requested everywhere—begged for. And your wife…well you won't be able to peel her off your shadow."

Richard however, isn't acting with the same enthusiasm. "Maybe you don't remember Sheryl pop, that's not her style. She doesn't follow anyone, certainly not me. I can't get her to do a damn thing she doesn't agree with."

"No, she's not your mother…that's for sure," Senior becomes mellow. "God rest her soul. But she's not entirely scary either," he resumes spirit. "Give it time. She loves you. I know it."

"Pops," Richard exhales, "there's something else."

His father listens but Richard hesitates. "What is it? Let it out," he requests.

Ring, ring, ring…Richards phone buzzes.

"Please son, shut that thing off. You know how I can't stand being interrupted."

"It's Carl…I can call him back," Richard mumbles, turns the phone off and then continues. "It's the Disney hub. There was collapse this morning—worse than the other ones. Carl's on it as we speak, but the ground—is it possible the central region just can't support the infrastructure?"

"Listen," the confident man positions himself to the front of his desk, "our geological research and development teams—private surveyors and engineering firms are all in agreement," he attests while sitting on the corner of his desk, one foot touching the floor. Straight in front of his son, he guarantees with both hands up, "after many years of judgmental investigation they're all convinced, our method and materials will endure. Our designs establish a new era of accolades. Even the Army Corps of Engineers believe so. They and others cannot find a single reason to believe we are doing anything harmful. All of them stand behind us."

"I know, but…"

Eight

Snack time comes early for Sheryl, but then she is always ready for a bite of something. She secures a can of tomato juice and a bag of potato chips from a vending machine, and then cracks the drink open—takes a sip and meanders for a place to plunk down. In luck, there is a vacancy near the window but that's the only inspiring feature. Her break room is ordinary, something less than a public cafeteria. Cheap vinyl sheets jackets the floor and plain florescent lighting lays-in between dreary ceiling tiles. Though she can look outside, most of the scenery is of a mall's back area across a shabby alley. The tables are ordinary too but easy to wipe—that she appreciates. However, the chairs are rigid and uncomfortable.

"Is this seat taken?" a voice surprises.

She looks—Arnold is here.

"Hey…no, it's yours," she waves a hand at an empty chair.

"Is it safe?" he cracks. "I noticed you squirming."

"Yeah, our spectacular lunch facilities. I conveniently left that part out of our meeting. Oops!"

"Well, at least they're easy to clean," he notes, rubbing a hand across the tabletop.

She chuckles under her breath, impressed with his awareness for cleanliness. "I'm sorry about earlier," she sighs. "He's a bit of an ogre."

"Jeff says you're the tyrant," Arnold delivers with a straight face.

She glances out the window, "of course he did."

"I'm just kidding—I mean…he was kidding," Arnold giggles.

"I know. He's like that," she turns to reengage. "How was breakfast? Did you get the special pancakes?"

"Hash browns…he didn't tell me about the stacks. I knew the prick was holding out," Arnold jests.

They share a laugh.

Sheryl nudges him, "Yeah, you're starting to get the hang of our bizarre mentality."

"So, you don't actually want to hear about my meal!" he changes flow.

"Not really—want a chip," she jiggles the opened bag toward him.

However, he doesn't reach. "I'll take it," he says.

"Well, you need to grab one. I'm not feeding you, and I'll be damned if I'm turning the whole thing over. I just opened it," she exclaims, rattling the bag faster, enticing him to seize one.

"I'm talking about the job," he elucidates, putting a chip in his mouth and crunching it.

"I know," she admits. "But do you have to be so dramatic." Poking fun, she gives a silly expression.

"You knew—like your psychic."

"Well I do catch on fast," she grins. "But no. Jeff called when you left the diner."

Arnold scoffs, "he is a prick!"

"That's what I keep saying but no one believes me," she motions a 'whatever' gesture and eats another chip.

Then Arnold's character enriches.

"You know," his tone deepens while reaching to the bag again, "he speaks very highly of you."

In 'southern-belle' style she declares, "I have that effect on him—he's well trained." She pokes fun and then returns to normal. "The only man I could do that with. Isn't that a bitch?" she wisecracks. "But we do have the same goals—the environment you know. So it's easy, and HE IS an amazing hydrologist," she emphasizes and pauses to swallow—he waits for continuation. "Thanks, I'm glad you're on board," she says with sincere appreciation. "This means a lot, and not just to me."

"You're welcome," he formally obliges, and then resumes jesting. "So... when do I get abused?"

"Hasn't that already happened?" she jabs.

They laugh again.

"So, I need to ask," Sheryl alters temperament. "Did you come here for the sun and fun? The tropical landscapes are amazing, I know...and the beaches are filled with 'good time' girls but that doesn't seem to be your thing." Changing the subject, she personally inquires.

Noticeably, he chokes on those words.

"I'm not saying your gay—that came out all wrong," she recants, holding her hand to mouth with embarrassment. "I'm so sorry! What I mean is—there is more to you than those kinds of superficial things. You don't strike me as a player type—you know, so what's the deal?"

He clears his throat, "is it that obvious?"

"Yeaahh! The way you talk—there's substance to you. You're not materialistic...so spit it out."

He regains control.

"Well, there is a special lady," he coughs.

"I knew it," she explodes to a big smile. "I was right, I was right. Details—give me something to chew on."

"Not much to tell really. We're emerging from the rebuilding phase."

"Uh huh you've been fighting. I know where you're coming from."

"Yeah, but we're on the right track and to tell you the truth... this job, will help, so," he stumbles for words but gains speed quickly. "My being here isn't just helping you. This will keep me in Florida, where I need to be. Anyway, I'm here so let's just get down to business," he requests, trying to dodge the subject.

She notices the swerve and internally submits. "Great, my kind of worker—business first, personal life never," she withdraws from questioning him. "You can give me the particulars when you're ready," she changes subject.

"Well, about the sinks—here's what I think," Sheryl goes right into established territory. "Facts are facts and evidence always leads somewhere or to someone. I really don't want to believe my husband is up to no good, but this department deserves the truth."

"You mean you do?" Arnold points to the obvious.

"Yeah, whatever," she dismisses the idea. "But this is deeper than me."

"Okay, but what if I learn that 'ODG and company' is destroying the environment. What Then?"

"Then, I take it to the board," she clearly states. "Lawyers get hired, and the media runs wild and…"

"And ODG gets shut down," Arnold cuts in with a harsh tone, warning her of a possible outcome.

She turns away, "Perhaps! Or maybe they're mandated to adjust procedures," she looks back. "The company is used to changing their strategy and amending polices—nothing new. They'll survive—at a huge cost but they will go on. More importantly, nature remains intact."

"I see…you're all about the environment."

"Am I making that evident?" she laughs playfully.

However, Arnold continues in a grave tone, "or they get locked in legal battle and their colossal project gets put on indefinite hold. I've seen how this type of thing plays out Sheryl. First, investors pull out and then drastic loss of profits follows leading to lay-offs. Assets sold and buildings vacated. All of a sudden, the VP isn't married anymore. Is that what you want?"

"I've thought about that," she mentions to a cautious pause. "But it is what it is," she maintains to a caustic end, staring right at him.

"You can't mean that. You're not that cold," he glares straight back. "I don't think you've thought this all the way through."

"Well, we're not there yet. So let us first get the truth, and then I'll deal with reality later. Okay. That will give me time to…"

"Hey, hey, hey…" she's interrupted by a swiftly approaching voice. "There are my two favorite people," Jeff hollers while strutting in the room. "Has Arnold made a decision?" he questions, causing a few other heads in the room to turn.

Upon reaching the table, he snags a bunch of chips without asking.

"I already know you called her. Thanks buddy," Arnold jeers.

"You told him?" a stunned Jeff asks.

Sheryl only returns a raised brow.

"I thought you only shared secrets with me," Jeff whines, taking a seat.

"You're not the only one anymore, get over it," making a twisted face, she boasts. "What do you want anyway?"

"Why do I need something?" he grasps more chips.

"You always want? Let's not do this dance…okay."

"She's no fun anymore," he tells Arnold with a mischievous grin.

Arnold doesn't desire involvement with their little spat, giving Jeff a blank stare.

She makes another silly face, sticking her tongue out.

All right, Jeff shakes it off. "Did you catch the latest alert?" he blurts, picking up the empty bag to glare in to it. "Who ate all the chips?" he rattles.

Sheryl and Arnold gawk at him.

"We weren't watching," she smacks him on the hand. "Leave the chips alone. What now?"

"Well, it's a good thing you're sitting down," lifting the snack bag to his face he mutters, shaking the remaining crumbs into his gaping mouth.

"Dude, you've got a canyon," Arnold puns, cowering at Jeff wolfing scrapes, some specks falling onto his face.

"This is the best part," Jeff struggles to talk while chewing. "The end of the bag—all of the extra… salt is down there. Everybody knows that."

He tips the bag again but nothing comes out, so he crumples it into a wad giving it a light toss to the table. Finishing with a gulping swallow, he rubs his hands together above the table to get off chip dust. Then he lets out a satisfying 'ahhh'.

The other two simply shake their heads.

"Jeff, the news—can we hear it now," Sheryl blurts, as if demanding that he focus on the issue.

Jeff abruptly gives her his attention. "Lake Marsha, in Orange County…" he begins.

"Old broadcast," she casts. "And it's in Orange Tree Community. That happened last night. I know it dried up. I haven't discussed it yet but yes…" she tries to complete his thoughts.

However, he prevents that. "Yeah, yeah," he dithers. "So, you know one of your husband's job sites is across the street."

"So what…!"

"It's at Universal Studios," he delivers bluntly.

"Sure…they have projects everywhere."

"They're digging."

"What's the point?"

"It's only a hundred yards from that lake."

"Okay," she throws a hand up.

"Does he always tell a story like this?" Arnold probes.

"Pretty much, he can't avoid it. It's like playing twenty-one questions with a toddler," Sheryl whines.

"Hey, I treated you to breakfast, traitor," Jeff prods an elbow into Arnold's rib.

"The news Jeff…!" Sheryl exclaims, getting irritated with the delay.

"Okay!" he blurts. "They had an exclusive at ODG's work site—inside Universal's fairgrounds, a few minutes ago," he informs. "You could literally see the dried-up lake from that location."

"Is this going to get worse?" she murmurs.

"Yeah, your husband's site is now a huge swimming pool. That's what I'm trying to say," he blasts.

Sheryl suddenly changes character.

Arnold takes serious notice as well.

"The report indicated they hit an aquifer—all work had to cease until further notice. They've been dealing with it ever since this morning and as of yet, all efforts haven't stopped it from getting bigger. It's all over the news. Where have you been?

Sheryl's agitation grows, tension mounting.

"Alright, let's not jump to conclusions," Arnold delivers comforting words and a calm hand to her shoulder which he jostles around, encouraging extra solace.

She doesn't seem to mind the contact.

Jeff nearly has a cow. "You're already at the touching phase," he jeers. "It's only his first day."

Arnold returns an evil glare.

Jeff retracts. "Kidding—just joking," he apologizes—sort of. "Not really…I am upset."

However, Jeff alters character quickly. "It's a mess out there Sheryl," he too becomes gentle.

Although Jeff thought he joked appropriately, she is taking it hard.

"You really didn't know. Richard hasn't called you?" Jeff says softly, realizing her mood.

"Why…why would he call? Does he even know?"

"Well…about that," Jeff hesitates to even say anything else, but he does. "He was there—first thing this morning. The report cited that the VP of operations visited, specifically to inspect the disaster. But he wasn't available for comment—said he left without offering a fix too."

That was the last straw for Sheryl. She plops her head on the table and moans, then rises with inkling, "that was the phone call he got this morning." Her eyes reveal surprise realizing that.

Arnold interjects again, "here's an intelligent thought—maybe this ordeal happened after the lake incident—a simple coincidence."

"Or they ruptured an aquitard and a lake got sucked dry," Jeff disrupts like usual, "and an old man can't use his boat anymore. You have to at least wonder, right…right—I know I do."

"Wow Jeff, can't you see what this is doing to her?"

"Trust me, she can handle it." Jeff callously replies. "And you almost didn't agree to help—your one to talk."

Sheryl has become pale, as blood leaves her face. She goes limp and slouches, merely staring into an imaginary space.

Arnold looks at Jeff and gives him a silent look and a gesture indicating that he make this right—help Sheryl out.

Jeff breathes deep. "Sheryl, you've got to call him," he pleads. "You've got to know. We all do—Arnold especially. That's why he's here, duh," he tries to relieve her anguish with humor.

Sheryl doesn't respond.

"Earth to Sheryl, come in Spock," Jeff heckles.

Arnold does not seem pleased with Jeff.

Finally, she moves, siting up. "Ugh," she drones getting louder, and then issues a brassy sigh, "Ahhh…ODG caused it and he doesn't want to tell me. Where's the honesty? Please remind me! Why do I trust him?"

"Relax," again Arnold tries to ease her frustration, speaking eloquently. "I've been there—where you are right now. I didn't finish telling you about my girlfriend but we had issues too. Mostly my fault I admit, but we both compromised each other's trust. Attitudes skyrocketed—I abused her expectations and then other misconceptions developed. Before we knew it, neither of us was able to handle simple problems. We weren't prepared for the grief—ended up on different paths. Luckily, I was able to figure it out and all I did was come to terms with her outlook, began to understand her point of view. That's when I realized…we could satisfy one another. Sure, we struggled through irritating discoveries along the way, but I gave it time and she eventually allowed me back in. Together, we busted through the barricades of despair and now, we're rebuilding a relationship stronger than ever."

Jeff is in awe, his jaw dropping, eyes star-struck. "Wow, I'm really starting to like this guy. He's good. Can you help me too?" he pleads. "There's this girl— well, she doesn't know me, but…"

Sheryl without concern starts speaking over him, abruptly cutting him off, "That's touching?" Sheryl provokes. "I'm happy for you. But I can't get beyond some of his crap," she stands. "But I'm not sitting in the passenger's seat any longer, that's for sure," she vents, removing her cell from her lab coat and strides toward the door. "We'll catch up later. Arnold, good talk…thanks."

"Can I get some appreciation?" Jeff whines, "Anything?"

No one acknowledges him.

"For all I do, that's what I get," he mumbles.

Arnold snickers, half-smiling.

In the hallway, Sheryl dials a number. Holding the phone to her ear, she waits for an answer, but there is none. She tries again, but still no response. Back and forth, she paces like an irritated schoolgirl. Once more, she fails to reach Richard.

"Urgh…" she aspirates and calls a different number.

It rings, and someone answers.

"Hello." A female voice answers. "Richard Olson's office, can I help you?"

"This is Sheryl. Can I speak to my husband?"

"Oh I'm sorry," the girl consoles and then gets bubblier, but with a devious nature. "I haven't seen him. I think he's still out on… um…-prior commitments. Can I take a message?"

"It's almost noon?"

"I'm not his warden Mrs. Olson," she sneers using a prepared appealing nature. "I take messages, draft memos, make appointments and try to keep him…content," she explains, with seducing connotation, almost beckoning an improper implication.

"And how do you do that Ashley? Keep him satisfied?"

"I'm not sure what you mean, Mrs. Olson. I just do my job," continuing the derisive behavior, she taunts a verbal altercation.

"Of course you don't," Sheryl hisses. "Well then, draft this letter, 'Richard, call you wife. It's urgent.'"

"Sure thing, I'll let him know. But can I just say one thing—woman to woman?" she exaggerates sweetness.

"I've never been able to stop you in the past, shoot—what is it?" Sheryl issues with artificial interest and a put-off attitude.

"Well, Ricky is…a good man. He works hard and his job is stressful. And he's important and good looking," she adds the last part with zing. "I think he needs to feel more significant—to that special someone of course," she flirts with mysterious wording. "Perhaps some carefree attention and cheerful concern would be nice. Maybe a little more than that—if you know what I mean," she rouses, hinting something. "You might get more from him if you…."

Sheryl, now infuriated, stops her from going any further, "Ashley, you'll refer to him as Mr. Olson. He is your boss and I really don't need your advice. Even for you, I think this conversation is inappropriate. Just tell him I called?"

"Sure, I just wanted to help."

"How long have you known me, several years? In that time have I once asked you for assistance with my marriage—any guidance at all?"

Suddenly, silence is on the line.

"Exactly," Sheryl persists. "You know…I'm quite used to your snickers but this prying approach is over the top. Are we on the same page?"

"I guess so," Ashley suspiciously yields. "I'll let him know you called."

Now, more upset than ever, Sheryl's worry intensifies. However, she finds a way to struggle passed it as she always does.

In her office, she meets with her right-hand men. "Let's get that team together. We're going in. ODG—well it sucks to be them and Jeff," she states his name in official tone, indicating her passion is alive.

"Yes—what?" he questions while hanging at the door like a kid who just wants to skedaddle. Arnold already parted so Jeff was anxious to leave as well.

"Send your water samples to the private firms, 'Biometric', 'Bluewater' and 'Elab'. You know, for the toxins you can't identify. They may have the resources—worth a try anyway. Have a courier get them there today."

"I'm on it, chief," he salutes and darts away.

Nine

"It may not be as stable as we predicted," Richard argues.

His father scoffs, "this project didn't start from a guess son—the earth was properly analyzed."

"I'm concerned with the stratum," Richard contends, pacing before the domineering figure.

"That was surveyed too," senior boasts, presenting a stern hand—then heads back to his chair. "But you know that," he reminds. "The center of the State is solid as a rock and that's final. The technology we've incorporated is unsurpassed, beyond its years—our leak detection devices, hydro-valve mechanisms, not to mention the carbon fiber, molecularly bonded, reinforced steel that we use—is undeniably the most elite thing going."

"I know the drill dad," Richard extends hands way out wide. "I've issued those same statements a hundred times myself."

His father grows perturbed with the friction. "Just get that hub installed!" he demands with a closed fist to the desk. "I'm sorry to lay it out that way, but it's a key component to the infrastructure," clearly he stresses the location's importance, and then takes a seat to calm his spirits. "Continue with Sheryl—be sure she remains happy, and the department head too. By the way…how is that going?"

"Still under the radar," he replies.

"Good…you see. All is fine. Let the news do their thing. Before you know it they'll be on to something else," he kicks back. "This will blow over. Nothing can hold us back now," his confidence exudes.

Richard stands, his concerns defeated. After giving a nod, he makes his way to the door.

"Rick," his father calls. "You know where we keep confidential records."

"Of course pops."

"If you're not sure…go through the data again."

Richard takes note and leaves his father's office.

In the hallway, Ashley seizes him while presenting her wares in tempting fashion. She is an attractive young woman, seductive and alluring by nature—glamorous without effort. She doesn't need to do anything in order to grab a man's attention, but today she's 'working it'. Wearing a tight-fitting blouse, stretching across every curve of gifted breasts and exercised tummy she poses with incredible deportment. Her skirt, too short for respectable impression, is revealing her voluptuous rear and news anchor legs. One she extends out to the side through an open slit, so her delicious thigh protrudes—a stocking's elastic band squeezing smooth skin. Her costume jewelry is shimmering, such as the pearly gold necklace she toys with while tilting her head in just the right manner to deliver the prettiest, most welcoming smile.

"Hey, I've been waiting for you. Can we talk?" casually griping the inside of his elbow, she eases him along.

"Sure," he responds, "in my office."

With a bright smile, she flips her flowing blond hair to the side, and sashays beside him. Although branded with a coarse personality—others might say is a constant need to outshine equals merely to obtain success, even if it means stepping over losers, she captures his approval regardless.

"Do I have any messages?" he asks. "And I need you to set something up with the Disney staff, ASAP—the hub directors," he notices something and redirects thought, "and what's that smell? It's delicious!"

She smiles even more so, as they enter his suite.

"Um...slow morning...no messages," she assures without hesitation. "But I'll set up that meeting," she adds and then vagaries into a seductive voice, "That's the perfume you couldn't resist. The one we tried in Tallahassee awhile back. Do you still enjoy it?"

"From the showcase window, right..." he fumbles. "Uh, yeah...it smells good...um; I like it...its sweet and effervescent."

"Fizzy," she giggles and steps to him. "That doesn't describe perfume silly."

"Yeah, I knew that," he smiles, trying not to show nervousness.

"You can get a little closer," she squeals with a twinkle in the eye. "Smell it....enjoy!" Inching closer she makes it easy for him to do that, and more if so desired.

He is enticed, drawn to her feminine features and apparently ready to ignore the secretary-boss relationship. Staring at her beauty, he seems defenseless.

She feels the passion.

However, he pulls away, "are you sure there were no calls—nothing?"

She simply nods 'no' and takes a settling breath while he sits at the front edge of her desk.

"Alright then, what did you want to see me about?"

Immediately, she sits next to him, her elbows and fingers gently grazing his. Resuming the presence of a playful sweetheart, she fosters the essence between them, commencing frisky chitchat. Aware of it or not, he is encouraging her attraction, simply by allowing their evoking conversation to play out. He should know that verbal caressing is as seductive as physical contact when persuading intimacy, more so when the other is already enchanted. In addition, such closeness can promote deeper feelings, and affectionate touching will surely create greater promise.

Topics change, but never does her attention drift. Eventually, she gets to the point.

"Well, the American Management seminar is next week," she reminds him while clearing her hair away from her neckline, exposing fragrant skin.

He glances.

"You said you would take me," her willing behavior is radiating magnetism.

He gazes upon her blemish free face and bedroom eyes.

"I know you're busy but..." her moist ruby lips slightly sulk, puckering like a bruised little girl.

His eyesight moves on them.

"I really need the credentials," her fingers caress along her luscious neck, all the way to cleavage.

His vision follows there too.

Once again, he fights temptation, "oh right, you need a sponsor." Catching his wits, he avoids a mistake.

"Not just any benefactor, the most prestigious firm in Florida," she squeaks. "And we could spend some educative time together. Kind of like college cramming, stay up till the wee hours drinking too much coffee or... whatever," she bats her eyes.

"Sounds like you might be...?"

"What," with a devious smile she instigates, "are you thinking...?"

"Nothing," he stands. "I'll see if I can clear it with Sheryl."

She did not like hearing that. "You seem a bit tense," quickly she gets behind him, commencing a gentle massage upon his shoulders. "What's to explain...it's just another business trip?" she whispers in meticulous tone, so close he senses her tongue skim her lips. She feels his shaky breathing and enjoys it, evident by the dreamy smile he cannot see.

His heartbeat surges faster.

Again, she perceives that too through her curvy chest, pressing against his back. With an alluring sigh, she delicately removes a spiked shoe and kneads his pants leg, a nylon clad foot roaming. Like a purring feline she swaths her extremity around his, lifting his cuff with toes. Gradually, his head turns back, her sultry eyes glaring at his—her lips bear down and he is not resisting. Willingly, she relaxes for him.

Suddenly, 'Mr. Olson...call on line one,' emits over the intercom.

He breaks from her clutches and without a parting remark, heads to his adjoining office at the rear. Ashley stares, sliding her foot back into her toeless pump and gnaws at her upper lip while removing a clip-on earring. Instead of acting bothered, she breeds a mischievous aura like a bad girl envisioning a long awaited present. Possibly, she believes romance is inevitable.

Ten

Awake before the alarm clock delivers its cue, Sheryl's eyes are wide open. Another day has arrived, but something is off. She breathes deep and winces at the ceiling, her eyes are woeful and so early in the morning—'Harmony Central' is not perking as usual. Straightaway, she hides her face in a pillow and presses it hard against herself. By the sight of her stomach convulsing, she is no doubt crying. She tosses the soft headrest to the floor on the right…wet eyes looking left to observe the other half of the bed untouched—Richard has not slept there, cushions fluffed and covers drawn tight. Another glimpse reveals his nightstand is bare too—no watch, no wallet, or keys lay atop it. Where is he?

What is Sheryl wondering? Could it be that of anger, not seeing trouble earlier? Might she feel responsible, not giving him enough feminine devotion? Perhaps, she has been too busy or living in denial of the truth. In any case, she knows trouble will linger and that difficulty cannot be resolved unless first acknowledged. She recalls, that is the greatest hurdle—either betrayal is too subtle to notice, or so flagrant that most ignore it. She thinks, 'Which am I? My defenses are indestructible but didn't see a thing coming?'

Yet here she is, dealing with ruinous behavior. She considers, 'now what? I have felt the wrath of betrayal—I can't ignore it.' Then she thinks, 'at least the coffee smells good, why not get some?' Though Richard's voice has not summoned her, she rises. Today, Sheryl does not need coaxed from bed.

In the kitchen, she finds him at the niche—routine as always and today, pays close attention to his character.

"You're up early," he peers overtop the paper to acknowledge her.
She does not respond while en route to get some hot beverage.
"Is that a new night shirt?"
No rejoinder from the cold woman, her back turned.
"It looks cute—sexy," he flatters.
She releases a deliberate sneer.
"You're awful quiet," he increases pitch. "What's the matter?"

Suddenly she turns. "Do you have anything to say for yourself?" in unforgiving tone, she scowls and scrutinizes him—he readies a reply.
"About what…? Oh yeah, my back is hurting," he moans, lending a pressured touch to his lower rear side. "I need a solid surface to lie on," ignoring her sharp attitude he complains without eye contact.
She increases her impatient gape while taking a large swallow—her eyes draw together.
He covertly eyeballs her too.

She senses he is only pretending to read the news as he flips a page.

Speechless seconds dawdle as she prepares for battle, swigging coffee.

He too feels conflict is near, but does not let on. Unprotected and grazing like an animal in the strike zone of a spitefully aimed arrow, drawn and ready for release, he does nothing.

These two have had many showdowns.

She knows his answers will be primed for retaliation, and that his resilience has brought pardon before. However today, the spousal hunter is ready for predictable excuses. She has ammunition to oppose those habitual responses and her intense stare reveals that mood—escape is not possible. She takes her customary seat, nipping at coffee. Another swig goes down and then, 'bang', the mug slams to the table. Some coffee splashes out, splatting on the news— immediately her hand crushes his newspaper flat.

Now he, the startled prey, is face to face with predator.

"I'm talking about you not coming home last night?" she blasts. "Lets' start with that—Oh...and how was work?"

"Sheryl, this isn't the first time I stayed late. There's a lot going...and you were asleep when I got home. I know how you need your rest. I didn't want to wake you," trying to seem unruffled, he tries to straighten the paper.

She pushes it down again, "you were at work?"

"I was reevaluating our systems and going over previous land studies—for you."

"For me..." she jeers. "That just makes everything okay. So, how'd you hurt your back?"

"They don't make chairs like they used to."

Again, he tries smoothing out pages.

"You're not joking your way out of this," she yanks his paper away, smashes it into a ball and tosses the wad across the table, "try reading that now."

He looks at it rolling away.

"Look at me," she shrieks, grabbing his wrist.

He has no choice but to return a dazed gaze.

"What the hell is going on? You said you would never lie! You told me I was it!"

The tirade begins with one hand flying in the air and then another. "I trusted you. Like your honest! You portray being faithful...but you're not. You said I was enough! C'mon, I know we have a few problems, but really. Oh well, it's all gone now," she wipes away a tear.

He reaches to comfort her but she pushes him away.

"Was work...'HARD' yesterday?" her anger persists. "Was it...'WET' too? Did you get satisfied? I hope she's worth it," she grabs the clumped paper and hits him with it.

He flinches to deflect part of it.

"Whoa, whoa, whoa," he finally seizes both of her flapping hands. "What are you talking about?"

"Ashtray 'what's her name...'" Sheryl hisses, squeezing his fingers with all her might. "The bimbo with the trashy mouth, are you involved with her?"

"No, of course not!" he adamantly defends.

"Oh Really...! So why didn't you return my calls," she struggles out of his grip. "I even left a message with your floozy and oh yeah, you didn't come home—if that's not a red flag. It adds up. Just stop lying. It's over," she waits for his answer as another tear drips.

He looks at her with compassionate eyes.

"Oh give it a break—you can stop pretending," she finalizes, mouth puckered, eyes displaying disgust.

"Sheryl, I think you have the wrong idea. I don't know what brought this on, but I never got a call from you. I didn't get any messages," he tries to rectify.

"For Chrissakes, that's your defense," she cries and laughs at the same time. "I called—don't say I didn't and that bitch took my message. But I shouldn't be surprised she didn't give it to you?"

"I'm sure there's a good reason."

"Oh yeah, there is, you just haven't admitted it."

"No...no, that's not it. I promise."

"There's that word again," she rebukes aloud.

"Listen, if you wanted my attention so bad, why didn't you leave a message on my cell?" Richard changes flow of the conversation, focusing on a different issue.

She seems to bite, lowering her tone, "I don't know...it just rang. I didn't let it go long enough for voice mail to kick in I guess. I expected you to pick up." Her voice escalates again, "you should have seen the number and called back."

"Sheryl, my phone was off. You know how my dad is."

Upset and looking away she cannot stop shaking her head. "So where were you?" she tries to calmly state.

"I was working, by myself...I told you."

"And your phone was conveniently off," she scoffs.

"Sheryl, check the number you dialed. Let me see your phone."

She reaches into her purse on the bench beside her, removes her phone, and pulls up the recent call log. She shows him.

"That's not my number. The last digit is a six, not a nine."

"Oh crap, you're right—I dialed from memory. I was in a hurry, you know how I get."

Richard is relieved, "See...and you thought all those terrible things."

"I still am. There's still something up with your sex-retary, we both know it."

"Can you at least give me a chance to find out what happened? Don't I deserve that? Are you going to roast me alive over a misplaced note? That doesn't sound like you, not the woman I married—always compiling research, getting proof and evidence before passing judgment. You never leave a stone unturned. CSI can't hold a candle to you, but with me—no you don't want to dig for the facts."

"Oh, you think you're so good, playing to my intelligent side. The truth is all I want, along with your fidelity but therein lays the problem. She rests her head in her hands.

"Okay, I'll give you the benefit of doubt," she looks up, "for now—but we're not done. There's still the problem of a dried up Lake."

"Well that's what I thought you were upset over," he throws hands up. "But I am glad you asked about the secretary thing first—you're more concerned with us," he chuckles.

She scrunches a face, snubbing a nose at him.

"I am important to you is all I'm saying. I do come first," he brags and attempts to hold her hand.

She smirks and pulls away. "Don't get ahead of yourself cowboy. I'm still pissed. You're not out of the sink yet. Speaking of which, what's your side of the story? I know all about the rupture at Disney, and you were there.

He ponders with relaxed composer. "We didn't do it," with clarity, he claims. "I know what it looks like…I do," he confesses. "I told my guys how this would look and I also knew—I'd have to deal with you sooner or later. I had hoped though, just not now."

She lifts a brow.

"But that's the truth," he says, appearing honest. "That breach was well after the lake dried up. I can't prove it…but…"

Then he hesitates, showing a sudden inspiration, producing a strange guise accompanied with a bizarre smile. His eyes light up.

"I know that look," she confronts his altered behavior. "Whatever you're thinking, stop. I won't believe you…so don't even try"

"Well actually…" he struggles with his impulsive notion. "Is there a way you could corroborate it?"

"Whaaat!" she screams.

"Not exactly you, someone from your department?" he quickly says and waits, gesturing beggars' hands, palms up.

Sheryl is about to erupt. "Oh my God—you're asking for my help?" flabbergasted she rattles with fury. "You lied to me—are still lying. You disregard my intellect every chance you get, avoid my warnings and never heed my advice—don't trust my judgment on the 'one thing I know best,' the environment. And…" yelling at him again she repeats, "you didn't come home last night because you're probably a cheating F'n bastard. Yet, after all your bullshit, you still have the nerve to ask 'ME' for help.

He flips an 'oops' hand gesture while his chin rests on the other and tries to respond with snoopy dog eyes.

Nevertheless, she will not allow it.

"You want me to protect your good name—help spare ODG's image and most likely your wallet too...Do whatever you can to keep the bottom line low—right,' unbelievable."

"When you say it like that," he lowers his head and scratches it, "I sound bad."

"You think," she says. "The thought of you appealing to my good nature is way past awful. Actually, your behavior is a few levels below despicable. If I could find a way to verbalize twisting a knife deep into your gut causing you to bleed out, I would.

"I think you just did," he frowns.

"I want you to experience some pain...but you won't will you? You just don't feel misery...why is that?" she stares at him. "Oh wait...no need to answer. I remember now," she opens up with surprise. "You're too busy to deal with emotions...yeah, that's it!"

For a moment he sits, staring—not sure what to say.

She returns the same feeling, placing her head in her hands, also out of words.

"So that means you'll help?" he shrinks into his seat, yet pressing onward with his inapt request using a big smile, looking like a chastised little boy waiting to be let outside again. He knows she has a soft spot for that pitiful act.

She shakes her head and peers out the window, admiring the splendid countryside.

He patiently waits for a reply, knowing the longer she takes to give an answer the better it will be for him.

"I can't believe I'm going to do this. I must be an idiot," she brings her feet up to sit on them. "Okay, I'll help." She turns to him. "But don't think this little union changes anything. There's a lot you haven't dealt with yet...and I'm not about to forget it."

"Of course, no problem," he declares. "We'll get through it—together," he's quick to provide words she would want to hear.

She looks at him, almost appearing persuaded.

He very likely feels relieved.

"Jenny didn't come home last night," unexpectedly she changes the subject. "I'm worried."

"How do you do that?" he reaches for her hand.

"What's that?"

"The kids, no matter what's going—you put them first. The world could be falling apart but their needs are more important. That's what I like about you."

"So you like me now," she chuckles and notices their hands have joined—he caresses a thumb over hers.

"You know what I mean."

"I don't know what to believe." Then speaking of their clenched fingers, she continues mistrust, "This doesn't change anything. I'm not sure about you anymore and truthfully—I'm not certain about me either. Maybe, I've changed too."

"What are you saying?" Richard is suddenly feeling discouraged on a different level.

The mood is faltering as she removes her hand from his and with great caution, she takes her wedding ring off and places it on the table, holding one finger atop it. She looks at him with tear-filled eyes and slides it forward, leaving it to rest before him.

Now, it's as isolated as he is. As Richards beholds the discarded gold hoop—the bond that ties them together, he melts. It is obvious that this action comes to him as a complete surprise—a devastating blow. He is in utter disbelief.

He turns his vision to her and waits for a reason.

She looks back at him with a shattered aura, "I'm saying, right now...until whenever...I can't be your wife."

Eleven

Birds are chirping, and from the sound of it, several varieties. Some sing with flamboyant style, others shriek repeatedly or discharge single peeps, but together all tweets produce a marvelous parade of visceral communication. The most prominent vocals are Scrub Jays, Sparrows and of course the Northern Mockingbird. Harmonic tunes released by these songbirds make waking up a unique event. A standard greeting to woodsy residents, but to a new listener it's a symphony, a delightful ensemble from the gentlest winged creatures. Amidst this display, a branch cracks off and falls, rustling to the ground. Squirrels scatter across leaves, through brush and scurry up trees—their little claws make a distinctive clatter. One excited creature jumps onto a tire, but why is there a Jeep parked in the woods, covered with dew?

"Bobby!" a girl whispers near a boy's ear, lips grazing his cheek as he lay.

No response from the motionless fellow, so she kisses his face and then again, but still he sleeps. She places a peck at the ear canal and softly drones his name, "Bahh-bie..." Then she rubs her nose against his, but her enthusiasm has no effect.

There's not a single reaction.

Eager to wake him she lifts from under the neck and presses her lips to his, oscillating with zeal. She wets her lips and tries again, then delivers a gentle lick to his. She pants and blows on his face but only a quick snore results, followed by a brisk swat.

"Wake up you idiot!" she lets his head flop and then shoves him like an annoyed schoolchild.

"What, what is it? Is there a gator? I'll get 'em," the boy wakes in disorder.

"Go brush your teeth," she criticizes and rolls over to unzip her sleeping bag. Then, she crawls out to do the same with the tent door.

"Where -are -you going Jenny?" The drowsy boy utters through a gapping yawn and rubs his face to gain clarity.

"Out," she drones and exits.

He starts kicking his own sack away.

Outside she stands to stretch and smell the morning air with deep unwinding inhale—eyes closed and arms out wide the freshness exhilarates her. Barefoot, she begins through the woods looking around with wholesome appreciation whilst in the same skimpy nightwear as home. That's okay—no one is around.

"Jenny, it's too early, come back," the boy pouts flopping at the threshold, too sleepy for pursuit.

"Get up lazy!" she yells, and then mutters to herself, "This must be what Mom is always talking about."

Then she darts away.

"What?" he calls to deaf attention—Jenny has already gone to a lake. Sunrays are casting such beautiful streaks upon the glassy surface and while passing through the hovering fog, beautiful colors display—making the spectacle as serene as heaven. Anyone would want to see—she is captivated.

"It's breathtaking," she dunks a toe in.

Gentle ripples disperse.

She smiles because as expected, Bobby's footsteps are treading close. "This is the first time I've woken so close to nature," she yelps to his approach. "Look, fish are jumping," she points with excitement as he stands beside her.

"And you've never spent the night with me before either," he ignores her delight, trying to secure her interest.

"Yeah, your snoring is amazing," she banters and issues a 'whatever' hand flick, then enters the water going in up to her thighs.

Bobby is left befuddled. "What the heck was that?" he snickers.

"Never mind," she yells. Then she submerges and resurfaces holding her chin above water. She looks at him with a mischievous stare, "C'mon in," she tempts and swims to lure him in.

The boy stands still.

"It's warm chicken little," she harasses.

"You're acting like your mother," he shouts.

For a moment, she is absorbed in the thought of that possibility, but regains jubilation, twirling and thrashing around. "And you're acting like my Dad," she returns razz.

"That's it!" He could take no more and jumps in, but shivers upon entry.

She laughs but soon he is up to his chest and paddling onward. "It does feel good," he agrees, swimming closer.

"Told ya," she mocks, smiling with giddy enjoyment and swims away. "Come and get me," she squeals moving faster.

He takes pursuit and either, she wasn't trying to escape or he was a much faster swimmer because he caught up quickly.

She splashes him in the face to keep him at bay.

He returns fire, and then lunges to dunk her.

Coming to the surface shrieking, she wraps her arms around his neck and with water draining from her face, they lend each other an intense stare. For a time, they were carefree, playing like young animals.

Then a nearby rope swing grabbed their attention. Each took turns slinging into the water—sometimes willingly, at other moments pushed. Nevertheless, they always tried to go as high as possible. Then, when out of breath, they drifted with only their heads above water, cuddling to get warm and flirting with innocent love.

Eventually, they head to shore and rest. Jenny begins preparing a blanket taken from Bobby's jeep along with snacks she mindfully prepared for the excursion. As they lie next to each other, they contemplate life as kids their age do.

"Bobby...what do you want to be when you grow up?"

"Rich," he assures.

"Besides that—how are you going to make money? What will you do?"

"I don't know...maybe I'll be a race car driver or a surfer."

"Seriously...!" she nudges him and sneaks a bite of his sandwich he held over his chest. "Those aren't even options for you. You can't drive and you haven't even tried surfing."

"I can drive. Anyone can do that," he takes a chomp too.

"Uh huh, right—you didn't miss a single pothole on the way in here."

"That's called 'four-wheeling,'" he explains and prods her shoulder.

She snatches the snack from his grasp.

"Whatever?" she disregards his silly fantasy. "I just don't want to become my parents. They fight all the time." She lies on her back and looks toward the sky.

"About what?" he nestles by her side, positioning to get comfortable—and to get his dwindling sandwich back. She relinquishes it easily.

"Like everything including me and Jake—how everything should be done her way. But mostly they argue over their jobs...all the time," she scoffs. "They can't agree on anything, but me," speaking confidently, "I'm not going to be like that."

She rolls over and stares with a serious expression. "I don't want to take on the world's problems or solve national issues," she flops back down, returning her sight to the sky. "I want to have a small shop selling toe rings or popsicles out of a cooler on a bike—something senseless you know. I could make baby clothes. That would keep me near my family. I'd need little kids to practice on and to model my work, so that would be perfect. I wouldn't be my parents though, that's for sure," she turns again to look at him straightforwardly. "What about you? Do you want kids?"

Then, they both gaze into passing clouds.

"I don't know. I don't think about it. I really don't want any now... I mean, I guess later though, you know in the future that would be okay," he fails to explain because he has no clue what he wants. "But kids are okay...even though they are like little rebels," he adds.

"Yeah, I know what you mean. My kid brother Jake is definitely radical."

Suddenly, she props herself on elbows and pokes him in the ribs.

"I've got an idea. Let's go see Jake. He and his friend are making a raft, you know for the contest. I want to see it. I mean...now I'm fascinated by the thought of it. It's outdoorsy, adventurous, and a little spooky. What do you say?"

Bobby displays a grandiose smile, nothing short of perfect boy next-door teeth. "Sure. How can I resist you?" he articulates with great admiration. "We'll go...but first..." he puts the last morsel in his mouth and pauses while possessing a sly gaze which he delivers on purpose and with curiosity.

"What?" with an elated smile she returns the moment's glow, wondering what is on his mind?

He merely swallows—staring into her eyes and then on her lips…and then leans into her moist body. He kisses her on the cheek near her ear.

It tickles her, she laughs.

He caresses her face with the back of fingertips and gently sighs.

"I hope you're not thinking what I think you're thinking," she places a hand against his chest, applying only gentle pressure.

"Well, I just wanted to…" he stammers, while relishing her form.

"I'm not sleeping with you yet?" she firmly addresses that issue.

He giggles.

"I'm not kidding," she repeats.

In a flash, he jumps up. "Last one to the swing has to clean up," he takes off running, laughing like crazy.

Surprised, she picks up a small rock and hurls it at him. "You jerk…I'm going to get you for that."

Laughing and shouting they resume childlike play, this time running about the woods. Circling around trees, playing tag and chasing one another he taunts her at every instance. Sometimes he grabs hold of her and tickles.

She giggles wildly. Again, they frolic like the children they are.

However, had they not left their spread so soon—they would have seen it. If they were not carrying on so loudly—they may have felt it. At their picnic place, the ground trembled—vibrating and pulsating, again then again. An idle person lying would surely have noticed. Even their water bottle jostled and the liquid inside shuddered—forming ripples. At the lake, bubbles surfaced near the border and yet more rose. Sinks typically release pockets of trapped air, and over time it raises, but this event had too many for that to be the case, and Jenny would know. Another judder happened and then tiny waves moved away from shore, into the deep, the opposite direction of normal travel. A few squirrels leaping over the blanket stop in their tracks. They look around and dart their heads back and forth, quickly as if something was wrong, and they were desperate to view it. The tiny creatures were concerned. However, the two rousting kids were unaware.

Twelve

"I'll get something to eat later mom," Jake's testy voice rambles while shoving a few of his belongings into a backpack. "I've got to go. The raft isn't finished... and we don't have much time. Junior is waiting and probably his dad too," he rationalizes to his flummoxed mother, standing in her son's bedroom doorway. He bends to tie his right sneaker and then with sack in hand whizzes past her while she clutches the doorknob. Swoosh, he scrams down the hall and is out of sight before she recovers from his careless bump—shoving her aside.

She yells. "Building stuff isn't the only thing in life—you're just like your father," and for a moment, she is still, barely shaking her head. Then, she looks at her hand, only a band of pale skin around one finger indicates there was a ring on it.

"I'm heading out," Richard's voice resonates toward her.

She holds back a response.

Then the front door opens and she looks at her finger once again, and issues a comforting exhale. "Rick," she calls, but only the faint sound of a door closing comes back to her.

Then an engine starts.

Immediately, she goes to the front window, parts the verticals and peeks to observe him pulling away. "Can't take the heat huh," she smirks, watching him drive on.

A glance at her wristwatch reveals tardiness is on the horizon, so she lets go of the window covering, but from the corner of her eye, through swaying gaps, she spots break lights. To see if he is coming back—possibly, he has forgotten something, she regains good sight of him. "Maybe he does have something to say," she mumbles. However, just as that thought occurred, he instead stopped in front of a house twenty or so front lawns away and worse, a woman at the end of her driveway is greeting him. Sheryl soon realized his intention was to encounter this young dame, who is dressed too glitzy to be a stay-at-home mom.

This female trots to the driver's side window and leans to address him. Straightaway, she poked her head in the vehicle and longer than a brief moment. Sheryl's temper is quickly rising. "What is she doing?" she drones. However, obstructed by automobile steel, and too far for decent scrutiny, she could not really see what was going on. It was apparent to Sheryl though, that those actions were inappropriate, and could only imply one thing. Certainly, it was all the suspicion she needed to revisit her earlier thoughts of him being a double-dealing man. Immediately she established a plausible look of jealousy.

Her eyebrows scrunched together and mouth puckered with teeth gritting as she blasted the verticals from her grasp. Watching him, part from that woman was too much to bear, she was so cute while waving goodbye. Sheryl has seen that type of gesture—holding a graceful hand next to a brightly smiling cheek, moving all four fingers up and down rapidly at the knuckles with an elbow bent into an appealing body—including the sexy hip shift to the side can only be a sign of too much adoration.

'Her eyes were probably twinkling as well,' she assumed. Angrily, Sheryl tramps away releasing a harsh, "Grrraaahhh" with hands clenched and slamming to her side. Her breathing is getting more erratic too while pacing from indignation. Groaning and vexing to no one she breathes deep and places her face in her hands. Just then, music from her cell begins playing. She grumbles at that too but stomps to answer it.

"Yes Jeff…you just can't wait until I walk through the door can you?" she snaps.

"Whoa, what crossed your path this morning?" he shields.

"Nothing, what do you want?"

"Oh wait; you had a talk with hubby. It didn't go well I gather?"

"Worse…"

"So, shoot the next guy?"

"You know me too well," she pauses, "I'll tell you about it later. I can't…think about it right now," she lowers brashness. "What's going on?"

"Well, you can thank me later but I know you probably forgot…with the ruckus and all. I almost did too but…"

"But, what… what should I be so thankful for Jeff? I really don't have time for Q & A. Please…just get to the   point."

"Well, you have about an hour. Uh…UCF…remember the graduating class of future geologists and environmental tree huggers like us—you have a seminar with them today…remember."

"Oh crap," she tosses a hand in the air. "I did forget. The 'University of Central Florida'…I'm not even ready," she scoffs.

"Relax…don't worry, you'll be fine," he pacifies her. "Take your laptop and all the notes you've kept. Show them some visuals and trust me…you are always ready for this subject. You don't need to prepare. You're capable of discussing this jargon in your sleep. Just do the same thing in front of all those kids. They'll get a kick out of it."

"Very funny Jeff, seriously…"

"Hey…I'm not kidding. You know your shtick inside and out. Be yourself and talk about whatever comes to mind. They'll love you."

"You think?"

"I know so…except…" suddenly he halts to a peculiar pause.

"What else you pain, I was just feeling encouraged…now what?"

"I shouldn't even mention it but…"

"Jeff," she boldly states his name like an irritated mother, "stop hedging."

"Sheryl, it's probably better that you don't find out until you get there…"

"Jeff, spit it out," she hisses and he detects her growing rage.

"Okay, okay…Wynyard…he's going to be there too, for moral support he says."

"You talked to him—are you serious?" she shouts. "Why didn't he tell me about this? How long have you known?"

"Well...he actually just planned it. Believe it or not...he was just here, and um...saw all of your notes on your calendar."

"That bastard...he's snooping around my office?"

"Yeah well, that's essentially how I remembered too so...sorry. Hey, at least now it won't be a total disaster, you can still make it.

"Ahhh," she releases mild sarcasm, "I guess you're right."

"So you're both going—together. It could be fun."

"No, it just got worse. And thanks for your pointless pep talk."

"Hey, that's what I do Sheryl—help."

"You're such an idiot Jeff. Why do I put up with you? That's what my husband always says."

"Because I complete you, that's why. Not like that, but you know what I—I think you get it...right?" he heckles with humor, but changes to an earnest tone. "Listen... seriously. Don't let this guy get to you. You do what you want, nothing less. Whatever that is," he stutters. "Okay? Just be, you and I know," he heightens character. "I don't need to say that because we both know you're really good at being yourself," he concludes to a soft-spoken point.

Looking up at the ceiling with hand on hip, she contemplates his suggestion. "Okay, I'll see you later, but uh... take Arnold with you to Universal. See what you can find. Catch up with me later and uh...thanks."
She hangs up and sets the cell on the boudoir dresser, still standing in dreamy posture.

Then she transforms her attitude as always.

Thirteen

Sheryl was quick to get ready, no different from any other day. Grabbing essentials and coffee on-the-fly she's out the door and driving on 192, but this time up to the desolate marshland 441 route and then to University Drive. Despite nearly forgetting the important colloquium altogether, Sheryl reaches the school with time to spare. The auditorium was near empty as she entered moving directly to front stage. On it was a stand equipped with cables for connection, so she places her laptop there. She notices the projector, screen, tables, chairs and computer necessities were well prepared for her arrival. Within minutes, she was ready to engage the expected audience of about five-hundred students and dozens of faculty members. All that remained was to deliver a professional presentation.

"No pressure," she whispers while scouting the surroundings, mostly noting people taking seats.

Some staff, each who gave insightful instructions, greeted her.

It was not obvious to anyone else, but she was quite nervous and otherwise had a great deal of unsorted clutter on her mind.

The audience was taking form, but with time to review, she sits to the rear of the stage and makes a few notes. Apparently, focusing on subject details was helping her to gain a grip on her emotions and the circumstance. Finally, she seems to be settling down. Then, her boss takes a place, front row just off-center from the podium. Suddenly, she is focusing on the growing numbers of listeners—almost every seat taken.

Wynyard waves to acknowledge her.

She releases an internal sigh.

All eyes are upon her, and concentrating on that burden was unnerving her. Therefore, she returns her focus on the reminder cards, but she fumbles and drops a few. She kneels to pick them up but at that moment, she looks to the crowd and embarrassment envelopes her.

Moments later, a male affiliate from the stage-left faction steps forward, places a small pad on the lectern and begins delivering a short introduction…then subsequently invites her to the stage.

Applause commences while she walks to the pedestal as eager pupils watch and listen. She is straining internally, for the courage to deliver an adequate and interesting dissertation. However, once thrust into action something inside takes over. Removing the microphone from its holder, she goes mobile—vocalization quickly improving and fitting mannerisms following. Initially intimidated, but now moving confident she begins to give them what they came for—knowledge of nature.

The professor covered environmental challenges, uncontrollable shifts in the ecosystem, natural and manmade obstacles, changing conditions and the concerns they present—all while fortifying her theories with case study, supportive philosophy and in-depth analysis. She amplified the oration with current affairs newsworthy of correlation to produce substance and intrigue; aligning both hypothetical quandary and notorious factors while merging themes of common knowledge.

She delivered a collection of narratives to tug and draw at their attention to build trust and enhance the audience's fascination with every word. Before long, the entire assembly felt she knew her occupation well. Then, her slides and videos produced graphic effect while related stories from personal memory brought it all together. Her presentation of Florida's historical background not only explained the advantages of its pristine ecology, but she confronted future worries with reasoning of why and how local individuals should get involved. A broad discussion produced the necessary wisdom for everyone to grasp more than just a few fundamentals. Of course, she topped the exposition with her favorite argument, 'sinkhole mystery.'

"I touched on this earlier," she reminds. "But I like to save it for last because...well, I believe them to be the greatest threat to our landscape, not to mention our personal safety. Let me say it out loud, 'sinkholes,' commonly referred to as 'sinks.' They occur more often than the average person is aware and have been since the earth's creation...and don't ask me how that happened," she jokes. "That's a completely different subject."

A unanimous chuckle emanates from the crowd.

"But while sinks are normal," she continues with certainty, "that doesn't mean they're harmless or happen without help. Let me explain."

"First...why do they materialize? Well, simply put, the earth erodes. That's the clear-cut reason," she points to the audience, and moves on. "But to clarify," she gestures with a palm up, half-raised to the side. "Groundwater levels drop during dry season and sometimes for long periods. Therefore, the dirt withers. It dries out...right. It weakens, shrinks and becomes loose because the cohesion of wetness is no longer present. Many feet below the surface, this free soil can descend, particularly if there is a cavity below it and especially if there something moving and pulling at it. What I'm talking about here is aquifers— travelling tunnels of water. I'll get back to them in a minute," she pauses.

"Essentially, this void is aching for something to fall into it, and how much depends on the amount of solid rock there is to support, acting as a bridge. Even then, it will only hold for so long. Now, to exacerbate the effect, when rain penetrates this dry soil, which is hanging over a pit remember, it becomes wet and heavy and so...huge amounts can plummet because nothing is holding it up. You've seen them on the news, most are small gobbling up a car but occasionally they consume a house, or worse. These types of sinks are called 'cover-collapse,' and indisputably they cause the most financial and personal damage, because when they occur in populated areas, destruction is usually extensive. Most don't get names, because there are so many, but others gain popularity like 'the Devils Sinkhole,' in Hawthorne, Florida. Kids play in this one because the water is clean and deep, and rope swings create fun, which they use to jump in…and for the most part…very safe.

"The USF area, where we are today, is an active cover-collapse region. This campus has experienced more than thirty sinkholes in its forty years of operation, about one per square mile per year. Well-known sinks are all over the world. Her voice elevates to highlight one, "the Great Blue Hole off the coast of Belize is amazing. When you get a chance, look it up on-line. Jacques Cousteau declared it one of the top-ten scuba diving sites so yes—they make exciting news too.

But, I'm concerned with the ways we encourage the ones we don't want."

"The erosion I speak of sets above a hydrogeological framework, consisting of lime rock, compressed animal life and shells which we call karst. It is chock-full of tunnel formations—very large openings down to just crevices or even porous matter. Nevertheless, they carry all of our fresh water. As I mentioned a moment ago, these are known as aquifers and Florida…yes our State," she points a finger for effect, "has the most productive such system in the world.

"Our drinking water is obtained from them but these vast passageways do have a few disadvantages. One, they are usually unobstructed for many miles which at the onset is a great benefit. However, while the water is usually fresh and clean, if contaminates were to enter the stream they could end up far away very quickly and undiluted. It's like water going from one end of a garden hose to the other. Irresponsible landowners and many industries put us at risk when they let chemicals and waste get in…or worse, put them in on purpose. You can imagine the possibilities, right?" she asks a rhetorical question to make listeners think.

"These aquifers transport enormous amounts of water every day. Some, of course, just dribble but others…move rapidly. We categorize this varying speed and volume of water carried using a scale called, 'magnitude,' and listed from one to eight."

Putting a graphic display on the screen, she references that information. "A 'magnitude one' conveys the most amount of water, passing more than sixty-five million gallons per day; that's a lot right? A two, delivers six million to sixty-five million gallons per day. A four is only one hundred gallons per minute, a lot less but still quite strong and finally an eight which could be less than a pint per day—barely a trickle. This brings us to their second shortcoming.

The unassuming movement of water also eats away the very ground we stand on, and though these tunnels are rocky, do not presume they are indestructible. They are actually quite delicate. That's nature operating poorly, or at its best— depending on how you think. But today," she takes a needed breath, "we have something else to contend with. I'm referring to, 'construction.'

It's all around us—more prevalent every day. It doesn't take much to disturb the already 'volatile makeup' of an aquifer," she says using a quote, unquote gesture. "Construction can easily damage them by blocking or altering their direction. By that, I mean the current—the flow of water within them. More often than not, this activity is responsible for today's common sinkhole. Digging too deep, too often and in so many areas has displaced a lot of dirt which nature would not have executed alone. I think we all need to open our eyes to this fact, and start reevaluating structural building procedures and the impact they are having on our environment. For this discussion that's about it. Are there any questions?" She concludes, ending the one-way confab.

Immediately hands begin rising.
She picks one in the front.
A young man stands and asks, "How big can the diameter of an aquifer get?"
"Good question,' she commends him. "They come in all sizes from too small for a snake to pass through to immense and vast cave environments. Next question," she urges, picking a girl not far away.
She stands and asks. "Have people been inside them?"
"Another great question...! Yes, divers do sometimes go in them, exploring for changes and problematic situations. They usually gain access to them from the coast but some have entered via sinkholes where aquifers emerge, known as springs. I should add that some have currents too fast for safe exploration...much too dangerous to be in."
"How many are there?" the same girl asks, taking a seat.
"Gosh...there are so many, most haven't even been identified," Sheryl seems like the question is difficult. "Too many to say, they're everywhere. Much of Florida is private land, thereby unexplored, so there is no way to know for sure. I can tell you this though, there are seven hundred identified freshwater springs in northern and central Florida, and all of them end at a hole somewhere...but statistics show there could be as many as ten thousand undiscovered springs probably of magnitudes five or less, and again, mostly on private property. Numerous others could emanate from river beds like in St Johns River, extending the greater portion of Florida, and all uncharted."
Sheryl then asks the audience, "is there another?"

"Are we in danger?" a boy shouts, standing in the back. "I mean, it seems holes can open up anywhere. Is there protection? Who's looking out for us?"
"I'm glad you brought that up," she addresses. "Many people ask me that, you're not alone. We hydrologists and others at the Department of Environmental Protection (the DEP), we work hard every day to test, retest, survey, and evaluate the earth using increasingly better equipment and more improved methods. We help pass regulations to limit construction. Private company's also assist so there are many factions looking out for your interests but the fact remains...no one can calculate how the ground underneath our feet will ultimately react to shifting currents, tectonic plate movement or man-made

events. Forecasting an event like sinkholes is more difficult than predicting tornadoes and common weather patterns.

Do you know why they call it weather?" she asks. "Because meteorologists don't know what they're talking about." Again, she receives a humorous hum.

"Listen...I don't want to discourage anyone from living their lives," she advocates. "No one should stop doing that but you must understand the challenge. Dealing with nature is one thing, but other forces can encourage sink occurrence as well.

Think of it like this. Jenga, the game where each player takes a turn removing a block from the lower portion of a tower built of many intertwined layers. The object is to pick any one you want and place it on top of the stack balancing them as you go higher, making the structure taller and taller. Its instability intensifies as the height increases and eventually... it tumbles down right? Well, disrupting the earth is much like that. How long until we remove that one piece which makes the game...over? Constructing that one planned community, erecting that single building or just digging somewhere you shouldn't—that could be the final move and this contest is being played multiple times each day across this great State. I'm being a little dramatic and scary but the truth is... construction is everywhere and it's not going away. That's reality. To answer your question, our department is evolving to increase what we know for the inurement of public safety."

Sheryl thanks the students for attending and ends the lecture.

The students leave via exits at the rear and sides while Wynyard saunters a path towards her, presenting ample applause for a job well done. In dashing attire, plodding off the last step to stage height, he makes his way to accompany her at the projector.

Placing her belongings into her leather carry case, she glances his way.

"Well, well," he begins with hands in pockets, standing aloof exhibiting an astonished tone. "I've seen some speeches, but that was remarkable. You must have prepared for weeks," he praises with exaggerated tone.

"You might say I whipped it up," smiling, she zips her bag closed.

"Yes, you are inspiring but then...I'm always stimulated by you," he lowers his voice.

"Now's not the time," she snarls, avoiding eye contact. While slinging her bag over shoulder, she does give a brief look. "I have a lot on my mind," she complains.

"Right...!" he hails with displeasure. "The Olson saga continues. What did he do this time?"

"You know Scott...you're taking too much pleasure in my plight. That's not becoming of a gentleman," she turns to walk off stage.

"Well, I've never been accused of being courteous to competition, I'll give you that."

That makes her stop and turn. "My husband isn't a contest..."

"No he's not," he arrogantly cuts her off.

She sighs to a pause shaking her head. "What I mean is…he's not competing against you—no rivalry. You're struggling with yourself. I've told you…I'm not available," she affirms and continues to the exit. "If that changes, I'm sure you'll find out."

"But that did change," he blurts. "Did the rum cause memory loss?"

"It's Gin…arrgh," she hisses—thrusting through the door.

He simply smiles, appreciating her sashay, and mumbles, "at least she called me by my first name."

Fourteen

Peering into the late afternoon sun can be straining on the retina and optic nerves, particularly on a sweltering summer day without a cloud in sight. Blinding glare is a nationwide problem and the Sunshine State has the most intense rays in the country.

Numerous Floridians have alleged, "you can literally feel it beating down on you."

Richard, a safety instructor, is aware of the many accidents blamed on relentless daylight. On the roadways, it can obstruct the view of traffic lights and signs, but more importantly of other vehicles. Hazardous situations worsen and crashes occur when people can't see well. Therefore, he tweaks his truck's visors in defense. As the road veers, and changes direction, he must also reposition the adjustable flaps to shun those flickers and alternating flashes. Still, they find a way to strike his face at problematic angles and inconvenient moments. Though he is wearing dark sunglasses, contending with the sun is still an aggravating procedure, but unavoidable. Concentrating on traffic under these conditions is tough enough, but other annoyances will increase that peril, and today there may be a nuisance on his mind.

"What is it going to take to get through to you?" he mumbles aloud while swinging a visor to the left. "I don't get it," he scoffs, shifting the shade yet again while passing a yellow light without prudence. Then through another intersection, he accelerates too quickly.

"I work hard, play by the rules, provide a good life...oh yeah, and support her every need," he continues in defiant tone while changing the car radio for the nth time. Shaking his head with displeasure, he carries on, "but this is what I get—doubt, suspicion, and tossed to the wolves like tainted meat." Scratching his forehead, he glances toward the station playing yet another song he dislikes. He reaches for the dial, but suddenly—he has to slam the brakes.

The car in front stopped to let a pedestrian to cross the road—Richard has locked—tires screeching. He is aware that his truck is surging ever nearer to the rear end of that vehicle, but with no time to stop, he braces for impact—gripping the steering wheel tight trying to resist the momentum thrusting his body forward. Closer and closer the squealing mass of steel skids with him frozen. Unable to take his eyes off, he can only express panic as time begins to stand still. Anyone who has been in an unfolding accident knows that the moment leading up to collision is both endless and yet occurs so fast. Almost as if, nature is allowing the brain a precious extra second. Somehow, in the midst of this extremely short interval, he thinks of Sheryl mentioning something about that. Then, at the last possible second, an incisive thought causes him to swerve while pumping the brake pedal.

Like magic, he narrowly misses the catastrophe and fortunately, there was no traffic in the adjacent lane. However, the cross walker, caught in the potential strike path of the screeching four-wheeled weapon, ran like crazy to reach the curb and then beyond that. Thankfully, Richard stopped short of the flabbergasted man and came to rest beside that immobile car, although inches apart.

As the female occupant drives away, Richard notices her giving the one-fingered salute…but he was out of sorts, too shaken up for a return apology.

Cautiously, he moves the vehicle off the road to gain composure. Traumatized, he sits for a moment with both hands clenching the leather wrapped helm. Eventually, he calms and reaches into his pocket to remove something. It's his wife's wedding ring, which he gazes at with unexplainable relief, and then squeezes it.

"You saved me," he softly breathes. "I remembered your wisdom."

Bowing his head into the steering wheel, he murmurs again, "I promise… I'll make it right. I swear."

With that, he has a reflection. He elevates with transformed attitude and thinks with clarity. "I wasn't paying attention to the road and disaster almost happened—I'm not considering her..." he continues to contemplate the connection between this mishap and his troubles with Sheryl. "You win," he nods. "You won't call me…I'll call you…gee, she always gets what she wants," he smiles with pleasant disbelief.

After returning the shiny hoop, he takes out his cell phone and begins dialing, but at that moment, a call comes in. He went to cancel it, but recognized the number.

"Yeahahh, is everything okay?"

"Dad!" a rattled voice exclaims.

"Jenny, what is it? Are you alright?"

"Yeah, I guess so. I'm with Bobby. He's okay too and we're both okay…okay, so don't go and get all weird like you do."

"Alright, "he issues a non-committal promise. "But you sound worried."

"Well, uh…his car…" she wavers.

Her dad cannot hold back. "Did you guys get into an accident? Did you call the police…do you need an ambulance…where are you?" he's quick to interrogate.

"Daaadd… really, we're okay," she blurts. "It's not like that. It's just that Bobby's car is in a huge hole."

"WHAT!"

"The ground…it just…opened up," she yelps. "It happened so quickly, but like I said, we're alright. We got out without a scratch…but…" she begins loosing thought.

"Oh my God…! Give me the details later. Where you are?" he orders.

After jotting the location down, he heads off to the rescue. He is in a rush, but no doubt driving more cautious than earlier. Upon cornering the last turn onto a dirt road, he spots them standing near the helpless jeep—literally, the back end was sticking out of the ground. They are at a distance and the terrain is bumpy, so he approaches with care and has time to observe. They're jovial, more like lovebirds rather than victims. Bobby is dancing about his daughter while rotating one of the back tires. 'Very strange under the circumstance,' Richard thinks. The irritated father scowls, and while avoiding scattered ruts and rocks he maintains reconnaissance, wondering what is making them so giddy.

"Did you feel that? "Bobby shrieks at Jenny, and then looks down at the ground while assuming a crouched stance with arms out wide, as if stabilizing his balance. "Oh my God—there it is again," he warns, harnessing a confused appearance while darting his look at the sinkhole, to her, and then at the surrounding area. With seriousness, he places a hand on the Jeep. "I think it's moving," he alerts. Ultimately, Bobby couldn't sustain the charade any longer. He begins laughing to reveal that he was only playing.

"That's not funny," she stomps her feet. "Stop it you jerk. You might actually make it fall in."

However, he pays no attention and continues mocking the situation, pretending to feel additional vibrations that do not really exist. "Yeah, I think I'm starting to shake all over," the boyfriend chuckles again, and starts dancing senselessly while singing an old relevant tune. 'I can feel the earth...move...under my feet...I feel the skyyy tumbling down...I feel my...'

Jenny promptly steps up to him and delivers a peeved shove to bring the pitiful Carole King impression to a halt. "Cut it out you idiot, my dad's here," she scolds.

At that moment, Richard exits the truck and has an intense stare brewing—eyebrows drawn together with wrinkles bulging and nostrils flaring.

Bobby is the first to confront the parent moving with deliberate purpose. "Hello Mr. Olson. Thanks for helping with the...uh..." he extends a hand with exuberance.

Richard merely sends a stern look, hands on hip. "Save it Bobby. When your dad finds out about this you won't be 'bebopping' around', what is the deal? Doesn't this bother you?" He squawks.

"I'm just making the best of it sir," he cowers placing hands in pockets, no longer acting silly.

"Is my daughter's life important to you?" the unyielding father moves to inspect the damage.

"Daddy...!" Jenny interjects, hoping to reduce the reprimand.

Richard gives another strict stare.

The worried lad looks toward his girl, but she only returns a wary shoulder shrug.

"Yes sir," the boy responds more properly.

"Well, let's make that 'A LOT' more obvious, shall we!" the dad disciplines.

The boy's eyebrows rise and mouth scrunches as he nods with definite agreement.

Dismissing the boy's exploit, Richard begins studying the submerged vehicle. Jenny takes her father's side.

"You're lucky the doors could open," he tells her.

She looks up at him with woeful eyes, "yeah, I know," she agrees standing aloof with arms crossed.

"You're fortunate it didn't go deeper."

"Yeah, I figured that much," with big regretful eyes she concurs.

"It's remarkable I wasn't far away."

"Yeah, good timing huh?" she admits, gnawing at her bottom lip.

"You should be thrilled that you got out unscathed."

"I am," she eagerly replies and quickly changes subject—pleading in sincere tone, "do we have to tell mom?"

The father laughs, "Ohhh yeahhh!" He smiles. "That's a given."

"You don't have to seem so happy about it," she peddles puckered lips and a nervous crackly voice.

"I think your luck has run out. There's no way to keep this from your mother," he shakes his head. "That's not possible, trust me…I've tried keeping secrets over matters having much less significance. She's got sonar you know— ESP and not just clairvoyance or telepathy but some kind of damn mind-reading ability," he gestures a hand flick off the side of his head. "I don't know what it is she has going on but I'm telling you, 'you can't hide it?'"

"I know dad, she's weird. So are you gonna tell her?"

"Oh no, I've got my own problems. Have you listened to the way she speaks to me? Besides, I won't have to tell her," he heads back to his truck.

Jenny argues, "why not?"

"Because you're going to do it," he laughs again.

Immediately, Jenny winces and stares to the woods.

Richard removes a clevis hook and cable from his winch, and begins chuckling. "Oh, this is going to be good. I might even make some popcorn," he jokes, and then stops smiling to resume a half-mean glare at Bobby.

"Thanks dad. Enjoy the show," Jenny's sourpuss face complains.

"Bobby," Richard exhales. "Get over here. Hook this up to the rear of your jeep."

The boy takes the heavy clasp and metal hawser and initially struggles with the application, but manages to secure it as requested.

With the aid of a tough truck and a robust tree, the two males labored with emergency extraction. At first, it did not seem possible, but their tenacity got the vehicle out and it only suffered superficial damage. Bobby even earned a few brownie points for his accommodating effort. They were all relieved.

Fifteen

"This is the most time I've spent with you, in a long while, huh," Richard relaxes. "It's just my work you know, I'm busy…"

"It's okay dad. I get it," Jenny looks at her father, sitting beside him at their kitchen nook. "But why are you and mom fighting so much?"

"We're just on opposite sides of an issue."

"What's that, construction?"

"Somewhat, and other matters—listen, I piss her off too but she's so unwavering about things though," he chuckles. "I used to think that was cute."

Jenny prods, "and now?"

He thinks carefully as a car is heard entering the driveway. "And now, it's your turn to bite the bullet," he changes the topic.

"I've got to get a shower," she swallows, and tries to leave the table.

"Sit," he keeps her seated. "Take your medicine. You can do it."

They both face the front door as footsteps approach, keys jiggling…then inserted to unlock the door. Jenny becomes uneasy as it opens and items hit the floor, noise resonating. Shoes slide off, a fatigued groan follows and a purse plops. Jenny eyes her dad one last time. Just then, Sheryl turns the corner and makes contact with the idle pair.

"What are you doing home so early?" she asks, but Richard doesn't reply, "Still have nothing to say…great," Sheryl scoffs. Then she notices Jenny's quiet behavior. "What's going on? What happened?" she moves closer. "Somebody better start talking. You're never home at this hour," she points at Richard. "And you," turning to Jenny she acknowledges, "don't have conversations at the same table with your father.

Where's Jake? Is he okay? Did he get hurt building that raft? Why didn't someone call me?" her anger swelling as she throws a hand up. "Richard, if something bad happened," she pauses, holding back extreme frustration. "Either of you can speak now. Who is going to be first?"

"Did I tell you?" Richard expresses.

Jenny gives a meager nod.

"And this is when you start explaining," he nudges the sunken girl.

Sheryl draws attention to her daughter.

"Mom, before you get all worked up," Jenny explains with the help of cautioning hands.

Richard inserts a smug gesture, "too late for that."

"Spill the beans," her mother demands, standing with her arms crossed.

"It's really not a big deal. I was at East Lake Tohopekaliga this morning with Bobby."

"And where were you last night?"

"That's not the issue."

"It is now—where were you?"

"Uh…the same place," she reluctantly exposes.

Sheryl turns her vision onto her aloof husband, "were you aware she spent the night in the woods?"

"That part I didn't know," he smiles but Sheryl is not amused. "This isn't about me," he defends.

"Mom, listen. Dad saved us," Jenny enlightens.

"From what…?" Sheryl utters with obsessive tone.

Jenny proceeds to tell the story and then when finished, tries to escape.

"See you guys at dinner," she starts darting.

"Not so fast. Sit down," mom grabs the fleeing gal, pressing her back down. "Did you have sex?"

"No mom…geese. Don't you trust me?" Jenny whines.

"Don't lie Jenny…I can't forgive that."

Richard looks away.

"I said no Mom—Dad can you talk to her."

He does not say anything, but he does give Sheryl a concerned look.

"Alright, we'll discuss this later. I want to talk to your dad now. You can go," she releases the worried girl. "But I'm not done with you yet," she hollers at the absconding teen.

Now Sheryl's attention is completely fixated on the lonesome spouse.

"Why are you looking at me like that?" he defends. "This is an unrelated event."

"Secrets, you're just full of them," with disdain, she accuses.

"I'm not keeping anything from you. This just happened."

She shakes her head, detailing there is something else on her mind.

"Forget it," he thwarts her attitude. "I can't do this."

"No, you listen," she arbitrates. "I need your honesty—you're going to give me closure," she sits across from him, piercing into his eyes. "Is there anything you have to say?"

"No, I tell you everything, eventually, but I do. There's nothing to hide," he asserts.

"Yeah, you keep saying that, but that's not good enough," she breaks to inhale. "I might be able to get passed some things but…?"

"Listen, I was thinking," he moves into another subject. "I had a sudden thought today. And…I want you to take your ring back."

"Just like that, huh," she is quick to anger again.

"It's just that I…"

"Look…!" she stops him. "This is about me now." She lowers her voice, "I don't want Jenny to hear, but I know…"

"Okay, there is something," he admits with reluctance and takes her hand. "But at no time did I," he stops and breathes. "I didn't want to hurt…what I mean is…" he is having trouble getting something out.

"What the f' are you saying?" she anticipates a horrible confession.

Just then, Jake busts in—again their conversation put on hold. The boy begins jabbering about his raft and the fun he is having building it. He mentions, "Junior's dad, Mr. Nash, was a boat builder and has been helping as well...and he called the craft 'unsinkable.' I can't believe we're getting this kind of craftsmanship." He gets a drink from the fridge and turns on the TV. He starts to continue, but another news alert captures attention.

"Jake, Shhh. Please turn this up," his mom implores.

"Well, there you have it folks. Runnymede Lake is sick. Fish and wildlife are dying fast, and the residents believe the water is poisoned. Some elders say this problem has been around since the drug giant Hizamitu Pharmaceutical purchased Novan Company back in the mid-sixties. Even back then, some preservationists thought that countless drums of medicinal waste were buried near this area—but never proven. Has the onslaught of construction now unearthed those chemicals, releasing mega-toxins into the water supply? Will this be the next lake to disappear? This is Katie Burroughs and that was our top story...now, over to Stan for the weather."

Sheryl's aggravation only grows and Richard takes notice.

"Sheryl, you have to stop," he tries to nip it in the bud.

"Richard...that Lake is right around the corner from us. Our son has played in it—fished in it. Jenny was at a lake near it last night. Will your own child have to die before you wake up?"

Sheryl walks away leaving him seated at the table.

Richard is greatly perplexed.

On the front porch, she dials a number.

"Jeff...Sheryl," she quietly speaks.

"I know. I recognize your voice, duh," he affirms. "Are you calling about Runnymede?"

"Yeah... you saw it too?"

"Uh-huh. Listen—Arnold and I will get there first thing in the morning. We'll run the whole gambit. What else would you like us to do?"

"Just proceed with the usual."

"I know the drill. I'll do my best."

"Thanks. I can always count on you."

Jeff senses something unusual. "Why are you whispering? What's wrong? You're never this amiable. You're scaring me," Jeff pokes.

"Just at home—kind of in the middle of...stuff."

"Ahhh, right...I see," Jeff returns in a character like that of a detective feeling suspicion. "Something else is brewing," he says, "but I'll put a lid on it." He changes subject, "so how did it go at the University?"

"I wowed the crowd, just like you said. They never knew what hit them."

"And Wynyard—how was he?"

"I blew him off. I left so fast he won't speak to me again," she tells, but sounds upset.

"I doubt that," Jeff chuckles. "If I know that guy, and I think I do. He doesn't give up."

"Yeah, you're right," she sighs and alters topic. "So, did you find anything at any of the ODG sites? Did Arnold get inducted?"

"He's been educated just fine—in true DEP style," he laughs. "But we didn't find anything. You can rest easy," he assures, then deviates. "Sheryl, if you want my opinion, Richard might be telling the truth. If they're violating any codes, ethically or otherwise, I can't see it."

She does not respond.

"That's good news right," Jeff probes for a response, "happy, happy,"

Still there is silence.

"Hey, you still there,"

"Uh yeah," she staggers into a reply, not sounding thrilled, "of course it is."

However, her visual appearance is telling otherwise.

"Okay…goodnight," she ends the call.

Upon hanging up, she looks over her shoulder with a menacing stare.

Sixteen

"Is it dark or what?" a man's voice comments amidst inaudible droning.

"Umm…this is normal—the moon's hidden by an overcast sky," another male describes the situation. "So, do you like it"?

"I can't see anything?"

"No you—I'm talking about this State—hello, you there? The flatness, the heat, the sand, you know…the perpetual rays, girls and rum runners—are you okay with leaving that other world behind? You seem distant—kind of checking things out in a weird way…like right now. It's as if you're…trying to make sense of a confusing situation. Are you questioning your relocating here—as if you made the wrong decision?"

"I'm just inquisitive, but that doesn't mean that I'm thinking crazy."

"So you're truly happy?"

"Is anyone really okay with their lives? There's always something to complain about," he continues with stoic resolve. "But what matters is how you deal with the gloom and doom."

"Well, there's some philosophy that will save the human race. So you're not just a blind bloke walking?"

"Yeah, well I can't see much right now."

"Not out there you won't, there's only marshland beyond your window anyway. Hey man, I could use another cup. Do you mind?"

A dome light comes on and Arnold is unscrewing the cap from a thermos. He begins pouring coffee into a cup that Jeff is extending his way. Arnold helps stabilize the wobbly goblet while Jeff maintains control of the vehicle, concentrating on the path lit up by headlights.

"So, you didn't say… are you glad to be here?"

Arnold sets the container aside and Jeff places his beverage into a holder. The radio is off and the sound of wind rustling past the car is quite apparent—tires are humming too as Jeff returns the interior to darkness.

"Well it's different, but yeah, I like it," Arnold continues with a gaping yawn into his cupped hands. "This is a fun place. There's a lot to do. Plenty of water activities and endless outdoor stuff but as far as the part with girls—I have the one I want thank you! It took me a while to figure that out…almost too long, but she took me back after pursuing her here."

"So she left you?"

"I was dragging my feet. She would say I had…'commitment issues,' so I was put on notice. She dropped everything and went home."

"So she's from Florida! Where's your family?"

"Salt Lake City Utah, the beehive state—more copper, gold and oil than most know about…and the birth place of the Sundance film festival. Of course, the yearly celebration is now held in Park City," he educates, and suddenly shifts

71

focus. "And before you ask, it's not like everybody from there is a Mormon either," Arnold states with a modest snicker.

"That wasn't even on my mind," Jeff chuckles. "Seriously!" he asserts and glides past the comment. "But what is the—why the interest with earthquakes?"

"I grew up with their adversity—not like I was in a family business. As chance would have it, I always had the misfortune of witnessing the havoc they wreak. Wrong place...wrong time...whatever the case, I was close enough to feel the destruction, but far enough away to live through it. Experiencing something like that first hand, at such a young age, left me lost and I don't know why—but I had to know more. They didn't make sense to me until I learned that studying them might help people. That's when I knew what I wanted to do with my life...and with that comes hope—the possibility of saving one life. So that's what I tried to do."

"Yeah...?"

"Yeah, but dreams change," Arnold pauses. "Some quests take you through...unexpected feelings."

"And you threw in the towel for beaches and relaxation. That passion is over huh," Jeff boasts. "There's a new vision on Arnold's horizon. Is that it?"

"No, not at all, I'm still living that goal. It's just that...I have realized there's more to life than discovering ways to save masses of nameless people. Sometimes...all that matters is rescuing that one person who makes you happy. And once you believe they're the only one who can do that..."

"Okay...wow. You explained the whole being in love thing. What's the big take away from hunting seismic activity?"

"Truthfully, I have more questions than when I started," Arnold confesses while staring at bugs dart across the artificial illumination. Like a shooting star, they zip through the car's headlights. For a moment, he seems lost in thought. "I can tell you this though," regaining poise he continues. "There are several fault lines, much more dangerous than the notorious San Andreas."

"But I thought that was the big one?" Jeff seems surprised.

"Not really, that fault just gets a lot of attention because there's been more activity in that region and it's in...OH MY GOD...California!" Arnold jests aloud. "But check this out, the Wasatch Fault in Salt Lake City is one of the lengthiest in the world, at a stretch of two hundred and forty miles long it can deliver a punch of seven-point-five on the Richter scale. It has slipped more than seven miles over seventeen million years."

"That's pretty far!"

"High actually," Jeff corrects. "It caused the mountains to rise along that ridge line, and it's due to go off again. Now the Cascadia Subduction Zone, it has thirty times the destructive power of San Andreas. It's a six-hundred and eighty mile stretch of colliding landmass located fifty miles off shore along the coast of Oregon, Washington State and British Columbia. When this thing gives way, you will see tsunamis surpass the one in Sumatra 2004—tidal waves a hundred feet high. I'm not kidding, look it up. The last time it shifted was in the year seventeen hundred, and speculation is...any day it will unleash again. Talk about widespread destruction. You know the longer the timespan between quakes the worse they are when they occur—it has been three-hundred and twelve years now. So think about that."

"Alright, you obviously know more about earthquakes than I need to hear," Jeff's eyebrows rise, and with natural light emerging, Arnold can see it. "But now you're here…just left it all behind."

"Like I said, my future is here. The way I see it—my prior life was only practice for the real mission. The journey changes when the right person enters your life. But how do you know when that happens?" Arnold lifts a hand, "Glad you asked. "When you don't mind changing your objectives—when you realize you're not giving anything up but rather gaining more—when you figure out that your life was never complete before you met—when you experience real physical pain without them…that's when you know. It's hard to explain but like they say, you'll know when it happens."

"No, I think you nailed it…really" Jeff smirks.

Arnold continues.

"When you believe you aren't a whole person on your own…that you're truly better, and more effective with this someone else around—you don't feel like you left anything behind. It just confirms that you never had anything to begin with…until that moment."

"So your girlfriend is the new mission?"

"Yeah, I guess that's what I'm saying."

"Okay, enough already," Jeff gets disgusted. "I don't feel like this is a guy talk anymore. Football, hockey…let's talk a few stats or something. I get it…you love this girl. It's sick I tell you. Couples surround me. First Sheryl, and now you—all I have are stories of work and my neighbor's cats."

"What do you mean about Sheryl?" Now Arnold is being the nosy one. "I thought they were on the rocks."

"Yeah, it appears that way. That's the way she presents it anyway but I don't know, they're both stubborn like that, workaholics and always on opposite ends of every issue."

"And cheating—is she involved with Wynyard? What happened back at the office? He came in and she had us leave. What's up with that?"

Jeff pauses, "I'm really not sure, but I don't think so," he seems to be guessing. "She doesn't have much in common with him. He isn't her type but he is persistent, I'll give him that. If there was anything between them though, I think I would know it. Maybe there was an 'uh-oh what did I do' moment somewhere along the way you know, but no, I'm pretty sure that whatever it is…it's harmless."

"Sounds like you're not sure," Arnold mocks and gets restless. "What about you? He changes the subject. "Where are you from?"

"Born and raised right here! Well, Key west anyway. I'm a Hemingway fan, tried and true."

"Are we about there?" Arnold looks around, "I need to stretch".

"Actually, we are," Jeff veers, pulling off the road just as tangible light breaches the horizon.

"Hey, I think I can make out the appearance of a lake up ahead. Is that Runnymede?"

"No, that's East Lake Tohopekaliga, Runnymede is behind us and it's only a bathtub compared to this body of water. As soon as full light comes up though, you'll see it better. We've actually been circling around it for the last few miles. This side road faces the bigger one, but from here, we have access to either one. It's a short walk, just past those trees," Jeff points to their rear.

As they get out of the company utility vehicle and stretch, they both joke that it is much too early to be collecting poisoned fish. They engage a few puns and complete their coffees, but they soon refocus on the task in hand.

"Sheryl only lives ten minutes from here," Jeff mentions. "She's basically a straight shot south on 192."

"So why isn't she doing this then? Oh right, she's the boss," Arnold answers himself.

At the rear of the vehicle Arnold opens the swing gate, the cargo light comes on to illuminate their effects.

Jeff slides a cardboard box closer to their proximity and begins removing the contents. Several pairs of latex medical gloves, masks, booties and over garments; specimen cups with screw caps, Ziploc bags, permanent markers, blank stickers and a few other items.

"Securing potential life-threatening substances should never be taken lightly," Jeff enlightens.

"One must be precise, but also safe," Arnold acknowledges.

"You got it my friend—time to earn our pay."

Each grabs a one-sized fits all superpolymer coverall and suit up, utilizing the attached protective hood as well. They are now completely white like a researcher from the arctic region. Promptly, they begin treading toward the water. At first, their feet crunch in the loose pebbly ground but quickly the stepping becomes squishy, as the earth turns marshy while entering the tree line, a brief distance away. They pass through it as quickly as they entered and emerge near the north side of their destination, Lake Runnymede. Immediately, they spot dead fish. Carcasses rest on the perimeter partially submerged, bobbing back and forth from the pushing of gentle waves. Others are drying out, laying further up the banks incline. Many still float in the lake along with high quantities of scattered trash. Debris also aligns the border and trickles into tall grasses just beyond.

The sun is now providing well-needed light—helping to distinguish items as they effort to collect and characterize soil, water, rocks and rubbish for analysis. Jeff begins marking bags with proper location and various useful data. He asks Arnold to return to the truck to retrieve a few larger ones more suitable for the securement of the bigger specimens—a big Blue Catfish and a huge Stripped Bass. He isn't gone very long when Jeff's cell phone rings and he has to remove a glove in order to view it, so Jeff is a bit agitated when he notices that Arnold is the one calling.

"What?" he answers with abrupt tone. "You've only been gone a minute—okay, okay—the bags might be in the back seat instead of the cargo area...but they're in there somewhere."

"No, that's not it—I think you better come over here," with a sincere and troubled voice Arnold informs.

"Why...for what?" Jeff tries to interrogate but Arnold quickly cuts him off.

"Come to the truck now," he unloads and hangs up.

Jeff is beside himself, mumbling under breath for the entire jaunt over there. "The new guy must be crazy. Who does he think he is? I have to come to him—and then he hangs up on me? Who does that? I'll make him walk home, that's what I'll do...for a couple miles anyway. I can't let him get hurt though, Sheryl will kill me. I'll just scare him, yeah, that's it..." he continues subtle ranting.

Marching up from the rear of the vehicle, he sees Arnold a good distance in front of it, standing near the edge of the other larger lake. Hastening past the SUV Jeff announces his arrival.

"This better be good because I don't want to be here all day and..." just then, before completing another word he moderates his walk to a slower meandering pace, cautiously moving forward with a jaw dropping stare. Changing his character from annoyance to something greater than amazement, he sees what Arnold is gawking at—and becomes captivated as well. Upon reaching the new colleague, he simply rests a hand on his shoulder.

"Does this happen often?" Arnold scoffs. "This place has more surprises than Utah?"

"No," Jeff responds prudently. "It never does." Reaching for his phone he falters, "I...think Sheryl...will want to hear about this."

Seventeen

Wet and wrapped in bath towels Sheryl turns a doorknob and gently pushes on the ingress, but only enough to peek. Through the crack, corridor illumination strikes the backside of a young body lying beneath comfortable blankets atop a full-sized bed. Long hair drapes over a large pink pillow and then streams off the edge. The other end of the cushion, clutched by a youth who is facing away and into the adjacent wall, still in dream state. Sheryl witnesses that Jenny is fast asleep and is pleased. Across the hall, she peeps into another room. Jakes is out cold as well. Mom can rest easy—both kids are home safe.

Satisfied, she grins and moseys to the master bedroom and finds Richard buttoning his shirt. As she passes him they make pithy eye contact, but neither has anything to say. They are not in a cheery mood, but don't appear upset either—possibly each is experiencing emotional quandary over recent arguments.

Once in the bathroom she removes the clumpy head dressing and shakes out her hair—blonde locks are left swathing her face, partially concealing the eyes. Piercing between those loose curls she ganders at her image in the mirror, and then directs vision toward Richard. He also faces a mirror in the bedroom, which is opposite his nearly naked wife, and while zipping his pants he notices her reflection watching him. She draws some tresses away to allow him a better view of her—clearly, she is aware he is spying her.

He reaches for a tie and begins to don it. She grabs a makeup case and removes some of its contents…and again they glance at each other through their looking glasses. She brushes on face powder and adds eye shadow and the glimpses remain. She applies mascara and spreads shiny gloss across her lips…he spies on her while fiddling with cufflinks. Their stares are beginning to gain each other's appreciation.

"You don't need any of that," he comments and begins toward her.

Rubbing her lips together, she combs her hair with long downward strokes, and she does not take her eyes off him.

He extends his wrist and exposes an unclasped shirt cuff.

"You always have trouble with this one," she gently sighs and stops grooming herself to finish it for him. While pulling away he takes hold of her hand—she lets him while conveying a curious look.

"You're gorgeous without it," he says. She looks into his eyes and he to hers. "Other women are envious of you," he further cajoles her beauty and then releases.

He walks to his dresser—she contemplates the last few seconds, but many issues are on her mind. They are complex yet simple, convoluted and certainly not resolved which accounts for her mysterious expression. Nevertheless, she appears to be transforming.

Now, her change of character could be one of surrender, and it might be more of need but then again desire may be the culprit, or just the basic will to conquest female seekers. Either way, her attitude has noticeably become playful. Leaning against the edge of the doorway she acquires a stealthy view of him— he's securing his wallet and car keys. In that moment, she lets the last towel drop straight to the floor. Now nude, she takes a few steps to stand on the carpeted portion of the floor, delicate and supple. Presenting herself as available and with hands to the side, she takes a quivering breath before softly calling her husband's name. He turns and straightaway has an involuntary reaction, forcing him to stop in his tracks. He simply relishes a delicious gaze upon his arousing wife, and the nature of her exposed invitation.

She steps closer—he begins to put his keys back down.

Then, her cell phone rings. They both look toward it on the nightstand—it rings again but they return gaze upon one another, still beholden to the moment.

"Do you have time?" she appeals to the moment, revealing a provocative mood.

Their eyes meet and lock as she coasts yet nearer.

The device rings again and his attention is drawn to it.

"I won't answer it," in craving tone, she sighs, grazing a hand across her breast to further entice and stimulate him.

He looks back at her…ogling her shapely figure from head to toe, but her amorously snaring eyes—those he cannot stop looking at.

Her passionate stare is imprisoning him.

He too takes a deep captivating breath.

The phone rings once more and yet again.

"Answer it," he thoughtfully remarks. "You know you can't let that go."

Pausing for a sec, she scrunches her mouth, then releases a vexed exhale through the nose…but she nods okay and moves to retrieve the phone.

Richard waits.

"Sheryl, you have got to get here, right now!" the caller's voice shrieks with desperation.

Richard could hear it too.

"There is a whirlpool in East Lake Tohopekaliga—it's about to swallow a fishing boat—I'm not even kidding."

Sheryl puts the cell to her shoulder and looks at Richard. "It's Jeff… it sounds serious," shrugging shoulders she utters, minus the usual enthusiasm.

He gives her an encouraging kiss upon the forehead and then looks at his watch. Ultimately, he turns and departs leaving Sheryl bothered.

"Are you there?" Jeff hollers. "Hey did you hear me," he repeats in a pestering tone. His voice bursts from the little speaker.

Sheryl merely stares into an empty hall, not paying much attention.

Jeff's voice explodes again.

She finally places the phone to ear. "Yeah, I got it," she snaps. "I'll be there—in the meantime call the authorities—set up quarantine—just keep it safe for now," she blurts and hangs up, and directly heeds to a window and impatiently parts the blinds. She sees Richard driving away and irritably watches until he is out of sight.

It was not long before she was standing alongside her workmate, examining the lake and the latest untimely interruption.

"Is that the same boat?" she questions with arms crossed and a perplexed guise. With a sketchy attitude, she glares from shoreline out to a small craft, slowly drifting.

"Yeah, I guess it got weaker," Jeff also gazes upon the barely spinning vessel.

Sheryl's eyebrows rise as if saying, 'this is what you got me down here for?'

Jeff notices her discontent. "The suction was stronger a few minutes ago, I swear," he attempts to establish the fact—she's not convinced.

Just then, the whirlpool begins swirling faster.

"I told you," Jeff jumps in glee of being right.

Quickly the spinner picks up speed…wider and deeper the center becomes—swiftly drawing the rickety boat to the middle. One end sucked in as the other flopped about, struggling to stay afloat—breaking apart, disappearing.

"Crap! I don't believe this is. Kids swim in this lake—this isn't good," Sheryl yelps, flipping a licit hand gesture toward the dismal scene. Suddenly she has an internal 'ah-hah moment… 'Jenny was here last night.' She puts her hand to mouth.

Jeff disregards her demeanor, as promised. "Well, the police are roping it off," he points to the officers dispersing plastic yellow caution tape from tree to tree around the lake.

"That's good…thanks," she suspends her thoughts to glare at him. "Jeff, what does this have to do with Runnymede or ODG? What's the connection?"

"Honestly, I can't find one. They don't have an active operation within miles from here but if they are blasting to dislodge hard rock—that could loosen soil farther away too. Who knows what's occurring down there?"

"Could I have been wrong? Maybe they're not causing these problems. Perhaps I have been too hard on Richard"

"It's too early to tell, just remain positive okay. You'll get to the bottom of this…you always do."

"You're a good friend you know."

"Yeah, I keep telling you."

They both have a needed laugh and each pauses briefly for personal deliberation, though Jeff is eager to reengage.

"So…I interrupted you guys didn't I?" he pries.

She looks at him with a dismayed face.

"I just know these things," he grimaces.

Sheryl shakes her head. "No I don't think so, Rick was preoccupied anyway," she chews at the side of her lip.

"Right, he just had a lot of work to get to," Jeff agrees with melodramatic certitude.

"I just don't get it," she gestures. "Dropping the towel has always done the trick."

"Okaayyy…" Jeff looks away.

"Sorry for the visual," she apathetically apologizes. "But I was all out there—you know what I mean?"

"Well, my call did get in the way."

"That's beside the point—he wasn't going for it anyway. I could tell," Sheryl whines.

"Well, maybe you just don't have it anymore," he teases.

She scoffs wildly, "don't mess with me Jeff. I'm not in the mood."

"Okay…golly. I'm just messing 'wit cha'. But you are getting a little flabby," he continues jesting while looking her up and down.

She gives him an evil stare.

"I'm just saying…maybe you should start jogging or working out. You know—keeping up with tight 'twenty-somethings' takes a lot of work."

She promptly gives him a shove.

"I'm kidding—you're fine. Can't you take a joke?"

Then another voice arises.

"Sheryl, this is the chief of police," Arnold touts an introduction. Vying for her attention, he walks up from behind.

She turns. "I appreciate the quick response captain," she shakes the uniformed man's hand.

"No problem, I'm just glad there aren't any casualties—say, how does something like this happen?" the officer politely enquires.

"Well, that's an easy request…but what causes it—now that's the fifty thousand dollar question," she professionally responds, and moves into her educative mode. "Basically, a breach in the lake bed is letting water pass into an aquifer which carries it away," indicating with her hand she points toward the whirlpool and explains. "This one appears to have a sizable vortex resultant of a significant downdraft, meaning it's draining at a fair rate.

"How long before it's all gone? The water I mean."

"Well, it may not deplete, at least not yet," she sneers at the twirling eyesore. "From what I see, the level of the lake isn't going down—my guess is there are other springs keeping it filled, probably an equal amount of water is coming in to counter balance the outflow.

"This cycle may continue indefinitely?" the awestruck man asks.

"It looks that way," Jeff butts in.

"Which is why everyone needs to stay out, especially children," she warns. "These things are compelling, tempting to get close to and kids will want to play in it...but that luring nature will eventually drown most novice swimmers."

"Because it pulls them down," the chief requests clarification, showing concern.

"It could." Jeff points out.

Sheryl somewhat disagrees. "The danger is really the constant resistance of swimming to get away that kills," she adds. "Ones strength can be zapped pretty quickly when struggling against that current, that's how most unaware victims usually meet their fate. This one does have some strength, but it could become a maelstrom at any time."

"That's a large, very powerful whirlpool," Jeff explains.

"Is that possible?"

"Not likely, but they are unpredictable," she asserts.

"Tell him about Lake Peigneur," Jeff nudges her.

Sheryl objects, "Jeff!"

"Sheryl, he should know."

"What is this lake?" the police officer urges for explanation.

Sheryl is reluctant, but continues.

"November 21, 1980...Louisiana," she begins with Arnold listening closely, as if he had never heard the story before. "It's a manmade disaster though, and not what we have here—but I'll tell you anyway. An oil company, on Lake Peigneur, drilled a fourteen inch wide hole down through the lakebed fifteen hundred feet and accidentally penetrated into the Diamond Crystal Salt Mine."

"You can look it up on 'Wikipedia' or better yet 'YouTube,'" Jeff excitedly interrupts, adding validity to the account.

"Anyway," Sheryl continues giving Jeff the eye. "The lake started draining into the mine cavity and very quickly—the inrushing water also dissolved the massive amount of salt making the reservoir bigger and bigger—so it was able to take in more and more water. The downdraft was so powerful that multiple large ships, 'barges' were drawn to it and eventually became submerged—a couple of them actually got sucked all the way down and into the mine."

"The cavity was huge," Jeff butts again. "Mythbusters once had a show— they debunked the possibility of something like that happening—a devastating whirlpool that is," he highlights with a detesting scoff. "But the Peigneur episode...yeah, that really happened, so...so much for that flimsy theory."

Sheryl gives him another strict glance. "Of course, it's possible under the right circumstance and that day was it," she confirms. "And to make matters worse, the force was so strong, the Decambre Canal reversed direction—the water in the Gulf of Mexico actually started flowing north—even more water came in, devastation was further enhanced."

"Landslides occurred," Jeff rams in again, demonstrating with his hands. "A one-hundred and fifty foot waterfall came out of nowhere and huge trees fell over like toothpicks," he animates vividly.

"He's right. The disaster was immense. The mine was a complete loss and by the time it was over, sixty-five acres of terrain was destroyed, sucked right into a giant hole."

"Is that even possible?" Arnold moans.

"Ask the eighty year old man who survived it," Jeff contends. "It was only a ten foot deep lake that this old fart was fishing on. He'll tell you all about it. If he's still alive that is, but if not, that's on YouTube too," Jeff throws in a blasé remark.

"Alright, alright, I get it," the cop stresses. "These things can be dangerous but what I want to know—is that going to happen here? How do I prepare?"

"I very much doubt that this turns into anything like I just described," Sheryl eases. "None of those conditions exist here, but it could get more hazardous than it is. As far as doing anything though—we'll just have to ride it out. Maybe it will stop on its own."

"'Lake Jackson,' in Tallahassee developed a sinkhole under it and part of it dried up. They're now thinking of trying to plug the thing up," Jeff declares, giving the officer an option.

Sheryl gets perturbed again. "But it is dry now, and easy to get to—filling it in is possible because there's no water to contend with," Sheryl clarifies. "But still, the costs don't benefit plugging and doing anything like that."

She begins walking away from the lake, urging them to come with her. "Listen, just keep people away for now," she directs the chief. "I'll send a team to investigate possible remedies, but until then we just need to keep vigil," she assures that's all for now.

Having done all they could to secure the area and forewarn law enforcement, Sheryl instructs her people to meet back at the office. Jeff and Arnold drive away, but upon reaching her vehicle, Sheryl's attention is deviated once again.

A female reporter with her cameraman at bay is quickly encroaching, intent on reaching her before she leaves. "Mrs. Olson, Mrs. Olson," the reporter lets out a breathless squawk. "I'm Rhonda Smith...with KBTV news. Can I have a word with you?"

Sheryl promptly turns, acting compliant. "We've met. I know who you are. What would you like to know?"

"Can you explain the reason for the unusually high number of sinks, or the scattered contamination found in them and what about this whirlpool, how did it develop?" holding a microphone to Sheryl's face she pressures.

"Listen!" Sheryl persists in a professionally agitated manner. "These occurrences are within nature's average range."

"You're saying this spinning threat is normal?"

"I'm trying to explain that...the environment has many challenges to contend with."

"So, none of this has been encouraged by man...like construction companies," she quickly digs deeper.

Sheryl is notably curious about the question, "That possibility is under investigation."

"What are you doing, exactly, to figure that out?"

"Well, that work is complex...there are...numerous avenues...to research," she falters for a proper assertation.

"Have you found any of it to be connected to human flaw?"

"I'm sorry. That is all I can say. Now, if you'll excuse me...I have to get going," Sheryl takes a few steps and begins to enter her vehicle.

"You sound unsure," the reporter nags, following closely. "Is there something you can't divulge because you have ulterior motives? Frankly Mrs. Olson, is there a conflict of interest between your job and your husband's company? Your last name is Olson, isn't it?" Rapidly she discharges an inflammatory suggestion.

Sheryl abruptly turns and adamantly fires back. "Nothing could be further from the truth. People's lives come first and they always will. Now please, I have nothing else to say until our investigations are complete."

Upon closing the car door behind her, the reporter immediately starts tapping on the window. Repeatedly she raps while waving the camera operator to walk away. Noticing the camera is no longer present, Sheryl, though irritated, finally rolls her window down.

"The camera is off," the newsperson submits while lowering her microphone, out of possible use. "Off the record, don't you think too much construction might have something to do with these events? I know ODG is at the heart of your investigation—aren't you just a little worried?"

"Off the record...'Rhonda'—I don't know more than you and if I did, personally I wouldn't share it with you. I have no knowledge of any suspicious activity—that you can print, okay?"

"Does he share everything with you?" crouching lower she probes.

"I don't have to know every detail. I'm his wife, not his defense attorney."

"Do you know about the weeklong corporate bash he's attending in Atlanta next week? I hear it's quite the... celebration—for select staff only," flaunting a prissy smile, she eagerly reveals this company secret.

"What are you talking about?" Sheryl demands with unsettled intrigue.

"I guess he doesn't tell you everything. Maybe that's not the only thing he's keeping from you."

Walking away the happy reporter delivers a candid chortle. "As his wife, you should probably find out more...don't you think. Thanks for the commentary Mrs. Olson. Have a good day."

Sheryl, yet again, has more on her mind.

Eighteen

Jeff and Arnold are laying out specimen bags onto a polished steel surface. Once again working sanitary, but wearing different protective gear, as their surroundings are sterile as well. Various pieces of equipment situate the room they occupy. Compact machines sit upon tables and larger ones standalone but all methodically placed and aligned in rows. Hermetically sealed lighting hangs overhead, brightly illuminating the effects below while air quietly permeates large grills at the front and rear. Above those openings are placards labeled 'HEPA Filtration' and dangling in front of them are red plastic streamers gently swaying toward the ventilation. They indicate that aeration is on and adequate.

"How are we doing this? Teach me Obi-Wan," Arnold adjusts a procedure mask, his voice muted by the paper barrier.

Jeff isn't bothering with his. "Arnold, you will now witness why I am so reverend around here," Jeff exaggerates his abilities while standing tall and proud—stretching a surgical glove tightly between the fingers letting it snap when done.

"You mean revered," Jeff corrects, "as in respected and admired."

"Ahem, yes of course…that's what I said. These darn masks," clearing his throat, Jeff begins showing Arnold around the room, pointing at devices along the way. "We will view larger samplings under microscope, propagate cultures inside these petri dishes which will be ready in about twenty-four hours, and then analyze the subsequent bacteria growth. Test tubes will hold solutions and dilute chemicals to cultivate these sugary…uh, slimy things," he holds one up to show, "I can't think of the name right now but anyway, moving on."

He sets it back into the organizer tray and directs Jeff's attention further down the line. "Centrifugal machines will spin the crap out of whatever we put in them, obviously to get out the denser colloidal particles and then we'll further isolate chemical physicality by breaking that composition further with dissolving agents. Are you following?"

"Oh yeah…right behind you," Arnold gives him a weird expression.

"Good. Well, over to the next line—pollution detectors will unearth hydrocarbons, methane, combustibles and the levels of fluoride, chlorine, arsenic, pesticides, pharmaceuticals, lead, cysts, natural gas and plastics. Then we will use chromatography to pull molecules from remaining compounds. Then, we'll further analyze those isotopic elements for a variety of lesser-known but more hazardous contaminants. Once thoroughly studied, we will do it all again called, 'verifying data.' You don't plan on going anywhere for the next few days, do you?"

"I'm sorry I asked," Arnold seeks refuge near a stripped fish lying on the countertop.

Meanwhile, Sheryl enters the hygienic apparel station, taking a seat beside shelves of sterile garments. While glancing over the choices of boxed clothing she spots the two men and they notice her presence as well.

Jeff promptly shuffles to the transparent wall separating them and presses a button, bringing his face close to a speaker passage.

She grabs over-shoe booties and begins to put them on.

"So what took you so long?" he taunts her. "Oh wait…the reporter. How'd that go?" he chuckles. "Did you give her the usual, 'I'll get back to you' excuse?"

"Have you finished analyzing those fish yet?" Sheryl gives a crass reply, disgruntled with Jeff's humor. Struggling with a shoe cover that will not fit, she tosses it to the ground.

"Yeah, I cracked the case…you can go home now," he wisecracks. "What the hell happened to you?"

"She asked me if I knew about my husband's trip to Atlanta next week. Now, why would she say that?" Sheryl throws a hand at the wall.

"You never mentioned he was going anywhere."

"That's the point. He hasn't said anything about it."

"Oh crap!"

"Exactly…he's definitely hiding something from me…or someone."

"Well, maybe she interviewed him and picked it up in idle conversation. Perhaps she just wanted to get under your skin…to get you to talk. You know…it's their job to rattle people. That's when we accidentally reveal things."

Jeff tries to appease, in his own strange way.

"No," leaning back she exhales. "It didn't feel like that. She was pleased that I didn't know."

"Sounds like you need another talk with hubby."

"I haven't finished the first one yet," she blabs, "not really anyway. I don't know what to do."

"Hey, we have fish." Jeff jokes.

Sheryl gives a chafed look.

"Sometimes you just need faith. I think that's what Jeff wanted to articulate," Arnold enters to interject a thought.

"Yeah, I was going to say something like that," Jeff nods talking with insincere tone.

"Thanks for the suggestion," Sheryl picks up another bootie, "but trust isn't my strong point right now."

"Hey, what guy isn't cheating on his girl these days?" Jeff laughs.

Arnold gives him a strange look and Sheryl shows disgust.

"What? I'm just noting that you're not alone," he defends his words with unashamed character. Then he lets them continue unabated.

"Stand up and get some answers," Arnold continues. "You don't have to be mean. Just deal your cards and play them out. You might have a better hand than you think. What are you scared of anyway? You would not think twice about jumping in front of a bus to save your kids. Do the same for the man you married."

"If it doesn't work out then you can throw him under the bus. What…I can't help it," Jeff groans.

"You're cultured and accomplished," Arnold persists while eyeing Jeff…who indicates that he won't interrupt again. "And where is the 'take no crap' lady that hired me?" Arnold asks.

"Whoa…that's pretty bold?" Jeff snickers.

"The jury's still out. But yeah, thanks for the honesty," she reaches for scrub pants

Then Jeff speaks more normally. "Go…take care of your life. We got this. These fish aren't swimming away," he offers with improved sentiment.

She hesitates to act.

"That's not an option," Jeff aggressively states.

"Okay, I get it," she gets up moaning, and heads to the door dragging her feet.

Jeff punches Arnold in the arm, "make me look bad," he scoffs.

Once plopping behind her desk, she stares at the far side of the room, mumbling possible remarks that she will say to Richard.

"So, what's with all the women? Whom are you going to Atlanta with? Just tell the truth for once…I can handle it. Are you involved with someone?" she concludes in abrupt tone, shaking her head. Then she tries a different way to start the conversation, somewhat more lenient using proactive hand gestures she talks to herself. "Alright, listen…you don't have to continue this charade, and I'm okay. Things happen…no, I get it. No, no, I'm alright." She tries yet another, "this is about the kids, and they're almost adults anyway. So let us end this the right way. Urgh…!" she lowers her head to the desk.

"Goodness Sheryl, why are you having so much trouble?" she asks herself. "Just talk to him. That's it, here we go," she rises and dials his number, checking it twice. However, before calling, a receptionist announces over the speaker, "Wynyard's on his way back, and he's not alone."

"What is it with this guy?" she grunts and closes the phone—totally annoyed.

Moments later, there is a knock on the door and before she could say 'come in,' Wynyard enters along with two other men, dressed in black suits.

She notices they are moving with confidence and appointment.

"Okay," Sheryl moans with tangled tongue showing a befuddled expression. "Scott, what's going on? What's with the strong-arm approach? This is odd."

"Relax, no need to be traumatized, it's not like that. This is 'informal official business.' Mrs. Olson, this is agent Callahan and Groves, with the Bureau."

Sheryl notices that her boss is acting quite formal, but she stands to perform a customary greeting—they simply return a detached handshake, not smiling.

"The FBI," Sheryl puts it out there. "What do you want with the DEP?"

"It's a simple matter," the elder agent begins, "just a few questions, to clear the air."

"I don't understand. How can I help?"

"Well," he steps forward with palms rubbing together. "Let me get straight to the point. You had water samples tested by a private firm. I want you to show us where they came from."

"Alright, that's not a problem, agent..." Sheryl jitters about. "Uh..."

"Callahan mam," he clarifies.

"Right, of course, agent Callahan, but this is a little weird. Sinkholes and general contamination have never captured the attention of your agency in the past. Why the sudden interest from a couple men in black?" She states but then cannot hold back a laugh. "I'm sorry—it's just that you seem like the movie..." she pauses, "anyway, why are you questioning me about this? Was there a mutant alien egg found in the water?" she laughs again.

They don't.

She regains poise. "Alright, so how did you get wind of this issue? Let me guess." She points a finger at the lawman, chuckling, "if you tell me you have to kill me."

Both agents force a brief giggle, but quickly stop to a tense stare.

Sheryl is getting a creepy feeling.

"Mam," the second agent steps-up and glares while leaning on the corner of her desk with sincere posture. "We have public interests to worry about, sometimes that requires a bit of confidentiality. We have eyes and ears everywhere, even on little out-of-the-way testing facilities like this. We need answers—your timeliness strongly requested. Please, for your well-being as well as your...ahem...just tell us what we want to know."

"Is this guy for real?" Sheryl directs a thumb. "Do you guys still act like this—threatening people?"

"Okay Groves," Callahan interjects, placing a hand on the over assertive man's shoulder, encouraging him to back away.

Reluctantly, Groves eases off.

Callahan gives Sheryl a blissful grin to let her know the situation is okay. "Mrs. Olson, there is always a matter of concern circling around the populace that most people don't need to, well...concern themselves with it," peacefully he assures. "Sometimes knowing too much can actually cause more problems than it solves. Most folks just want to go about their day receiving food the way they order it, believing gas will be available when they want it, and...at night, they want to know that the moon isn't going to fall on them while they're sleeping."

"I'm not most folks or just a member of the public, agent," she vexes to explain.

"Callahan mam, but call me Tyler," he urges.

"Okay Tyler," staring into his soul she grumbles.

Wynyard seems worried.

"I'm not just part of the society you speak of. It's my job to protect that population," she pauses. "This backwoods lab that you unkindly refer to—it ensures I do my part and therefore, I do the same thing you do. So...if there is something out there that may bring harm to my team, I need to know. Their safety is not only my concern, it's my obligation and I take that duty seriously."

The two suits look at each other with that familiar official 'non-verbal' stare of consultation, and then deliver each other an identical affirmative nod.

Callahan continues. "Mrs. Olson," moving closer he speaks with sensitivity. "Are you familiar with the threats that this country tackles every day? Between foreign and domestic there are no less than one-hundred and ninety-seven different avenues of danger to contend with at any given time," he ogles after delivering the statement.

Sheryl laughs. "Is that a real number?" she scoffs, as if that was absurd.

Her boss gestures 'I don't know.'

Groves with crossed arms issues an evil stare.

"No, I made it up," Callahan lampoons the data. "But the point is do you know about the threats?"

Sheryl replies shrugging shoulders, "I guess, not all of them."

"Your water samples contained explosive properties—TNT, dynamite, fireworks…whatever. A compound that blows-up was found—any idea why that would be in there?"

"Oh my God…!" Sheryl throws up her arms and retreats back to her chair, laughing like that was silly. "Is that what this is about? Are you kidding me? Remnants from civil wars, decaying leftovers, old gunpowder barrels, tossed shotgun shells—that's what you're worried over?"

She shakes her head and chuckles. "Everyday someone is finding century-old crap like that lying around. I'm sure there are sticks of crumbling dynamite in a hundred different ponds, disintegrating and leaching into the water supply," she cracks again.

Groves lends a fake chortle and Callahan constructs a peculiar smile too.

"Yes, I'm aware of the crazy things in the water," moving to the back corner of her desk, Callahan sits and crosses his arms. "But we believe there is more to it than that."

"What makes you think so?"

"It's a gut feeling," Groves positions for respect.

Wynyard becomes edgy.

"You're here on a hunch," Sheryl scoffs. "This just keeps getting better."

"Groves don't help." Callahan eyes his partner then turns to Sheryl.

"Mam, don't you find seismic activity in this area to be an odd circumstance, and increasing levels to be more unusual, possibly alarming?"

She looks at the agent with gravity, but does not reply. Suddenly he has her attention.

"In fact, don't you have evidence on these occurrences?" he invites her to become nervous.

"How do you know about that? I haven't concluded any such theory, let alone published it?" she looks to the side, agitated.

"Do you have test results on this matter or not Mrs. Olson? It's a simple question. What about the new person out there, where is he from...uh Utah? What is his field of expertise? Would you like to enlighten us why you need him or do you want me to guess?" Callahan smiles, "I'm pretty good at it."

Sheryl is now aware something is going on.

Wynyard paces.

"What did you tell them?" She looks to her dismissive boss.

"Sheryl, they would have found out anyway. Just tell them what you know," Wynyard tries to console her with a tender hand.

"Don't touch me," she pulls away and blasts, "you know there isn't one conclusive aspect to my report."

She sits at her desk to reflect, but only for one second. "This is a witch hunt. I can't believe you would stoop this low...not even you. If there was anything I ever respected about you, that's gone."

"I didn't," he tries to speak.

However, she will have none of it—holding a hand to his face. "Save it, I'll deal with you later."

"Mrs. Olson," Groves squeezes beside the elder agent, "your information."

Callahan eyes him—number two yields again.

"We're not actually here to invade your life," Callahan soothes. "We're not concerned with trivial local matters. If this turns out to be a State issue, I'm out of your hair—just like that."

"Okay..." Sheryl tangles with emotion. "Like I said, we really don't know what's going on...but my husband is..." stammering she struggles to find the right words. "He's the VP for ODG, the developers you've seen on TV— building everything in sight. They're constructing the trendy pipeline project or unpopular...depending on what side of the fence you're on. Some speculate they may be engaged in unscrupulous methods to complete projects faster. But until there is proof, it's merely rumor, okay," she ascertains with confidence. "You have to understand, I'm married to the guy and honestly... I haven't seen or heard of anything to put a finger on." Then she points toward Wynyard, "Regardless what this asshole told you!"

They eye each other.

"So, what is this devious practice?" Groves presses.

She stops to contemplate again inhaling for resilience while strongly considering the ramifications.

"Using explosives to dislodge hard rock," she reveals, "making it easier to remove, but you have to recognize, if that was being employed we wouldn't just feel it, it would be heard as well...and not a single resident has complained about such noise. With all of the reporters probing for the next big story...well, there isn't one. Anyway, I am looking out for the environment too, that's what I do. So, if I had knowledge...I wouldn't keep it a secret," she explains in earnest behavior.

Wynyard smirks and looks away.

"Or would you?" Groves takes a step closer and starts to grill.

Callahan holds a hand to him, keeping him at bay. "I'm sure you wouldn't mam, but it seems we'll need to speak to your husband and uh, like I mentioned…have a look where those samples came from."

Sheryl glances at her boss and bites a bottom lip.

Nineteen

Feet stride a carpeted hallway, several pairs. A throat makes a clearing sound, a hand fiddles with keys inside a pants pocket and elevator doors close behind. Cascading water emanates from the distance as a cell phone drops into a purse. A doorknob twists, the partition swings open and extremities swagger in, one by one. Behind a counter, a young woman's eyes widen.

"Welcome...to...ODG, can I help you?" she slowly greets, reluctant.

"We're here to see the VP," a male voice responds.

"Do you have a...?" she stops in the middle of a question—something is grabbing her attention. Leaning toward them, over the tall desk, she gives curious stare. "You do know it's not bright in here, right," she asks.

Groves and Callahan standing firm before her, turn and look at each other with blank expression, both still wearing very dark black sunglasses.

"Richard knows we're coming," Sheryl's voice announces from the rear. Stepping forward she further makes her presence known.

"Oh, Mrs. Olson...I didn't see you."

"It's okay. No need to buzz him."

"Alright," the nervy girl points in the direction they must travel.

Trekking down a hall Sheryl leads the way with Callahan and Wynyard following, Groves lagging behind. Upon entering her husband's office, Ashley is sitting behind her desk filing one of her nails.

She looks up, rather surprised, but doesn't say anything.

Sheryl snubs her too while walking past, no cordial greeting there—nor was one expected.

Of course, Wynyard said, 'hello'.

Callahan issued a standard nod but Groves took a bit longer—gloating over the attractive female. Curiously, he becomes taller and more gallant as he struts along her desk, swiftly imparting vigor into his step.

Indeed, Ashley relishes the attention and gives him a bright smile, causing the delirious wonk to walk backwards, to make the moment last longer. He returns an interesting grin of his own before catching up to the group.

"Glad you could join us," Callahan jabs his dallying partner.

"What?" Groves acts oblivious.

Callahan shakes his head.

The group now stands afore Richard, who takes sharp notice of their arrival, but remains seated. Holding a pen lengthwise between fingertips and thumbs, he quietly waits for someone to speak.

"Rick," Sheryl begins. "These men are with the FBI—they have some questions." She seems a bit detached delivering the off-sorts introduction.

"Yeah, you mentioned they wanted to speak with me," he stands, "but no explanation."

Groves gives her a look of disapproval.

"It was a brief call, I didn't say a thing," she tells the grim-faced stature.

Richard embellishes. "Lunchtime just ended, you obviously haven't had yours...why the urgency?" he tosses the writing utensil on desk and moves from behind it. "I feel this is a planned attack," he flares. "No warning—coming here with the full force of the FBI and your department head too."

Wynyard, standing aloof feels pressure and begins to look around.

"For God's sake, I'm your husband. You could have conferred with me before resorting to this measure," he scoffs. "Are you taking the kids too? Is that the next provocation? I guess I don't know what you're capable of."

Sheryl scoffs. "Has that gotten me anywhere...talking to you?"

"The Feds Sheryl—what are you thinking?" With hands in pocket, his angst grows, standing directly at her.

"Oh don't get in a wad," she blows off his attitude, turning away. "You should know. They sprang on me too." Crossing arms, she defends.

"Right, they just waltzed into your office."

"As a matter of fact they did," she tilts her head.

"Are they delivering divorce papers?"

"Sure, why not."

"Well, have em' slap a ban on digging while you're at it."

They eye each other with harsh spirits—back and forth, they clash to each other's sarcasm.

"Maybe they're here to shut you down," she blasts.

"Now that's something you'd like to see."

"Easy does it there boss?" Callahan wedges between the contenders, and extends a hand for greeting, "sounds like you two have a whole lot of issues and I promise...I'll let you get to them as soon as possible."

"Richard, it's true. Sheryl had no prior knowledge," Wynyard jumps in. "They made the same inquiries at our office—based on a few tests results they got wind of. You've met Callahan, this is Groves."

Sheryl smirks with disinterest and steps back to permit introductions.

Though unsure, Richard lessens his attitude. "Alright, what can I do for you?"

"Let's everyone take a seat," Wynyard suggests.

Groves seizes the opportunity to rattle, "We simply need to know what your operations consist of. How you are doing them? Where your sites are located? When they commenced? Who's in charge and details of other erroneous employees...names, dates, times—a chronological list too, events citing any known or unexplained occurrences...and a really good explanation of why the media has such concern with your company?"

Immediately, Richard gets insulted. "Whoa…what the hell is this?" taking offense Richard leans forward with unsettled concern.

"Groves, what did I say?" Callahan pulls his weight.

The younger agent withdraws to his chair.

"He's been like that all day, I don't know what to make of it—like an untrained animal," he enlightens but stays on topic. "Mr. Olson, we're not out to fluster harmless people—following everyone's move, tracking their financial transactions or whittling our way into every nook and cranny of their lives. Not unless we need to," he laughs thinking that was funny.

However, Richard remains solid.

Sheryl has a worried look though.

"Relax, we're not doing any of that," he persists with an ominous giggle.

Groves snickers—Callahan clears his throat. Groves normalizes again.

Callahan continues. "But I would like to know a couple of things, if that's okay with you. I promise…the media doesn't have to know."

"Go on." Richard seems willing to listen.

"Why are people concerned with your company, uh…digging and such—help me understand."

"I see my wife has misled you too," he briefly shifts eyes to her. "But I can't help you. Our procedures are like a coveted recipe, a company secret. That's how we keep our competitors behind us, but also why there is the hoopla that you speak. Chasing the leader pisses people off when they can't catch them. Am I right," he looks at Sheryl again. "People will say and do anything to get information, and then they effort to destroy the company when they don't get it."

Sheryl scowls.

"I see why you're having marital issues Mrs. Olson," Groves leans toward Richard. "I don't think you're aware of the FBI's full power. We can fabricate issues out of thin air—render innocent people guilty—cause companies to fold and need I say—make things disappear. You could be in violation—be picked up without a warrant…perhaps never see the light of day. We have more men, time and weapons—some you have never heard of, and an endless supply of funds. When our pen writes—peculiar things happen," in disrespectful tone the agent hovers, administering an intimidating gaze.

"Alright, sit down Groves," Callahan laughs, and delivers a reassuring smile to restore tranquility. "Like I said 'he's a big scary bull dog with a pretty deep bark, but no teeth—had em' yanked out after biting a little old lady. Don't mind him. He's just a restless pooch."

Groves eases off.

"Nonetheless," Callahan nods. "What he says is true, but I would rather skip that nonsense and have a discussion like men, the way they talked in the olden days and just…well, put this situation behind us so we can all go home."

"They used to kill people over talks like this," Richard points out.

"Okay then—not that far back." Callahan snorts. "Anyway, the sooner you reveal your company's hush-hush procedures, the quicker you can get back to digging and Sheryl here—she can return to saving trees and grass.

"Just what do you want?" Richard presses.

"Mr. Olson, let me get to the point. Do you use explosives?"

"What?" he exclaims.

"You know, TNT, Pop sticks, C4, blasting powder."

"Or something more powerful...?" Groves inserts, "anything with big boom."

"I don't know where you're getting your information agent, uh…" Richard stammers.

"Callahan," the agent clarifies.

Sheryl butts in, "he told me to call him Tyler."

Richard and Wynyard each give her the eye.

Richard continues. "Those things aren't part of our application," he explains while looking at Sheryl. "That's what you've been thinking this whole time?" he flares, "why didn't you just ask me?"

She gives a cold stare.

Richard persists with the FBI man. "My Company is earth friendly for Chrissakes. Okay," he pauses for a refreshing thought, then changes tune. "Okay, let's talk about what we do. Frankly, I'm tired of the B.S."

Richard stands to spell things out.

Sheryl pays closer attention.

"The conduit structure and materials we use are state of the art. The technology was a combined effort between the best engineers and scientists coming together, some from other countries. Dozens of patents spawned new and improved inventions, including the gas-sensor leak-detection system, a small apparatus installed into the piping every few hundred feet. The slightest leak initiates an extraordinary valve system to close, which is proprietary equipment, and it isolates troubled areas in several ways. First, modules keep gas blocked ahead of the breach preventing further seepage, then the fractured segment of conduit locked down—escaping gas trapped within an outer stratum. Only the inner most core contains the product. Happening upon a break, gaseous material will never really reach our atmosphere. This method both protects the environment and allows us to reclaim the gas—not a bit lost. Next, internal modems, routers and signaling devices send important data through additional wireless repeaters, then across every cell tower utilizing existing technology—ultimately every department gets alerted via computer systems, within our agency, and some outside our organization like the DEP."

Sheryl's eyes light up hearing that her department has a role.

"That's right," he informs her. "Even your division will receive phone calls, texts, and desktop alarms. Factions responsible for emergency repair—appropriate personnel and maintenance staff will get details to react immediately. Latest software allows perfect description in vivid detail—how a disruption occurred precisely identifying the exact location of the issue. In addition, a printout describes the methods for accurate repair with a list of tools, materials, equipment, and manpower required for proper deployment. On the fly thinking is not necessary...nothing is left out. Even the names, phone numbers and email addresses from the engineers to product suppliers and their manufactures provided. The location of supplementary gear and resources also supplied. The best part is—all automatically updated with each change of employment, status revision or any modification to the chain of command...from top management all the way down to the most basic worker. You can even have the program tell you what everyone likes to eat if you want. Every problematic situation is accurately evaluated...spot on, prior to onsite assessment, allowing restoration to commence immediately without human review or estimation delays."

Sheryl has growing interest.

"Sounds like you have all your bases covered," Callahan commends.

Richard divulges more. "You see, the conduit system consists of a thick outer layer constructed of non-corrosive, impermeable steel combined with flexible carbon and nylon composites which protects and houses inner reinforced tubal layers. The second encases the sensors and mechanisms, which injects and extracts product, but this channel has no product within it. This is an inert vacuum-sealed layer if you will, and finally the center core contains the free flowing gas. Pipe segments can be isolated, filled and or vented simultaneously to enable one hundred percent of the product to remain without the unwanted inclusion of air or oxygen. This also allows a safe working environment for repair—welding if necessary with no mishaps and then the gas pumped back in. Portable tanks placed nearby will house the product until needed for reinsertion. Nothing goes to waste.

"So what happens if the gas is shut off too long—people will just go without?" Sheryl butts in with a pessimistic attitude. "A sinkhole could wipe out a large section. What then?"

Richard nods for a moment.

He has something to say about that too. "Yeah, that was a main concern for us too, but you may be displeased to know—that issue was debugged. First off, the conduit structure is self-supportive. Should the ground collapse, it would likely stay intact anyway...however, if it doesn't, repair is quick with the availability of numerous prefabricated parts. Filling the hole is easy. However, if restoration does take longer than expected—this is when the hubs kick in. Every gas station, college, manufacturing and industrial plant, and various other sites are set to become a location for huge reservoirs, large storage tanks of natural gas. Protected and tamperproof as well I would like to add. Disney is one site, you may have heard," he snickers. "Anyway, each hub is capable of feeding back into the system to maintain adequate flow. Customers won't notice a thing upstream of an issue or below it. Combined centers will keep up with demand for weeks, if not months to the entire State. No one will be the wiser of ongoing repair efforts. Adequate time will always be available."

"Wow, you guys stand to make millions from increased gas consumption," Groves states in amazement.

"Billions," Richard happily corrects. "When you consider the new products undoubtedly to be created, it may be more than that. Appliances and cars alone will soar off the charts, every home and institution will require conversion. Consumer and worker safety programs will enter redesign, alone launching over nine-hundred billion dollars into the economy. Will there be jobs? Oh my God," he praises. "This country will have so many needs. Here is the best part. ODG will be in every piece of it."

"Oh my, a new era is on the horizon," Sheryl mocks.

"This all sounds great Mr. Olson," Callahan admits. "I can't wait for the car myself. Personally, I've already looked at the ones in Utah. But uh...you haven't mentioned anything about explosives."

"That's because we don't use them. That would be crazy. Perhaps you're aware that gas and fire don't make a pleasing combination, not to mention taking the chance of damaging our expensive installation. Why would we risk that?

"People do the darndest things don't they?" Callahan gently laughs.

Groves agrees with a nod.

Callahan exhales and relaxes back, rubs his chin and contemplates. "But...I tend to believe you," he concludes.

Sheryl gets upset. "That looks like the face of honesty?" she jeers with disapproval.

"Yeah," Callahan stands, "a company like this would jeopardize more than installation setbacks if they engaged in activity like that."

Groves is complacent.

"I'm glad somebody finally gets it," Richard delightfully seems relieved.

Sheryl seems more fumed—that Richard is getting recognition.

"Don't kick back yet," Groves warns. "We still need you and your wife to help locate the source of our quandary."

"I'm out of suggestions," Sheryl throws a hand up. "I have other problems."

"She's right, we're done," Richard supports. "There's no way I can get involved after this ambush. I feel trampled on."

Sheryl sneers at her husband. "Now you know how I feel," she pauses. "The taste of helping someone who just pissed you off is pretty sour, huh?"

Richard has no words to express.

But Wynyard has something to say. "Richard, the DEP wants you to cooperate—don't have a choice really. You know how politics operate— corporate image is probably the last thing to worry about, and we don't want the media to get wind of a few, abnormalities...do you?"

"What are you saying, Scott?"

Wynyard simply smirks and looks down.

Richard sits. "Are you going to play that card again?" he scoffs. "After all of the hoops you made me jump through. I did everything you asked. You promised I wouldn't be threatened with your environmental warfare— scare tactics. This is bull."

Sheryl catches the comment and becomes very curious, paying close attention. "What was that?" she questions, moving closer. "Tell me you just didn't admit to consorting with each other."

Richard, places his hand over his chin.

Wynyard simply stares away.

Sheryl's awareness grows deeper.

"It's just business," Wynyard turns to defend.

"I can't believe this. I've been betrayed by both of you."

"It's not like that," he argues. "I was protecting you. Having intimate knowledge of your husband's venture with the DEP would jeopardize your job. What kind of story would that make?"

Sheryl looks at Richard. "I suppose you were looking out for me too?" she rebukes.

"I know you don't see it that way, but…"

"Shut up. I don't want to hear this right now," she cuts him off, turning her back.

"Richard, your father doesn't need brought into this. He's getting too old for this crap, eh." Wynyard continues, "Is he here? He plays a great game of golf, a personal best—under eighty just last week. You should join us next time."

Sheryl looks at Wynyard, astonished with his brazen subtle tactic to get Richard to concede.

"I get your point," Richard exhales.

"All this time," Sheryl shakes her head, delivering a reserved stare, "I've been kept in the dark by my own department."

She again bites a bottom lip while looking away.

"Hey, aside from helping Richard get permits a little faster than normal, treating inspections delicately, dispensing a few valid certificates before final review and bending some already flexible regulations—it's all acceptable…nothing illegal transpired. Let's move on."

There were a few moments of turmoil during these discussions, but the Olson's began to settle. The agents moved back in.

"Okay team…this is what we have to do," Callahan gives a wide smile.

Ultimately, the group departed, Richard was left sitting on the corner of his desk. He stares at the closed door in contemplation and reaches into his pocket. Again, he removes Sheryl's wedding band and ogles it—sparkling in his opened palm. Abruptly he clutches it and exits his office, then leaves the suite and makes his way to the balcony. Downstairs, he could see the agents speaking with the building receptionist, but it was just those three. Then, beyond the plants and florae, he spotted Sheryl with Wynyard…and they seemed a bit too close. He was touching her hair and grazing a cheek, and she was responding to it. Then he proceeded to put his arm around her as they walked out.

Dejected, Richard puts the ring back in his pocket.

Twenty

Morning fog hovers above a forest floor concealing plant life and marshy conditions. It looms as individuals mosey through it and relax at the base of trees or atop rocks. Jeff is walking amongst them handing out coffee in foam cups and grateful moans resound. Nearby, Arnold places an empty cardboard tray into a large trash bag and proceeds to hand out the remaining sugar glazed doughnuts from the last box, stuffing one into his mouth before they're all gone. Idle chitchat grows among the partakers as caffeine and sugar enter their blood streams. Fast food wrappers and paper bags lie crumbled, pitched like basketballs, somewhat close to the trash bag. Some have finished their beverages—others are savoring the steamy brew. A few dozen people huddle into three or four member cliques and while decaf is not on the rise, the sun is as streams of light pierce treetops, continuing to ground, dissolving low-lying haze. As daybreak strengthens, so does restlessness. Conversation breeds, voices elevate and tolerance for immobility diminishes.

"Are they going to get this show on the road?" someone blurts to Arnold.

He stops to acknowledge them, licking sugar from his fingers. "They look ready," he replies while looking toward parked vehicles. "I see movement. I'll go check."

"Where's the FBI? Why aren't they here?" one man calls out while Arnold trots away.

"Still sleeping, that's where," another voice criticizes and the crowd laughs.

"If this is so important, they should be here."

"Yeah, with their galoshes on—traipsing through the woods right beside us," the first man sounds again.

Arnold looks back listening to every word as he approaches Sheryl, standing at an automobile. "They're getting impatient," he tells her.

"Yeah, I hear. They'd rather be home and I can't blame them," she relates while testing several pairs of two-way radios spread out on the hood.

"It only takes one person to get everyone riled," Richard steps in. "Get this thing started—we'll work out the details as we go."

Sheryl glares at him for a thought processing moment, but grabs the talkies in a rush and moves to the group.

Richard keeps to her side as she confronts the group.

"Gather round everybody," she announces and a semi-circle forms in front of her.

"Harmony's festival starts tomorrow," someone blurts. "Will we be done in time for that?"

"Yeah, and I have a recital to go to. Can I be excused?" a woman standing up front shouts, causing a united laugh.

"Okay, okay, I know this effort is above and beyond," Sheryl paces to the left. "But thank you all for coming. I'd rather be in bed myself," she pauses. "Now, some of you already know, but for the rest who don't, we're here to conduct a search for the FBI."

Boos wave the crowd and continue.

"I know…yeah…" Sheryl walks to the right. "I get it…I do," she relaxes to help quiet them down. "But hear me out. You were each chosen because of individual skill."

"What ability would that be?" a man yelps.

"Well, I'll tell you," she begins but she is superseded.

"That question comes from Carl, my general superintendent," Richard moves up. "There are basically two groups out here—with ODG I have surveyors, supervisors, dive teams and construction personnel."

"And with the DEP," Sheryl adds, "we have researchers, environmentalists, the forestry division and land conservation staff members."

"And what's the task?" an attentive female ranger in uniform speaks up.

"Well, simply put…there is reason to believe a stockpile of explosive material is lying around out here somewhere. Chemical compounds are leaching into neighboring wetlands," Sheryl educates.

"Seriously!" the girl shows concern. "What type of stuff—how dangerous is it?"

"Honestly, we don't have much to go on so we need to be careful…that's why I have you out here. You are all specialists and I assume will search and act accordingly when encountering something unusual."

Jeff blurts in joking fashion, "professionals?"

"Well, I'm not sure about you," Sheryl razzes him.

"So how do we look for this stuff?" a voice enquires?

"Which way do we go?" another seeks information?

"Is there a plan?" someone else expresses.

Others start conveying concerns, "Do we have water—how about supplies?"

"How long can we stay out here?"

"It's summer time, what if we get lost?"

"Alright, alright," Richard jumps in to diffuse the irritable sentiments. "Everyone, bring it in," he motions while Sheryl passes out walkie-talkies along with a list. "Finish your coffee—we're going to break off into teams, each will have a leader equipped with a radio to maintain contact with other squads and especially the base station—that will be Sheryl. And please, learn who you are placed with?"

Sheryl perceives positive mumbles and nods. "Good, here's the plan," she moves on. "Team leaders will report to either Carl for ODG, or Jeff for the environment group. They are your main source for information and can direct you further if needed. Stay in your groups and for those without radios…keep your cells handy. There is a decent signal out here."

"Communicate with everyone frequently—just to chat…it'll help pass the time," Richard adds.

"Yeah, don't think you are a bother to anyone. Stay engaged and work together—nit-pick, whatever it takes to stay safe."

"I can handle that," Jeff blurts. "I learned from two of the best."

Richard and Sheryl immediately lock eyes—in silent reaction.

Nevertheless, Sheryl continues on, passing out a few maps. "If you have GPS…use it," she states while opening a map. "Everybody look. This is our starting place," she points. "Here's Lake Sheen. Big Sand is to our immediate right and you'll notice that it's surrounded by homes—a community. Be cautious over there, don't invade personal space while scouring," she emphasizes.

"Our plan is to move north-west from hole to hole stretching to Lake Mable, Tibet, Reams, Lake Speer and so on, systematically covering every water hole whether on this map or not. Just be sure the ones on our list receive attention, indication is they are most likely to have what we're looking for. Keep in mind, we are not crossing over I-4—it's about a mile away to both the south and east. So, for the team going to Big Sand, cover these several lakes and then start moving north. Of course, by the time you're finished you'll be quite a bit behind the others, so call for an ATV to get you caught up.

"I thought this effort was all on foot," someone shouts.

"It is. I'll explain in a minute," Richard answers.

Sheryl continues. "Our destination is Lake Apopka, Harris, Eustis, Yale and Griffin. They are the largest and the final ones. Just to let you know, that's about twenty miles away."

"You're kidding!" Jeff winces.

"I'm afraid not, but it's completely doable. We'll each have water and everyone is used to outdoor activity—another reason you were chosen. I will be checking in with each of you every half-hour. Does anyone have any questions?"

"How are we getting back?"

"Right…that's a good one. There will be a bus and some cars waiting at the rally point—anything else?"

"The ATV's…what are they for?"

"Well," Richard interjects, "the divers will be on them."

"What?" Jeff and others whine.

"I know, I know that seems like visual punishment but walking in flippers isn't easy," with a smile he delivers. "Hey, they have a lot of gear to carry—along with your water, first aid, vitamin packs and a few other basic needs. If someone collapses, well there's your ride back but don't get any funny ideas. If you don't show signs of first-degree heat stroke…keep walking. Please note…we do have a qualified medic on staff so don't think you can fake it," he jokes.

"Oh yeah, if you have sunscreen and a hat, use them—larger the brim the better and keep a wet scarf around your neck. The frogmen have those too so speak up if you want one."

A few people raise their hands.

Then the quest began. The divers linger a bit longer to suit up and prepare the terrain vehicles but the others branched off into their groupings and headed on their perspective course.

Immediately, team leaders begin checking in with Sheryl to ensure communications is working properly. Some ask for trivial details again, others engage unrelated gossip.

Jeff and Arnold can be heard laying out routes and plotting coordinates.

Eventually, everyone begins methodically examining each area reached. Rocks are over turned and larger heavy ones surveyed. Debris is sifted but dense foliage and piles of lying branches poked with anything long and rigid. Old decaying wooden structures long since abandoned scrutinized, carefully rummaged if safe to enter. Bodies of water thoroughly circled searching for anything contradicting nature while divers search the depths especially cloudy areas. Their underwater lights are vaguely visible from above but their transmissions describe finds of old soda and beer cans to rotting shoes, books and clothing.

On land, horrified comments tell of decaying animal parts, but completely dried bones receive toying for fun of it. Further reports of washing machines, dryers, cars, and numerous manmade items submersed in the murky basins become too frequent. Zone after zone within every locale visited, the searchers use the same procedures, documenting every trace of human impact.

Hours soon pass and eventual afternoon rays become intense, casting few shadows large enough for one individual to catch shelter from the growing heat. Shade is hard to find, their movements now pelted with penetrating and blistering summer sun. Coffee, the earlier beverage of choice, replaced with water and each bottle seems to empty more quickly than the last. Some pour quantities over their heads to sooth their simmering souls, while others keep their neck scarves moist with a generous douse. Many simply use their shirts the same way. Divers keep supply plentiful and the rest spare no expense using it as they see fit. Straw hats, typical of Florida beaches, are now in full use. Preserving motivation is nearing the desperation stage, staying hydrated and remaining cool are the most important factors to ensure the cause continues. From abyss to void, bush to brush, cavity to hollow and burrow to meadow every reachable stretch of terrain scoured. Nothing was left untouched.

Ultimately, the northern most point was reached and with a few hours of good light to spare.

Search crews are exhausted. Everyone has walked exposed to the elements all day except for the divers, but even they are growing fatigued. To worsen their weary souls, not a shred of evidence they set out to locate has been uncovered.

Each must be wondering, 'Have we reached that halting period?'

Few have eaten properly or replenished vital nutrients. Peanuts, protein bars and various snacks do help sustain physical strength but do not do much to keep moods elevated, not for long anyway. Steps have become shorter, less frequent and more wobbly. Rocks and fallen trees are prime sitting attractions. Breaks in action take longer, and the time between them is diminishing. Shear willpower is the only driving force left.

"A hot shower and a cold brew...! That's what I need," a man shouts.

"A sit-down at the absolute nearest restaurant is on my mind," a woman adds.

Just then, the words they wanted to hear.

"Guys, lets pull it in," Sheryl's voice emanates over radio."

Everyone is relieved.

"Roger that Sheryl," Jeff gives a tired reply.

"Silver lake, that's our rally point," she continues. "Everybody sound off."

"Roger that. Convene at Silver Lake...Arnold out."

"10-4-almost there now," another squad signals.

Carl chimes in, "ditto, en route."

Then teams seven, eight, nine and ten each respond.

"DEP personnel accounted for," Jeff relays to Sheryl.

Then four, five and six call in.

However, two more groups have not checked in.

"Team three," Carl transmits, "do you have a copy?"

"Three here—we acknowledge. We're probably the furthest out, north of Griffin. Gonna need some time to pack up and get there," they add.

"10-4," Carl responds. "Sheryl did you copy that?"

"Yeah, I heard...but where's Richard? He's the last one."

"Hey, how bout ya boss, give me a shout—over," Carl broadcasts again. A moment of silence passes with no reply so he sounds again, "Richard, do you have my copy?"

After another moment of silence, still nothing.

"Boss, come on back now," more loudly he stresses.

Everyone looks around for Richard.

Sheryl is especially observant. Then, static crackles over the airwaves and each anticipate the beginning of his transmission. Sheryl is poised for reply.

"This is three again Carl."

Everyone sighs—that wasn't Richard talking.

Sheryl grows more concerned.

"We left him hours ago back on the south side of Griffin, probably closer to the rally point—over," three sounds again.

"Copy that. Thanks," Carl replies and calls out to Richard again, but still no reply.

Sheryl could take no more. "Damn it Rick, if you can hear this you better say something!" she exclaims—the airwaves remain silent.

"Rick, are you there?" she yells—her voice swelling with torment.

At this point, everyone remains vigil for his reply, each wondering if something perilous has happened. What else could it be, why is he not responding?

Then, another transmission comes through.

"Two here—keep your panties on. I'm coming up behind you. I got you in my sights." Richard sounding jovial with his reply continues, "I got your damn copy."

The awaiting listeners exhale with relief, but Jeff mumbles under his breath, "Dick, what an ass. It's no wonder they have problems"

"What the hell Rick? What are you doing?" Sheryl blasts him over the air—looking in his probable direction. She sees people in the distance but they are too far for recognition.

"So you do care," he cracks. "You haven't called me Rick in days."

"You're a dick," she announces over the radio. Everyone laughs.

Not Jeff though. "That's what I said," he mumbles.

"Relax babe, just having a little fun," he projects with a superficial attitude. "I'll be there in a sec.—team two in transit. ODG personnel accounted for," he signs off.

Sheryl waits at the rally point keeping vigil for the others, and of the image trekking toward her whom she believes is Richard. Encroaching from the horizon, his likeness is hard to distinguish as only a silhouette is discernible. As he nears, she tries to avoid showing concern but cannot evade noticeable pacing. In short order, he is the first to appear but she does not greet his presence with enthusiasm and neither does he have much to say. Instead, they turn their attention to the others arriving close behind. One by one, teams reach the rally point, except for the third crew, which have a greater distance to travel. Sheryl and Richard congratulate everyone on their individual efforts and then listen to each tell of their experiences. The good and rough moments are told in storybook fashion, describing personal incidents both funny and troublesome, but inevitably, they all end the same way…what they sought out to discover was not found.

Twenty-One

"Jeff, Arnold," Sheryl changes theme. "Can you and the rest stay here, Carl too, and wait for the remaining personnel?"

"Sure, but where are you going?" Jeff throws a hand up.

"Richard and I have to get back—we have paperwork to produce for the FBI pricks. Official business, you know how it is."

Richard listens from an adjacent conversation.

"Okay people, let's conclude this fun. I have great news. It's been a long day and ODG wants to show their appreciation for your deeds by paying for dinner—for everybody," Sheryl surprises everyone and the crowd claps.

Whistles sound as a very curious Richard moves alongside his wife.

"You can have Carl pick up the tab, right?" she whispers into his ear.

He simply remains apathetic.

Smiling, she murmurs again, "smile honey, wave…let them know you're thankful."

After issuing her a clandestine look of irritation, he reluctantly grins and acknowledges the happy group, conveying his gratitude. "Is this your form of payback?" he hisses low enough that only she could hear.

"You know it," she smiles brilliantly.

"Uh, absolutely," Richard loudly tells the group, confirming the idea. "I was going to suggest it myself, but she beat me to it."

Jeff and Arnold look at each other with questioning stares. "She's getting better at this bullying thing," Jeff quietly tells Arnold.

"When you guys get back to your cars, there are several great places to eat within a short distance, diners with outside seating," Sheryl informs the elated group.

"That's perfect because we smell," a shout is heard

"Right on Boss," Carl yelps.

"Here's to ODG," a voice praises.

"I'm gonna eat gooood," another resounds.

"Oh, you guys deserve it," Sheryl compliments. "Just make sure the rest go with you okay! Richard and I are going to leave now."

Some issue dreary 'awes,' disappointed that the two are departing.

"I'll bring you a doggie bag," Jeff yells.

Sheryl and Richard begin toward her company vehicle, and of course, he was exploding with something to say.

"Official business…is there something I should know? What are you up to?" he cross-examines her.

She remains composed. "I just wanted to talk."

"And dinner for thirty people—how does that fit in?" he complains.

"Oh they deserve it. Besides, you can afford it. Don't be such a grouch. You made their shitty day better."

"When did this idea come to mind?"

"Since this morning," she chuckles.

He does not seem amused.

"Oh come on, you know if I had of asked you upfront…you would have caved anyway. Admit it."

"Whatever," he grunts. "So what did you have to say?"

"I thought we could finally hash some things out. I don't want to avoid this any longer."

"Argue—here among the trees on an empty stomach?" he takes a brief hiatus from the short walk. "You can't discuss anything when you're hungry."

"That's true—which is why you're going to feed me too…a huge, expensive five course meal somewhere at this city's finest with wine…no, champagne," she changes thought, "with escargot and caviar."

"I am?" he resists the self-invitation.

"That's right—nothing tawdry either. And as much as I want."

"So you think I'm going to roll over, just like that?"

"You are and…" she stops at the car door and heightens her attitude. "You're saying I'm not worth it?" arms crossed she demands an answer.

"Sheryl, you know what I…"

"Stop right there," she alters her character. "Don't get yourself in a dither. I'm not fit for fine dining and neither are you. I really thought we would just pick something up and take it back to your office."

"ODG headquarters—every environmentalist's nightmare. You want to go there?" he scoffs.

"It is on the way and didn't Carl drive you this morning? Where did you guys hook up before coming here?"

He nods, "at the office."

"So, your truck is there too, right?"

"You did your homework, as usual," Richard sighs.

"Get in, you're riding shotgun."

Richard shakes his head.

Sometime later, she is applying a modest gaze, trying to gain Richards attention. She amplifies the tactic with discriminating countenances but he remains inattentive, sitting in the passenger seat.

"Wow…it's not that bad," she jeers at the preoccupied man. "I just told them we had paperwork to do."

He only gives a menacing stare.

"Yeah okay, I also obligated you to buy dinner."

He scoffs.

She smiles and smiles.

"Oh come on, did you see how excited everyone was. You made their day. Jeff was beside himself and even Carl was happy. That is why you furnish him a company credit card…right?"

"I won't even get to enjoy it," he gripes, she laughs.

"Oh they're starved," still smiling she reminds him. "Besides, how much seafood could they eat?"

He grunts.

"And you do need to get your truck."

"Uh-huh," He groans.

"We've got twenty or so minutes, where do you want to stop?"

"What?"

"Food, we have to eat too."

"Is this what you wanted to talk about?" he complains.

She shuts the radio off and places both hands on the wheel, seemingly to get more serious. "How about burgers and fries—that sounds good, 'let's talk' grub…alright?

Sheryl, still grinning, has become off-tone and sarcastic.

"What's another hundred bucks?" he drones.

"Right…you're probably tapped out after paying for that big bash in Atlanta," she cynically brings up that topic. He abruptly reacts with an astonished look. "Oh, that got your attention. So I guess it's true."

"I was going to mention it when the time was right," he starts defending.

"What time would that be…when you're on the plane?"

"How do you know about that anyway?"

"That's how you're going to sidetrack this conversation, by asking me how I know about it. This is what worries you?"

"Damn, can't I ask a simple question or does cross-examination belong to you alone?"

"So is this a good time…you know, to fill me in on the details of this secret celebration?"

"It's not some party? It's a seminar, a regular deal for aspiring managers in the construction and development field."

"Don't treat me like I'm ignorant…"

"I swear. Why would I lie?"

"So who on your staff is going?" she interrogates.

Richard sighs to a curious pause, but does not answer. He is nervous.

"Who's going with you?" she repeats loudly.

"Ashley…but it's not like…"

"What…?" she screams nearly veering off the road.

"Whoa…!" Richard shrieks grabbing the wheel to help stabilizes the vehicle.

"You and her alone for an entire week a thousand miles away…and you thought I would be okay with that?

"Would you please relax and listen to me. I'm not going. I never was. That's why I didn't bring it up."

"Oh my God…you're unbelievable?" she denounces the excuse.

"Someone is obviously trying to get under your skin."

"Well, it worked," she yells at him.

Then Richard's tone becomes genuine and solemn. "The truth is I made an idle comment months ago without considering the..."

"Your right, you haven't been thinking for a long time."

"What the hell does that mean?"

"You know, I wish I could believe you but I'm pretty good at reading between the lines. You can just stop pretending. Frankly...you can stop coming home too."

"Wow!" Richard exclaims reclining backward. "What was the sentiment back there at the rally point? You sounded upset when you thought I went missing. What was that?"

She does not respond, fixated on the road.

"So that's it huh!" he scoffs, thinking that he has figured something out. "I get the boot but you get off Scott-free, or should I say Scotty-free—I assume that is your plan? Make me the bad guy so no one will think poorly of you."

"Are you desperate?" Sheryl deflects the allegation. "What disturbing thought is flowing through your warped imagination?"

He looks at her with accusation, but she does the same to him. Then his phone rings. He pulls it from his pocket.

"That phone," she sizzles with anger. "I can't stand it, if you answer that thing—I swear I'm going to run off the road and conveniently...one of those telephone poles is going right through your door."

"It's Ashley," he mentions using flared ironic tone. "I'll let it go to voice mail."

Sheryl immediately panics, "Oh no...no,no,no,no...you answer that right now."

"But you said..."

"I don't care what I said; I want to hear you talk to her. Answer it."

"Okay, but you asked for it," Richard gives her a 'whoop-de-doo' head gesture. "Ashley, what is it?"

"Richard, I just got off the phone with an OPD officer," sounding frazzled, she informs.

"What? Why?"

Sheryl is paying close attention with meddlesome expression.

"They just had a few reports of people claiming they heard a small explosion at Lake Apopka."

Suddenly, Sheryl's phone starts ringing too. Reluctantly, she answers, taking her away from their conversation.

"They asked if our company was in that area. I told them you were...have been all day," Ashley continues.

"Why does everyone think we blow shit up? Are you sure he said this just happened?"

"That's what he said," she confirms.

"Okay thanks, I'll check it out…bye."

Just as Richard gets off the phone, Sheryl finishes her call as well.

"Are you happy? Did you hear anything inappropriate?" he jabs.

However, she is perplexed. "I think Jeff just told me the same thing. They felt something from the bus."

Her phone rings again.

"It's Callahan," she exhales. "What can I do for you agent?"

"We're on our way to Lake Apopka, can you have a team meet me there. There's a development."

"I heard…but how do you learn of these things so fast?"

"Never mind, we'll be there in a few minutes."

"Well, our staff is on highway nineteen as we speak, they're pretty much there already. But Richard and I left a while ago, do you want us to turn around."

"No, do whatever you were doing. I'll call you if we need you."

Click, he hangs up and Sheryl looks at her phone, dismayed.

Both she and Richard call their team members, informing them to meet the FBI at the Lake. They mention it probably will not take long they explain as past experience shows, usually nothing comes from these reports. Everyone moans, but cordially react well to the request.

Then, Sheryl and Richard continue as planned and before long, they parked at their destination.

"Would you really have wrecked on purpose?" Richard asks while grabbing fast-food bags, closing the car door behind him.

Sheryl gives a peculiar grin without reply.

"I didn't think so," he confidently asserts.

Just then, a man appears from the center court.

"Dad…?" Richard greets his father. "You're leaving late today."

"Yes, I had to hold the fort down with you gone. Hello Sheryl," his father turns to her. "I'm glad to see you two are having some quality time together."

"I'm not sure that's what you call this," she snickers, "but we did spend the day together."

"Yes, this is the longest Richard has been away from the office in a long while."

Sheryl smirks on that comment, "Yeah, we were about to discuss why he spends so much time here." She looks at Richard but he avoids that stare.

"What are you doing here? Shouldn't you be heading home?" senior asks.

"My car is here—just dropping by to get it and take care of some paperwork for the FBI."

"Yes, how is that going?"

"We'll let you know. Circumstances are still unfolding," Richard says as he begins walking on. "I'll talk to you tomorrow pops."

"Okay," the elder Olson replies, watching them depart until vanishing beyond the bushes.

Twenty-Two

Foodstuffs, napkins and plasticware lay atop a large table. Paper bags open and ruffle with contents being removed, then sandwich wrappers crackle while pulled back to bite the meal within.

"All these years, I've never been in here," Sheryl mutters with a full mouth.

"It's our conference room," Richard informs, also trying to swallow.

"Leather chairs, marble accents and African Blackwood under our elbows, that's a nice touch."

"No... just Mahogany," Richard corrects, "but it is African."

Suddenly, Ashley's voice announces over the intercom, "Richard, is that you? Are you back?"

"That's Mr. Olson," Sheryl mumbles under angry breath while making a distorted face.

"Uh, it's beer-thirty. Are you interested?" Ashley asks in her usual character.

Sheryl immediately scowls at Richard with glaring gotcha eyes, which he tries to ignore while pressing the talk button.

"No, that's it for today, maybe another time. Sheryl is with me," he begins to explain, but suddenly chokes on a bite of food.

Sheryl obviously insulted by his untimely gag on words.

He slurps a drink and performs a grueling swallow to conclude with hoarse tone, "We have FBI reports to finish up."

"Oh," sounding surprised she returns. "Sounds like you're already eating too. Well okay, say hi to the misses for me. Have a good night."

"Okay, bye," Richard sounds off.

"Right," Sheryl pounces on him as soon as he releases the switch. "Explain to me again how I have nothing to worry about. If that's not 'come on let's do it', I don't know what is?"

"She didn't mean anything by it."

"Really, are you that out of touch or just playing dumb? You lead her on with, 'maybe later.' What the hell is going to happen then?"

"I conducted myself professionally Sheryl, no point in making it seem like..."

"Like you spoke discreetly in front of your wife to prevent her from catching on?" pausing to take another bite, she then continues, "Have you been with her?"

"What about your boss Sheryl—I've seen you two?"

"I can't help it if the guy won't leave me alone—you know I tried to talk to you about him...but"

"But what Sheryl?" he stops chewing to scowl at her, but he changes to persist more humbly. "You know what, just forget it," he sighs into his chair.

"Did it start before or after I let things go between us? I can forgive you if it was after. I wouldn't blame you—I know it's my fault. Like you said, I've let the kids down too."

Appearing glum Richard simply sits idle.

However, Sheryl's spirit becomes agitated. "First of all, thank you for not trusting me," she attacks, pushing his half-eaten burger across the table. "And second, you are an asshole. Scotty's just being an annoying, very hopeful prick. That's what I wanted to tell you, but you never seem concerned with my day. And if your lack of interest doesn't get in the way, there's always another interruption—the kids, work, a new sinkhole…and I…"

She breaks to contemplate—dealing with strong emotion, she is becoming unsettled.

Richard waits, growing disturbed as well, wondering what is coming next.

"I didn't want to screw things up for you."

"What are you talking about?" he asks as if completely baffled. "How are you protecting me?"

"Never mind," she suddenly gets elusive.

"No, what does that mean?" slurping through a straw and then passing it to her he questions, paying close attention.

She takes longer than usual to respond.

He nags her, "this is supposed to be an open talk, remember?"

She takes a drink and of course an extra moment.

He is on edge.

After another deep breath she exhales and looks at him with sudden candor, "I've always known you were in the tank with Wynyard," she blurts and resumes sipping soda, turning away as if worried about his reaction.

"You mean," he teeters for a reply.

"Yeah, him helping ODG, massaging reports, exaggerating timelines, holding your hand—I'm aware of it all."

"Why didn't you tell me?" he leans in. "You acted so surprise earlier."

"I couldn't risk it. Can you imagine the media backlash if they found out? And Wynyard might have used it to get closer to me—perhaps threatening to expose you somehow."

"He wouldn't do that."

"Not intentionally, but he can let his mouth run."

"Yeah, he is a loose-cannon," Richard admits. "So you kept your awareness secret?"

"Umm, to protect you and all my investigations which would be deemed worthless? If I issue findings in favor of ODG…I'm just skewing reports and giving you a free ride. That's what the media will say and why I brought Arnold in. He will be seen as objective and fair—which he is by the way."

"So you let Wynyard keep thinking he has the upper hand with you… and you're okay with that?"

"I can put up with his bullshit."

"But what about the press, their stories, and how do they get details so fast?" he adds.

"That's not me," she sustains. "I don't want them around anymore than you do."

"But they know things, and you have been snooping around my jobsites."

"Of course I'm investigating. I'm not saying I wouldn't hammer you about egregious crap if I found out that you were involved with it, or worse the cause of it. I would—but the difference is I would speak to you first."

"Okay, the FBI. What is the deal with them?"

"That's Wynyard's doing. He got a hold of my preliminary findings and turned them over as soon as they came knocking on his door. I tried to keep it out of the limelight, until my guys could figure the glitches out."

"What kind of problems are you referring to?"

"Jeff has been recording these…tremors, small quake activity."

"And you thought I was the reason?"

"I wasn't sure," throwing a hand up she asserts. "But aren't you curious about these things too?"

"I don't know…honestly I don't worry about the things you do. Events happen to the environment all the time. But…"

"But what…?"

"But if you care, well then…I guess I will too," he pauses while they both take a moment.

She seems to like hearing that.

"So you knew about Wynyard?" He mentions again, adding a thrilled smile.

"Yeah, I did…but he can't know that. I care about your career, 'YOU JACKASS.' I really do. Your future is my future too but if I visibly get into the middle of this, he might do something …"

"So, it wasn't you leaking to the press."

"I told you I wasn't. So you can relax, and there's nothing between me and Wynyard—you're so stupid." Pulling away, she reclines with bad attitude. "But what does it matter…" she pauses again, but with apprehension.

Disappointment returns to her face as she looks into his eyes. "I remember you used to be interested in me like that, showing up at my job unexpected. Telling me I was beautiful."

"It's just that I…" he tries to speak.

"Stop!" she cuts him off, "you still haven't told me about Ashley, or the neighbor for that matter?"

"Who…?" He seems mystified.

"Like you don't know," she scoffs. "Down the street, the girl on our block…she greets you at your car every morning."

"Have you been spying on me?"

"Watching your husband drive away isn't snooping. So, what's going on?"

"That's Susan Carter," he groans.

"Am I supposed to know who that is?"

"She's the president of Harmony's green building committee; you've met her several times. She's campaigning to have a hub installed in our community. You know that infrastructure I build. She hasn't stopped nagging me since learning about them—Harmony could supply gas to other communities for miles around. She's been pestering me non-stop about it."

"Oh…" Sheryl settles down. "Well why didn't you tell me?"

"…Because lately you've been beating me up over every little thing. What would you have done hearing I might be installing a five-hundred thousand cubic meter gas tank in our own back yard?"

"Great, I guess I should be upset on a completely different level. You can't disclose business dealings with me either. And right where your family lives no less."

"C'mon Sheryl…it's not like that."

"I've heard that before."

"Listen, you would have been in my face to no end, knocked on her door and harassed the committee non-stop and like you said…"

"You're right," she admits, raising a hand. "I would have lost it." She laughs, acknowledging that truth but quickly gets serious. "Well, that leaves just one more thing doesn't it?"

"Ashley," Richard exhales.

"Yeah…you really seem to be avoiding that subject. Why can't you tell me about her?"

"I did, you're not paying attention."

"Well, I'm listening now. What's the explanation? You know, she actually gave me advice about you… that I should recognize what a good catch you are. She tried to tell me how to deal with my husband." Sheryl's voice mocks, 'from one woman to another.' Yeah, she said I should know."

Richard looks at her funny, expressing disbelief.

"I'm not making this up," Sheryl flares. "I feel there's something going on—a reason for her conniving attitude or is my mind playing tricks on me? Tell me, why does she protect you? It's almost as if she got a taste of it and now can't let it go. We still may have cheater in the midst. So, you and she, what's the truth, final answer," Sheryl fixates on him with intense gaze.

"Just one shot huh?" he exhales.

"One try, that's all you get. But keep in mind—I may not be forgiving as you so before you answer, just tell me what she means to you."

"She's my employee, a good secretary…"

"Where are you going with this? Stop doing that?" she blasts. "This is crap okay."

"Sheryl, I know you don't have any reason to believe me. I can't prove a thing and I know she is incredibly hot, the life of the party…extremely seducing, attractive and a knockout…"

He reaches for her but she slaps him away.

"Yeah, yeah, you mentioned that part…she's good looking, I get it…are you even trying to earn my trust? Do you want me to believe you?"

"We'll, she's probably desperate and plain obsessed—you know how some women get. Maybe I got a little too close once or twice but I swear..."

"How close...?" in harsh tone, she demands.

"Just like you with 'Windbag'. You know the deal."

All of a sudden, over the intercom, Ashley's voice emerges again.

"Nothing happened, that's what he's trying to say. I can tell you he is a complete drag. In fact, you're both pathetic," she utters in serious character. "Oh, I tried. What can I say? I guess I understand now though. I know where his heart really is. If I had been paying attention from the beginning, I would have realized that much earlier—you two are made for each other. Sheryl, can you forgive me for being such a bitch?"

Right now, both Sheryl and Richard are completely surprised. She is sitting with mouth opened wide and Richard is expressing utter annoyance. They just realized Ashley had listened to their entire conversation and they are quite stunned.

"I think I can work on that," Sheryl stammers, unsure where this is going.

"Richard. What about you?" Ashley asks for clemency.

"That depends. How long have you been listening," he questions with boss authority.

"That depends. Should I be looking for a new job?"

"Ashley, I'm not ready to get rid of you, you're reliable. I just don't know what to make of this."

"In that case, I heard everything, all of it—a girl has to know what she's up against, you know and now...I get it. You guys...are the real deal, made for one another or whatever. I can tell by the way you argue—even though you're both mad at each other, you still care about each other anyway. It's like...you can't stop it. I'm jealous okay."

"Really, you heard everything...the entire conversation?" Richard scoffs.

"How do you think I get all of the information I do? People don't just give it to me!"

Sheryl scrunches eyes hearing that, and starts to wonder. "Do you know a reporter named Rhonda with KBTV?" Sheryl asks.

"She's my roommate. Why?"

With the passing of that comment, Sheryl and Richard both eye each other.

"Good night Ashley! This time leave," Richard orders.

"Yeah, I'm going and uh thanks for the hot comment. At least I got that goin on. But you should know that I'm not desperate, just vein and maybe a bit of an opportunist. Ciao."

Ashley signs off and Richard is sure to check that the intercom is off too, this time by unplugging the power cord.

"She's worse than I thought," Sheryl moans. "I wonder how many times she's done that."

"I don't want to think about it," Richard gasps and then turns to his wife delivering a brilliant smile. "So, am I off the hook?"

"How do I know that you didn't plan this?" Sheryl contends but now with a smile. "You could be the world's best scheming asshole."

He moves closer. She allows him. "No way I'm that smart."

"True, you never think that far ahead."

Then finally, they give each other a simple but pleasant kiss.

Upon turning off the lights and closing up office, the two reunited souls head down to the parking lot. While walking, Richard is playing with Sheryl's ring inside his pants pocket. He looks at her thinking that he should give it back, but decides it is not the right place or time.

Standing under a light pole situated between their vehicles they hug once again, seeming more like the lovebirds they used to be. Abruptly, she gets an idea, and while holding hands she exudes a titillating gleam.

"I know that look," he laughs. "You want something."

"Hey, why don't we go to all three days of the festival, you know as a family?" she pleads like a little girl.

"Oh you can work it too I see," he smiles. "Are you sure?" he takes her in for another heartfelt embrace. They kiss.

She voices with her face against his chest, "yeah, why not? We can make it a long weekend. We haven't seen Jakes raft yet and the kids will be happy to see us together again—and our teams deserve the extra time too."

"Yeah, okay," he agrees. "We'll tell the kids as soon as we get home—it'll be like old times?"

"New times," she concludes as they kiss and hug again.

"Better than old," he adds.

"I don't know, old wasn't so bad," she breathes against him.

"Just one thing," Richard mentions.

"What?" Sheryl looks up to stare into his eyes.

"Are you making dinner tonight?" he smiles.

"Are you kidding?" pushing off his chest she laughs. "After all this, you're buying me that Riviera experience—a feast on the intercostal. You've got a lot of making up to do."

Both laughing, they embrace again.

"Well, since I'm spending a fortune on all those other guys...I guess I can splurge on the most important person in my life too annnd... maybe give her something special."

"Now you're talking my language," she smiles and they kiss. "What kind of surprise are we talking about?"

"Uh, well...it's...ah," he struggles with words. "It's something you'll be happy to see."

Ring, ring, ring Richards phone sounds, interrupting their moment.

"That phone, it never fails," Sheryl spews, whirling a hand in air.

"Yeah Carl, how's it going, what now?"

"You're not going to believe this boss…"

"What is it…what happened? Did somebody find explosives?"

Sheryl listens intently.

"No…it's worse. We found a floater…in the lake."

Richard turns to Sheryl displaying great concern, "as in dead, Carl?" Richard's eyebrows narrow.

"What going on?" she interrupts but he ignores

"Boss, they're not letting us go. After we pulled him out—the FBI took over. You need to get back here…a.s.a.p."

Richard closes his cell, exhales and places a hand on Sheryl's arm simply stating. "Babe, it looks like dinner has to wait."

Twenty-Three

Camouflaged SUV's and Jeeps maneuver through a marsh near lakeside, making substantial noise. Their engines revving to maintain horsepower as all four tires spin insatiably, gripping to gain traction on a soggy surface. Mud flings high into the air and far behind leaving two impressive tracks, squished into the soft ground as the taskforce proceeds in unison. Mufflers roar and the smell of exhaust fumes fill the once serene and clean air. Several Humvees also roam the perimeter providing surveillance. Small arms mounted atop and manned at the ready indicate full-scale protection is underway as well. Armed guards stand watch over parked vehicles with a dull black finish, some all-terrain style with high ground clearance and grilled front bumpers, winches, and high-powered spotlights. Other soldiers are securing the area by spreading concertina wire around the lake. Nearby, more of the razor sharp rolls wait on the bed of a M35 cargo truck. Inaudible directives arise from numerous directions as troops fortify their positions.

Sheryl and Richard witness the organized scene unfold as they park among an adjacent group of civilian vehicles. The DEP bus is in line of sight too, but it sits empty.

"What the hell is going on?" Sheryl asks her husband. "Army personnel, what are they here for? And how did they coordinate this so fast?"

"I don't know, but this doesn't happen unless something big is brewing." Turning to his wife, he exhibits an alarmed expression. Then, near the guarded vehicles, he notices a group of people.

"Over there, I think that's our guys," he points.

"Are they holding rifles on them? I can't believe..." astonished, she is at a loss for words.

"I think we better get over there," he affirms. "Let's go."

Cautiously, they leave their vehicle and begin walking to their friends and colleagues, but they did not get far.

An armed guard stepping from behind a flanking vehicle confronts them, "Stop right there folks. This area is off-limits," he issues a stern warning while pointing an M-16 rifle.

"We're with the FBI," Richard explains. "Well, we're working under their authority rather."

"We are in charge of the people you have over there," Sheryl adds. "We scouted this lake just a couple hours ago, for agent Callahan. Our guys found the body, we know about that."

"The FBI wants to speak with us," Richard pleads. "And we need to see our friends."

Directly, the MP transmits over his radio explaining the situation to his superiors. Then a crackling voice emits back, "Hold them with the others. I'll process this up the chain."

With that, the guard escorts the dazed couple to a makeshift tent and holding area where their group waits.

"Hey Carl," Richard blurts, quickly moving to greet the restless coworker. "Are you being held against your will?"

"No, at first maybe, but they said we could leave."

Sheryl closes in. Jeff spots her and joins the conversation as well.

"What happened? Why didn't you call earlier?" Richard asks.

Jeff answers, "It all happened so fast. One minute we're bringing a dead guy to the edge of the lake, and the next we're being rounded up."

"They wouldn't let us call anyone at that point," Carl includes.

Jeff further explains, "We came to meet the FBI right. They said, look on the north side of Lake Apopka, where some residents thought they heard a blast and felt a thud. We all looked around for a while and then Carl sent in the divers and almost right away that dead guy surfaced."

Richard and Sheryl listen intently.

"We wanted to keep searching, but got yanked away...and here we wait," Carl continues. "All I know for sure is he isn't one of ours, or with anyone we associate."

"How do you know that?" Sheryl asks.

"His equipment—it's out of date. The mask, regulator and protective mechanisms are old—gear that isn't used anymore."

"The tank hasn't been certified either," Arnold, stepping in speaks out.

"I thought you don't do water," Jeff scoffs.

"I don't, but I did get scuba certified."

"He's right," Carl notes. "He had to be filling his own air tank too. It wasn't serviced—no dated safety checks.

Respectable divers wouldn't use what this guy had on, unless they were forced to."

"So, was he blown up? How did he die?" Sheryl seems confused.

"Concussions don't leave external signs of damage," Arnold details. "Unless you were right on top of the blast or got hit with shrapnel, only a medical examination could tell."

"And he didn't have any obvious wounds," Carl affirms.

Richard begins thinking.

Sheryl crosses her arms glaring on and Jeff impatiently paces.

"This is a national matter," Arnold lays it out there.

Richard and the others turn to him.

"What do you mean?" Jeff asks.

"You all know what I'm saying."

Everybody stares at each other with menacing quandary.

"I'm gonna get some answers," Richard positions at a doorway to look at the lights and action, scrutinizing for a way to get closer.

"I'm coming with you," Sheryl follows and peeps outward as well. She grabs his hand to affirm her conviction and as they stand poised to spring, the intensity of ensuing conflict grows.

Noticing the comfortable clinch, Jeff jeers, "Are you two holding hands?"

Sheryl looks back and gives a shoulder shrug with an elated smile. "I'll tell you later," she whispers, and then the two dart toward the lake, hand in hand.

Jeff and Arnold left staring at each other.

"What are they up to?" Jeff lends a dirty look, "They haven't been like that in years."

"It seems she took my advice," Arnold grins.

Confused, Carl is at a loss, "What are you talking about?"

Searching for a member of the FBI, the Olson's move toward the lake—progressing between vehicles and around temporary barricades. Looking left and then right they scout further ahead.

"Stop right there," a man wielding a rifle wearing a maroon beret steps in front of them.

Halted again and startled, they remain speechless as the determined lone guard nears close, but then...

"At ease soldier," a familiar voice sounds from the rear.

They turn—its agent Callahan. "I'll take it from here," he continues. "Go back to your post and tell the others to get on the bus."

"Yes sir," the GI complies.

"What the hell is the military doing here?" Richard requests resolve.

"I thought you'd be happy to see me," Callahan laughs. "You know, if you need more time, I could have let that trooper have his way with you," he jokes.

"We're delighted?" Sheryl fakes happiness—clearly disgruntled too. "We've been out here all day...for you, and now guns are being pointed at our face. What could be wrong?"

"Listen, things are developing rather fast and I can't discuss it right now. Come this way," he urges them back toward their vehicle.

"Wait a minute," Sheryl steps aside. "You infringed on our well-being, took advantage of our good nature, made us search for...whatever, and we supplied you with teams for this emergency and now you don't have time for us."

The agent stops walking and stands rather casually, looking at the tangled pair. "People," he exhales to a passive state. "It wasn't necessary for you to come back all this way."

Richard scoffs. "We just sent you personnel, remember," he resists the dispassionate shove-off. "You called us to assist. Don't we deserve answers?"

"C'mon guys, it's not like that. This has turned into a Federal crime scene now, civilians aren't…"

"Needed," Richard interjects.

"What I'm mean is," he corrects. "There's a lot going on and my boss's chief is in on this now."

"Who's that?" Sheryl asks but gets no answer from the lofty agent. So she puts it another way, "Are you saying the president is involved?"

"I didn't say that," he gets defensive, placing persuasive hands on their shoulders, again encouraging them to withdraw to their vehicle. "Both of you know how it is when things have to be kept under wraps. I will get back to you as soon as we find something out. Besides, you should be thankful this is out of your hands—just yesterday you didn't want anything to do with me."

"What are you going to tell the media? They'll be all over this," Sheryl offers an intelligent thought, throwing her hands up.

"We're just protecting the environment. That's all they need to know," the agent smiles.

"That won't be good enough for them, trust me," Richard assures.

"We'll, news agencies have already been informed," Callahan smirks, "and they won't be coming."

Sheryl exclaims, "So that's it."

"That's it," he offers an assuring hand, showing them the direction to their car. "We'll take it from here."

As a helicopter lands nearby, throwing noise and wind in all directions, the three stare at one another.

"That bird's for me," the agent yelps in a raised voice and turns to see it.

"Okay then. Are we free to go?" Sheryl yells.

"Yes you are."

"Well, we'll be enjoying our hometown festival tomorrow; with our kids so if you need us…don't bother."

"Like I said mam, we got it. Thanks for all your help. I thank you…your nation thanks you. You've served your country well."

"Spare me the patriotism lecture. I've heard it all before," Richard barks as the whirling blades begin reducing speed and sound.

"Well, I thank you anyway, truly, it's been a pleasure," Callahan acknowledges, and then turns making his way to the helicopter.

Everyone watches as military personnel carry a stretcher with a body bag on it, and then load it in—Callahan shouting while climbing into the copter.

"I want to know where he lives, works, what town he was born in, the name of his kindergarten teacher, who his great, great grandparents are and every single one of his hobbies—his favorite food and what the hell gives him gas. Yesterday people—let's go."

Once aboard, it flies away.

Twenty-Four

A gentle breeze compliments a perfect sky with only thin clouds drifting overhead. The sunshine breaches those high-altitude layers easily, mere vague shadows cast on the warming terrain below.

Nearing the fairgrounds, rows of flowers are in full-bloom with red roses highlighting the floral arrangement—they stand prominent, bursting for attention. Children sit engaged in board games and playing jax, several randomly chase each other and play tag while a few run down the family dog dashing away with a Frisbee. Flawless vivid green grass leads up to a walkway with an arched wooden trellis overhead labeled, 'Harmony Festival—it's a wonderful day in Harmony.'

The day is vibrant, as is the renewed spirit and zest for life that the Olson's feel. Amends and togetherness will spotlight this fun filled afternoon. Richard and Sheryl seem content while trotting through the entryway, faces smiling and clenched hands swaying, but it seems one of their kids is not as enthusiastic.

"What is it Jenny?" her mother nudges the frumpy teenager but no reply is given, she is looking at her feet.

As the family strolls into the park, an entertaining young girl waves some colorful cotton candy in front of them. Shaped onto long paper cones it is perfectly prepared for enjoyment, purely to tempt a compulsory grab, and Richard was there to bite. He could not resist the easy sale.

"Three dollars," she says and he pays with bills from his shirt pocket.

Sheryl snatches a taste without asking. "The weathergirl said perfect conditions for the next few days," she tells the kids, but they don't seem impressed so she changes subject. "Tell us about your raft Jake."

Suddenly, she gets someone's attention.

"Okay, it's going to be the best part of the festival. I'm not even kidding," Jake's eyes light with enthusiasm. "Mr. Nash, you know Junior's dad. He made some improvements—a few seaworthy techniques and there's nothing but a win in store for us."

"So what does Chuck do again?" his dad asks, offering cotton candy.

"He was a boat builder, so he knows his stuff," Jake answers with zeal but refuses the sweet stuff.

"Oh," Richard lends an endorsing smirk and nod.

Sheryl bumps the boy with her bum, "When do we get to see it?"

"Later…because the contest is actually tomorrow, but we can check it out though," he eagerly suggests.

Then Jenny speaks up, "Do I have to walk with you guys?" she pouts.

"We just got here," Richard harps.

Sheryl interjects. "No, let her go find Bobby," She stops to look at her daughter, face to face. "That's what you want, isn't it?"

"Are you testing me or something?" Jenny gripes with cautionary character.

"Not at all, you can go, but uh…you're going to miss your dad winning me a stuffed animal."

"Oh geese, I think I liked it better when you two were fighting," Jenny hoots and takes off.

Then Jake blurts, "I'll show you the raft later okay. I have to find Junior. See ya," And he runs without asking, his feet racing.

"Hey, hey," His dad vies for his sons fleeting consideration, but to no avail…he's gone.

Sheryl turns to Richard and playacts a grouchy moan, "Well, it looks like it's just us," then brilliantly smiles and moves in for a hug, wildly wrapping arms around his neck with theatrical glee.

"Yeah, I thought we'd never get rid of them," he lets out a naughty laugh.

Then they too sprint like a couple of kids.

Waltzing through the park, they notice the event is larger this year, greater attendance and much more to do. Nibbling on a bag of popcorn, they meander past merry-go-rounds, slow sightseeing train rides and kids throwing softballs at flip-up cloth puppets. Then they walk past people shooting corks from rifles at old coke bottles and others throwing darts at small balloons, popping them to uncover the prize behind. Bobbing for apples and tossing Ping-Pong balls into goldfish bowls catch their interest too. Candy, pretzels, ice cream, sodas, hot dogs, burgers and numerous treats are abundant at every turn. Ferris Wheels, hot air balloons and roller coasters are just some of the rides on their list but feeding the pigs is an eccentric must do as well. There are plenty of things to do, and the Olson parents are experiencing as many of them as possible.

Thirst comes quickly, so the mature lovebirds stop for something refreshing.

"One large pride of the country…!" Sheryl orders at a lemonade booth.

"Fresh squeezed homegrown lemons and secret tradition coming up," the polite and bubbly female vendor says, grabs a large cup and adding, "with crushed ice in a tall mug and a few slices of juicy sugarcane. Mm-mm you know that's good."

Somewhat pooped, they sit at a nearby table under a large umbrella and drink from the lone cup, but through their own straws. Between slurps, they chew on delicious cane strips. Like teenagers, they giggle and ogle each other until the frosty beverage is gone and upon hearing that crackle of an emptying cup, Sheryl quickly lifts and tilts it to her mouth. She sucks down the remaining bottom nibble like a thirsty football player, hurriedly shaking it so Richard can't have a chance to get at it. He light heartedly scoffs and shakes his head while lobbing his straw into the empty container. Just as they were about to move on…a nice surprise happens.

"Hey guys," several voices come from behind, so they turn to see who."

"Arnold, Jeff...you guys made it," Sheryl shrieks.

She and Richard stand to greet them.

"And who is this?" Sheryl directs her vision to a newcomer.

"This is my better half, Maggie," Arnold smiles."

Sheryl squeals giving the cheery girl a hospitable hug, "Arnold! You never said she was so adorable." Then she gives Maggie her attention, "You've got to tell me about Utah." She insists while releasing her clutches on the overwhelmed woman. "I've always wanted to go."

Quickly, the group gathers at the same table and Richard brings a few more lemonades.

"Maggie, you have to taste this," Sheryl slides a tall cup her way. "It's amazing."

"The secret is a bit of added key lime juice and a tad of the shaved peel," Richard whispers, but way too loud for discretion. "Don't tell them I told you."

They all share a laugh.

Maggie confirms the flavor is incredible as did the rest and it was agreed to be all the hype as advertised.

Then...it happens. The phone rings just as it always does and Sheryl delivers Richard that familiar displeased stare.

"That's not my ringtone," he says. "I think it's coming from your purse."

Grasping her phone, she reads the incoming call. She scoffs, "its Callahan. That prick, I thought he was done with us."

"I couldn't have said it better. May he rot in hell?" Jeff broadcasts taking another swig.

Maggie gives Arnold a confused look, "Who's that?"

"I'll tell you later," he mumbles.

"I thought we were meaningless and obstructive civilians Mr. Callahan," Sheryl snarls.

"Mrs. Olson how is your lovely day—warm and cheery I hope?"

"It's just great agent...because you haven't been in it."

"Sheryl, I'm afraid I need your help," Callahan gets straight to the point, with usual serious character.

"Just like that, you must be out of your mind," in raised tone she blasts. The others eavesdrop—each manifesting a curious and troubled glare.

"I have a grave situation," he begins but she deliberately interrupts him.

"You always do—tell me, why should I care? Better yet, go bother someone else."

Richard is becoming irritated.

"Mrs. Olson I can't..."

"Can't or won't," she snaps again. Moments go by with no response. "Are you still there?" she groans.

"I know your upset, but I do need your expertise."

"Suddenly you need us—again, and we're just supposed to jump. Honestly, this is why you guys get such a bad rap," she scolds once more."

"It's about that diver Mrs. Olson."

"Well, we're not available till Monday."

"Mrs. Olson."

"Sorry, I'm here with my kids,"

"Mam,"

"We're having a blast. Did I mention that?"

"Sheryl,"

"Agent, did you pick up on that," she laughs, "I don't care!"

Suddenly, Richard grabs the phone away from her.

"Listen agent, my wife already told you that we're busy."

"What if you're not able to enjoy the next three days Mr. Olson? Callahan expresses a severe connotation.

"What's that?" Richard asks, becoming very guarded, "are you threatening me?"

"Mr. Olson, please listen very carefully. That diver—he's not your humble resident and he wasn't taking pictures or collecting seashells. If you have any desire to see humanity persist, you'll get here…right now," with grim conviction he warns Richard. "Do you understand?"

Richard breathes deep to absorb the moment, his eyes communicating great concern—transparent for all to see. His dark change in character noted.

Callahan continues, "This is a matter of life or death. Don't say a word to your friends and don't alarm anyone…just get here. You'll learn more then."

Richard, with blank expression makes one simple request. "Give me the address."

Twenty-Five

Arriving at a street corner in an Orlando suburb, Richard and Sheryl observe their destination from within the safety of their vehicle. Richard rolls Sheryl's window down with his electronic button so they can get a clearer look. They notice it's a regular three-story complex in a moderate community on intersecting residential streets. Gated entrances with security are absent.

Slowly, they drive around it for the once over. At the rear, the top two levels have balconies bordered with railing but the bottom floor opens to the backyard environment. A tot playground sets to the side and kids run about as numerous vehicles commute this common route—rows of close-knit apartment buildings fringe both sides in either direction, an uneventful neighborhood. All appears normal, except today there are a few black vehicles resting at the front curb—unmarked but easily spotted as official transport. A few squad cars from the local municipality positioned amid them as well.

Several people are watching the mild activity—some walking away stopped by police and pressed to answer questions. Other suits are knocking on doors but few of them open, however swaying curtains reveal someone is home. Workers wearing latex gloves carrying sealed bags and covered boxes routinely pass between a particular downstairs apartment and several vans parked overtop the sidewalk just outside the flat's entry.

Uniformed officers and plain clothed agents alike communicate via radios while directing efforts, securing the scene and keeping a focused observation of the vicinity. Although they are keeping a low profile, an untrained eye could still tell an investigation of some magnitude was underway.

Richard and Sheryl park at the shoulder behind a police car and promptly exit.

An odd sort of man walking by asks, "What's the hullabaloo all about?"

"We have no idea," Richard tells him, casually keeping an eye on the fellow as he walks away.

After critiquing the situation, the two start toward the center of commotion and swiftly—they notice a deputy is moving to confront their advancement—followed by two others dispatching as well.

"Here comes the sentry," Richard exhales, sliding his hands in his pockets.

"Just tell him the FBI called us here," Sheryl advises.

"Right, because that worked so well at the lake."

"Just speak with authority," she urges, placing a hand on his arm, "like you belong here."

He gives an encouraging nod and inhales preparing for defiance. As the encounter draws close, they stop amidst an open area.

"Listen, before you guys drag my wife and I off somewhere, let's get one thing straight," Richard begins with a stern hand directed at the three protectors. "We're not snooping or trying to infiltrate your frontline or anything like that..."

As suspected, his longwinded pretext cut off.

"Mr. and Mrs. Olson...?" the man in the middle asks.

That was not expected. They give each other an astonished look—shocked to be recognized.

"That's...us," Sheryl stammers.

"Follow me mam," the patrol officer delivers a hand motion and begins leading the way. "Agent Callahan is expecting you."

Richard valiantly comments to his wife, "was that commanding enough?"

"Oh yeah...that was good," she jokes, "nothing wrong with that. I knew you had it in you."

They both share an obscure chuckle.

Upon reaching the apartment, the escorted duo is drawing all of the attention. Several interested people were being held back by police—to allow adequate passage under the yellow 'Do Not Cross' barricade line.

Once inside they wait while one of the bodyguards proceeded onward.

"What's with the stuff being loaded into the vans?" Richard asks one cop.

"ERT's," he replies.

Richard is confused.

"Evidence Response Teams," the man clarifies. "They're securing evidence."

"It seems like they're taking everything in sight," Sheryl exclaims as an outside disturbance unfolds.

"I want to know what's going on," a woman protests, sounding rather upset.

"Please stand back mam—keep your children behind the line," a male officer instructs.

"I live in this building, I need to know."

"No need to panic. If it was something important, you would be notified."

"Where's the guy who lives here."

"Do you know him?"

"No, not really,"

"Well, if you have anything to say, tell those men over there," he says. "Otherwise, residents get information on a need to know basis. Until then, please get back."

Meanwhile, the Olson's are making unavoidable observations. Either the FBI's brash fact-finding efforts have turned the apartment upside down or the clutter within it is indicative of unkempt living. Pizza boxes and convenience food trash lay about, along with remnants of various uneaten grubs. Dirty clothes rest in disorganized piles, torn shipping boxes and wrapping paper are scattered, tossed in haste. Unrecognizable debris is noticeable in every direction.

A view into kitchen reveals the cabinets and drawers are absent of culinary life—thoroughly inspected they sit wide open. Only a few boxes of foodstuffs remain. Elsewhere, typical home furnishings such as couches, TV's, paintings, china cabinets, bookcases, knick-knacks and other living niceties are missing too. A plain dining table with two chairs is apparently the only furniture in sight and atop sets a computer, which two official personnel are exploring. Others scamper through stacks of documents, books and manuscripts at the opposite end of the table and yet someone else is rifling through a four-tiered filing cabinet. Numerous wood crates align the walls—they too ransacked.

Oddly, there are maps of Florida taped to bare walls—some type of writings on them. Also hanging, large pictures of underwater scenes—rock faces, floor bottoms alongside a calendar. A photographer is documenting those images on film while one agent flips through the calendar making notes of what he sees. Yet someone else is lifting prints from postal mail, address keepers and phone books—each scrutinized for every lead too. Drawers and lamps lay broken apart. Even cigarette butts, ashtrays, pens, pencils, markers, plasticware, discarded foods, traces of soil and the contents of trashcans—placed into specimen bags.

A wall clock lies in pieces, appliances rest disassembled and shoe prints remain protected. Personnel are examining the entire bedsit for hiding places—one man knocks a hole into the wall where he found a possible secret location.

At the door, beside their feet, they notice a couple of nylon and cotton mesh tool bags. Clearly, with the contents examined—evidence labels affixed.

Indistinct chatter emanates from every direction while the awaiting pair witnesses the remarkable display of gathering techniques. Amidst the conversations, one voice grows louder and more familiar. From a back room, Callahan emerges and he strides to encounter them.

"Hey folks...hope you weren't waiting too long?" he appeals to their presence with cheerful alliance.

"This is a massive feat," Sheryl commends.

"To say the least, we spare no expense...nothing left untouched or uncovered, and no one permitted to leave unquestioned," the agent confidently acknowledges. "That's out motto."

"You guys are really picking this place apart." Richard concurs.

"Every piece of physical evidence gets tagged, bagged and then closely examined," Callahan points out. "Yeah, you should see the toilet...or maybe not," he laughs. "It's not a pretty sight but the inside of the mattress isn't any better—you'll never think of box springs the same way again. Oh, here it comes now. Kind of smells doesn't it?" the agent jokes as they sidestep to avoid touching it while being carried by. "I didn't know they rusted like that," he derides the stinky bed.

"Whew...!" the Olson's choke on passing pungent odor and wave it from their noses.

"That taste won't last long. Don't worry," Callahan snorts. "Yeah…it's a madhouse in here," he removes his eyeglasses and begins cleaning them with a handkerchief. "This may seem like chaos…but it's actually an organized mission. No stone unturned—sooner or later we find what we're looking for."

He looks through his lenses to check their cleanliness, and then stares into Richard's soul while placing his frames back on, "Right this way." He leads them to the kitchen.

"Why did you ask us here?" Sheryl questions from his backside, "we left our kids for this. It seems you have quite enough help."

She gingerly steps over rubble, Richard warily follows as well until all come to a halt at the sink. Callahan abruptly turns, gripped in thought. The Olson's patiently wait for his response.

"Are you familiar with extremism, Mrs. Olson? How about you?" he gives Richard a terse head turn.

"I'm not sure we get your point," Richard is in quandary.

Sheryl shrugs shoulders and the agent exhales.

He almost seems perturbed. "You know, most people just go about their day," Callahan pulls gum from his pocket and offers a stick but each deny. After placing one into his mouth, he continues. "They never experience violence, cruelty or witness terror first hand." Enjoying the chew, he pauses, "But for those that do—even fewer will seize an opportunity to prevent tragedy. They're either too scared or don't know what to do. In any case, seldom does anyone avert danger even when possible to do so. Real life isn't like the movies." Callahan enjoys a breath, observing their attentive facial expressions. "The question is—would either of you do anything about a looming threat if you had the chance?"

"Listen Agent," Richard begins.

"Tyler, Mr. Olson," Callahan proposes.

"Great! We're on a first name basis now, I feel so much better."

Sheryl interjects, "Rick, let the agent explain."

Richard surrenders, "Go ahead—tell us what you have to say," he says, looking at Sheryl with doubt.

"I'm saying, people need to be protected—they can't survive on their own. No one would ever admit to it, but the truth is, most folks need safety initiated for them. The strongest and bravest citizens have always stepped up to provide it. So here it is…there's some shit going down and I am asking you to be one of those courageous sorts," placing hands on their shoulders he concludes.

"Okay Tyler. I give," Richard concedes in playful spirit. "What do we need to be concerned about?"

"What haven't you told us?" Sheryl, more worried than Richard, asks.

"Remember the diver?" Callahan hesitates, "his name is Saliha Achmede, a member of a known terrorist group organized by Yasser Qadeer, a terror leader."

Both Olson's are at full attention.

"He has been under the radar until yesterday—you're standing in is his apartment."

Suddenly, he has their curiosity.

"Okay…we're listening. So what was he planning?" Richard uncrosses his arms to place hands on hip.

"Not past tense Mr. Olson, his death doesn't stop anything. Someone else always takes their place," he complicates the matter with explicating hands.

"Okay, I get it, but how do we fit into this situation?"

"Come with me," the agent walks to the entry door. "I want you to see something." Crouching down he pulls a device from a tool bag, "What do you make of this—you're the construction pro?"

He hands it over. Richard examines it.

"It's a battery operated drill, with hammer action, uh…but not like one I've ever seen before," he squints, "there is no manufacturer or model number."

"What else?"

"It looks like it has been modified, built from scratch maybe."

"Go on."

"It's pneumatic and self-contained. It has both battery and air powered capability."

"What does that mean?" Sheryl asks.

"Well, it's small, lightweight, and easy to carry. When the battery runs out it can derive power from compact compressed air tanks. Usually tools like these are bulky, heavy and require long lines of air, but this one doesn't—simply screw in a canister and it's ready for use. I can see a few of them in the bag."

"Is that all?" Callahan presses.

"No. It has a half-inch chuck, capable of decent torque, a limitless air supply would keep it going indefinitely, possibly waterproof. The casing is…" Richard stumbles.

"Designed for underwater use," the agent completes his sentence. "And this tool, would it be noisy?" he asks.

"I don't think so. Depending how deep and where it's used, it may not be heard or felt at all."

"But it would get picked up on a seismograph," Sheryl murmurs.

Richard nods yes and they each share a concerned look.

"Okay, now look at this," the agent shifts focus to a wall map, actively pointing at it. "Mrs. Olson. What do you think this is?"

"Uh, it's a geographic chart of Florida," she states the obvious, "with a bunch of red dots and circles that someone wrote in."

"What do you think they represent?" Callahan compels.

"Coordinates maybe?" She is uncertain.

"Please, give it a closer look," he presses hard.

She breathes deeply and studies it, "perhaps they indicate areas surveyed—possibly something was found at those locations," she shakes her head, "it's hard to say, there isn't a legend—they could represent anything."

"C'mon, think like a bad guy," Callahan continues to push, tapping a finger on his temple. "This is where I need help."

"It's a trail...uh, money is buried there. I don't know," she flails and walks away.

The agent groans with displeasure.

"Ease off," Richard interjects. "You're not giving us much to go on and it's your job to unravel these things, not ours.

Callahan angers, "Clues...they're inklings," he drags them to the table. "Have you found anything else?" he addresses the two geeks sitting at the computer.

"Not really," one replies. "We've got a few more contacts, some pictures and a couple messages but nothing substantial. Either he didn't leave much or the valuable content is somewhere else."

"Alright, let the search rest for a sec—play that video for these people."

"You got it," the man begins typing on the keyboard. Swiftly clicking through folders, he locates the desired file. "Here it is," he voices and makes a single stroke on the enter tab.

While everyone jockeys for a good view, a video begins loading on the computer screen.

"It's an underwater scene," the tech informs.

Initially, considerable bubbles rise—possibly two divers' breathing apparatuses are releasing air. A beam of light illuminates the swarm of respiration and as it clears, a view of a stony vertical surface remains—it's coral or similar sedimentary rock. A gloved hand appears and rubs the rough façade, fingers pressing into the crevices trying to remove easily dislodged pieces. Loose sediment wiped away, the structure pushed and tapped for stability.

Small fish interested in the activity curiously swim near, first snooping and then dart off. Then, the individual brings a strange cylindrical apparatus into view, placing the tip perpendicular against the rugged wall—and the mechanism is attached to that drill from the tool bag.

Richard gives Callahan a serious look.

"That's a carbide core-drilling bit, with diamond tipped vents for smoother, easier cutting," Richard tells him. "The barrel diameter appears six inches or so—the inside of it is hollow. We use them to create holes in solid concrete such as walls and floors so plumbing and electrical piping can pass through. They're quite effective in removing huge chunks."

Sheryl pays close attention too.

Richard continues to educate, "They require a great deal of water to reduce heat and friction, but that's not an issue here—extraction time should be greatly reduced. Under usual circumstances, the process is virtually quiet with little vibration, which makes it the most preferred method of cutting in occupied buildings—it doesn't really bother anyone."

Callahan develops a curious gawp, and Sheryl takes note as they continue watching.

Then, while the device is being held in place, one hand grips the rear of the drill, squeezes the trigger and applies forward pressure. The large bit begins turning and instantly starts to penetrate the rocky wall. Slowly it spins propelling burrowed particles rearward, creating misty clouds drawn away by surrounding current. Fine residue is continually churned up and shed as the bit rotates, penetrating deeper with every revolution. Flawlessly it disappears into the pillar.

"Isn't that going in too easily?" Callahan questions the video.

"Core drilling—by nature it operates at low RPM and that material isn't as hard as tempered concrete reinforced with metal rebar."

"Limestone," Sheryl inserts, "it's comprised of shells, calcium and marine life—fairly soft stuff. It's actually porous and being subjected to eons of saltwater makes it more so—a lot less dense than cement," she explains.

Everyone seems impressed with her knowledge.

Richard nods, "Does this have sound?"

"Not a peep," Callahan gripes.

After the bit pierced through to completion, the operative implements a quick side-to-side jerking motion and the mechanism snaps loose, and he pulls it out. A perfect circular hole remained in the wall. Holding the bit downward, he then taps on its outer circumference with a metal object and the chunk of limestone slides out—formed into a perfect column. It is once again ready for use.

"That was fairly impressive," Richard reacts. "A hole, twenty or so inches deep—in a flash."

"Mrs. Olson, where do you think this video was taken?"

"Limestone is everywhere, I don't know."

As the video persists, a hand comes back into view and enters the hole as if checking the quality of it. Then, the camera and illumination pulls away turning focus to the right. For a moment, a glimpse of the rocky wall continued further away, fading into narrowing blackness.

Twenty-Six

"Your parents will be back soon," Maggie tells Jake as they stand near the concession trailers.

The boy is staring at the ground, pushing pebbles around with his foot—hands in back pockets. "All they do is work," the boy grumbles and kicks a small rock away.

"I'm sure they won't be long," she consoles the woeful lad. "And your mom can't stop talking about your raft."

"Really," squinting into the sun he seems surprised.

"I wouldn't lie! Scouts honor," smiling with radiance she raises a right hand. "Why don't you tell me about it?"

"Well…" he begins, but suddenly.

"Hey you two give us a hand," Arnold calls out as he and Jeff trek toward them holding trays overflowing with burgers, fries, chips and drinks.

Jake is quick to help lighten their load. He and Maggie both grab a few plates that were dangerously near the edge, but not before Jake stuffed a few tasty fries into his own mouth. Then, they all assemble at a nearby table.

"I'm starved." Jake blurts and Jeff chuckles watching the kid take a huge bite of his double stack.

"Slow down, you're gonna choke," Maggie opines taking a seat between he and Arnold.

The boy gives her an acknowledgement, but keeps gobbling recklessly anyway.

"Is Jenny coming?" Arnold broadcasts.

"I think she's content hanging with her boyfriend," Jeff answers.

"That's Bobby," Jake gurgles chewing food. "You won't see her for the rest of the day."

"Don't be too sure," Jeff banters.

"Why?"

"I mean…she's on her way over here."

Jake turns and sure enough, he beholds his sibling hand in hand with a boy walking toward them.

"And she's not alone," Maggie cites.

"Yep, that's my sister's squeeze."

"You sound critical, do you like him?" she probes.

"No, he's okay," he continues scarfing food as the arrivals approach.

"Hi Jeff," Jenny greets him.

Jeff stands with surprise, "Hey, you've gotten bigger—and sprouted a boyfriend too," he jokes and shakes their hands."

Everyone laughs.

"This is Bobby everybody!"

Everyone says hello to the boy with a big country smile.

"You probably don't know Maggie and Arnold, they're new to town. Arnold works for your mom," Jeff formerly introduces them.

"Lucky you...?" Jenny jeers, while shaking hands. "Sorry, it's just that..." she tries to clarify but stumbles for words.

Arnold promptly jumps in, "no need for explanations, it's okay." He squelches her desire to explain. "Sit down—join us, we have plenty for both of you. Seriously, we need the help—even Jake can't eat all this food."

The full-mouthed lad looks up, seeming irked.

The young couple gives a spirited laugh, and sits too.

Maggie stands coordinating food, "Bobby, take this one." She cheerfully hands him a plate, "this is a double decker. You're a stout boy...you shouldn't have a problem with that. Jenny, here take this one...uh; drinks are over there," she points. "Be sure to get a straw and here is a fork," she extends two of them, which Jenny grabs. "Ketchup and mustard packets are under the napkins," she sites and looks at Arnold. "Babe, pass a few of them please," she requests. "Now eat," she instructs. "No excuses. We don't want to throw away a single bite okay."

Promptly, everyone is eating with smiles on their faces.

"Mom does that too," Jenny addresses Maggie.

The others look on.

"What's that?" Maggie asks.

Jenny explains, "She makes things happen like you just did. Sometimes people kind of don't know what to do... so she takes charge and directs them."

"I'm sorry...I"

"No it's fine—it's good actually." Looking at her plate she further adds, "That's one of the things I like about her. She's so confident."

Maggie smiles as the adults give each other an engaging look.

Then Bobby nudges his girl with an elbow, changing the subject.

"So, where's your raft Jake."

"Why?" The boy gives a dispirited reply.

"Because Jenny and I want to see it,"

"No you don't," he scoffs.

"Yeah way...we tried to see it yesterday," Bobby tells with excitement, to uplift Jake's mood.

Jenny cuts in, "And Bobby drove us into a sinkhole trying to get here."

Maggie cringes.

"Is that why mom grounded you?" Jake laughs.

"I'm not grounded you idiot."

"So...how big was this sink?" Jeff butts in to divert attention away from sibling rivalry.

"It devoured half of the truck and dad had to rescue it, but we got out without a scratch," Jenny informs while avoiding her brother's stare.

"And you might say it needs a little bodywork," Bobby cackles.

"Oh my God, I'm glad you two are alright," Maggie offers her sympathy.

"Otherwise," Jenny directs her attention back to Jake and raises her voice, "We were on our way to see you and your juvenile raft."

Jake grimaces.

Jenny scowls back.

This time bobby gets between them, "I hear you could win," he emphasizes.

"Do you guys really want to see it?" The boy moans, and takes a drink through his straw.

"God as my witness," Bobby sounds off, raising his palm half-high. "Besides, your sis won't leave me alone until we do."

"Maggie, is it okay if I go show em?" Jake asks.

"I tell you what," she delivers a crafty smile.

"I know that look," Arnold shakes a head.

Maggie blurts, "Let's all go."

"Right now…?" Jake squeals.

"Yep, let's go. I'm giving the orders. Is that okay Jenny?"

"Yeah, fine with me."

Jeff drones, "It looks like we all have something to do." He stands to get a move on, but the others move too slowly for Maggie.

"Well, come on…let's go," she urges with heightened spirit. "Throw out our trash and put the trays back—chop, chop," Maggie claps her hands and instructs the clan.

They respond well and Jake was smiling. Everyone was happy.

Within moments, the group was off—Jake joyfully leading the way.

Twenty-Seven

"Understand detective—this footage could have been shot anywhere in the world," Sheryl bolsters.

"Agent…!" Callahan corrects her in scathing tone, "FBI people are 'agents.' We're not Dick Tracy policemen as sketched in comic books," he desperately wants her to refer to him as an 'agent.'

"Whatever, I can't help you!" she flicks a hand and retreats to the kitchen.

She left the annoyed agent staring at Richard, who seems content with his arms crossed.

"Now you know what I have to deal with," Richard chuckles.

Callahan throws hands up, gesturing for help.

"Don't look at me," Richard continues with a flail of his own. Bored with the conflict, he too breaks from his casual stance to go support Sheryl—bent over the sink she seems to be losing focus.

Callahan perhaps emptied as well, supports his weight on the back of a chair at the dining table. Apparently, at a loss for words he exhales to unwind. Nevertheless, as habit dominates his aspirations, he keeps going.

"Cracker," he yelps. "Have you found anything else on that damn computer?" Callahan irritably addresses the man at the keyboard.

"Isn't that a bit racist…DETECTIVE?" Sheryl yaps from the adjacent room with more than a hint of sardonic attitude. She and Richard reenter.

"He deciphers codes," Callahan tells her. "He opens computer files, figures out passwords and breaks through encrypted barriers," he retorts with similar behavior. "Get it…his nickname is cracker, as in cracking things open. Not everything is as it seems mam—he wants us to call him that. And for God's sake…I'm a FEDERAL AGENT!" he barks.

"It's true," the computer geek admits. "I kind of like the title—I'll keep searching sir."

"You see?" Callahan scoffs.

Sheryl rolls her eyes.

Just then, Groves roars in. "I got something," holding a key up high he grins.

"Aye, what do you have there, lad?" Callahan replies in decent Irish accent.

Sheryl seems surprised by the lingo effort.

However, Groves does not seem to notice. "I said it's a key," he repeats.

Callahan shakes his head at Groves for missing the humor.

Groves kept expounding, "It was taped to the bottom of a kitchen drawer. It must mean something."

"And what do you think it goes to?" Callahan tosses a hand.

"Um…" Groves stutters.

"Try the front door."

Groves walks to the front door, sticks the key in—it does not fit well and worse, it's now stuck in the hole.

Callahan laughs.

While Groves vexes to remove it, another agent enters and discretely sets a phone book on the table.

"Sir, I don't know if this is important, but several storage units are circled on three of these pages," he calmly mentions, tapping a finger on them.

"Good work," Callahan professes.

Groves becomes irritated—upset that this guy was getting praise—he doggedly yanks the key out of the doorknob. "Hey...I found a key," he argues for consideration too. "Somebody hid it on purpose. It has to be important," he persists.

But Callahan ignores him—still addressing the other agent. "Follow that lead. Make phone calls. See what you can find out and make it snappy."

As the young man begins walking away, Cracker raises a hand. "Hey wait," he yells. "Come back, I think I saw something." Facing the computer, he starts rummaging the files once again, opening and closing them in succession. "I saw something...what was it?" mumbling to himself he types persistently. "No, that's not it...no, not there either."

Richard intently stares, Callahan and Sheryl seem less interested but Groves and his enthusiastic counterpart is absorbed.

Cracker continues. "For some reason, you just sparked my memory," he carries on in a low voice. "I can't recall what it is right now but I will find it." Typing faster than he speaks, the moment seems to linger. "I got it," he shouts. "There it is," he shrieks and turns the screen for easy viewing.

"It's a picture of our dead guy, only he's still alive...so what?" Callahan scoffs.

"You're the supervisor," Cracker makes fun of his boss. "You don't see it."

The others come closer for a better look.

Callahan describes the photo, "I see a man with an arm around the neck of another dude, probably another terrorist. That's what I see."

"Okay and..."

"Two guys smiling for the camera," Richard jokes.

"What's that behind them?" Sheryl calls attention to the background.

"Thank you," Cracker blurts. "Who's the real agent in this room...boom?" he hoots and high-fives Sheryl.

Callahan scowls.

Cracker winces. "Sorry sir," he apologizes but explains. "This didn't register with me earlier but now I get it. There is a storage facility in the background. If I blow this up a few times..." click, click, click he presses a button—all their eyes draw concentration to the expanding image. "There...you can see it now, 'Everyday Storage.' I can clearly make out the name."

"That's one of the storage companies identified," the newest agent confirms. "And there's only one in town. Sir, it's not far from here," he points to it on the first page.

Groves lifts his eyes to the ceiling, sneering at his incredible find.

"What did you say your name was kid?" Callahan asks the young agent.

With a slight stutter he answers, "Bill sir...Bill Braxton."

"Well good job Bill. That's detective work."

Sheryl lifts her eyes hearing him say that. "I thought you said you guys weren't dicks," she sarcastically taunts Callahan.

He simply smiles back at her, amused with her wit.

"Let's get on it—good work...what are we waiting for people...move out," he reinforces that everyone should hurry and the agents scurry.

The Olson's begin to leave as well, but Callahan has other plans.

"I'm afraid I need you to tag along."

"We have a life to get back to," Sheryl argues.

Richard agrees. "We left our kids at the festival...which we promised to be part of," he adds.

"Our colleagues are watching them. In the middle of the day we left with barely an explanation," she throws her hands up.

Callahan becomes serious. "Do you see all these investigators?" he references the activity in the room and urges that they have a look around. "We don't employ these skill sets unless there is a threat."

"Maybe the guy was an explorer just digging for minerals or fossils, or perhaps he was a surveyor," Sheryl mocks.

"Mam, with all due respect, you have your head up your butt," the agent squelches the outlandish thought.

Richard becomes defensive with the agent's tone.

"No offense. Don't get riled up," he pleads, easing Richard's worry.

"Are you sure this is a terrorist network?" Richard conveys doubt.

"It's far above the ground floor. I can tell you this isn't a joke."

"Well I don't see it." Sheryl remains steadfast.

"You bleeding hearts just don't get it," Callahan bumps her ego again. "That's not an insult," he quickly lifts an apologetic hand, but moves closer to deliver a contrasting attitude anyway. "Tree huggers are overly sympathetic people by nature. They're simply fearful of offending anyone and as such, refuse to see true dangers because of those timid beliefs. But there is counseling for that," he concludes with an insensitive jest.

"You think I'm a liberal, inspector Clouseau," Sheryl fires back characterizing him as a silly investigator.

"Conservatives shed blood too mam," he's quick to react. "Don't read that far in to it. Just know that you are on the brink of some major shit and this time...you might be on the end that suffers the most," he attunes his dialect and begins pacing.

Flummoxed, Sheryl moves away and fixates on the map to twiddle in her thoughts.

"How much longer do you need us?" Richard intervenes, "seriously, what can we offer?"

"I believe we are at the threshold of a treacherous plot. Somehow, I think you two have a vital strategy to solving it. Think...what was this guy doing in the water?" Callahan hammers the question again.

"There's nothing left for us to do. Let us get back to our kids," Richard pleads while Sheryl is studying the map, this time with more interest than before.

"Sir, don't you feel responsibility to your country..."

Richard interrupts getting more flustered, "My country, are you kidding? Like I owe it..."

"Guys, guys—hold on a minute," Sheryl brings their feud to a halt. "Look at this. I think I know what these marks indicate."

Straightaway they unite at the wall while she continues, "I didn't see it at first because I thought they represented something on land. Okay, this is going to sound crazy," with mysterious temperament she speaks and their attention is high.

"What?" Richard barks.

"Come on, what are they?" Callahan pesters while maintaining an avid nature.

"Alright," she begins, "many of these red dots are barely off the edges of ponds, lakes and known sinkholes right...and then they trail away. But these blots aren't on footpaths or roads though."

"Well what then?" Callahan urgently requests. "What the heck are they?"

"Okay, didn't you come to us because you found explosives in the water?"

"I did, go on."

"These marks," she hesitates to take a breath, causing them to impatiently hinge on her exhale. "I think they represent where this guy has been drilling holes...inside aquifers. Maybe, he put dynamite in them and the stuff inside is starting to leach."

"That substance would be nitro glycerin," Richard informs.

Callahan hears that but seems disinterested. "Well, that's kind of..." he stumbles for words. "You mean in the..."

"Yeah, the underground tunnels of water flowing all over this state," Sheryl completes his discombobulated thoughts. "I know...I told you this wouldn't make any sense, but I recognize the pattern. I've viewed aquifer layouts many times—often that's all I do and these patterns resemble them to perfection."

"Alright, I agree." Callahan professes. "But what danger could this present?"

Richard steps up with a possibility. "A six inch wide hole would fit quite a few sticks of dynamite, several bundles end to end tightly bound. That would displace a lot of rock in a compact area, but honestly... that wouldn't cause widespread devastation."

"What if he was planting something more powerful?" Sheryl proposes.

"Well, there are water gel explosives, which would fit nicely in any configuration," Richard mentions. "There's HMX, RDX, C4 and countless other substances.

"The list goes on," Callahan adds, looking concerned.

"But none of them would do much more than disturb small areas," Richard expresses.

"It would take several tons of explosives to do any real lasting damage," Callahan notes with a strange look on his face. "It wouldn't fit in a hole like that…but there is an 'awful lo-aa-hht' of holes," he concludes.

Richard continues, "Yeah, thirty to fifty pounds of TNT would make a sizable crater."

"But a few sticks might punch through a wall, right?" Sheryl asks.

Richard lends a confirming nod.

"This is what I'm thinking," she continues.

"A breach in numerous aquifer walls could change the entire underground ecosystem. They could literally flow into one another altering current directions and flow rates…lakes may spill over or completely drain. New sinkholes might occur everywhere."

"Like what's happening right now," Richard gives an ominous stare.

"Exactly…!" she points out. "Some would happen right away…others not for months or years down the road," she forewarns. "Everything that I thought your company was responsible for…" Sheryl hesitates, looking at Richard with apologetic eyes.

He gives her silent forgiveness through an encouraging stare.

"I hate to break up the emotional ride…I really do," Callahan blurts. "But can you both come back to me."

They quickly oblige.

"Thank you," he submits. "So you're saying…only changes might happen—what Mother Nature produces." The agent seems to knock her idea.

"Yeah…except on steroids," exhaling heavily she becomes annoyed. "This eco system isn't a joke detective. It's delicate."

"There we go with that again," Callahan rubs his head. "I'm just saying, that plan seems a bit foolish, even for a terrorist."

"Agent…these dots are all over central Florida," she rebuts, with total seriousness.

"Thank you," he pauses to comment on her use of the word 'agent.'

"As… I… was… saying," she displays irritation. "The most abundant underground streams in the world are right under our feet. If they don't continue working just as they do, then landmasses will undergo abnormal forms of erosion, at an incredible rate. Even if the ground doesn't fall through as a direct result of a…" she holds her hands up motioning two fingers on each, 'quote unquote… explosion.' Over time, soil and rock displaced over great distances. Years from now sinkholes will form that otherwise wouldn't, possibly larger and more devastating than we have ever seen. Every structure is in jeopardy, manmade or not... houses, malls, you name it. When they start occurring...no one will be the wiser to who the real culprit is. People will believe that nature is just doing its thing, simply another disaster," Sheryl concludes expressing great fear.

The agent returns a half-hearted smile though, looking away.

She turns toward Richard for emotional support, but he too starts backing away...and she notices the dismissive behavior.

Suddenly her husband is acting as if he saw a ghost.

"What is it?" she asks. "I know something is on your mind...you believe me don't you."

He looks at her, expressing fear...or shame.

Callahan looks on.

"Tell me," she pleads.

Richard sighs. "You know when I told you I was reviewing company data?"

She nods.

"Well, I saw reports that indicated..." he falters, "that there are serious fractures in the Karst—all over Florida."

"What?" Callahan is confused.

The ground, under our feet, what Florida is made of," she explains—becoming concerned. "Like what do you mean?" she asks Richard.

"Cracks," he yelps. "Throughout the State...they're everywhere—fault lines others would say."

Sheryl's mouth dropped. She cannot even speak and Richard—he too is showing anxiety.

Suddenly, Callahan dominates tone. "Okay, hold these thoughts. They're really interesting but..." he jests, putting the brakes on the debate to look at his phone. "But right now, we need to go."

Twenty-Eight

A glass door with an aluminum frame opens between manicured shrubs on the left and right. Exiting from it is an aging white haired woman. Pudgy and fragile with declining eyesight she carefully observes the sidewalk below to ensure safe footing while waddling outward. After adjusting her thick framed glasses, she holds the egress agape until another nears close enough to hold it. Callahan is right there to help the elder with the weight of the door, and several others follow suit as they pass the threshold as well. Above the entrance is a sign reading, 'Everyday Storage.' It has a few burned out light bulbs but the business name is legible nonetheless. She leads the group around the corner of the building, a short distance away.

"We're going to building 'E'—it's the last one," she announces and without wearing dentures, her mumbling voice is almost inaudible. First, they encounter a security gate, which she unlocks and confirms that everyone goes through before rendering it shut once again.

Groves takes a second to look at the locked door.

"Don't worry," she tells him. "You can get out without a key…you just can't get in." Then she turns to the group and announces, "still, some people wake me up in the middle of the night because they think their stuck. If they'd just tried the knob…" she complains with mild contempt and resumes walking.

Cracker and Bill smirk at Groves who seems tense.

Sheryl smiles at Richard, to let him know the plainspoken female humors her.

"It's a long walk," the older woman informs. "But if I can make it back and forth umpteen times a day, you guys can do it at least once." Out front, she strides, slowly as her age dictates. "I would use the golf cart, but there's too many of you so follow me and keep up. I don't want any stragglers."

Everyone silently giggles as none has a hint of trouble maintaining stride with the dawdling gal.

"Yes mam," Callahan politely harmonizes with her pace. "Thank you for the personal tour and might I say you look lovely today."

"No need to butter me up, sassy. I've already got a man," snapping off a caveat she alerts him.

"Uh…yes mam," the stunned agent stammers, disbelieving his ears. He turns to deliver a stealthy chuckle to the others…but they are already quietly laughing at him. That abruptly triggers his hilarity to change into delivering them an evil stare.

They persist snickering at him anyway.

The group quickly controls their glee and continues toward the rear of the facility. On the left are parked motorhomes, trailers and boats arranged in orderly fashion and to the right of the parking lot are metal stowage structures. A total of five comprise a single row, each painted purple and orange.

"Garage type roll-up doors of all sizes are on both sides of these buildings," the manager explains.

Everyone takes a gander.

"Each one is an individual storage unit. You can drive a vehicle right up to it—makes unloading easy. You'll notice there are a few regular doors positioned between them. They take you inside to the air-conditioned interior spaces. See the light poles?" she changes subject. "They stay on all night. The fence has barbed wire on top of it, all the way around. It's secure here."

"Any cameras...?" Groves asks.

"No, none of that, but I see everything—understand stuff too," she professes with complete confidence. "Like, I knew this guy wasn't really Bob Smith. Nobody looks like him and goes by that name. Give me a break! He was a towel head for sure. I'm not that stupid," the manager clearly speaks her mind. "But half of the people that store here don't divulge who they really are though. What do I care? As long as they pay, that's what it takes to rent here and he was a good customer too, on time and always paid in cash—my kind of tenant."

Suddenly, the agents are paying close attention to her unexpected disclosure.

"Crisp twenties and always gave me the few dollars left over. I should have known they were criminals. Yeah, he wasn't always by himself," she enlightens another detail. "They were constantly in and out of here at odd hours, sometimes all through the night, but not my business. This is a twenty-four hour facility and people have the right to come and go as they please, after all it's their stuff—two and three in the morning doesn't matter to me. Besides, people work during the day so night activity is normal. I never know when someone wants to access their unit—not my job to care either, but I see all of them anyway...if I don't, the computer tells me what time they open the gate and I always check it. Only a few come in that late. Got some kind of business this guy did— delivery— shipping or something like that. Whatever, here we are," she concludes, standing in front of a large roll up door. "This is a 20x30 unit. One of the biggest we have but like I said, I can't let you in. If you don't have a key, you're gonna need a court order to cut the lock. That's the rules," she chuckles. "I love saying that."

"We understand Mrs....Uh..." Callahan stutters.

"Just call me Lilly."

"Right Lilly, we do have one. Groves...!" he shouts. "Here's your opportunity to impress."

Quickly the itching agent steps forward and hands over that key he found— finally he is getting some respect.

Callahan shows it to Lilly and smiles, but she simply gives him a blank unending stare. He looks around to see if he is missing something. As silent moments pass, he becomes more confused.

"Well, I need to see you use it," she blurts. "You all could be a band of thieves for all I know. Open it or come back with legal documents."

"Okay, right of course," he judders. "Here we go." The agent grasps the shiny circular padlock and tries to undo it, attempting a couple times but it does not open. The key goes in, but it doesn't turn. He gives Groves an annoying look as he pulls it out.

"It's not opening," he grunts, banging the lock against the metal door.

The others release a frustrating breath as well.

"Lilly, we have got to get in here," Callahan urges with importance using extreme hand gestures. "What's it gonna take to make you look the other way?" He hints there may be something to offer.

"You have to pull it back a little," she calmly states.

"What?" He is now more puzzled.

"Don't push it in all the way—the key I mean. Pull it back a little after inserting it, just ever so slightly. Then try it again. And be gentle this time," she finishes with a bright grin. He looks at the group. They simply shrug shoulders offering no support. He does as suggested, placing the key in again.

"Carefully," Lilly persuades. "That's it. Now pull it back a bit and turn."

He follows her recommendation to the tee, and whammy….it opens.

Everybody is amazed and none more than Callahan who lets out a relieved sigh.

Groves nudges him in the arm to bring recognition to himself and Bill lends a slow clap to offer respect.

"Whew-hoo," Sheryl releases a happy tout, "way to go Groves."

"It's a design flaw," Lilly tells everyone. "That's why I stay to watch people open them. It happens all the time. Well, it's all yours now. Just make sure I get that death certificate. I need it for my paperwork," she boldly broadcasts while toddling away.

"No problem," Callahan earnestly responds. Then he returns to squawking. "Groves, fame is short lived in this institution, get this thing opened."

Cracker promptly helps him and the metal gateway rises.

Straightaway, even an amateur officer could tell they have stumbled into a significant find. At the very front of the unit stood wooden racks vertically placed side by side, each with a dozen rapid-fire assault rifles. Next to that set numerous stacked crates of ammunition, some not related to basic weaponry. Intermingled are many curious chests, containers, boxes, luggage—further inside are other unrecognizable items. Sheets drape over many things blocking view but a small passage across the frontal span of the unit allows entry to the interior. Everyone is motionless—shocked and amazed by the sight.

However, the reaction is brief.

"Groves," Callahan issues a throaty demand.

"Yes sir."

"Call this is in—get a forensic team here a.s.a.p., and some more blessed agents. Tag these weapons, dust for prints, run every damn serial number and find out what this artillery is for and where in the hell it came from. This facility is quarantined."

Groves did not react fast enough for his superior.

"Now…!" Callahan screams. "And get that lady her death certificate."

"Right away," Groves quickly disperses.

"Braxton, Cracker," Callahan redirects focus. "Let's begin checking this out. Be careful, pay attention for traps, snares, anything deceptive. We can't get too involved until infrared, radioactive, explosive, and x-ray equipment arrives."

"And the dogs," Cracker adds.

"Yeah, them too…no stone unturned."

"Got it," Braxton agrees and carefully enters the unit.

Cracker cautiously waits, as he peers into the darkened space.

Callahan turns to the Olson's, "Please, stand by," he requests with stern influence.

Suddenly, Bill is already calling out.

"Cracker, there's a computer system in here."

Twenty-Nine

Reconnaissance units and bomb squad teams just wrapped up combing the storage facility grounds. Now, forensic professionals can safely examine the storage unit and commence criminal study. Tactical vehicles still maintain surveillance at every corner and dogs remain engaged too. After searching for imminent dangers and obvious hazards, they continue fact-finding efforts for remains and other physical evidence. However, the primary emphasis for subject matter experts was the large unit in building 'E'. The arsenal cache dismantled and systematically carted off along with the contents of every crate and carton. Numerous activities overlapped each other, meshing the exercise into a broad undertaking.

"This place was set up like a studio," Callahan expresses, huddled around a table with several agents to include Cracker, who was working on his new project with utmost resolve.

"He put in a bed, appliances, a TV and installed overhead lighting," Groves adds.

"This arrangement resembles his apartment," Braxton points out while Cracker enthusiastically keystrokes buttons.

Oddly, the computer whiz just complained to his self about underestimating an encryption and then mysteriously seemed delighted with his progress. For sure, he was engrossed within his own realm because he was both asking and answering his own rhetorical questions every few seconds with half-spoken resolutions.

The crew does not pay much attention to him, as they are familiar with his behavior.

"It's clear he was living here," Callahan asserts, but quickly shifts focus speaking sternly. "Okay people, let's put our heads together…what do we have so far? Groves, any comment?"

"Well, we found slapper blasting caps," he holds one up. "The 'electronic bridge wire' type, quite efficient at initiating a spark in conventional weaponry—they fire quickly," he notes. "EBW detonators are safe from stray voltage like static electricity, so they're primarily used in applications where radio signals or other energy currents might cause premature detonation. The goal was to produce a rapid detonation but also a predictable one. And they're modified, like everything this guy used."

"What are they used for?" Callahan questions, but young Braxton steps in to reply.

"They're for igniting HMX and C4 compounds…basic military explosives. Nowadays our adversaries use them in IED's," he assures as the group stares at him, perplexed with his apparent knowledge. He notices their curious grimaces.

"What?" he boasts. "My MOS was 89 Delta—explosives disposal. I've seen a thousand of these things."

"How old are you?" Groves rudely interrogates him. "You've been with the agency for what...a year? What could your brief experience have taught you?"

"I did two back to back tours in Iraq, straight out of high school, and then I came here."

"Why the Change—let me guess...you couldn't be all that you could be any longer?" Groves laughs.

Braxton gets defensive. "Let's just say three of the five men in my squad didn't make it," he educates Groves, speaking with serious pitch. "One fatality was a kid younger than me, barely eighteen and two of his limbs couldn't be found when he met his maker."

Groves' face begins to lose jovial expression as Braxton expands his scornful sentiment. "Disarming live bombs comes with a definite risk, but you've probably seen that stuff on TV, eh," he jabs. "Yeah...well I lived it. Every day I wondered if my number would come up and my parents couldn't stop praying for me—hoping that I wouldn't become the next casualty."

Groves looks down at the ground.

"Oh, it gets better." Braxton continues. "My father died while I was serving and my mom believes that his worrying about me is what killed him and well...she didn't handle life very well after that. After she stopped blaming me...she couldn't live with the thought of losing her only son too. She went to skin and bones drinking day and night—nothing left but wreckage. So yeah, I got out and if you're thinking I'm a coward—you can cram that thought right up your ass," he firmly retorts.

Groves' mocking smile was completely gone at this point, replaced with a face of regret as Braxton stares him down.

Callahan finally steps in. "Okay children," he separates them to refocus their attention. "Don't forget why we're here. We need answers. Groves, give the boy a break," he orders, ending the tussle.

Suddenly, a calm but eerie Cracker speaks up who is intently looking at the computer screen, "sir, you need to see this."

Promptly the agents gathered to take view of his findings, and each was in awe. None were speaking or expressing themselves. They were completely captivated.

Then with stoic tongue Callahan speaks, "Get the Olson duo in here."

Groves promptly complies.

"Honestly, how much longer will this take?" Sheryl bellows while being ushered in. "My kids are waiting for us."

"This better start moving forward soon," Richard inserts.

"You got your wish," Callahan bolsters. "The wheels just began turning."

"The only wheels I want to see spinning are the tires on my truck," Richard barks, thwarting the agent's suggestion.

"The same maps are posted in here too," Sheryl notes, walking past them. "There goes nature," she shakes her head.

"There is more at stake than the ecosystem mam. It's not dynamite you need to worry about."

Sheryl and Richard are curious as they approach the table.

"Whatever they are…they're fifty feet deep," Richard moans.

"Please, take a look," Callahan urges while pointing at the screen. Then, he notices some people standing idle in the back of the storage unit. "This is no time to slack," he yaps to get them moving, and then resumes his focus on the matter at hand. "Cracker, from the beginning please…"

"It's another video," Sheryl expounds.

"But not the same one," Richard points out. "His gloves are different and the hole is already drilled. Hey, what's that on the floor?" he draws attention to something.

Like before, the diver feels inside the hole, but then reaches down and gently secures an object—obviously heavy, using both hands to hold it up for review—now in plain sight of the camera.

Everyone sighs.

Sheryl says, "What the…"

Richard moans, "Oh my God…"

"Yeah, we can't believe it either." Cracker explicates.

Callahan just utters, "We have work to do, and no time to waste."

Cradled in the diver's cupped hands is a cylindrical shaped pipe, silvery metal, about two feet long—and apparently it's very heavy. One end has an electrical device attached to it—a square black box with a myriad of wires and a red blinking light. Carefully, he inserts the back end into the snug fitting hole and glides it in. Smoothly, it seats flush with only a faint flashing light visible. Next, he secures light brown putty and packs it around the circumference to seal it in. Once complete, the apparatus is barely noticeable. After picking up tools and left over debris, the diver swims away.

"What the hell is that?" Sheryl blurts.

Callahan becomes incensed.

"Do you know what they are?" she strongly requests again. Looking at the agent with a baffled stare, she crosses her arms.

He does not reply, so Richard adds some perspective. "The housing looks like a segment of conduit with capped ends—probably 5052 series aluminum. It has the highest resistance to marine oxidation, but 6061 or 6063 would be good too. Any of them welds easily, offering great workability and waterproof joints."

Sheryl looks at him with surprised eyes. "Won't that corrode?" she asks.

"Actually, salt water has little effect on these metals. Ocean water is PH neutral—totally safe for this material. Its composition is resistant—it'll last forever in salt water. Some of the finest boat hulls are made of it. As a side note, it's the third most abundant element after oxygen and silicon...the most plentiful alloy in the Earth's crust, 8% by weight of the world's solid surface."

Sheryl gawks at him with amazement.

"Yeah, who's the environmentalist now?" he puns.

"So you're saying..." Sheryl begins to read into it.

"Yeah, whatever these things are—they could have been placed in the water ten years ago...and they would still be intact today."

"But, you still don't know what they are...exactly," Sheryl looks at Callahan. "And what's with the metal? Isn't that weird?" she sighs.

The other agents seem overly reserved too as the FBI leader becomes non-reactive while strangely staring away.

"What is it?" she asks with fear in her voice. "There's a thousand of these things out there. Do you know what they are?

Callahan, still harboring withdrawn feelings ignores her.

Richard takes note.

"What are you guys holding back? You know something. What is it?" he strongly requests an answer.

"These bombs are under our feet right now," Sheryl complains. "I think we deserve to know."

"Why did you ask us here?" Richard barks but receives no immediate reply.

However, Groves steps forward. "We should talk."

Thirty

"Um...Homeland Security doesn't know about this?" Sheryl loudly heckles Callahan in an alley outside the storage unit. She gives him a derisive stare.

"Are you saying we're the only ones on this trail?" Richard keenly chimes in. "What about the CIA?" he drones but the agent remains negatively silent.

"The military, the NSA...anyone in the Federal Protective Services," Sheryl incisively adds, "are they aware?"

Callahan shakes his head and turns away.

"How about the secret service...a deceitful senator or an over the hill mayor...?" Richard presses while the agent continues to gaze into the distance—avoiding the obvious answer.

Finally he turns, channeling a grave look. "The FBI director isn't backing me either, okay? My own boss won't listen," Callahan groans.

Richard and Sheryl release a profound scoff as he continues. "But this is my effort...and I'll see it through."

"You're a traveling rogue, Richard sneers. "You aren't acting in any official capacity are you?" Adamantly he makes a gruff accusation while giving the angry agent a piercing squint, but then alters the topic. "What about all these people? You've allocated teams of people. Who are they reporting to?"

"I still have resources and a lot of pull," Callahan rubs his forehead. "My agency knows what I'm working on—others do too, but they think...it's unfounded—that I haven't enough proof."

"Don't you coordinate with other agencies?" Sheryl seems very confused. "Isn't that what you guys do?"

"Well...I did, but they were...I mean...I tried to explain but they all said the same thing. They needed strict intelligence, tangible supporting data or they can't get involved," he throws up a surrendering hand.

"Are you saying you spoke to them a while ago, before today? These developments were just uncovered—no time to talk to them about this. What facts are you referring to?" Sheryl pushes to understand.

Callahan is still acting strange, somewhat despondent.

"What are you not telling us?" she demands...then suddenly a wave of perception engulfs her. "Oh no..." holding a hand to her mouth she inhales. "This has something to do with the water samples, doesn't it?"

Again, his reply is lazy, like a kid asked about cookies missing from the cookie jar. Looking up and then down while rubbing his chin he stares at the base of the building—as if avoidance in on his mind.

"Tell us," Sheryl appeals to him, "what was in the water?"

Richard steps closer to him. "I think it's too late for the usual 'classified information' routine," he bellows. "If you want us to help...we need to know what you know—all of it."

Finally, the aloof agent reveals signs of battle fatigue, and moves closer to them.

"These matters are always a national security issue, you have to understand," the agent expels with compunction and starts pacing back and forth. "It's normal for me to..."

"Spit it out," Sheryl points at him. "We're your defense now."

He stops walking, relaxes and stares directly at them.

"Thorium, U-233..." he releases a heavy breath.

"Are you saying...?"

"Yeah...nuclear," he confirms. "Some of those bombs that you think are too small to create any damage." To Richard he gives a stern look. "They're leaking."

Sheryl is quick to react with incensed feelings, "Okay...just tell Homeland what you found here."

"They've already told me not to show my face again unless I had proof," Callahan again gets serious. "I need an actual device, centrifuges, parts or pieces—something physical. I don't have that and this administration won't hear jack about my theories otherwise. Certain individuals believe that my analyses are drastically inconclusive—just baseless beliefs. They say...I uncovered a natural occurring element, which mimics radioactive characteristics, and additionally, thorium can't make nuclear weapons anyway. The technology is gaining interest, but until now only in the battleground for producing energy. Scientific credence says a bomb can't be made with it, therefore, not a threat. It is worth mentioning though, thorium is widely available and most every country has tons of it."

"But you found a video of one," Richard reminds.

"What we have Mr. Olson...is a well-made movie—a Hollywood film pure and simple. It doesn't prove that the devices are real, or what they're made of."

"What?"

"That's how they'll see it. They want concrete evidence, and that video is no confirmation of an eminent threat. It may not even be authentic. There is no verification that a bomb has been created or planted." Callahan gets very excited as he explains. "Where are they? That's what they'll tell me. Have you seen one? No!" he exclaims. "I don't have a witness, a testimony or a taped warning from a terrorist—telling of this plot or expressing any demands...no threat or intimidation. Unless I find a physicality of nuclear fortifying...I can't substantiate any of this," he places his hands on hip. "They'll say its speculation...my opinion, and that doesn't have a place in their narrative."

"And what is that," Sheryl asks.

"Basically that everything is okay—Al-Qaida is dying, terrorism is on the run and every American is safe—all thanks to the new age President with Kenyon heritage. But guess what? Contrary to what most people believe, this guy won't get involved or put resources into action until mayhem already happens. That's his 'M.O.' His administration walks on eggshells hoping a tragic event doesn't occur. Do you pay attention to Libya and Egypt?"

They affirm with a nod.

"Unrest isn't even a valid way to describe it and not one federal agency is conducting any real mission to combat it. There is no investigation—nobody is concerned about Benghazi. Russia is next...you'll see," The agent points and adds, "Iran has nuclear technology right now and our side knows that. Many countries already did. Is it really so hard to believe that a mobile nuclear bomb exists? It's not only a possibility—they're already amongst us, right here...right now...directly beneath the feet of ten million unaware people. This situation is catastrophic...only no one at the top will listen without proof—and only what the admin deems proper. It's as if I have to place one on the desk at the Oval office to get any attention."

"They think you're a whack job, don't they? Is that what you're dealing with agent?" Richard grins. "Is that why you need us—to find your verification?"

Looking very weary, the detective sighs and slowly shakes his lowered head. "Our own country created small bombs like these many years ago...only no one talks about it.

Richard scoffs.

"Go ahead, laugh Mr. Olson. What was I supposed to do? Let it go!" Looking toward him, he avows. "But, you've seen enough to know better...haven't you? So what do you think—am I crazy?" The agent surges back.

"I think someone needs to hear about this. That's what I think," Sheryl steps between the two men. "Somebody has got to listen. There is a dead terrorist and a video of a bomb. Isn't that enough?"

"For most sane people it would be," Callahan turns. "But in this case, I'm afraid not Mrs. Olson. "This government is more apt to go after someone for not purchasing health insurance. They have no problem spying on millions of innocent people making mundane phone calls or laying down drone strikes on harmless Christian groups praying near public property," with sarcasm he jokes.

"If this isn't a threat...I don't know what is," Richard declares.

"Now you're seeing thing through my eyes," Callahan admires him, briskly grabbing Richard by the shoulder. "You're growing cognizant. You both are," placing a hand on each of them he inhales, delivering a wide curious smile. "Now it's time for the next step."

"Agent," Richard conveys distemper, pushing his hand away. "I don't like what you're thinking."

"Relax guys...I just need help one more time. It's a little thing."

With that, the Olson's share a thoughtful moment.

Callahan persists, "we've come too far to give up now."

"We're listening." Sheryl sighs, arms crossed.

Thirty-One

"We'll be home soon, I promise," Sheryl speaks softly into her cell phone, unwinding against a tree. "I can't tell you anything right now," she insists. "But I will when I'm able…I swear," she asserts. "No, I'm not in trouble," she pauses to listen, then responds. "Yeah, dad's okay too. We both are—just helping with an investigation is all." Picking at loose bark, she waits to speak. "Hey, thank Maggie for me okay…for taking care of you two so long…and tell Arnold I'm not sorry I pulled Jeff away," she releases a mild laugh. "He'll know I'm just joshing. No, I don't want to talk to anyone else right now. I've got to go, alright," she rests again to hear a parting remark. "Of course, I know honey…thanks. I love you too. Bye."

Richard steps closely behind her. "Which one was that?"

She shuts her phone and embraces it near neckline while cherishing an endearing emotion. "Jenny," she answers with dreamy tone, but converts her mindset quickly. "And she's more worried than usual. She said she loves me. When was the last time she did that?"

Richard gives a pleasing grin and begins caressing her on the back. "They both care, but it's a kids role to avoid being sappy, especially with their parents."

"Until something happens…then, even our detached offspring develop feelings?" she turns to face him.

"Nothing bad has happened," he assures.

"Not yet Rick, but she's just like me—she senses something!" Touching his face, she expresses deep concern as the sound of footsteps schlepping through the leaves closes in.

"Hey love birds," an irritated voice calls out expressing a fast-tracked nature. "We're ready to get started, and the day isn't getting any younger."

They remain fixated on each other while the nagging gets nearer. Sheryl chuckles.

"Coming Jeff," she nips and then playfully pulls Richard from the tree. They begin walking to meet him.

"Let me speak for everyone here," Jeff whines. "This was supposed to be a three-day weekend. I'm not happy."

Richard disregards the complaint to take notice of a hand waving from behind the grumbler. "John's here," he mentions.

"That's what I was saying," Jeff mumbles to himself, hands festering a huge 'whatever' gesture. "Doesn't anyone listen?"

As they look that way, the driver of a dual-axle pickup truck had parked by lakeside, and was lowering the tailgate. He steps up and into the bed and begins delving through it with Callahan and Carl assisting.

"Thanks for coming Jeff," Sheryl solaces the sullen looking soul while the three walk toward the truck. "If I didn't really need you, I wouldn't have dragged you down here," she tells him. "ODG will be taking the reins on this one. We only have to provide guidance—an easy afternoon. At least I got you out of the festival. I know you hate those things."

"Yeah I suppose. Hey, is this about the dead guy?"

"Well, yes but..." she hesitates.

"Is there another stiff?"

"No, that's not it," she tries to clarify but Jeff cuts her off.

"This deal is getting out of control, what's going on Sheryl?" Jeff's anxiety grows.

"It's okay. I'll get you caught up. A lot has happened since yesterday so I'll spare you the long story," she swears as they reach the vehicle. "But for now, just follow my lead."

"Agent Callahan this is John," Richard introduces. "This is the man I told you about. He can get you what you need."

"We just met," the agent acknowledges. "He was about to uncover some equipment. Maybe he could explain?"

"Yeah sure," John says and drags an unusual looking machine to the end of the bed and hops to the ground, taking a mild breath. "I'm an engineer at the robotics division with Olson, specifically, part of an aquatic research team. In short, I explore bodies of water for various hazards and how I do that is with this contraption," placing a hand on a strange mechanical device he touts. "This is my baby—a remote controlled underwater robot, employed and operated from the safety of land. Small and lightweight it can go about anywhere in H2O. Now, it won't manipulate objects—fix or repair anything, but it does have a remarkable monitoring system, which transmits real time recordable images. Everyone... meet 'Seabot'.

"I think he's speaking my language," Callahan marvels at the magnificent machine, giving an elated smile.

"When were you going to share this with me?" Sheryl whispers to her husband. "The department can use that. I need it...wait, does Wynyard know about this too?"

"Nobody knows yet," he smirks. "It's experimental, but you would have been one of the first to benefit...I swear," he quietly chuckles.

"Yeah right," Sheryl gives him a flirting punch in the arm.

"If you look on the back of my truck," John continues. "There's an eighty-four inch flat screen TV set up to view footage from six individual cameras mounted on the robot. Off to the side are lithium battery packs to keep the system powered—recording equipment and other electronics essential for operations like navigation." Then he grabs what looks like an iPad with joysticks. He toggles the knobs and the bot instantly responds.

"There, you can see the rudders and vanes moving," he demonstrates. "And here on the control tablet is a digital display used for steering and observing," he shows them. "It presents the actual images that the bot is capturing. It's filming us standing next to it right now," making sure everyone gets a good look he extends it outward for proper viewing.

Moving through the various camera sights, vertically up and down, forward and rear, horizontally left and right he exhibits how they appear on screen and illustrates that the cameras can rotate 360 degrees, for seeing in every direction. He notes that each angle displays on both the TV and control notebook.

"State of the art design," he hypes, then rolls into the mechanics. "There are two propellers in the back, several on each side and a couple in front as well. They rotate any which way like the cameras, for ultimate mobility. Handling this bot is tough to learn, but once mastered it can literally move any way you want it to—shift gradually from side to side, idle smoothly, turn gently or quickly scurry to fleet obstructions and danger. It can spin on a dime, reposition perpendicularly, horizontally or any combination thereof. It can hover and remain stabilized even against swift current," he educates with enthusiasm and the group remains attentive.

"One would think that it should look more like a torpedo, but oddly it's a rectangular block shape. Now, to the lens protection," he directs attention to one of them by touching its exterior shell. "They are guarded by a thin but strong layer of clear polycarbonate, rounded into a stationary dome. Behind them are the mini camcorders, which automatically focus as they rotate. At only two feet long with a six-hour battery life, this adorable metal creature can go most anywhere.

"Oh, it has LED lights," he remembers. "They only consume nominal amounts of power and they're intensity is managed too. The beams can be angled, narrowed, widened and shinned anywhere, directly where needed." Reaching for something else, he secures and elevates a circular shaped disc with several thin rods protruding straight out from each side. "This device has receiver antennae on the top and transmitter rods on the bottom," he explains. "While Seabot is in action, this gadget floats on the water allowing our control signals to constantly travel from the air, down and through dense water. It uses electromagnetic propagating waves at a low hertz."

"They don't need to know the technical details John," Richard interrupts, jumping in to advance the learning process.

"Right...well, it works like sonar. Military submarines use it. In any case, originally designed to assist divers while underwater, this system is for long-range usage from dry land. That's about it."

"Guys, we have to get this thing into action while we still have good light," Richard expresses. "It's about two o'clock now, which gives us a few good hours. Carl, John let's get it in."

"One more thing," John stops everyone. "I need to know what I'm looking for."

"Right, good point," Richard acknowledges. "Sheryl's team is going to direct you where to go with that. Sheryl, it's all yours."

Throwing the ball in her court, he steps aside.

"Um…" Sheryl stammers trying to find the words.

"Let me get this," Callahan rushes aide.

Sheryl is relieved, yet concerned with what he may say, but she does not stop the brash agent.

"John, a diver turned up unresponsive in this lake yesterday, uh…"

"…Lake Apopka," Jeff helps.

"Ahem, thanks."

"Are you saying he was dead?" John asks. "What killed him?"

The agent clears his throat. "We're still investigating that."

"Okay!" John accepts the reasoning with no further comment.

"Anyway, we believe he may have planted a little explosive device and Sheryl will guide you to where we think it is."

"What, a bomb?" Jeff bursts.

Sheryl gives him an evil stare to prevent further disruption. He backs down.

"Nothing to be worried about, like I said…it's tiny." Callahan vaguely explains.

"How small is small? What's it made of?" Carl inquires.

"Well, that's why we're here," Callahan replies with anemic faith, making Jeff nervous.

"Doesn't this kind of endangerment call for swarms of FBI personnel, SWAT or something?" Carl makes an observation.

"Dynamite, TNT," Richard clarifies, "that's all it is, only a stick or two."

Jeff's worry seems to ease.

Callahan gives Richard an inconspicuous thankful nod.

Sheryl delivers her husband a judgmental stare.

Jeff notices and gives her a concerned look too—he senses that may not be the truth.

"So if one goes off John, you only lose a robot," Carl jokes in that southern drawl of his, and he chuckles.

Richard laughs too but John is not amused at all.

"I'm just saying the blast won't be big," Carl defends his humor. "That we'll still be okay…you know living, breathing humans." He's trying to poke a little fun but John's feels no enjoyment. "Carry on, geese. I didn't know you engineers were so sensitive," Carl gestures a 'zip my mouth closed' for John's benefit.

"Okay, I'll find it," John tells the group. "Let's get started." Lifting his bot up, he heads to the water line." Grab us a few chairs please," calling back, he requests.

Sheryl looks at Jeff.

"Yeah, yeah, I got it," he proceeds to snag two folded chairs leaning against the rear wheel hub.

John promptly launches the bizarre submarine. It sets idle for a moment, but then slowly moves around and dives. With a click on the control tablet, images simultaneously appear on both the pad and big screen. Calmly, the unit progresses underwater showing grand detail of rocks, swaying grass and underwater life, even the label on a glass bottle lying on the lakebed is legible. Small fish caught on camera, swim closely to look at the unfamiliar organism, and then dart off.

John sits to stabilize for enhanced steering.

Sheryl joins him.

A few maneuvers later, the handler notes he is ready for bearings. "Okay, where do we go?" he looks at his guidance crew.

Sheryl and Jeff with map in hand remit instruction.

"Go over that way," she points across the lake while Jeff holds the large paper still.

John steers the craft accordingly.

Richard and Callahan step rearward to watch the action on the large screen.

"Are all of these dots what I think they are?" Jeff whispers in Sheryl's ear as they lay the chart on the embankment.

"I think so," she returns in cautionary tone.

Jeff breathes heavily, as if about to initiate a worried comment, but she murmurs again. "Now is not the time."

He understands his boss well and discontinues, but remains disturbed nonetheless. "Just help me locate the first one—I need your skills, okay," she reasons with him. "That's all we have to do."

He gives her an agreeing nod and points over the water. "Try a little further up," he dispatches John. "See if you can find an aquifer over that way."

Sheryl lets Jeff know she is pleased with an uplifting smile.

Off the bot goes steadily passing marine life with cameras filming. Callahan and Richard are fixated on the large screen while Jeff and Sheryl continue to guide John and his robot toward the opposite edge of the lake.

"Slow down, nudge to left a bit and get a look just beyond that protrusion," she instructs.

"Okay, slowing down," John describes the bots movement out loud, "hovering…backing up…okay got it." Then he toggles very gently, "here we go, getting closer. We should start seeing something…" he holds his breath while tactically maneuvering an unexpected tight spot underneath a bulging ridge.

"There it is," he lets out an 'ahhh' of accomplishment while easing beyond the constricted bend.

"That's it," Jeff gets excited. "Now, hook it around and see what's on the other side of that next outcropping."

"Going in...rotating, and...whoa, whoa..." John reacts to sudden thrashing and unwanted movement.

"What's happening?" Sheryl jerks too as the bot abruptly veers to the left, smacking against a coral wall—cameras losing focus, but only for a sec.

The men standing at the large screen flinch too.

"We got caught in a fast current, I wasn't ready for it," John voices. He moves the control levers again, one of the cameras shows the propellers changing direction and spinning faster. "I compensated and added some extra power," he murmurs. "Okay, alright...that should do it," he exhales relief. The watercraft is okay.

Callahan relaxes too.

Richard grabs the agents shoulder, unifying the sense of ease.

"There must be a large spring nearby," Sheryl brings attention. "Watch out for that bank!" she yelps. "Another obstacle is closing in fast."

John moves the controls and the vessel redirects to maintain course. He navigated the narrow passage perfectly.

"Whew, that was a good test," he utters.

"Yeah, but let's not do that anymore," Jeff delivers a tense laugh.

"Okay, shall we try that again?" Sheryl quips. "Go more to the left...yeah, that way. I see something up ahead," she points out.

"Right there, a hollow...is that what you're looking at?" Jeff remarks.

"Yeah, I think we're getting close."

"Try going inside it John," Jeff directs.

"Moving...going there now, the water is awfully cloudy though...I need to be careful," but as he gets close, he suddenly pulls back. "I can't fit." He breathes out fast, "the opening isn't big enough."

"A diver couldn't get in there either," Jeff mentions. "This can't be the opening we're looking for."

"Good point," Sheryl nods. "Let's try further up. There has to be another opening nearby. If this map is correct, we are very close."

Jeff contends. "It may not be accurate. Maybe it's a crude representation of something else or written in a way that only the creator understands."

She lends Jeff a passive nod.

"Possibly it's backwards or off by certain distances to throw somebody off. In this case...us," he adds.

Then a sudden surprise view.

"Whoa, whoa," both sound at the same time.

"Is that the objective?" John eagerly mentions.

"I think so," Sheryl admires the view. "It has to be."

"Do you see that?" Jeff points to the small screen.

"I sure do, that's got to be it," Sheryl sighs. "It's big enough to drive a car into. Let's go, John," she excitedly directs and nudges his arm, causing the bot to swerve uncontrollably. "Oh, sorry," she pulls away quickly.

John, gives her a peeved look, but recovers nicely, and advances onward.

"The water is much clearer," Jeff tells.

Sheryl analyses. "We're entering fresh water."

"Yeah, this is too cool. I've never been at the threshold of an aquifer before."

Though excited to be witnessing a seldom seen experience, Sheryl feels the apprehension of the ultimate goal. As well does Richard and Callahan who dash over.

"Do you think this is it?" the agent asks hovering too closely over their shoulders.

"Maybe—can you give us some room?" Sheryl pushes him back.

Jeff notices her brazen attitude—he is surprised.

At this point, John has the craft inside the tunnel. "It appears there is a current forcing us backward," he notes. "I'll increase thrust to compensate." The propellers respond.

"It's getting dark," Jeff mentions.

"Bright lights on," John responds, "illuminating all sides, cameras refocusing."

"The view is good." Sheryl tells him. "You're really good at this."

Jeff squints at her, feeling slightly jealous.

John smiles, "I'll keep moving slowly. Let me know if you see anything—I'll stop and check it out," he informs while holding keen sight of where the bot is going.

"Okay, you got it," she replies.

The craft effortlessly traverses the aquifer, cameras focused on interior walls and floor. As the light strikes upon them, colorful coral becomes apparent. Limestone and fallen rocks shine for many feet ahead, but only blackness lurks beyond the reach of illumination. Crevices, gaps, and potential turns loom every instance of the way—not recognizable until nearly upon them. Pockets of trapped air fill certain chinks in the ceiling and occasional tiny wonky bubbles mysteriously rise too.

"What an amazing site," Jeff drones.

"I've only seen this stuff on TV. I feel like I'm actually right there...wow," Sheryl expresses awe too.

John chuckles. "Yeah, I get that a lot."

Then Jeff notices something. "It looks like the tunnel is widening," he says.

"It sure is—it's getting huge. This is fascinating and the water is so clear. It's definitely a fresh spring," Sheryl notes and changes thought. "Jeff, what magnitude do you think this is?"

He hesitates, "a three...or two maybe."

"What's that?" John asks.

"It's basically how much water passes through an aquifer," Jeff clarifies.

The mechanical gadget continues on, passing rocks and fish—swiftly moving particles too. Dirt on the bottom is trace-free smooth and easily disturbed when the craft gets too close. Propellers whip up the loose filtrate and cast it into the steady current, swept behind the bot. Although no sound exists, the quiet and serene nature experienced regardless—undeniably peaceful. Could man have been here?

"There, what's that over there?" Sheryl alerts.

"I see it too, let's check it out," John maneuvers the craft for a better look, and then steadies it for sharper viewing. Closer and closer he moves, lighting up the walls while increasing focus…slowly the prospect becomes clear.

"It's just a plant," Sheryl sighs.

"It's growing out of a crack with some leaves flapping," Jeff moans as well. "Maybe this is a waste of time," he gripes, getting more irritated. "I'm mean, who in their right mind would swim through here, planting dynamite. Seriously, this is ridiculous. These shafts are endless—we could be in here forever."

"Some people don't have a conscious like you do," Callahan speaks to the unstable man. "Fanatics, radicals, assassins—I'm sure you get the picture. They don't care about the same things you and I do," harshly looking at Jeff he criticizes with an off-the-cuff tone.

"Are you saying this dead guy is a terrorist?" Jeff grumbles, and turns to Sheryl who is already giving him that look of hers.

He settles down again.

Callahan continues eyeing the critic though, whom he believes is acting rather suspicious.

Richard notices the touchy nature and urges the agent back to truck.

"There has to be something here," Sheryl mumbles. "It just makes sense." Forsaking Jeff's attitude she resumes vigilance and prods him in the ribs with her elbow, coaxing him to pay attention. "I can feel it," she raises her voice to get Jeff's eyes off Callahan. "Can we get a look of both sides of the tunnel at the same time?" she asks John. "The opposite wall is so far away. Go toward the middle."

"Okay," John responds. "I'm focusing in that direction…moving closer to compensate. You'll still be able to keep an eye on where we came from and also…"

Before he finishes speaking…Sheryl cuts him off.

"Wait, wait, stop right here, I see it. There's one of them," her tone becomes sure…and serious. She tap taps John on the shoulder.

"I don't see it," Jeff shrugs.

"Right there…do you see that? Look at camera three."

"Yep," John says.

"Where…?" Jeff counters. "Oh wait," he realizes. "You mean that thing…" he starts speaking more slowly as he understands what he sees, "with the blinking light…just…about…half-way…up?"

"Richard!" she shouts back to the truck "Are you guys seeing this?"
"Oh yeah, we have visual."
"Let's get some close ups of that," Callahan yells. "I need this taped."
"I'm recording all of it," John stresses.
"Every angle,"
"Each camera," he asserts. "You'll get everything."

John navigates yet closer—all eyes engaged, several cameras securing simultaneous views. It is apparent that the protruding object is man-made, a black plastic assembly affixed to the tunnel wall with several wires emanating from it and going back in. A faint blinking light in the center flashes about once per second.

"That's definitely what we're looking for," Callahan confirms. "Just like the video."

Jeff grows troubled. "What video?" he asks, but no one answers. He becomes more anxious. "That doesn't look like any dynamite I've ever seen Sheryl," he voices concern more loudly this time.

"Not now Jeff," she scolds and as a result, he enters a quiet state.

"I'd say we have verification…congratulations, Richard, everybody, good work…fantastic. But we need to confirm a few more."

Jeff again becomes perturbed with that comment too, "are you going to tell me what's going on? This is not normal Sheryl," he whispers to her alone, providing a notable nudge along with it. "I wasn't born this morning—how long will you keep this up?"

"As long as I have to," she scowls. "Now leave it alone and stay focused." She redirects her attention, "John, let's keep going."

Jeff remains irritated.

The bot glided a couple hundred yards or more and again they encountered another device, exactly like the preceding one. Over the next few hours, they spotted many of them, noting that each was marked on the map in precise fashion. Ultimately, the mission ended.

"The search was a success people," Callahan announces and then orders to have all footage placed onto digital media in common format. While the others chat about the exhilarating experience, the agent walks away for a private phone call.

Sheryl notices the secret talk and keeps watch from afar.

Eventually, he makes his way back to the group and stands before them, looking very serious.

"What now…we're starved," Richard exhales while leaning on the truck's side rails.

"I don't think we're going home Peabody," Sheryl yawns.

"Sorry people…not yet," Callahan issues disappointment.

They scoff.

"We'll get something to eat on the way, but some very important people want to speak with us…uh, just the Olson's," he grins.

Thirty-Two

Callahan exits his vehicle and turns the rear corner of it while buttoning his jacket as the Olson's get out of theirs, closing car doors behind them. The three begin walking a path through a parking lot toward an adjacent building.

"That was a quick drive, not far off Ronald Reagan Turnpike. I didn't know Homeland had an office in this city."

"Mr. Olson, that's the idea. They don't advertise it," Callahan pats Richard on the shoulder.

"What's with all the shipping containers?" Sheryl probes, pointing to the rows of cargo boxes encompassing the facility's large backyard.

"Just storage, you know books, old furniture—the occasional confiscated business and the belongings of a few thousand citizens."

They give him a weird look.

"Just kidding?" he laughs. "That stuff! You and I don't need to worry about," clearing his throat he mutters as they strut.

Sheryl is still studying the surroundings. "Actually, they are in the phone book but this address isn't listed. There's no 'Homeland' sign posted anywhere on the building either. I know their agency is nearby at the Orlando airport, highly visible, but this location is remote and hidden away—no doubt a private base or an EOC."

"Mrs. Olson, your observations amaze me. Emergency Operations it is. Truly, have you ever thought about investigations as a career?"

Richard, appearing guarded with the agent's fascination of his wife, places his arm around her.

"They want the landing strip close, but not too chummy." Callahan points in that direction. "That protects needless recognition, and preserves mobility which enables operations to run smoothly when action is necessary."

"The DEP uses similar strategy, so I'm familiar with the tactic, but what I don't get is why we need to be here?" Sheryl pauses on the sidewalk, waiting for some resolve.

"Relax. You'll provide additional commentary to strengthen the argument. Like I said, convincing these people is tough—this is where you two come in. Sometimes, civilians get a better response than we do." After encouraging them with a few uplifting words, they proceed to the building.

"Isn't this a matter of laying out a few facts?" Sheryl argues. "I mean, this is a huge national issue—seriously. Shake things up, make a few arrests, deploy bomb squads and evacuate people. You know…save the world."

"If only the process still worked that way," Callahan gives a dreadful stare. "But this administration has newfangled procedures now. Come, let's go inside."

They march up a few steps to an adjoining veranda.

"How did you set this up so fast? You said you weren't talking to any of these people," Richard comments.

"Mr. Olson, what I stated is they didn't believe my allegations have merit," Callahan corrects him with a pointed finger. "But recent developments may change their minds. You and your wife's testimony is part of that mood altering adjustment."

Upon approaching the front door, a man greets their expected attendance and promptly escorts them inside, to the rear. "The conference center is back here," leading the way he explains.

The three notice that many prominent personalities are gathering. Are they politically left or right, CIA or FBI, of public interest or private concern? A person's occupation or affiliation is impossible to distinguish by dress code alone.

Inside the chamber, a large semicircle shaped table aligns two-thirds of the perimeter, situated a couple feet below it is another smaller one centered and paralleled within it. There are numerous places to sit at each one. At the front of the room a rectangular bench sets, equipped for only a few people.

"Homeland will be sitting there," Callahan indicates. "They'll be facing the rest of us."

Sheryl sees that all stations are equipped and have adequate sight of a large screen drawn against an adjacent wall. A projector sets in the middle of the space and at the very front hovering over Homeland's area is a mammoth flat-screen TV. They grab the last few seats at the highest elevation—Sheryl sitting between the agent and husband.

Briefcases are opening, papers ruffling, computers booting and cell phones closing though some people are still shuffling for placement.

"This atmosphere doesn't feel like a time for chit chat," Richard tells them.

Callahan acknowledges a few people with a nod and meager wave but without words.

The mood is serious—all participants are devoid of smiles or laughter as they lend their attention forward.

"Who are all these people here to see?" Sheryl asks.

"Us," he replies while giving her a grave look.

She breathes deep.

Then the room goes quiet to heed a speaker.

"Good afternoon, I want to thank everyone for joining," a woman at the front table stands, addressing the attendees—all eyes upon her. "I am Dr. Karen Winslow, director of Domestic Nuclear Detection for Homeland Security."

Richard and Sheryl give each other a careful stare as the orator continues with gesturing hands. "And with me to my right is the Director of Intelligence and Analysis, specialist Robert Tester and to his right is Miguel Krylan the National Cyber Security Director. To my left is Enrique Charez...the Operations

Coordination Director and then to his immediate side is Darcia Davies with Public Affairs…and finally General Counsel Ilia Wong at the far end. She is of course our lawyer. It seems we need one for everything we do these days."

A gentle laugh arises as she continues.

"Unfortunately, the President couldn't be here because once again he's engaged…" she pauses to contemplate her word choice carefully, "well, he has other matters to attend to, and we still don't have a new Homeland Director. So let us begin with the issue. I understand that the Federal Bureau of Investigation's director, Paul Munsinger, has an urgent matter to discuss," pointing to him for recognition she remarks.

He briefly raises a hand to contribute identification.

"I hear we don't have much time so again, thank you all for coming on such short notice. P.S., I want to acknowledge the pilots of our private planes as well and though they aren't present, if it weren't for them, few of us would be here," she adds while looking about the room.

"Placed in front of you is a laptop, networked to the others in this room and to the screen on my far right. If you have media cards or USB drives, a port is available. They'll play automatically upon insertion while being displayed everywhere I mentioned."

Callahan removes a thumb drive from a shirt pocket and hands it to Sheryl.

She takes it as Winslow continues. "If you brought your own notebook…plug that in using one of the cords dangling about your station."

Richard hunts about to establish sight of theirs. "Either way, it's easy to present information, however you should be aware that all of your personal data will get collected in the process."

Sheryl stops, becoming alarmed. Many others do as well.

"Just kidding?" the doctor laughs but the room remains quiet. Nobody is amused.

"I usually get a boost out of that but I guess with the NSA breathing down our necks and tracing calls—it seems the subject is no longer a laughing matter." Immediately, she changes tone.

"People, there is a threat amongst us. At this time, I would like Mr. Munsinger to submit his much-anticipated intelligence report. Now, without further ado, let us examine the issue and please, keep the assembly civil. Director, the floor is yours," she points and sits down.

He stands.

"Thank you director," Munsinger moves his suit jacket out of the way to place a hand in his front pants pocket, and then commences with a severe temper. "At no point in history has a threat been as alarming as the one we face today. Unlike any other though, a real threat has been uncovered—placed right in our lap. For the last several weeks I have been working closely with an extraordinary investigative team that I placed in the field for the purpose of scrutinizing the impossible." He continues with composure, "I took a gamble and chose to examine something, having little information to go on."

Callahan scoffs under his breath, lending a discreet negative headshake to his boss's tribute. "Prick... he held me back is what he did," leaning into Sheryl he whispers as the poised man continues.

"They have worked feverishly. I only wish their conclusions revealed we have more time—that we caught this plot at the beginning of its development but sadly, I cannot say such. In fact, there may be little time before it culminates," clearing his throat he continues. "Regarding the details of this scheme, I will now turn you over to the man in charge of the assignment, agent Callahan." Munsinger directs the room's attention, everyone turns to acknowledge, "agent, please inform this influential body of your rather troubling information."

Callahan stands, pulling his waistline up a tad while displaying a tinge of arrogance. "I'll be honest. I'm not much for speeches so I'll get straight to the point," in harsh tone, he proceeds. "I approached some of you weeks ago but consideration wasn't offered to me then," looking around the room at a few individuals he delivers a wayward stare—to his boss in particular.

Munsinger simply looks down. Several others pigheadedly glance away too as the agent proceeds. "So you're aware of why I'm here. However, I have more information than I did earlier, but frankly...I'm still unsure that the forthcoming peril is soaking in. The fact that we are meeting here in Orlando...in the center of the pending disaster causes me to wonder if you're taking the situation seriously."

The crowd looks across the room and toward one another as if seeking immediate clarification.

Sheryl and Richard notice the room's ambiance begin tweaking into a mild fluster.

"For the rest of you, I hope you find this as urgent as I. There just isn't time for political debate or tolerant behavior." Remaining relaxed, he employs alarming rhetoric. "Drawn out discussions and an incessant need for more information or hesitation of any kind will merely allow destruction to befall us—completely unimpeded," he warns, leaning on the back of his chair, staring around the room. "Proper assessment and tough decisions need implemented...and quickly," applying a stiff pointed finger on the desk he issues.

A man raises his hand but retorts without being asked, "I think we all understand how to take part in a discussion, can you get to the point?"

"I thought I was," Callahan bites back. "What's your position? I mean...who are you?"

"Florida Senator, district 33," the man replies.

"35 also present." The chap next to him blurts.

"Miami-Dade areas, great," Callahan groans. "Democrats too…not that it matters but is anyone here from Orange County, Okeechobee or Osceola?" he complains but receives no answer. "Is there representation from central Florida…anywhere in mid-state?" he questions again—but still no response from anyone in the room. "Well of course not!" he throws a hand up. "The areas to be most affected—no compliance. Who put this together?" he states with pompous character.

"I'm the Lieutenant Governor, Amy Franks. I can speak for this area," a woman sitting closer to the front speaks up.

"Fantastic, but we're not getting a hurricane," Callahan scoffs. "No offense mam. It's just that the nature of this threat is beyond FEMA."

Ms. Franks retorts, "I specialize in disaster relief that's true," she gestures, "but I am also the ears for the Governor."

"Okay, I can accept that. However, this is above most of the pay grades here. Again…people simply aren't listening to me."

"I agree…can you move this along?" from the front table a male voice emerges. "You have five of us from Homeland waiting to hear you out. There's enough decision making capacity here, please continue."

"That was Mr. Tester, with Intelligence," Dr. Winslow refreshes everyone's memory. "Please use your titles until everyone is familiar," she requests.

"Very well," Callahan changes his tone and looks toward Sheryl and Richard.

Sheryl conveys to him with her eyes that everyone in the room is waiting.

He takes note and regains his fighting spirit. Using explanatory gesture, he continues. "We came upon an individual on a known terrorist watch list, Saliha Achmede, although after he had drowned. Details led us to his apartment and a storage facility, both nearby. We uncovered assault rifles, ammunition and paraphernalia for making bombs. Blasting caps, assorted detonators, signaling devices, wireless transmitters, and various related items," he stops, noting everyone's expression. "We also made a shocking discovery. He has planted bombs in Florida's aquifers and there is definite reason to believe," he stops again to assure everyone is listening, "that they're… nuclear."

Immediately, skirmishing began throughout the room.

"Is this a joke?" the Lt. blurts.

"It's no hoax mam. On the contrary, this cell has been doing so for years, probably since 9-11."

"Do you have proof of this allegation agent?" Mr. Tester shouts across the room.

"I do."

"How are you abreast of this while we haven't heard any such chatter?" he blasts again.

"Performing my job sir—I listen and follow leads, even when they appear an unlikely possibility…just like the rest of you should be doing."

Silence befalls the room.

Tester disagrees and interrogates. "Who's making them and how? What detonates them?"   "I'm glad you asked. I'll get to that in a minute," Callahan smirks.

"Yeah, I'm Krylan with Cyber Securities," another man at the Homeland table stands. "Have you any leads via the internet?"

"Such as…"

"Like web sites, twitter chatter, blogs…anything via those outlets or others describing this plot. There might be supporting schematics being circulated or documents detailing these bombs."

"No, we haven't followed that lead."

Tester, shaking his head, tosses a pencil down.

Krylan continues, "I think this is an avenue to be examined, immediately in fact. If what you allege is true, reinforcing facts will pop up. If you need assistance…I'll ensure you get it."

"I'll have my men contact you after this meeting…Uh cyber security correct?" Callahan asks.

Miguel nods.

"Thank you," Callahan concludes.

"Agent, how many bombs are there?" a formal speaking female voice at the table asks. "I'm Darcia Davies, public relations, should the populace need to know, what do I tell them?"

"That is a great question mam," he pauses. "The answer is about a thousand," he calmly states. However, he receives a dreadful collective moan, which echoes the room.

"And you're saying all of them are in the ground, waiting to be detonated?" Tester grills with a tone expressing great doubt.

"Right at this very moment," Callahan asserts. "I assure you."

"How big are they? What type of damage can they do? Why are there so many? How can they be detonated at once and when would that be?" throwing a hand in the air Tester angers, provoking others to join his reaction. "That would be important for us to know, don't you think?"

Many nod and rally in support of his questioning.

"Well, I have working theories."

"A theory…!" Dr. Winslow now criticizes. "You're not sure?" she says.

Now the crowd is becoming agitated due to the agent's apparent lack of evidence.

"Are you telling us that none of this has been substantiated?" Senator 33 blurts, instigating an immediate riling amongst the clique.

"This is a waste of time," a random voice calls out.

"Hardly what I expected," another sounds off.

"I told you, he's unreliable," erratic hollers roar over each other.

Callahan, unsettled, tries to relieve their ill feelings by speaking loudly, "every puzzle may have a piece or two missing but you can still understand what the picture is right?" He persists, but the room grows more restless...indistinct chiding and nagging chatter now stem in all directions.

"What makes you believe they're nuclear? Where's the proof?" Tester bellows over the crowd.

"There's more you need to know people, please if you'll just hear me out," Callahan tries to surge over private conversations, but the static only grows noisier.

Some, now standing and moving about, he's losing control. "Listen up...this is serious," he tries again to get the rooms attention but still he is ignored.

Then suddenly, 'slam, slam, slam,' a mallet strikes the front desk.
Everyone stops in an instant and the room goes silent.

"I want to hear more," Mrs. Wong speaks up. "This is why I prefer a courtroom," she explains with authority. "This juvenile rambling is not allowed there."

Everyone quietly retakes a seat. "Now, let's get back to the subject," she continues. "Mr. Callahan, usually these people don't act alone. There are always traces of financial backing, product and shipment trails, partners and various resources associated with every terrorist cell. I haven't heard any talk of this."

"Thank you Mam," the agent inhales a much-needed breath, and gathers himself. "We know there are at least two others acting with him, Yasser Qadeer and Kahil Yafil. Qadeer funds the operation, coordinates intelligence and monitors movements, but Yafil is the one who worries us. His specialty is engineering and electronics. We found custom built signaling devices and repeaters used to carry communications over great distances and through water—all activated with simple transmissions, powered with nuclear batteries. They comprise the triggering mechanism and can lay dormant for a span of at least twenty-five years, and still maintain full operation when needed.

Mrs. Winslow cuts in again. "Take me back to the bombs, how do you know they're nuclear? Warheads are quiet large—not easily carried. How are they doing this?"

Callahan considers his words carefully before answering. "Well, this is one of the pieces that requires a bit of imagination," he lifts his hands to the room, "please, don't come unglued again as I explain." He jitters for proper explanation. "What we uncovered is smaller than contemporary wisdom would say they should be."

Some individuals start to grow uneasy already, but remain attentive.

"How small exactly? The technology requires that..."

Callahan cuts her off. "Respectfully mam, I'm aware of the parameters for nuclear fission as I certainly know you are. These weapons are usually large, but they can also be small and portable too. Please allow me—as your education must have taught you, our own country developed them. The M-28 Davy Crocket, designed in the 1950's, fired a 51lb. warhead capable of a 20-ton TNT explosion... four to eight times the power of the 1995 Oklahoma City bombing at our federal building. They termed it a recoilless portable rifle. We called it a tactical nuclear weapon."

The room is quiet.

"Our W54 warhead weighed about the same and maintained a 250 ton explosion. How's that for easily carried damage."

A slight moan emanates the crowd.

"So you see…we have made them small but that wasn't good enough for America. No—we had to develop one that could wipe out an entire country. Hey, we can conveniently drop them from a plane though. How long did we think we could keep this technology out of our enemy's hands? The ones I speak of are about six inches in diameter and two feet long, assuredly large enough to cause severe damage." As he concludes, there is only silence.

"Okay, we're listening." Dr. Winslow concedes."

"What a minute," Tester again disrupts the flow. "If this guy is dead, why is the threat imminent? I still have not heard any evidence to support your theories. You haven't explained how you know they are nuclear or for that matter, that they exist at all."

Callahan becomes disgruntled.

"Continue Mr. Callahan, what else do you have?" the doctor demands, trying to calm Tester.

Startled but not down, he carries on. "Before I bring my facts together, I first want to introduce you to Sheryl Olson," he indicates her sitting beside him. "She is the ecosystems director for the DEP and her husband Richard is here as well—you may know him as Olson Development Group. They were vital to this investigation."

Sheryl looks at him as if grateful for being included.

"Right now I would like them to show you footage that they acquired. I believe this will greatly help. Sheryl, would you please?"

After the agent's foreword, Sheryl stood and briefly spoke about her occupation and role in this investigation. Richard explained how he obtained the upcoming film. Then she inserted the media card into the laptop and played everything they had recorded, including the videos from the terrorist's computer. Immediately the audience was captivated and remained so for the duration of the presentation.

Thirty-Three

A fingertip strikes the enter tab and every computer screen goes dark, leaving observers engrained with the last image they saw—a device merely designated as a nuke. Poignant silence endures except for deep breaths followed by exhales that mildly resound within the Homeland's conference center. Everyone remains seated while reflecting on the last few minutes, some staring at the large screen, others at a blank monitor. Casually, eyes begin to explore each other, trying to make sense of the general sentiments that Richard's videos have imparted. Surely, one has to be wondering, 'what do they mean?' Moreover, 'what happens next?'

Callahan notices that reactions are scarce, so interpreting the solemn stares is challenging. Sheryl, still standing and devoid of countenance as well, looks around the room, then toward Richard, and then to the agent on her left. He closes her notebook and urges that she sit. Then he stands and prepares to speak. The crowd, still gripped, turns their eyes on him. However, he is beat to the punch.

"Boosted fission," Dr. Winslow speaks out. Quickly, she draws the attention, as she stands to explain. "Fusion boosting is achieved by introducing tritium and deuterium gas. Solid lithium deuteride-tritide, has also been used in some cases, but gas allows more flexibility and can be stored externally into a hollow cavity at the center of the sphere of fission fuel, or into a gap between an outer layer and a 'levitated' inner core—sometime before implosion of course. By the time one percent of the fission fuel has fissioned, the temperature raises high enough to cause thermonuclear fusion, which produces relatively large numbers of neutrons speeding up the late stages of the chain reaction and approximately doubling its efficiency. Deuterium-tritium fusion neutrons are extremely energetic, seven times more so than an average splitting, which makes them much more likely to be captured in the fissile material and lead to complete fission."

"What are you saying Doctor?" Tester removes his glasses.

"Well, making small and powerful nukes is a reality. The agent is right. The U.S. has made them already. It's not hypothetical and at this point, based on what I have heard so far, we have to assume the worst—particularly in light of these newfound fault-lines. Each explosion could destroy the circumference of a football field—two stories deep or perhaps ten times that. Unable to analyze one though, who could be certain?

"You agree?" Tester complains. "These contraptions could actually be nuclear—cause severe damage."

"It's possible," she looks at him with complete candor, and then back to the audience. "The smallest nuclear test on record was conducted right here inside the U.S, at Operation Plumbbob, 1957—a detonation equivalent to fifty-five tons of TNT. It was developed as part of an experiment to create small, easily transportable strategic nuclear weapons," she hesitates inhaling slowly. "Pascal-A' is another, the world's first underground nuclear explosion. Yes, it was set off beneath the earth as well and it was twenty-five times stronger than the Federal building calamity. If you recall, that blast killed one hundred and sixty-eight people. So I'm guessing—but I believe we could be looking at a couple hundred yards of complete obliteration with each detonation—moderate destruction may reach four times that circumference and light damage could spread for miles. However, radiation is always the greatest concern, which…depending on wind and nature may reach unthinkable distances. But… if there is any good news…fallout could be reduced due to the depth and density of surrounding water," returning sight to Tester, she begins closure. "So yes, the damage could be catastrophic. Perhaps several square miles of prestigious Florida landscape becomes dust with each discharge…I cannot be certain, but I don't believe we have the liberty to know. Lives are at stake."

At this moment, the look on Callahan's face is one of relief. Finally, he has reached someone and even the Olson's release a smile.

However, Tester has other plans. "Well, the way I see it," Tester maintains opposition. "There is no overwhelming evidence that these devices are real or even exist. It could all be a hoax, a well-made episode for Lifetime TV."

Callahan looks at Sheryl, "What did I say?"

"This agency," in vulgar tone Tester refers to the FBI, pointing at Callahan, "has a few water samples with thorium in it…so what? That has not yet been used to create nuclear weapons, or been proven viable for the purpose. Mrs. Olson pointed out that this element occurs naturally anyway, and in quite abundant amounts. It's logical to assume that it seeped in that way. Radon rises from the ground too, am I correct?" he asks rhetorically. "We know that this gaseous substance is everywhere, causing all kinds of problems. It kills people in their own homes. Is it our job to do something about that too? Maybe there is a dumpsite out there somewhere with a crap load of decaying arc-welding electrodes, thorium is used to make those as well."

Callahan looks at the ground.

Sheryl sighs, rubbing her forehead.

Richard seems deflated too. They know what he says is true.

Tester pauses for a moment, reviewing everyone in the room, and most are hinging on his next word, including Winslow. "This is my suggestion. Procure one of those devices and analyze it, determine its composition before we get worked up into frenzy." Adamantly he issues, staring directly at the FBI man.

Callahan bows his head and nods slightly. Then slowly raises a hand, palm up. "I can see how you would come to that conclusion," he speaks sensibly. "I do." Then he hardens tones and engages clear eye contact with Tester. "But I have to strongly disagree with you. This threat is real. Evacuate, then we can risk trying to obtain whatever you think is relevant. This would allow proper time to search them out and diffuse them without the pressure of losing innocent lives—over half the state."

"How do you expect we ask ten million people to get out? Do you have any idea the level of chaos that would create?" Mrs. Davies points out. "All of central Florida—old people would have heart attacks, which would be a disaster as well."

Callahan fumes. "Would you rather they all disintegrate mam? Would turning people into dust be mayhem more to your liking?"

"Mr. Callahan, please," Dr. Winslow pleads.

"Seriously," Tester scoffs. "Since they have been planted for so long as you say, explain to me why we don't have more time?"

Callahan is becoming unnerved—the Olson's are at a loss too. They look at him, but can only console with him with their eyes. The agent takes their glances and again musters a dispute.

"You're worried about the ramifications of being mistaken?" he blurts with utter disgust. "I can't believe the sentiments I'm hearing. Many, many unknowing people are on the edge of doom and you sit here…all of you…arbitrating as if this is a simple divorce case. There's something you're not remembering," Callahan defies all in the room. "He wasn't acting alone. His accomplices are on the run. They can detonate every one of them with a single phone call."

"What…what are you saying?" Winslow asks.

"How is that possible?" Mrs. Wong requests.

"Then why haven't they done it already?" Krylan suggests with cynical tone. Tester scoffs.

"Because, they're fleeing…trying to get out of the State," Callahan contends. "Their colleague who performed the installations is dead, so the plot can't expand any further. When they get farther north, maybe Georgia…we're out of time," he sighs, and then continues. "We have road blocks in place at all the major routes—surveillance at train and bus stations—airports are covered too. Numerous counties are on alert—descriptions and pertinent details given, which will slow them down. But if we don't find them, one by one or all at once, they're going off."

"How is that possible?" Senator 35 asks. "Cellular signals barely travel through this building let alone underground."

"The repeaters…like I said. Equipment these days is amazing. Undersea optimization of signal enhancement has emerged. Companies like Cygnus are a dime a dozen. These electronic devices are simple—receive a signal, then transmit it again at a higher level, enabling communications to travel to the other side of obstructions and around obstacles—in addition to extending them over incredible distances. In air or underwater, analog or digital broadcasts are amplified, reshaped and retimed to perform complex functions in combination to complete a network of spreading transmissions. Ultrasonic waves have been around for years—nothing new. Hell, dolphins and bats navigate the same way." Callahan laughs with cynical flare.

Richard stands. "The robot I used to capture those images uses the same technology," he interjects.

He gets a few stares.

"Then catching them may not be enough," Krylan bolsters an opinion.

"Why not?" Winslow asks.

He responds. "If the detonation trigger is a phone call…then any computer could have been programmed to execute that function, even years in advance. But find the numbers, and I can deactivate them."

"Is this true?" the doctor asks.

"Agent, bring me their computers, I need to search them," Krylan demands.

Callahan seems tangled with the idea. "I see your point, I do…it's just that…"

"Give them to him," Charez chimes in with an attitude—ready for physical fight if necessary.

Others begin motioning for action as well.

"I agree," Winslow matches the request. She too fuels the spirited argument even further.

Again, the debate turns fiery, but in the midst of disputing correct course of action, a voice suddenly rebounds from the front speakers, and quite loud.

"Stand down people," it calls out, and the accent is familiar.

"Mr. President?" Dr. Winslow acknowledges.

A solemn sigh swirls and the room goes silent.

"I didn't know you would be joining us?" she says.

"I've been listening for the last forty minutes," he attests. "And I'm a bit dismayed with your attitudes, and with the attention you're giving this situation."

Just then, his image accompanies the vocals, appearing on the TV behind the Homeland table. He is adjusting his headset as crew personnel make corrections to the monitor in front of him.

"Okay, okay…I can see just fine…leave it alone," the President slaps them away while speaking harshly to a production member, and then mumbles abroad in wooly tone to others in his general surrounding. "No…I don't need makeup. My skin is perfect, geese you people are something else…this is a serious issue people. Give me some daaamn space."

"Are you golfing sir?" she notices greens are exposed in the background?

"I was Doctor, but you guys ruined that at the sixth hole. And I was on course for a stellar performance too—under ninety, that's for sure," he chuckles.

"Sorry to have… interrupted you sir," she hesitates, speaking with a disbelieving tone.

"Don't be silly. The United States takes precedence over…"

Suddenly, he redirects his concentration. "That's too tight!" he chastises a helpful hand. "What have I told you?" He nudges them away from the camera. "Now, where was I. Oh yeah that's right, National security."

"Mr. President...we are involved with a matter of utmost ..." the doctor begins, but shut down.

"Really...I don't give a shit," he rudely interrupts in scolding tone. "I just proved that over the last six years didn't I?

"Sir...!" Callahan brusquely interjects, possibly out of turn. "With all due respect, I don't believe that you have been quite focused on the subject due to your concentrating on knocking those little balls into cup sized holes."

The President's appearance quickly shows dislike for the agent, and his assessment. "I don't like your tone agent. That's not what this discussion needs," the President quickly retorts, looking into the camera lens with great suffice. "Business doesn't always require physically sitting at a table in order to deal with something. And I'm a busy man."

"But this is not a trade agreement sir," Callahan fires back.

"Pay attention agent, I'll be the judge of what makes a matter serious. And frankly right now, I believe you need to relax, take a deep breath, assess reality just a little bit deeper and stay the course."

"Sir, this situation is way past critical," Callahan battles for acknowledgement. "It's life-threatening...peril is imminent," he argues with passion.

"Do you have a problem referring to me as President, agent?" he returns as if offended, utterly ignoring the previous comment.

Callahan, irritated, does not reply, but he does stare boldly at the screen.

"Let's see if we can issue a proper address next time, shall we?" the President demands in very sober character. "Let me explain something to all of you," he continues with rough temperament for all to hear. "Many crises occur in this country every day and we deal with them. What's new? For that matter, people are blown up and shot at, thrown off buildings, run over, and tortured to death in other countries all the time. Somebody loses a head every fifteen seconds or so but I don't see any of you waving your arms in the air about that," he pauses.

"Agent...what you brought to us is nothing short of an excerpt from a 'C' rated movie...someone trying to start a riot or worse, and we've seen our share of those films, haven't we? Having said that...of course, America will stand tall against chaos, as it always has. Only I am not going to engage in evil methods created by fear, thus causing me to deliver a poor disarming attempt of a non-existent threat...especially with such lack of intelligence. Is that clear?"

A few obedient responses circulate.

However, not from Callahan, he is gathering an attitude.

"Mr. President, with all of the admiration I have for you...your being stubborn."

The room grows silent, jaws drop, no one is moving.

The President constructs a humorless expression and opposes with an acute defiance, more so than Callahan. "May I remind you of who pays your salary agent?"

Callahan responds very quickly. "Actually the people pay my wages sir, including the ones in this state who are needlessly being put into harm's way and may I 'REFRESH' your memory, many of them voted for you. They deserve nothing less than the truth."

The President laughs. "The truth!" he smiles with a very condescending nature. "They will agent, if necessary. But only when I deem appropriate and fitting to do so—and even then it will be the facts that I deliver, not your conspiracy theories, do you understand?"

Everyone in the room is cowering, except Callahan.

The President continues after an intense stare down. "Right now you need to do your job, which is to get the information that Director Tester just said he wants. Only then will we have further debate on this issue"

Nevertheless, Callahan has not yet given up. "May I remind you of what the outgoing DHS secretary said," he blasts. "She warned us of a disaster to hit this country, the likes of which this nation has never seen? This is it," he pounds the desk. "And I'm sure you've spoken to her about it. Tell us what those conversations revealed and…"

However, the President cuts him off, displaying adamant, near reckless intent. "Do you know why I won reelection agent? Because I am smarter than you, that's all you need to know. "Furthermore, there's no place in my administration for name calling." Increasing his temperament, the President clamors, and a strictly aimed finger precedes his words. "Now…I have voiced opinion on this topic numerous times in the past and you people just don't get it. It's derisive, dismissive, and disdainful. Frankly, it's merely a scathing attempt to deliver a moot point. You are so predictable."

Others in the room form a blundering look upon their faces wondering who he is referring to, and to what his implications represent.

The President pauses to collect his temper, quickly looking away and then back to the audience. "Whatever?" he scoffs and throws a hand into the air.

Then his mood tweaks into a supreme 'God like' nature. "I fundamentally have an issue with it," he reprimands. "So get that information and we'll go from there. This is an order without debate…okay."

"Yes sir," Callahan bites his tongue.

"That's an order Mr. Munsinger. Is that clear?" directing his attention to the agent's boss, the President re-checks the comprehension of his instruction. "Try to remember who appointed you to your position…uh I did. Will I have an issue with one of your employees?" the President harshly poses an irrefutable question to render his words understood.

"No, Mr. President," the director replies. "There won't be a problem."

"Good. Now we're reaching across the aisle," the President laughs. "That's non-partisan behavior...am I right," he asks aloud in grand rhetorical fashion under a disingenuous calm chuckle.

The room remains silent beyond reproach.

Seconds seem like minutes and not a voice speaks out. Everyone looks about the room at each other, waiting for someone to comment, but not a word spoken. Chastised into speechlessness, Callahan sits down.

"Has a cat got your tongue?" the President titters, smiling with victory.

Just then, a soft but provoking voice arises.

"Maybe we can shut down cell towers," Sheryl peeps, taking a stand.

"What is that?" the President Demands clarification, maintaining a nasty glare. "Who are you?" he boldly asks.

She seems a bit embarrassed.

Richard is certainly squirming.

"I'm Sheryl Olson with the DEP Mr. President. I was merely implying that we could shut down communications, instead of evacuating. You can blackout telephones, emails and really all transmissions."

Suddenly she has the room's undivided attention.

Richard is surprised too.

She continues. "The bombs can't be detonated then," she states.

Callahan slowly nods his head, beginning to smile.

Many others are showing positive gestures for the idea.

"We would have all the time we want then, wouldn't we?" she optimistically avows. "Um, shut down the internet—all of it...until this situation is figured out," she concludes.

Suddenly, sighs of relief fill the air.

'That's a fantastic suggestion,' across the room a comment carries.

'I agree,' another voice calls out.

Callahan places his hand around her wrist and smiles.

Richard gives her a fist pump.

Winslow lends a happy grin too—even Tester cannot dispose the idea.

Amy Franks delivers covert silent applause, signaling agreement.

Remarkably though, the President seems to share a different outlook. Harboring what looks like disappointment, nearing reckless abandon he confronts the mysterious newcomer. "We'll keep that in our back pocket," he assures her using sarcastic connotation. "It's a great concept however and dare I say, 'you are the crowd pleaser.'" with insincere appeasing character he praises her. "But let me tell you," he raises a slanderous voice. "Your ill-planned suggestion is thoughtless and would needlessly alarm and infuriate— more importantly it would endanger too many people within your great state."

Smiles quickly turn to frowns among the cluster as the President persists. "If all that you mentioned stops, so ceases government, business, industry, schools and the economy. Not to mention the lives put in widespread jeopardy. For most people like the elderly, disadvantaged, and disabled—those procedures would take away their only form of contact with emergency and auxiliary services." Smirking with great annoyance he continues, "Aannnd...since there isn't enough confirmation to warrant the belief of a real concern...I can't support or encourage such extremist and radical actions—that's what I call terrorism. I will not sign off on that. I refuse to release such drastic and inappropriate measures. Am I clear?"

Using rash overtone he reminds everyone that he will not tolerate a suggestion so dangerous. "So... that's the end of it. Use the next forty-eight hours to establish better intelligence, something concrete and we'll talk then. In the meantime, I'll put together an independent and impartial committee to hash out the details and investigate the FBI...I mean, examine their allegations," he laughs again.

"Mrs. Winslow, I expect a full report on my desk by the end of the week...well, next week because this one is over already. And don't forget...I have a vacation coming up so it has to be before that or I won't give it any attention for about two months."

With that, the TV turns to static and audio stops as well. Those who were standing, collectedly take a seat. The room is silent—no one has anything left to say.

Thirty-Four

A few people enter an empty room. Ms. Franks is the last one in and gently closes the door behind her, first checking the hallway to see that no one else has followed.

"We can speak in confidence here," she turns to a group, huddled for secret conversation.

"What the hell was that?" Sheryl whispers loudly, pacing the tight space. Her voice quivers. "That wasn't someone acting like a President," she complains.

Richard settles her with a caressing hand to her shoulder. "Let's hear what the Governor has to say," he pulls her close—she regains composure.

"Listen," Winslow explains, "he doesn't believe we'll ever be struck by terrorism, not on his watch. He thinks those factions are under his control—people from similar territory or something. He imagines that they respect him."

"That's nonsense," Callahan suggests.

"It is, I agree," the doctor admits. "But everyone is in the tank for him and not just the media, politicians too. They stand to lose a lot of ground if the President fails...so they back him at all cost."

"That Tester guy supports him," Sheryl scoffs.

"Yeah, he's one of the puppets...what gave that away?" Winslow jests.

"Doesn't the President worry about his reputation?" Richard throws up a hand.

"Career politicians do have a community standing to contend with because they will remain in the public eye long after this administration is over," the doc further explains. "But this President doesn't care about his perception, despite what you hear on TV. He got to the top and that glory has a scheduled end. He simply wants to make as many changes before that day arrives. His job is merely an assignment, one that has a point of no return—does that strategy sound familiar. His philosophy—dishonest missions succeed too. His Presidency has been such a joyride, a boundless tour free of opposition for so long that he truly feels above failure, and why not. His fiascos went completely undisputed or turned into honorable endeavors. Reporters tout his greatness at every turn, even things that are normally considered miscarriages of justice."

"Yeah, well this shit storm is going to make Benghazi seem like a children's skirmish over a pack of gum at a neighborhood playground," Callahan blasts, delivering an inappropriate gesture.

Sheryl looks at him funny.

"Substantiating the problem though, that is always the obstacle," Winslow attests.

Munsinger opens up. "In life, we often know things that we can't prove, but should that inherently make them less real?" he divulges.

The dismayed group seems to understand him.

"I'm guilty of requiring a disproportionate amount of detail too, right now in fact. For that, I'm sorry Tyler," he apologizes.

Callahan imparts a thankful nod. "But that's in the past," Placing a hand atop his boss's shoulder he assures one thing. "Now, we make it right."

"No," Munsinger stops him. "The President isn't about to do anything," he continues in grave tone. "His speech was all show and I don't want you to risk your life. I can't let you down again."

Ms. Franks steps in with comforting words, "it's okay, and we've all been there at one time or another. We can't fret any longer. We must find a way to deal with this situation, and quickly."

Winslow agrees-they all do.

"And I think I know how," the Lt. continues. Suddenly, postures begin to straighten up.

Sheryl asks, "How?" Everyone listens.

"This isn't tricky," she starts. "Through the Governor, I have direct influence with police and fire departments, emergency services and rescue divisions throughout Florida. I can issue high alert at the state level. Orders for the shutdown of communications can be given on a moment's notice, but getting all of this coordination functioning at a sufficient level will take at least twenty-four hours."

"You don't need the President's approval?" Sheryl questions.

"No, but our efforts have to be planned before we send people fleeing. To ensure safety during outage, government agencies can use conventional radios to maintain correspondence within departments up and down the state. For starters, that will aid the flow of exodus. Continual advisory loops will play on television and the radio, which help people understand rally point locations, and so many other pertinent pieces of information. But of course, this is going to require your cooperation agent," she directs attention to him.

"I'm listening," he responds.

"First, can you assure me that these things are real?"

"I can attest!" Sheryl confirms.

"I've never believed anything so much in my life," Richard expels.

"Agent," the LT says again. "And you?"

"Yes, of course. I stake my career on it," he replies in earnest.

"Fair enough," she exhales. "Then, I'll get the inner workings set up, but I need you to cover the Governor's ass by presenting this threat on national TV, offering the public something more tangible than you did here today. People need to witness a physical shape. Manufacture something if you have to, even if it's not the real deal but…"

"No, no way," he quickly lifts a hand to halt her proposal. "I can get you an actual one, disarmed. Seriously, it will be easier than trying to make a fake one anyway. I can have it first thing tomorrow morning, but that's when I want migration to initiate. I'll speak then," he boldly contends. "So you've got twelve hours."

"What are you trying to...?" Sheryl begins questioning, but the agent overrides her.

"I've got my resources...and my reasons." He abruptly changes topic. "The question is, 'why would the Lieutenant stick her neck out?'" He requests explanation while looking right at her.

"Let's just agree that I have my motives too," she simply states. "And 9-11 will pale in comparison if someone doesn't act. Let me ask...if any of you could have stopped one of those planes before it took off the ground by killing the terrorists...would you have done it?"

Everyone takes a moment to reflect. Motionless they stand, silently thinking about the thought. Then, one by one each make gesture to confirm their answer.

"Exactly," she says. "Well, this is our chance to make it right...this time—we stop those bastards.

Thirty-Five

"Tyler, what is happening to this county's leadership? The last few hours have involved an absentee President, unexplainable disorder, methodical hostility, and an upheaval in the standard practice of protecting and serving. The ringmaster appears to be our leader...and I voted for him," Sheryl complains with backside leaning against her truck door—a parking lot light illuminates her face while she crosses arms in a huff. "He's supposed to safeguard people from any threat, even the slightest ones no matter the cost," she adds.

"This isn't the government you grew up with," Callahan comments on her idealistic view with his hands in pockets—his shadow casting near Richard who was leaning over the truck, elbows on the hood. "It's about time you started dealing with it. Politics have changed," the agent explains. "And you know what? Many people like the new direction, especially those who benefit from assistance programs and others merely trying to protect themselves from forced expulsion. Of the remaining populace, thirty percent either don't have a clue or want one. So, who's going to hold our elected accountable?" he throws hands up. "Most people only care about what they want...what's good for them today," he concludes.

"As long as I have my IPhone, Ipad, TV and car is what you're saying the attitude is?" Richard sarcastically exhales.

"Yeah, that pretty much sums it up. Give me my entertainment or else," the agent complains. "They don't know what Syria is doing or who in the hell that is—in a few years the Constitution may be rewritten right under their noses," he sighs. "That doesn't matter right now. We have to worry about something more immediate than stupidity and neglected foreign affairs."

"What's the plan?" Sheryl exhales.

Callahan seems grim as he hurls one of his illustrious ultimatums. "Well, for starters...you and your family are getting on a plane," he points, "just over that fence. I'll have one waiting for you, tomorrow morning."

"What? No way," Sheryl balks and moves about with displeasure. "My oath was to serve and protect...like yours."

"We can't leave," Richard scoffs and rises to express his apprehension.

"Yes, you can." Callahan grins. "You'll love New York this time of year," he tentatively jokes.

The Olson's are displeased, displaying silent dejection.

The agent notices. "Besides, you've done enough," he adds. "And your country is indebted. I mean that, truly, I do."

"And our friends, what about them," Sheryl grumbles, "our relatives, our neighbors?"

"Acting like it's happy times…that's the play?" Richard hassles the gruff agent.

"Run like hell is what I would call it." Callahan laughs to show good humor. They do not.

"We can't take a back seat now," Richard protests.

Quickly, the agent resumes seriousness. "Enough," he stops the conversation's direction. "I know you have good intentions. I'm sure about that, but tactics change and usually when unexpected. Listen, I've got this crew," he lowers tone to express truthfulness. "These warriors don't care if they live or die. Any reason they had to live is long gone, their families too, hell…they should have been killed as well, decades ago, but for some plagued reason they weren't. Extreme danger is the only thing that makes them forget bad memories, or reminisce the good ones. Heck, I don't know what it does for them. What I am saying is….It's someone else's turn to carry the load now. So let them."

Sheryl and Richard stared at each other, eyes filled with varying emotions from worry to relief…wrapped in a confusing web of awareness that is raining down hard. They have absorbed many details, difficult to make sense of, leaving insufficient choices and yet fewer remedies, possibly none at all.

However, Sheryl is more willing to resist the request. "I can't flee, but the agent is right," she decides. "Richard, take the kids, I'll stay behind," she nearly begs.

"I'm not leaving without you—stay or go we live or die as a family. We're not separating," Richard lays down his demand—holding her dearly. "The kids would never agree to leave you."

"You two are something else," Callahan vividly points out. "Two days ago you couldn't tolerate each other and suddenly, you can't be pried apart with a crowbar."

"Agent," Sheryl explains. "We never stopped loving each other. Sometimes people…"

"Yeah, I get it," he throws his hands down. "You're both staying, but remember. You have to act normal until the word is given. Go back to your community celebration, appreciate the kids through morning and be ready to depart—don't try to be heroes. You may jeopardize this whole arrangement."

"Festival, how in the hell can we do that?"

"You either go now or leave later, I really don't care," Callahan flares. "That's your choice okay, but evacuation has to be organized and announced from top officials. Until then, you need to be routine."

"What about you? What are doing?" Sheryl asks.

"Mam, I'm just one of those numb soldiers living without a family for too many years," he reveals. "I live off that risk and fear—why I'm bitter. What happens to me is not important. I'll be doing exactly what makes me feel something."

Struck with shock they can only admire the contemptuous man as he turns and proceeds to his car. Richard and Sheryl quickly speak amongst themselves, eyeing the agent as he begins backing up. Upon pulling away, Sheryl suddenly waves for him to stop. He rolls down his window to listen. She makes an inaudible request, to which he agrees. "Anything for you Mrs. Olson, just don't cause a riot tomorrow," he yelps—driving away.

A short time later, the Olson's, driving home were tired but remarkably wide-awake. The radio was off and travel seemed pristine. Calm and quiet finally surrounded them. Sheryl called Arnold asking him to take her kids home but he already did—it was late. When she and Richard got home, everyone but the kids was solemnly sitting in the kitchen. The five sat and talked as if the world were ending.

"You have to go," Sheryl tries to drive the message home.

"And leave everyone behind. I can't do that," Jeff resists.

Maggie agrees as well.

"It's not fair to have advance knowledge," Arnold weighs in. "My conscience would get the better of me. I know the head start only amounts to a half-day or so, but I'm going to wait like the rest."

"The roads will be jammed," Richard notes. "You'll see it differently then."

"You're staying," Maggie reminds Sheryl. "You'll have to deal with traffic too."

"Well, that's the thing. We have a plane waiting," she discloses. "We made a deal."

"At least for our kids," Richard points out. "They leave first thing to Texas. We'll follow sometime later."

"Somebody has to show them the aquifers," Sheryl carefully adds.

"Nobody better than you right," Jeff scoffs. "And Richard has an underwater bot. Perfect." He grunts louder.

"We'll be protected." She eases Jeff's worry. "There are safe havens in the State. Helicopters will take us back and forth, and the bot operates from any remote computer. We'll be out of harm's way."

"You need me," Jeff argues.

"No... I don't," she firmly states and looks away.

He shakes his head, "you're lying. I don't believe you."

"You're all boneheads," Richard cynically chuckles. "But I get it...I really do."

Their discussions lasted for a while and not much was resolved before the three colleagues left for home. Afterwards, Richard called Carl, John, Ashley and his father.

Sheryl called Wynyard as well, but to their amazement, none of them wanted to leave early. Senior Olson added he was too old to be running like a quail.

Richard and Sheryl sat, looking at each other, feeling both disbelief and pride for their friend's principles.

"I never thought my worries over ODG would bring me here," she protests, reaching across the table to grasp her husband's tired hand. "All along, I was hoping your company would be cleared. That seems so petty now."

"Nothing you do is irrelevant," Richard smiles. "You care and thanks to you...I do to. Anyway, our kids will be safe at Nanas; at least we're safely getting them out of here."

"Yeah, I guess...but what if they give us a hard time."

"They won't. Well, of course they would if we told them what's happening. But we won't be far behind and they'll come to understand."

"I don't know? You know how Jenny is."

"Yeah, she can be belligerent. But she's just as warm too...weird," he laughs. "Anyway, just make sure everything they need is ready. They'll be on that plane before they know what hit them."

After the two parents made final decisions, they groggily made way to their bedroom. But they didn't notice, on the way down the hall, one of the bedroom doors was slowly closing.

Thirty-Six

Atop a nightstand, an alarm clock plods its solitary assignment. Sound asleep, its keepers unaware that only a few seconds remain until that awful, yet familiar noise discharges. Then, it happens. Loud buzzing emits toward Sheryl's pillow covered ear—evoking the intended reaction. Immediately, she stretches an arm and begins slapping the device, several times to locate the button that disarms the screeching menace. Just as quickly, she falls back into position wanting to sleep longer, hugging a fluffy cushion to help return her to dream state. However, she saw the 5AM readout so her eyes cannot stay closed. Though groggy, she is mindful of what lies ahead and her wide-open stare indicates such. Briskly, she flings the covers from her body and sits on bed's edge. For a swap on roles, Richard is still snoring so with a nudge she awakens him.

This morning is most austere and to amplify anxiety, there are no perking noises or aromatic java scents to sooth their challenged spirits.

"I'll make coffee," Sheryl moans and heads to the doorway. "You get the kids. Just don't let them out of your sight."

Yawning and stretching trying to acquire focus, he too arises. "On it boss," he replies with minimal effort, dawdling behind her.

In the kitchen, Sheryl had just opened the coffee can when an unpleasant remark reached her ears.

"Sheryl, the kids aren't here," Richard's troubled voice resounded aloud.

Abruptly, her weary persona changed into perceptive concern. "What?" a disturbed utter departs her quivering lips. In a rash, she slid the container across the counter and as it banged against the backsplash, contents spilling, she was already near the kids' bedchambers. Upon reaching Jenny's room, she found Richard rummaging through it.

"I checked on them last night. They were here," motionless at the doorway still holding the knob she rants.

"Well, they're not here now," narrow-mindedly he snarls.

"Are you sure they're just not..." she stammers, swinging the door behind her while darting to the private bathroom.

"She's not in there," he criticizes, and begins to say something else but instead, notices a paper stuck to the back of the closing door. He pulls it off. "Over here," he hollers.

"Oh, you found them," she lets out a relieving sigh. She reenters relaxed, but he does not give her a comforting feeling. She moves closer, gazing at his displeasing posture.

Simply, he hands the paper to her. "You need to read this," he says, and she does so aloud.

'Mom, Dad. We are not leaving you. We go together or not at all and don't try to find us. I'll call you later...J&J.'

"Oh no," Sheryl delivers a bleak sigh. "Are you kidding me?"

"They heard us talking last night," Richard courses a hand through his hair. "It's Jenny, like you said."

"Do you think she...?" Sheryl begins pacing, engaged in thought.

Richard tries to remain calm, though he is conveying a glum appearance too.

"Sorry," she recants the attitude. "I'm just..."

"It's okay," he consoles her.

"Well, what do we do now?" She scoffs. "People are waiting for them."

"We find them?"

"Where, where," she yells, then cowers to sit on Jenny's bed.

Richard sits beside her. "Get ready, we're leaving."

"What...where..."

"No time for that," he asserts. "Get dressed and make a call to buy us time."

A short time later, they are pulling out of the driveway. Sheryl is on her cell, Richard behind the wheel.

"I told you this was a bad idea," Callahan's voice insults.

"I don't need your Dr. Phil crap right now," she retorts.

"Okay, okay, listen," he changes tone. "I'm sure they're alright, probably hiding nearby. Just secure them and get here when you can. We have more than one plane you know. Call me when you're on the way."

"Thanks," she hangs up.

Richard, slowly driving the neighborhood has already engaged eyesight of every nook and cranny illuminated by lighting. Unable to reach the kids via cell yet again, Sheryl joins him with greater observation. They stopped by Junior's house and found his mother outside with the dog. She informed them that the kids weren't there—her boy was still asleep.

Mrs. Nash seemed very surprised by the nature of the Olson's early visit and began an inquiry of her own. They felt her concern, but didn't have the heart or time to explain, so they made a casual excuse and carried on.

The worried parents continued casing the vicinity, including the parking lot, playgrounds and teen hangouts at nearby Harmony High. They looked in the tunnel connecting school grounds to the neighborhood too.

They called Bobby's home as well, but again the kids weren't there either. Sheryl tried Arnold and then Jeff. Richard called his father and Ashley too. Each was up and watching the news, preparing for departure, but none of them saw Jake or Jenny.

Then, Richard had the bright idea of going to the festival fairgrounds. It was too early for opening, but it was nearby.

Now on foot, they check closed booths, empty tents, vacant buildings and private kiosks but find no one. They interrogate a few workers setting up for the day and joggers passing through too, but that revealed the same. Minutes of scouring barren fields become wasted lengths of time. Repeatedly, the rattled parents called Jake and Jenny's names until their voices crackled.

The sun, now rising, makes sighting farther distances more possible but nothing changes. Discouraged, they return to their vehicle where Sheryl, sensing hopelessness, sheds quiet tears.

"We'll find them," he tries to solace her.

She wipes under her eyes and vents. "We're running out of time. Callahan will have a bomb soon, announcements and chaos will follow that. Millions will be scurrying then…we'll never find them."

Richard listens but sits idle grappling with thought. He has nothing to say. Then, a moment of vision comes to him. "I know where they are," his posture rises as he heralds the location.

But Sheryl fears another let down and cannot get optimistic. "Where," She groans?

"At the raft… that's what makes him feel safe, right."

Sheryl begins to exhibit a gleam. "I should have realized that too," she exclaims. "That contest is all he lived for, Buck Lake…hurry," she pushes on his shoulder.

"I'm going," he screeches while spinning tires kick up gravel. "It's a short drive. We're not far."

They arrive within minutes, promptly exit the truck and begin trudging through tall grasses to obtain a good view of the water. They can clearly see across the lake, but there was no sign of the kids.

"This is too small for a raft race. Are you sure this was the site," Richard asks that she search her memory.

"I don't recall now, I…" she mumbles. "Oh wait; this is where they were building it. Junior's dad already transported it, I remember now," with revelation, she states. "He said the contest was being held at Cat Lake, Lake Conlin or Cat Island…something with a 'C'."

Richards takes note. "Okay, let's go. Those lakes are to the west on Old Melbourne Highway, heading north," he comments while they hurry to the car.

Sheryl is right behind him. "Right, that road goes between two of them…I know the place."

Shortly they arrive. Cat Lake is on their right and Lake Conlin on the left as they pass by driving south, but they see nothing from the vehicle—both directions reveal emptiness. Then the road begins veering east, pulling away from Cat's view. While going over a small bridge, crossing over Conlin, they notice the water is very shallow. Richard slows and turns around to go back.

Sheryl gives a questioning stare.

"There's deeper water on the north side," he explains, "where Conlin joins Cat Swamp. We'll have to walk it, but that has to be the place."

'The water dries up going further south,' that's what Jake said," she affirms. "That is where the event is planned…the north side of Conlin," she expresses, feeling a sense of luck.

Richard nods. "We'll have to stop here," he advises.

"It's okay, just pull over—hurry," she fidgets while grasping the door lever, waiting to exit.

Once again, he parks, but in the most remote terrain thus far. Quickly, they get out and traipse to the lake's edge, pushing aside tall sward along the way.

"This lake is a good size," she sighs. "And I see rafts on the other side."

"Me too," Richard points out—but then he sounds deflated. "It must be a mile away though—might as well be ten."

"That has to be them," Sheryl objects. "How did they get over there?" She yells her kid's names.

"It's too far, they can't hear you," he bellows.

She fiercely looks at him, and then briskly starts walking to the left, then to the right.

"We can't walk there either," he states.

She ignores him and continues combing the area.

"What are you looking for," he scoffs.

She gestures for him to stop talking and then snaps a retort. "We have to get our kids. Okay, that's all I know."

"I do too, but…" he begins further argument.

"Check it out," she yells, ending his behavior. "I spot a dinghy."

He looks and is shocked to see it, tucked neatly around a nearby embankment.

"Come on, let's go," she directs while wriggling it to a more accessible spot.

In a jiffy, they were adrift, Richard providing propulsion.

"Couldn't you find one with a motor," he grunts, vexing with the paddle.

"Did you ever think you'd be rowing me across a lake?" she teases.

"With only one oar in a boat that drags like a brick, no…that never came to mind," already out of breath he retorts, stroking from one side then the other. "Even a kayak would be better than this slow trudging thing," he jokes.

She smiles—feeling her kids are within reach.

Richard expended a lot of energy and some time, but eventually he got them close enough for visual. Homemade crafts docked at the shoreline—possible giggling sounded beyond—no one else around.

"It's still too early for the coordinators of the race?" Sheryl mentions. "They'll probably be in a powerboat anyway, and I don't see one.

"But we're in the right place…these are definitely kids' handiwork." Out of breath, Richard labors. He relaxes to let the dinghy coast.

"Yeah, they're a bit shoddy, made from weird stuff. Milk cartons are helping that one float," she observes, and then notices his fatigue. "I was willing to help you," she reprimands. "I can take it from here."

"No, I'm the provider in this relationship remember," he blabs, and resumes rowing to get nearer.

"Okay, you're the man," she mocks and turns to view the shore. "Jeennnie…Jaakke," she screams, then believes she hears faint rustling. "Jake…Jenny, is that you?" She calls more loudly. After a few seconds without reply, she yells again. "Jake…Jenny. Can you hear us?"

Once more, both parents shout but the silence only increases.

"Which one is Jake's raft?" Sheryl impatiently asks.

"I don't know. I never did go see it. Damn it—I'm a bad dad."

"Don't say that, you're not," Sheryl scolds. "You're busy, like every parent. Take a look at what you're going through right now, trying to save them." Then she notices something. "I see someone over there behind those bushes. They're hiding," she utters. "Push this thing to shore, you're almost there," she urges Richard to hurry, and guides him between two rafts.

She jumps on land as the dinghy comes to rest. "Come out," Sheryl yells while walking toward them. "Kids, I see you. Show yourselves. Don't make us wait any longer."

Richard catches up to witness the indistinguishable figures. "Sheryl…let me do this," he requests, tired and out of breath.

Conceding, she stands in restless posture atop the upper slope near tree line.

"Kids," he pines for consideration while bent with hands on knees. "I know you guys are upset, but let us explain. We wanted you to be safe. We aren't separating for good," he continues talking calmly. "Mom and I won't be in danger, and we wouldn't hurt you like that," Richard stands erect. "Come on, hear me out. Talk to us."

Silence lingers. Richard looks at Sheryl and gives a quick shrug.

She steps to the heavy brush and pushes thick leaves and climbers aside. "Get out here," she screams. "I'm not fooling around any longer. If I have to come through this crap you'll be sorry."

Those harsh words had an effect. Immediately, sounds of feet crushing dried leaves began, followed by snapping twigs. Then, a young hand pierced through the brush, pushing it away, and then another showed. A foot and lower leg came through next. Soon, the children's appearance became recognizable and both parents expressed similar amazement at the same time.

"You're not our kids," Sheryl utters with complete shock.

"Who are you?" Richard, in a state of bewilderment, asks the panic-stricken teen boy and girl.

Intimidated and standing at attention they amiably rendered their names— explaining they were only hanging out, not doing anything wrong.

"Relax," he directs them with care—placing a gentle hand to the boys shoulder, trying to ease their fears. "We're simply looking for our kids. We thought you were them."

The youths simply look back with nervousness.

"Maybe you know them—Jake and Jenny," Sheryl questions. "Our son built a raft for the Harmony contest, like the ones over there. Have you seen him? This is the competition site, isn't it?"

"No," the girl earnestly replies. "These are just the relics."

"The race was moved to Alligator Lake," the boy adds, "on the other side of highway 192."

"Because Summer has been so hot and dry, the water is deeper over there," she said. "There's more access and plenty of viewing areas too."

"You didn't know?" the boy concludes.

Sheryl and Richard immediately look at each other with utter disbelief. Richard scoffs. Sheryl merely closes her eyes expressing dread.

"Damn it," Richard bellows and paces away, causing the teens to fret.

"Sorry kids," Sheryl apologizes, trying to calm their confusion. "We really need to find our children. There's a dangerous situation developing," she remits but changes tone. "Listen, don't worry too much but both of you should get home quickly, okay. Stay tuned to the news," she strongly advises. "I can't tell you why right now. Just go."

Thirty-Seven

At the edge of Alligator Lake, mere miles from their parents, Jake was reminding his sister of his raft's well-built and rugged abilities. That's how he referenced the structure during a long-winded narrative of its many attributes. He was hoping a judge would happen by to give him accolades for the construction, and Jenny would witness the praise to provide testimony. Until then, both runaways accepted that this jaunt only afforded a temporary retreat from their fated arrangement—a diversion that would ultimately end. However, neither knew that the timing of their venture was most unfortunate. Moreover, agreements between adolescents rarely conclude without a snag.

Jenny just mentioned it was time to end to their excursion as agreed when her attention redirected to several other contestants arriving to inspect their makeshift floats as well. While engrossed in their affairs, Jake unexpectedly untied the dock line, and the raft began drifting.

"What are you doing?" she shouted, taking several steps toward him causing the raft to wobble, necessitating a quick grab to the nearest rail.

"Test driving it," confidently he responded. Moving past his sister, he tosses the limp coiled rope on deck.

"We shouldn't be doing this?" grabbing his arm she fiercely states, urging him to retract.

"Yeah, yeah I know…Mom and Dad will be pissed but I don't care," he pouts. Pulling away from her grasp, he commences to push off the lakebed with a long pole. They glide even further away, moving more swiftly. "I've been building this thing for months," he bellows.

They travel yet closer to the center of the lake.

"But you heard what they said last night, what if it's true?" she argues.

"They were going to send us away Jenny," he continues thrusting.

"Yeah, maybe they have good reason."

"Listen…you were the one that planned this whole thing. Now you want to change your mind," he ardently shoves harder.

"I know. It seemed like a good idea at the time," she concedes, but tries to change his mind. "We have to go back."

"Not yet."

"Then, let's at least call mom. She should know where we are," the girl argues.

"No way," Jake yells. "She'll put a stop to everything and somebody around here needs to see what I built…people who matter. Besides, I thought you wanted to get back at mom and dad for leaving us, to convince them to go too?"

"I know, I know, but I'm having second thoughts. Something doesn't feel right—just like with Bobby the other day. I have to see him before we leave," she lashes out

"Jenny, you worry too much. I mean think about it. If there was something bad about to happen, don't you think it would be all over TV? And why isn't it? Because nothing is going on, that's why," he answers for her.

She thinks about that for a second and begins to calm.

"Why isn't Junior here?" changing subjects she asks.

"He'll catch up. Don't worry about him."

"Alright, just for a little while okay," Jenny yields. "But I need to see Bobby."

The boy does not respond.

"Okay Jake," she yells. "I mean it."

"Yeah, yeah, I got it," he replies, disregarding his sister while persisting onward.

Meanwhile, Sheryl and Richard are laboring to make it back to their truck. It's visible, yet so far away, and this time Richard is leaning back, relaxing—snickering at Sheryl who is rowing so slowly that the distance between them and their destination does not appear to be narrowing. She notices his flippant gawk and it overwhelms her. With a sullen look, she extends the wooden oar back to him.

Richard is paddling once more while Sheryl catches a justified break. Though she had helped row this time, returning seems to be taking longer—and they mention such to each other. Intermittently, they swap turns, which allows each to check in with friends via cell phone, but there were no updates to convey. None of the TV networks has reported anything. Wearied, they take a break together.

"Callahan needs us to help locate it," Sheryl groans.

Richard wipes his brow and agrees. "We'll be back soon. The truck is close and then it is just a minute to the kids. We're almost there," he assures his unsettled wife.

Richard knows their kids are close in terms of straight-line distance. Roads and terrain separated them, but the two lakes that each was on were almost neighbors. Although they have a car, traveling to get them will be quick. The path known—securing them and evacuating was inevitable. Then, helping the FBI save Floridians is all that remained.

However, life is never that easy and sometimes…situations are worse than bad. Without warning, it happens.

This was a wonderful Saturday morning and the festival was about to enter full swing. Around the State kids are playing—people jogging, fishing, shopping, eating, reading, walking—riding bikes, having picnics, heading to the beach, and beginning all sorts of fun activities. Most have been up for hours. College campuses are alive with foot travel. High school teams prepare for battle and various sports functions have begun with players and spectators engaged. Parks and recreational centers everywhere have numerous people waltzing in. Hunters, fishermen, nature explores, shoppers, tourists, teachers, professors, service workers, consumers, and so many others across the Sunshine State are going about their affairs. Many more simply remain in their homes, tinkering about or relaxing as they do every weekend. Yet all at once, each of these inhabitants had their attention yanked away in shocking fashion.

Thirty-Eight

Sheryl detected a shudder—Jenny experienced it at the same time and both had worried reactions. However, the father and son were each wielding their oars, exerting themselves—neither sensed a thing. They each thought the edgy females were letting their imagination run wild. However, while taking a moment to examine their surroundings, it happens again. Clear to all, something was wrong.

"What was that Jake?" Jenny whined.

"I don't know. I've never felt anything like that," the disoriented boy affirms.

Cautiously, they peek over the edge and stare beneath them.

"It's like the water is dipping and then pushing up at us," Jenny makes a nervous observation.

"But that's impossible," the boy maintains—his alarmed look says otherwise.

Again, they encounter a bobbing action and this time shouts circulate in the distance.

"Did you guys feel that?" a voice carries from a neighboring craft.

Jenny yells their way. "Yeah, we did." Returning vision to the water, she murmurs. "But what was it?"

Again, a more notable shockwave occurs. On this instance, it reverberated through the tiny drift. Moments later, another resonated with greater force than the last. It rang through their bodies with evil purpose—squealing voices crossed the waters in all directions.

Releasing her grasp from the wooden structure, Jenny shakes her hands and fingers in an attempt to remove the heebie-jeebies.

"What are you doing?" her brother whimpers.

"I don't like the way this feels," she whines.

"You're starting to scare me," he screeches, feeling defenseless and exposed. Completely baffled by the frightening manifestations caused without storms, his concern grows. Then, just as Jenny places her hands back, another impact bumps them up and the water oscillates—nearby screaming intensifies.

"What the hell is going on?" Jenny cries, arms wrapping the center mast, clutching dearly to ensure footing.

"I don't know...I don't know," the brother yelps. Clutched to the steering rod he remains, cautious and still, hoping there will be no further repercussions. As they wait to see what happens, tears form, reinforcing the overall fear their faces convey. Confused and afraid they gaze at one another, but from the corner of her eye, Jenny notices others paddling fast—scurrying towards land.

"Just get us to shore Jake," she blurts, but he doesn't react quickly enough. "Now Jake now," she yells with an elevated sense of danger. "Start pushing—

get us out of here," she urges with violent resolve, scowling a dynamic expression of vulnerability.

Then another jerk rocks them. "Faster Jake faster," she frantically hounds him. At last, the young boy heeds his sister's plea and generates the conviction needed.

The teens are tangling with unknown terror, but their parents are too. Identical evil is befalling them.

Sheryl is balancing, gripping the bow's edge with one hand while placing her cell in a pocket with the other.

"What did Jeff say?" Richard inquires, vigorously paddling toward shore. Her response hindered by sunken emotion. He presses again.

At last, she faces him, inhaling slowly to gain quiet sobriety. "He said, 'explosions in the Ocala area.' Reports are…" she can't finish saying the words.

"Oh my God," Richard exhales and stops rowing. He hunches over from distress as well as fatigue.

"It's starting," she sighs, sitting with head drooping while rocking to the lakes whim. "It's too late," she grumbles and shrouds her face with quivering hands.

Richard, trying to catch his breath, examines the sky behind him.

In the midst of losing optimism, their cell phones begin chiming, first hers, then his, and yet more come in so they play them.

Arnold and Maggie's message is panic, describing what was happening in chaotic fashion.

Ashley is frantic too, her crying and yapping isn't clear, but Richard knows what it means.

Carl and Wynyard both left similar accounts.

Communications kept coming, but no time to hear any more.

"We have to find our kids," Sheryl avows with compelling expression.

Though tired, Richard recognizes the urgency and resumes rowing, but with every stroke, the vibrations worsened, and far-off rumbling was beginning to echo too.

She looks over his shoulder. "I see smoke," she advises.

He simply returns a devout regard for the danger and rows harder. Then, his phone receives another call and it grabs his attention. "That's dad's ringtone!" he blurts.

Sheryl takes it from his pocket so he can keep moving them along. "Go ahead dad—you're on speaker. We can hear you," she eagerly tells senior Olson.

Straight away noise and calamity overshadowed the voice, but they could tell who it was.

"I'm going down son," the old man screams—war-like sounds blanketing the background. "The house…in shambles," he yells broken verbiage. "Wherever you…boy…love you…get out…"

Suddenly there was a loud whoosh and the call went dead. Sheryl can only give blank stare as her disbelieving husband stops propelling the dinghy. Breathing heavily he lowers his head. They both comprehend that the dear man perished, but the severity of their own situation is quickly escalating too.

"Keep going," Sheryl directs. "We have to find our kids," she commands—desperation consuming her—witnessing unnatural clouds rise on the northward horizon.

He is slow to respond.

She grabs his wrist and delivers a most provoking stare.

Richard acknowledges and again clutches the oar taking action as the water beneath them bubbles.

Just then, another cellphone rings.

"It's Callahan," she's quick to answer. "We're too late?" she bellows into the cell, but immediately notices the same noise as senior Olson's situation.

"They're going off. We've been hit," he cries out. "Our building is...great damage—plane...no good...airport...ruin," his words coming through broken—yelling, grappling with chaos.

Richard, though curious, keeps paddling.

Sheryl tries to ask something but the agent cuts her off. "Don't talk! Listen," he yelps, as if running for cover. "Head south. Get your...south."

She listens carefully, but understanding him is difficult.

"You're at the edge of..." Callahan struggles. "Go east and south." Suddenly, a loud clang disrupts the transmission, and language becomes more fragmented. "They started...ex...on the north end...where...map indicated," he attempts to explain with heavy breathes through evolving turmoil. "They are simult...ly going southward...you might...time. Get your family to..." The agent hollers. Sheryl efforts to understand as visible plumes of smoke disrupt her attention.

"What about you guys? The evacuation—what's going on with that?" She asks and waits for reply, but there is none. "Callahan," she yells, but still no response. "Agent... agent... are you there? Tyler damn it can you hear me?" she screams but only static and inaudible clamoring is returned.

Richard, struggling to maintain stride listens with great concern.

Then again, she closes her cell and frets over another loss. Richard shows the same fear, each oar stroke becoming tougher and slower.

"He's gone too," she expels, swelling with emotion.

Out of breath, Richard rests and dissolves into gloom as well—distant bombs resounding and smolder expanding. "He was a good man," Richard blathers.

In agreement, she nods, looking up—something on her mind.

She labors to express herself until getting the words out. "When we were alone yesterday, Tyler and I," she delicately begins. "He told me I reminded him of his wife, the one he lost," wiping tears from her cheek she muddles to continue due, but involuntary crying holding her back. "He said he had great admiration for you too," she gasps—Richard sighs. "He said we have the perfect marriage, the one he always wanted. That you were the man he strived to be, but…" she takes a brief pause to collect herself, crumpling yet deeper into unhappiness. "He said he couldn't deliver…because the job always came first."

"He's was a better man than I thought." Richard confesses.

Clearing her throat, she adds. "You're the man among men, he said." Richard takes hold of his wife's hand. "And now he's gone," she whimpers.

"Hey…" he tries to calm her but she persists over him.

"Your dad…and all of our friends too, their all dying," she cries and collapses into despair.

"Sheryl," with rigor, he speaks, "we'll find the kids but if God wants us to perish so be it, then I say that should happen as a family."

Suddenly she puckers up. "No," she shouts. "I'm mean yes, get Jenny and Jake, but we can get out. We can make it out of here."

Richard stares, confused with the bold statement.

"We have to take them south. It's the last thing Tyler said," she clarifies. Regaining senses, she wipes her nose.

"What?"

"He said we're near the southern edge of the bomb field. It's happening just like map indicated, from north to south. We have time," Sheryl excites him with renewed enthusiasm—all he needed to hear.

"Keep it together baby," he consoles, sweeping the blade through water once more. "We're getting our kids and getting out of here," he declares. "There's no time to mourn now, our kids need us."

With transformed spirit, he surges on—she nods to signify concurrence.

"Call the kids again," he yells. "They have to be experiencing the same thing, they won't avoid you now."

"Good call," she acknowledges.

Meanwhile, Jake and Jenny's situation is worsening.

"What is that stuff," Jake bawls while fostering steady pushes with the cane as they wake atop choppy waters.

"They're mushroom clouds you idiot, from nuclear bombs. Just like Mom and Dad talked about. I told you."

"What should we do?" he cries.

"We have to get back." The girl replies with utter urgency. "They're going to be looking for us."

"How do you know that?"

"Because they love us you jerk. Now keep pushing."

"I am hurrying. This thing is built for stability not speed," he barks, but thrusts with total certitude anyway.

"Just get us to shore Jake. We have to find mom and dad. They're the only ones who can get us out of here."

They are about a half-mile from shore, not far under normal circumstances but an eternity under distress. They can see the docks from which they embarked a short time ago, and some people on it appear to be screaming and urgently waving back at them.

"What are they saying," Jake calls attention to their signaling efforts. Jenny listens but cannot quite understand. The screams become more frequent and more serious as she minds them.

"They're saying 'get out', something about a pool," Jake mutters, causing Jenny to look around.

Suddenly, she displays a grave stare. "Jake look," she desperately cries and points behind him. "The water…"

To their complete dismay, the lake's surface is beginning to rotate.

"Jake, we're heading into a whirlpool," Jenny screams. "Push faster," she yells and kneels to help paddle with her bare hand, but the twirling only draws them nearer.

Slowly, the craft begins assuming the more powerful current's path. Still, the teens battle it. From shore, a vigilant man tells his stunned children, "I've never seen one so large or start spinning so fast…not even in the movies. And those poor kids are smack dab in the middle of it." The family only lingers for a moment. "We have to go. There's nothing we can do," the hardhearted father exclaims. "We have to save ourselves," he grabs his kids by the hands and insists that they leave—watching the monstrosity grow as they run.

However, Jake and Jenny have not given up—not in a position to do so. They continue fighting the increasing turbulence, exhausting every ounce of strength they have. In the midst of these unreasonable forces, Jenny's cell phone rings. She cannot answer though, trying to move the craft toward safety one inch at a time, valiantly thrashing water behind her.

"Answer it," Jake yells.

She's unresponsive, her face is very close to the sounds of challenging water, and it's mesmerizing her. She realizes that the energy tugging at them is getting stronger. To make matters more threatening, a drainage hole is becoming visible, growing wider and deeper. The phone continues to ring.

"It might be dad," Jake screams at the immobile girl. "This could be your last chance to say we love them. Just answer it Jenny…I got this!" the boy screams, shoving the tip of the thin shaft against floor bottom, over and over again.

She responds, cautiously removing the cell from her pocket, "its mom," she yelps as water sprays up—the craft wobbles, now wet and slippery.

Jake nearly lost his footing and sharp movements force Jenny's body to the craft's core, but she held on with one hand while answering the phone with the other. Clutched around the mast she brings it to her ear, but hard shaking rocks them once more. This time, she let go of the phone to grip the structure with both hands. Jake fell to the deck as well, still holding the steering staff. Both watch as the phone slid in one direction and then another. They each try to grab it as they toss about but to no avail—it skidded into the rushing waters. They could only stare at its departure—helpless and horrified. Too terrified to cry or scream, the siblings impulsively crawl closer to each other and cling. Powerless, they can only comfort one another as they witness a wall of water rise above them. With fear intensifying and the speed of circular motion increasing, the bottomless void nears and the whirlpool's perimeter broadens. Waking faster and faster toward impending fate, the youths' can only pray.

Thirty-Nine

"Jenny's not answering." Sheryl frets. Fearing the worst she harnesses a tense grip upon the mobile device.

Richard notices the letdown. "Don't worry, we're almost there," he exhales breathing heavy and often. "They're okay...I know it," he asserts, hoping to strengthen her moral fiber.

Sheryl glances toward her children's destination, briefly witnesses eerie smoke rise and then returns her view to the shoreline. "Just a little more," she jubilantly expresses. "The truck is close. Hurry! Hurry," feeling a tad of well-deserved joy she stands and anticipates debarking, though her elevated spirit fades too soon. "We're not advancing," she scoffs in subdued tone and attempts to understand why. "We've stopped or something." Intuition compels her to look around.

"Of course we're moving," Richard argues, but a serious screech halts him.

"My God Richard, behind us," she warns—he turns to see. "A whirlpool is sucking us in," she yells.

"It's huge," he grunts and paddles with extreme dedication. Quicker and quicker, he sweeps the slim blade from front to rear scooping as much water as possible, but it seems they keep going backwards. He shifts to deeper, longer, more penetrating strokes, trying to gain any type of forward movement.

In desperation, Sheryl peers into the water and notices something, and it gives her a good feeling. "It's shallow," she blurts and steps onto the bow.

"What are you doing?" Richard yells as she leaps. To his surprise, she lands about waist deep holding her cell above head, but now he is drifting away, slowly traveling into the eddy...four feet back, then five...six then seven.

"Quick, jump in," she hollers, "now before it's too late." Yelling louder her vocals express urgency, "take your cell out of your pocket, just do it."

Knowing this is the only way, he promptly does as requested. Upon doing so though, Sheryl's wedding ring plopped into the water. It was in the same pocket and she saw it fall and splash too. He must have snagged it while removing the phone—looking down he tries to spot it.

"Let it go," she screams as he drifts even further.

"But I see it," he calls out.

"I don't care." Yelling like an angry wife, she thrashes water with her empty hand. "Jump off the damn boat. Leave it," she shrieks as loud as possible. He tosses his phone—she catches it...but he doesn't jump yet.

Don't worry," he decides, staring right at her with courageous eyes. "I'll be right back." He dives in to get the band—her screaming 'no' as he leapt.

Although, once his body disappeared into the water she stayed quiet and motionless, anticipating his return. Two seconds pass and then four. Eight...then ten go by but he doesn't resurface and the empty vessel is on course to going down. Fourteen, fifteen, sixteen the moments tick away. Worried, she steps toward his entry and more time goes by. She moves yet nearer to search for him, but strong current pulls at her legs, nearly knocking her off balance so she halts and backs up. His safe return is fading fast, but she remains hopeful.

Meanwhile, their kids are in great jeopardy. Faster and faster the craft spirals as the vortex narrows, furiously pulling them toward center—and the winds rustle across the wooden flat. Higher the water surges roaring like a wild beast. Now, the poor forsaken teens can only see the cloudless sky above—no longer able to detect which is north or south. The people screaming from land, removed from vision, their voices are gone too. Complete equilibrium is lost. Jake finally lets go of the useless steering mechanism and tussles to his sister's side.

"Jake, what can we do?" Jenny cries—the whirlpool wall rising above eyesight. Lying clutched to the center post she watches in horror.

"Just hold on tight Jenny. Hold your breath as long as you can and don't let go," he renders what little comfort he can.

Both remain clenched to the raft, and each other. As they bounce and bump toward approaching fate, they pull each other closer.

"If we're lucky, we may get whisked to the side and pop back up," he explains a wishful thought. She listens, having boundless confidence and complete trust in her little brother.

"Is that possible?" she asks as a tear rolls down her cheek, whisked away by a gust of wind.

"Yeah, totally," he assures as they both glare upon one another—lost expressions. "I've read how that can happen," he informs her and looks away.

"What was the name of the book," she politely poses, but he can't remember. Jenny's blank stare tells the answer though—she knows he is trying to solace her.

Then, he grabs the deck rope and wraps it around them and the center pillar too, several times before tying it secure.

"Dig your feet in…like this," he urges and shows her how he is doing it. She follows and does the same as well—wedging toes between boards to anchor in.

"Are you hunkered down? He asks as water begins covering their feet and legs, engulfing the very surface they're strapped too.

She simply nods affirmation. He signals 'that's good'. Jake checks the rope one more time just as their last minute runs out. The raft is now vanishing into the constricting tunnel of water and its tightening power seems unimaginable to the teens as they spin yet faster.

"I want you to know, you're the best brother," Jenny speaks heartfelt feelings through quivering lips—her long wind driven hair flows past her face as she clutches his hand—wet, red, scared eyes adorning him. "I love you Jake," squinting from the coarse whirling bluster she utters.

"I know Jenny...me too," he returns sentiment. "Breathe deep, okay, and hold it as long as you can, until you pass out if you have too," he instructs one last time—she complies, tears dripping—mouth scrunching from fear.

Ultimately, the water has reached their chins and the last second of resistance has arrived. Together, they take a final massive gulp of air as they enter the twirling shaft of doom. The mighty vortex consumed them and the little toy raft spun and sank like a tiny piece of paper plummeting down a bathtub drain. Instantly, it suffered damage. The strong weight of twisting water tore the external rails right off. Within seconds, the top of the mast snapped and half of the bottom ripped off too. Though the kids remain clamped to a small intact section, the gushing turbulence was more intense than anything they have ever experienced. Along with pieces of wood, they hurl within a rapid current—only one breath to sustain them.

No person has lived to tell about such a thing—fate no doubt sealed. Despite being under a few short moments, the duration seems forever. Bumping back and forth the residual edges of the craft grazes against objects, but still they hold. Swooshing downward, then upward and violently tossed around repeatedly, they refuse to let go. Nothing is recognizable. Unknown objects rustle past, debris knocks into them but so far, none has done them in. They cannot see one another and neither can they talk but each must wonder how long they can withstand this torture...without air.

Then, all of a sudden, something smacks against them with such force it makes them release some of their precious breath, and more pieces of valuable buoyant wood were lost. Worse yet, it's stuck on the deteriorating planks continuing to squeeze the air out of them and they can sense the structure is losing the last stage of stability. Jenny detects it wrap her knee, like it has latched. Jake feels it on his leg and around the waist. He tries to dislodge it but it will not budge. This could be their demise, but the near lifeless teens cannot do a thing about it. The dynamics around them are too great, so they do what they must—contend with the unbearable pressure until they can no more.

Forty

Back at Lake Conlin, Sheryl was still wading waist deep expecting Richard to reappear, but she knew time was running out. The dinghy just vanished into the swirling center and now the undercurrent wants her too. With no other choice, she enters dry land, but looks back for Richard every step of the way. Plopping against the vehicle's front wheel, she rests while maintaining vigil. Now, explosions take the forefront amidst her lonely pause. Bombs are going off in deliberate sequence, each more formidable than the last. Their unnerving rumble echoes and smoke now bellows consuming most of the distant horizon. Her cell has not rung in a while, nor has Richards. She glances at them, still clutched in her withered hands, and notices neither have a signal. However, she pays this warning little mind.

"He kept it with him the whole damn time," she mumbles through a choked up cry and then zones out. Frozen in time she tries to postpone the inevitable grief which follows the loss of a husband—a best friend and lover. This terrible period seems to last forever and yet…passes so quickly. She now knows it is time to let go but doesn't want to. On her knees, she bows her head. Gradually, she begins cringing and striking clinched phones into the sand, one then the other. Faster she hits the ground—the harder they become and desperate weeping soon accompanies her madness. Sniveling soon turns into inflamed moans with absolute sobbing next, tears falling like rain. Getting angrier, her stomach convulses—discharging hideous groans, and with each passing moment, her uneasiness grows more regretful.

Mucus gurgles—it fills her nose and throat, gaging on her own spittle but she doesn't care—Richard is gone. Letting go of the phones she tightly grips a wad of sand with each hand and squeezes with all her might. Bawling turns into wailing and then uncontrollable shattered emotions take over—her soul destroyed. Gasping without restraint, she looks toward the heavens with incredible, utter disgust. Breathing the very air is difficult and paining because her tormented will is resisting the body's need for oxygen. So distraught she simply cannot get any air into her lungs. Eventually, human reflex forces an inhale and though it is filled with intermittent wheezing and broken intake…she seizes a most deep one. Silently, her quivering frame holds a large volume of air until it can no more. Upon exhale, she releases the loudest, most unimaginable ear-piercing shriek ever freed toward the sky. After another maddened breath, she unearthed yet another lengthy howl directed toward God himself, and then falls to the ground. Panting, she flops and rolls onto her back—trebling and crying with fits of anger amid intense pain.

"You took him from me," she screams toward the Heavens, several times while aimlessly throwing sand toward the sky. Then she stands in flamboyant fashion...still gasping she looks across the lake, gazing into the swirling monstrosity with absolute disbelief.

"Why couldn't you let that little piece of metal go," she screams at the top of her lungs, bending at the waist to release all of her breath. "I told you I didn't care! I told you I didn't care! I told you..." Then she collapses to her knees once again, repeatedly yelling at her absent husband until coughing and retching take over. Her life force of eighteen years disappeared into the shallows—along with him went energy she held dear. On hands and knees, crawling to nowhere, so sick with grief she vomits...then slobbering, choking and gasping resume.

However, logical comprehension at last returns to the breathless misery laden woman. She realizes she must put aside this tragedy to prevent another. Knowing her children may still be alive, her motherly character comes back to life. She wipes away drool and reconstructs that familiar feeling of adversity— oh so needed to carry on. Richard would tell her to go after them—she knows that. She pierces over the lake one last time, but gets no better result. The spinning water was too strong for a man already exhausted. She is aware of nature's destructive ability more than anyone is. The bottom of the lake simply opened up and there was no escape.

Reluctantly, she skulks into the car, shuts the door, starts it, and begins to drive away.

"Jake...Jenny," she mumbles, barely able to operate a vehicle. "Please God, let them be okay. You've already taken their father," again she breaks down, but this time prays. "I beg your forgiveness. Protect my children and return them to me. Prepare a good place for Richard too." Weeping returns as she appeals to Gods will, though moments earlier she was blasting him. Forced to recoup self-control to prevent running off the road, she stops driving once again.

Sheryl is unaware that God may have other plans for her and family. After recovering yet again, she begins to move the car forward—suddenly an unusual sensation happens. It starts at her fingers, moves to her hands and arms. Quickly legions of goose bumps were spanning her entire body causing her to shimmer into breathlessness. Hitting the brakes again, she examines the mysterious rash move up and down her appendages in synchronicity, with intent. By accident, she looked into the rear view mirror and the phenomenon stopped. Changing her view back to the front beyond the windshield it started coming back. While looking behind her it ceased again. Sensing a supernatural force was communicating to her, telling her to return, keep looking for Richard, she takes action. Without hesitation, she places the transmission in reverse and slams the accelerator. Upon returning to the scene of Richard's disappearance she notices the whirlpool is gone, but he is nowhere in sight. Remaining hopeful, she steps out of the car—certain he will emerge from the rough murky waters, but nothing happens. Only those distant explosions greet her presence. Believing she was wrong about her intuition, she sighs and reopens the car door.

"I told you…I need my kids," she hisses at the sky. "This is what you do to me."

Just then, she hears a popping thrust from behind her. She turns to see what it is. She was amazed to see that a geyser was spewing water high into the air, exactly where the whirlpool was. Her curiosity increased when she took sight of a configuration bursting atop it. Then total shock consumed her as it landed, floating on the lake's surface. Misty spray still settling, clouding her view, but it appears that someone is on it.

"I can breathe, I can breathe," a voice shrieks.

That grabs Sheryl's attention.

"Me too, oh my God we're alive," another howls with pleasure.

"We made it Jenny." A boy's voice screams aloud with joy.

Sheryl was pleasantly surprised. She couldn't believe her ears or eyes, but there were her kids—delivered unto her as she prayed. There they were.

"Jenny…Jake," she begins yelling. Immediately, they recognize their mom and are most happy to see her. Both wave and yell back.

"Mom, Mom," they call to her.

Finally, Sheryl has reason to smile.

On the tattered raft, the children discard the rope and begin to paddle but are startled when they identify what almost killed them. At the rear of the fragmented drift, barely clung to the edge and partially submerged was another body, and it was fast sliding further in.

"It's Dad Jake, help!" Jenny grabs her brother. Impulsively, they strain to drag him upon the raft—now comprised of loose wooden slats. They roll him over and try to wake him, but there is no response.

"Dad, dad…" Jenny mutters gently smacking him on the cheek. Jake lifts his father's head and places a piece of flopping wreckage under it, keeping his nose above frightening waters. By his side, they kneel and drift, Sheryl yelling to them without reply.

"He's not waking up," Jake states and in concern calls to his mother, "M-ahh-om…"

Jenny also yells through cupped hands. "It's Dad, its Dad, help."

Jake continues screaming while Jenny nudges her lifeless father, again and again.

Sheryl can't understand what they're doing, but she can see Jake motioning for her to come closer, so she begins wading deeper. As she gets nearer, she hears a word that sounds like 'dad' but she thinks they are merely asking where he is.

For the kid's sake, she tries to keep it together. "What do I tell them?" she mumbles under her breath and begins swimming.

Again, the teens call to her.

This time she knows they are talking about Richard, but she's confused—she can't see him.

"How could they know anything about him?" she wonders.

"Dad is on this raft—he's hurt. Get here now…" Jake's voice at last carries well and though understood, she can't make sense of it.

Realizing the imperative nature, she swims very fast.

"She coming," Jake informs his emotional sister, feverishly trying to do something for her father.

Sheryl arrives.

"He's not waking up Mom," Jenny cries as her mother edges alongside, water up to her neck. "You have to help him."

"Give him air, breathe into his lungs," Sheryl commands but Jenny seems confused. "Do it Jenny," she demands. "I can't do it, not from here and there's no room for me. It'll sink," she lashes out—the girl commences as asked. "Good…that's it. Give him another one," Sheryl instructs and begins dragging the scarcely buoyant pieces of wood to shore. Jakes sees what his mom is doing and uses a loose board to help push as well.

"You're doing fine honey," Sheryl keeps Jenny in good spirits. "Just keep going, we're almost there." The mother continues pulling the wreckage to safety, ensuring that Jenny stay focused.

Once on land they drag the lifeless man to a gentle rest where Sheryl administers CPR—a breath than compression…breath then compression, but it's not working.

"Is he alive?" Jake cries.

"I don't know." His mother gasps to keep working, but still no response.

"Why isn't he moving?" Jenny sobs.

Fearing that too much time has passed, she tells her kids he is in God's hands now—she can do no more and stops breathing air into him. Sadness fills their hearts.

Jenny caresses her dad's arm while tears burst from her pitiful face.

Jake lays his head on his father's chest, hugging him and convulsing profusely.

Sheryl is oddly less emotional, probably because she already experienced the pain of losing him once. She touches his face, straightens his hair and gently rubs her fingertips across his still pliable lips trying to encounter his vibe one last time. She lifts one of his hands and holds it dearly, shaking it softly to get a reaction to her sweet embrace, but there is none. In the background, explosions threaten, but the three seem less burdened with that now. She picks up his other hand to do the same but notices it is tightly closed. Carefully, she opens one finger then the next, and upon prying the third her wedding ring fell out. There it lay on his motionless stomach. Many emotions suddenly swelled inside her upon seeing the thing that lured her husband to his end. The kids take note of the strange occurrence as their mother comes to tears, her face grimacing with sorrow. She places it back on her finger and says the words, "I do…I always did," and then kisses his soft lips.

"I never stopped loving you babies," she whispers in his ear and kisses him again. Staring at her husband's precious face, she tells the kids he is still warm…then a large tear falls from her cheek, landing on one of Richard's peacefully closed eyes.

Suddenly, there is a cough and he's gasping for air—water expels from his lungs.

"Breathe," Sheryl yelps. "Breathe Damn it, don't you leave me."

"He's alive," the kids yell in unison.

Sheryl rolls him over to get the rest of the water out as he continues to gag.

"Daddy, Dad…" the kids remit joy.

Rolling back over, he resumes regular breathing, and though exhausted, finding Sheryl smiling back at him is all the relief he needed. The kids were gleaming too.

"You haven't called me that in years," he said.

"What?" Sheryl is confused.

"You called me babies," he smiles. The kids and Sheryl give each other a strange look.

"I did?" Sheryl realizes and then chuckles. "I did—and I mean it too," she hugs his wet body and helps him to his feet.

After standing and giving his kids a warm embrace, he looks into his empty hand, holding it out for his wife to see as well.

"I lost it—I'm sorry," he apologizes.

"No, no you didn't," she smiles holding hers out for him to see. "It's already back on my finger."

Lovingly they kiss with the kids joining in for a group hug.

"So, you put the ring on before you saved my life?" Richard jokes.

"What can I say," she says. The kids laugh.

"But I didn't get to put it back on," he groans.

"Hey, I'm always finishing your chores anyway," she puns as the family hurries toward the truck. "You should be used to that by now."

Forty-One

Forthcoming calamity recaptures the Olson family's attention—it approaches without resistance. As they flee, it is evolving and fast expanding right in front of them. A menacing haze on the northward horizon is rising and though the truck windows are up, those horrible detonations sound anyway—surreal concussions vibrate through the speeding vehicle too, despite the steady reverberation of knobby tires zipping along a coarse road.

Useless cell phones lie on the console and after Sheryl's failed attempt to dial-in a radio channel, the joy of family reunion is merely a short-lived memory. Nevertheless, Richard is ditching the lake that almost took his life— impatient and liberated he drives away, but why do they seem to be going toward disaster.

"Where are we going?" Jake imparts serious consideration while leaning between the two front bucket seats, bracing hands atop them to pull closer from the rear. "Aren't we heading straight into it?"

Jenny develops a most worried look noticing her brother's observation.

"We'll turn left, just a little further, then back onto 192," the father stresses, looking at his son for only a second so he can return eyes to the road. "And then we'll go south from there...don't worry. We'll be fine," he assures.

"We still have some time," his mom adds. "They're still twenty or thirty miles away, closing in, but we'll be on our way to Miami in no time. We just have to get a few more miles south of here."

"And then what?" Jenny complains. "Will we be okay then?"

"Yeah...we'll be safe honey."

"From there we'll grab a boat to the Bahamas or just keep going to Key West." Richard continues with positive reinforcement. "But I promise...we'll be alright."

"It's the only way out," Sheryl clarifies.

"But what about our friends," Jenny cries? "What about Bobby?" her sadness swells.

Sheryl is at a loss for words as she looks at Richard for support on this one.

"There's nothing..." her dad hesitates, "anyone can do," he expresses the frank reality while turning the steering wheel to follow a bend in the road.

The family stares at bellowing smoke on the right and continues turning their heads to watch as the vehicle follows the narrow dirt lane. Distracted, Richard's is absorbed on his daughter's distraught demeanor—tears flowing from her eyes. He begins to tell her something, but suddenly, he redirects his focus back onto the road and slams the breaks. There was a car stopped smack dab in the middle of the street and just before rear-ending it, Richard brings them to a gut wrenching halt. A dust cloud flumes and as it disperses, it's apparent that the immobile vehicle was also stuck inside a shallow sinkhole. The family is shocked—staring at the abandoned car with two others trapped the same way.

"Just go around it dad," Jenny yells.

Richard observes that trees and thick bushes reside on either side, creating an impasse.

"Try to squeeze through on the left," Sheryl urges and points to a possible opening.

He moves the truck that direction, everyone can see past the car pile-up and to their surprise, the intended route was unfit. The ground was literally moving—wobbling like the surface of a disrupted waterbed.

"Get out of here dad," Jake yells.

"Hurry," Jenny screams.

"Go back," Sheryl furthers the notion.

Richard throws the transmission in reverse and thrusts the vehicle rearward. With all four tires spinning freely he turns around on a dime, then hits the brakes placing the car in forward and punches the accelerator to tear off once again.

"I thought you said it was miles away," Jenny yells at her mother.

Sheryl and Richard give each other a very concerned look. The kids peer out the back window gawking at the quaky landscape trying to follow as they race away.

"What now?" Sheryl drones.

"This road also leads to 192 about five miles south of here." He comforts her with an alternative plan. "I tried the other way first..." he pauses, "because it would have been quicker. This way is a maze...but it doesn't matter now." He lets out a disgruntled sigh and looks in the rear view, whirling dirt spewing behind.

Tires dash along a pebbly surface, crackling and kicking up gravel. It clangs against the under carriage in mass unison as if a legion of BB's are pinging against dense metal.

The panic-stricken Olson family, in a tense silence mode for the past several minutes, had only the sound of menacing rumbles, guaranteed devastation taunting them. Then, Richard begins to slow and the others draw awareness.

"There should be a road on the right, just ahead," he voices and then sees it. "There it is," he points and decelerates to direct the vehicle that way but immediately comes to another unexpected halt.

Again, the group stares at their destination witnessing yet another impediment. Numerous large trees toppled over one another and several were blocking access to the road. In addition, all sides of the stack surrounded by water rendering the route inaccessible—the troubled family, demoralized again.

"You've got to be kidding me," Richard barks, slumping into the steering wheel with the sky resounding and the quivering earth shadowing their trail—a haunting reminder that hurriedness in order.

Sheryl observes her husband's faltering mindset and lends a witless sigh, demonstrating the same feeling.

"We're not going to make it out of here," Jenny cries, slouching at her window.

"Look at what you've already gone through…and survived," Jake leans in and solaces with a hug on her shoulder. "I'll help you through it again."

His mother watches in awe of her son's extraordinary endurance in the midst of disaster. He is transmitting nothing but resilience and positive approach.

"Your brother's right," Sheryl blurts, grabbing her emotions to convey the same sentiment –she continues alike with Richard. "Honey," she calmly looks at him, placing a comforting hand to his backside. "Get us out of here, okay," she implores his rationale.

He rises up, glances into the side view mirror and then the rear one and makes a dreary suggestion. "We can go back. The last road we turned from also heads east, a short distance closer to the crap up there, but there's a left turn in a half-mile or so from there. It leads to another main road six or so miles to the north," letting his head flop against the headrest he explains.

Jenny yells, "we can't go that way," her face filled with fright.

"It's chaos up there by now," Jake argues the same point.

Sheryl realizes the situation is grim, but senses that Richard is their only hope. She sees that his spirit is diminishing and naturally takes action. Appreciating that presenting him with an agitated attitude will not help—she casually guides the weary man.

"Baby, do we have any other options?" she petitions his withdrawn mood.

"No," he replies without zest while closing his eyes. "It does take us further to the east, but it's the last route we have." He rotates his head and affirms that belief with a stern stare.

She simply returns one of blank fear. The kids remain fixated on their defeated father with a similar bleak glare and remain silent hoping for better words of encouragement.

"Do it," she blurts. "Just go! We don't have a choice anyway—but I also have a feeling."

The kids look at her like she's crazy, and Richard rises to do the same. "Trust me," she persists with vigor and looks at all of them with an optimistic sparkle. "I've had a sensation like this before, and it didn't let me down."

Richard, not moving, is trying to believe her.

"Go," she shoves his arm, "I'll explain later. Don't waste any more time, okay."

Her attitude seemed to work and without delay, tires were kicking up unpaved road once again. The kids, staring through the back window suddenly shout.

"Oh my God, the ground just opened up Mom. You were right," Jenny screeches.

"A sinkhole—right where we were," Jake adds.

The four gaze upon each other both astonished and relieved as Richard peels out like Speed Racer. After making the indicated turn to the left, Richard again picks up velocity very quickly. Their destination to a safe route is only minutes away, a road traveling directly eastward, taking them further from the dogging devastation—surely providing safe travel to the East Coast.

Leaving only dust behind them, Richard pegs the speedometer, literally driving as fast as the vehicle will go. The wind is rushing past them with great force and the car is shuddering—steering wheel shaking. The engine is screaming and their hearts are pounding as they streak along a straight and problem free road. Further, they travel away from disaster at nearly two miles per minute, getting closer and closer to a reliable highway. Each of them on pins and needles—anticipating the sight of it—any second they should see it. While all hold on in a breathless state Sheryl's eyes widen, delivering a worrisome stare.

"How much gas do we have?" she utters.

Immediately, the kids administer raised eyebrows and lumps form in their throats.

"Dad," Jenny yells.

"Relax, we've got three quarters of a tank," he relieves their worries smiling back at them.

Sheryl lends a loosened smile too. The kids unwind and let out a sigh of relief as well—Jake, closing his eyes falls back into his seat.

Just then, Jenny screams and points toward the windshield. Sheryl and Richard both turn around as Richard slams the brakes yet again. Not far in front of their speeding car, the road buckled like flimsy rubber, and from it, spray and debris spewed upward at least fifty feet high.

Tires were locked and skidding. Expressions were fixed and writhing. There was no time to veer away from it and even less to stop. Hitting the protrusion at full speed the car and occupants soared into the sky. They flew through the air as if vaulting from a dare devil ramp—only there was no return decline on the other side.

Everyone held their breath as they ascended, hurling a great distance. Then, while descending they screamed until culminating into a slamming touchdown. First, there was a crushing impact and all shouting stopped...then a giant bounce followed by skipping, sliding and springing out of control for a hundred feet until the right front tire snapped off at the hub. Suddenly, that corner of the truck dug into the dirt road causing the rear to catapult. It twisted and flipped with brutal summersault action, tossing the family around like rag dolls. They were completely at the mercy of a higher power—gravitational forces wanted to rip the vehicle apart. Several times the crumbling hunk of metal overturned. It banged and clanged while propelling onward—battering them before silently coming to a rest in tall grasses. Unbelievably, they sat right side up, just off the road, steam hissing from the engine compartment—the motor no longer working.

Miraculously, each of them remained conscious through the ordeal and even more remarkable was that they not only survived, but also were essentially unharmed. They suffered a few superficial scrapes and many painful bruises but otherwise their wounds did not appear life threatening. Sheryl's head was pounding, Richards back was aching and the kids each acquired beaten ribs and shoulders...but they lived.

Dad kicked his door open and slowly got out nursing his body along the way. Sheryl climbed across and exited the same way. The kids simply crawled through openings where windows no longer existed, to which every single one was gone. Though they were thankful to be alive, grave danger persisted and they had not forgotten.

"What are you doing?" Sheryl yells to God up in the stratosphere. "You gave them back to me just to watch us all die. What kind of sick crap is that?"

Her family is shocked, observing her uncharacteristic performance.

"Maybe he just wanted us to be together when it happens," her husband slurs. Stumbling to her side, he tries to deliver a comforting arm.

Instead, she knocks it aside and grabs him at the front of his shirt. With both hands, she grips tightly, yanking him toward her with vigorous intent.

"I refuse to believe that," she energetically declares, holding her spirited face mere millimeters from his listless expression, staring him down like a Marine drill sergeant.

Jake comes to his father's aid by getting between them, urging his mother to let go.

"Mom," Jenny voices loudly, shifting focus to one real issue. "What's that stuff?"

"It's coming this way," Jake adds.

Each parent breaks from personal conflict, and musters a long glance at the settling cloud.

"It's...nuclear fallout," Sheryl reluctantly details.

"Depending on how concentrated the radiation is when it gets here...we could have mere hours to live before suffering to death," their father callously worsens the answer. "Our skin could melt off while we choke and gasp to a painful end, or we might not experience detrimental side effects until months from now...temporarily surviving but wishing we hadn't," he intensifies their pending peril with a pessimistic attitude.

"That's a real sweet thing to say to your daughter," Sheryl scoffs.

"Shouldn't we be running," Jake pleads, but then notices his father's injuries. "Okay, we could start walking," he modifies the method of escape. "We can make it to that road right," he argues. "You said it wasn't much farther," the boy contends for consideration. "We might find a car on it, or I don't know. Maybe someone will find us."

"What are we waiting for?" Jenny jumps in to support her brother's assumption. "Maybe the winds won't carry that stuff this far."

"She's right," Sheryl agrees. "It does seem to be blowing westward, at least for now."

The father nods and begins limping onward. Sheryl gets under her husband's arm to assist his movement. The kids trek along, clung to their parents side too, but the embraced family only takes a few steps before the ground in that direction begins to wobble as well—quickly becoming worse.

Yet again, their hopes dramatically fade.

Sheryl looks to the bog on the right and begins toward it. Believing they could walk directly east on foot through the marshes, she urges the others to enter. However, within a short distance they notice alligators looming, waiting for the next meal. Sharply, they realize that this path is also out of the question. Humiliated, they head back to the roadside and rest. Exhausted, out of options, and too tired of weeping any longer they sit motionless, free from the need to scurry—there is nowhere to go. Unavoidable danger now seems to be closing from every direction, so they simply wait for the inevitable to occur. Sheryl begins to console her grieving children when Jenny snaps yet again.

"Do you hear that?" she stands and jettisons an optimistic yelp.

"It hasn't stopped since it started," her father replies referring to the explosions.

"No, I hear it too," Jake rises to match his sister, looking at the sky.

Suddenly, the sound was clear to all of them and it's becoming louder, getting closer at a much faster rate than the explosive thuds, and it did not have the same roar. To their surprise, it was a low flying helicopter—flying directly at them.

Straightaway, the kids began waving their hands, jumping high and screaming as to bring as much attention to them as they could. Happily, it worked and the chopper landed not far away. The whirling blades drove harsh winds into their faces flinging sand and dirt along with it, but the four helpless people did not care. They were simply overwhelmed with joy.

The rotor vanes were still spinning when a man exited and began walking toward them. His stride was determined and when he removed his goggles and headgear, Sheryl was elated to see his face. Richard offered a wide smile as well. It was none other than the FBI agent, Tyler Callahan.

"Callahan," she jumps to her feet and darts to meet him, flaunting a shocked but happy voice. "I thought you were..."

"Yeah, I did too," he cuts her off as she clinches him with a tight hug.

"How'd you find us?"

"Someone taught me to navigate these parts pretty good," he smiles and as they release he looks toward Richard who just staggered up.

He too embraces the agent for a well-deserved greeting and then completes the reception with an honoring handshake. Both of Richard's hands interlock Callahan's—delivering ultimate gratitude.

"I never thought I would be so glad to see you," he tells the rescuer.

"Are these your kids" Callahan refers to the elated youngsters. "You guys made quite the ruckus today haven't you," he laughs and pats Jake on the back.

"You've got no idea," the boy jokes.

"Well, it's okay now," the agent changes topic. "Who wants to get out of here before anything else goes wrong?"

The kids scream energetically. "Get us out of here."

"Well go on then," he instructs with a hand gesture, indicating for them to get on the aircraft.

The kids take off running.

"This is about as much love as I can handle," the agent jokes to the parents. "Let's say we get out of here too. We can resume the celebration later."

The three move to the whirlybird, Richard limping as quickly as possible. Then they take to the air and as they flew higher, large areas of low-lying smoke were evident. It was not far from reaching them and it extended further north than they could see—and blasts were still happening too. However, as they flew away, the ground beneath was not visible—and since they were heading south away from the calamity, soon they could see no more. Jenny's weeping came back as she laid her head in mom's lap. Richard and Jake merely remained fixated—their eyesight drawn beyond the window.

Forty-Two

A camera zooms in on personnel wearing full-body suits, some outfitted in yellow rubbery ones and others in white but all completely protected head to toe. Gloves, boots and self-contained breathing gear are standard equipment and each ensemble appears made of impermeable material. Along the shoreline, they comb in squads, sifting through debris and turning over ruble. Partially submerged cars rest on the edge, most upside down and are a major interest to these individuals. Panning onward, toppled-over trees and bushes also fade into the water, but more disturbing are the barely visible rooftops, glistening just below the surface. Only the tips of a few homes crest above with rising air erupting around them. One spot in particular draws attention—close-up view shows volumes of popping bubbles—possibly, they represent a reason to be alarmed.

Just as troubling are the four lanes of cracked thoroughfare, further up the coastline, which simply disappear at water's edge. The broad divided highway seems to enter this huge lake with fascinating glide, yet the visible aspect is hard to comprehend. One worker walks across a section of the steep vanishing roadway while skimming the grounds with a testing device extended off a long shank. It seems he could slip and splash with one unsure step. Elsewhere, a few personnel scan the soil with similar devices while groups of two engage carrying elongated black zippered bags. The appearance brings an image horrifically familiar to human recovery. No other activity is present. Animals are not scurrying, cars are not driving and typical human endeavors are absent. Life as usual is gone.

Sounds of helicopters whirling nearby and overhead is prominent. Some are dissipating into the distance while others buzz closer. At times, cameras capture them hovering and lowering, trying to get closer to the bustle on the ground while others are shown skirting to another location or jockeying for better position. It is apparent that all are concerned with the terrain below. Each craft has a camera pointed downward with a crew gripped in fear or absolute sorrow and many have affiliation with news stations…their call letters' displayed on the sides. The noise below however is lacking, or at least not be perceived. Then, commentation joins the visual display and explains the alarming landscape spectacle.

"It's unbelievable, truly shocking…I'm at a loss for words," a restrained and doddering female voice crackles. A ruptured emotional state is hindering usual professional demeanor as she narrates with difficulty.

"That road down there is I-75—that's right," she chokes. "It completely evaporates into that…that miscreation. And those light brown shadows, they're the roofs of submerged homes but thousands more are no longer visible." The reporter's sentiments express distressed passion as she endures heartfelt explanation. "We are flying a few hundred feet above the ground, just east of Hillsborough Bay beyond the western outskirts of Tampa and we are... 'Oh my God...'", she fills with emotion, "witnessing absolute devastation on a level...I don't have words to describe."

After a heavy breath, she sighs, and vexes to continue.

"A massive sinkhole has swallowed a two mile stretch of the highway, both the north and south bound lanes. Along with it, portions of Highway 301, 60, I-4 to the North and others are gone too. So much land has disappeared that the bay now connects this new body of water directly to the ocean—and you can see it flowing. But that's not all."

Suddenly, the TV changes to a channel showing a close-up of body bag activity.

"No survivors found since Sunday," a male commentator informs. "They were taken to bio-shelters in Tallahassee and other states far from this forsaken place. Evacuation of nearly twelve million residents is underway, but it is slow going. Decontamination warehouses reached capacity days ago and northern Florida has become a chaotic gathering of lost humanity straining to escape."

The TV shows thousands of frenzied people rampaging on foot to move further north—all types of screaming unleashed.

"Around here though, you won't find a single native soul. Impact areas are desolate with only hazmat efforts in progress.

The channel changes again.

"It is estimated that six to eight million people have perished. The vacation haven is no more," a woman speaks with discord. "Could anything have saved them from the terrorism that caused this enormous sinkhole? For those that did get out, how long will they live? Radiation fallout has got to be off the scale."

Then the TV presents people suffering from open sores and thick layers of skin peeling off while coughing, choking and slowly dying.

The channel changes yet again.

"My parents were among them," a female cries, becoming distraught and unable to continue.

"We're sorry about that folks," a man's voice takes over while cameras continue scrolling. "Each of those dark bags has a deceased loved one in it, and it's hard to watch. Thousands of dead already transported to containment centers but millions will never be recovered, swept away by surging waters or blown to smithereens—probably both."

Briefly, the TV plays a similar scene elsewhere. Bags upon bags on top of more bags, mounding high and far, depicted in an isolated region. Large canvases stretch over other areas concealing thousands of placed bodies that did not receive the honor of a bag. Though arranged with care, the sight is disturbing, human characteristics perceived through the cloths, lifeless feet and hands sticking out of the sides.

"How many are left? We can only pray." The man continues as the channel changes once more –the same aircraft noises consuming the background of this station too.

"Journalists are still not allowed on the ground," a male commentator has trouble expressing. "Nuclear contamination levels have not yet been determined safe but as of our last update, they have fallen fast. The belief is that earth, rock and water soaked up much of the radiation before it entered the atmosphere— typical airburst fallout not generated. If there is a silver lining in any of this devastation, it may be that.

Okay, we are now flying over the Ocala National forest and for anyone who is familiar with it—the entire southern half of the preserve has become water. This is where the blasts began and where the Military's Pinecastle Impact Range used to be. Everyone in it is no more. The entire base and the land all around it have simply disappeared into the depths of the ocean." He pauses from grief. "I'm sorry folks, there's no other way I can say it. I'll move on… "

Lake George, once a relatively small body of water, that's it right there, is now the very tip of this massive new sinkhole. Earlier we showed you Lake Placid, the same one depicted in several movies. That was at the southern end of this beast. That means this gigantic body of water literally extends from Lake George all the way down to Lake Placid. That's a span of one-hundred and fifty miles people. And the width is a whopping eighty miles with an additional inlet protruding off the western side of it which leads into the Gulf of Mexico— another twenty mile stretch. I'm telling you, the sea now inhabits central Florida, a body of water in comparison only to one of the Great Lakes in the State of Michigan. I am not kidding! This hole is enormous."

The channel changes again.

"Lake Okeechobee looks like a five gallon bucket next to this monster; paling in comparison to this mammoth sink," a female voice professionally shrieks. "Many of you are grieving very badly right now I know…so I'll be gentle but I have to report the facts. I am hovering over what used to be the city of Orlando—at least I think this is where it was—hard to tell because there is only water for miles in every direction…nothing left."

She loses control and begins weeping, but maintains a proficient presence.

"This is very hard to watch. I understand that many of our listeners had friends, family and loved ones in these towns. I had relatives here too," she breaks down. "I'm sorry. I can barely keep it together—holding back the tears. I don't know how much longer I can keep my wits," the raspy voice continues, though noticeably difficult for her to do so.

"Apopka, Orlando, Deland, Sanford, Sebring, Frostproof, Plant City, Almonte Springs, Winter Haven, Lady Lake, the Villages, Kissimmee and St Cloud," she sobs to a pause and snivels—blowing her nose. "They are all gone…" she persists. "There is only water extending in every direction—where cities used to be…and there are many more yet to mention. Multiple towns and communities have vanished," she adds, trying to hold back intense anguish.

"Folks, I have just been told," she explains in cautionary tone. "We are going to increase our altitude so you can see the full extent of what I am talking about. We're simply going to ascend vertically."

As the helicopter rises, the view beneath them widens showing more and more area. The newscaster continues. "The new body of water extends north to south from Ocala all the way down to Sebring, and east to west from St. Johns National Wildlife Refuge to just a tad west of I-95—almost the entire width of Florida. The ocean current is literally flowing into Tampa Bay—swirling about in the middle of the state. Every street within a hundred miles dead-ends right into it this thing—broken homes around the edge, cracked in half rest on the shoreline. Hundreds of lakes have been swallowed…" she pauses and as the scene unfolds, it is clear that a huge body of water now encompasses a great portion of the State.

"Folks, this just in…I received word that NASA has recorded this epic collapse at over eight thousand square miles, slightly larger than Lake Ontario and some sources say it's just as bottomless too—possibly deeper than off-shore Gulf. They also confirm, 'everything within its border has been decimated. Every structure, all land and each county within its perimeter are no more.'

The channel changes yet again.

"Hello everyone, this is the latest from the Department of Homeland Security," an alarmed female anchor speaks, shown seated behind a station desk. "We are broadcasting to you live from Texas for those residing in Florida as…" she gets a little choked up. "Your local stations no longer exist. While complete details are not readily available, we have confirmed this. There was an attack on the State of Florida seven days ago, last Saturday morning. Roughly, a thousand nuclear bombs, planted within Florida's abundant aquifer system and concealed for years, began exploding repeatedly and successively one after another. Sustained detonations lasted nearly four solid hours—each blast the devastation of a small warhead. Survivors still being airlifted to Tallahassee and out of State, but I should mention, very few are left. An estimated seven million people instantly lost their lives, but we may not know the total effect of life-lost for months as millions more may soon succumb to radioactive contamination. If there is any good news though, and I just do not see how there could be…it seems radiation levels have dropped to tolerable levels. Nature's natural filtering process has already begun, but the earth and water still have many tests ahead. Whether or not this war zone can sustain life is yet to be determined. We simply don't know how habitable Florida is or will be and we will not know for months," she concludes as a colleague sitting next to her continues.

"Some cities around the outer limits are thankfully still intact," he begins. "These are the ones we're reporting on so far; Deltona, Summerfield (which are west of Lady Lake and the Villages), Clermont, Bartow, Bushnell, Dade City, Wauchula, parts of Tampa and a little place until this week no one knew existed, called Harmony. Harmony now sits on the southeastern edge of this massive lake. Check out this view from space…"

The TV shows the satellite image.

"It has a volume similar to Lake Erie and Ontario. Anyway, land rapidly fell into the water, but it stopped right at the outskirts of this little lucky city leaving it nestled and unharmed. It will be a long time before anyone can predict how Florida's real estate will be affected, and even longer before anyone cares. We will keep you updated as we get more details."

The channel changes again.

"Can you please stop watching that damn thing," Sheryl yells while entering the room, towel drying her hair. She walks past Richard who is simply fixated on the TV, sitting atop the foot of the bed with controller in hand. "They're already talking about property values and we're supposed to feel fortunate. I can't believe these jerks," she rants and briskly hurls a wet bath cloth at the wall.

Then, there is a knock at the door. Richard scoffs and reluctantly puts the tube on pause.

"Mr. Olson, we need to check you and your family one more time," a man's voice permeates from the other side of the egress, speaking in official tone.

"You people have probed and studied us a dozen times already," Richard stands and with three steps, he reaches and turns the knob to open the door—on the other side a man standing tall.

"We have to be sure, you understand," wielding firm hand gestures wearing typical agent attire he replies. "They'll be up in a few minutes," he informs and leaves.

Richard closes the door and rubs both hands across his face and through his scalp, concluding to a mild grunt.

"Was that them again," Sheryl hisses from the kitchenette around the corner, "NEST or whatever?"

"The Nuclear Emergency Response Team," Richard responds. "No, but they're on the way," he answers and returns to the TV, turning it back on.

"This is like the eighteenth time," Sheryl storms into the bed area.

"You sound annoyed."

"And you're not?" she scoffs, staring at him.

But he doesn't take his eyes off the television so she turns away with displeasure and starts pointing at things.

"And I hate this Hotel too and…and the damn ocean," she barks loudly, "All that water…I especially don't want to see that anymore. And you…" she stops in front of him again with a finger directed at his face. "I'm really sick of you sitting in front of that box. How can you keep watching—listening to that death? Eight days you haven't had enough. We almost died there—remember? Our family will never be the same," Sheryl vents, wildly gesturing both hands from the sides of her head.

The hotel phone rings. Richard answers it and listens.

"Okay, that's fine," he replies and hangs up.

"Who was that?" She sneers.

"Breakfast is on its way," he mutters with an aloof nod, still engrossed by the commenting reporters.

"Great, that will be the same freaking thing too?"

"It's your favorite—Bahamian food."

"Well, I can't eat…"

"You have to."

"People are dead Richard—millions, including all of our friends and co-workers—everyone we knew. Aren't you affected by that?" She speaks loudly, placing her face very close to his.

His eyesight meets hers, but otherwise remains unresponsive.

"Stone cold," she yelps and pulls away. "You're not the least bit upset."

"Of course I am," he drops the remote and stands, glaring at her, grabbing one of her hands, pulling her close. She doesn't resist and lets him draw her nearer. "But we were spared. There must be a reason," he calmly explains.

"Yeah, so we can suffer longer than everyone else," she sarcastically pouts, and breaks from his grasp to plop down at the top of the bed, curling into one of the fluffy pillows, partially hiding her face. One of her eyes remains looking at him with a precious glare, just piercing over the sheet like a little worried girl.

Richard enters the bed too, crawling closer. Hovering over her, he returns a heartening gaze of his own.

"We didn't get contaminated," he tells her with a reassuring voice.

"I'm sorry," she sighs. "I'm just not dealing with this as well as you."

"I know, I know," he lies beside and embraces her—nose-to-nose they lounge. He moves her hair away with a delicate swipe and smiles when seeing her pouty face.

"In all these years…you've never stopped looking at me that way," she presses the pillow corner down to expose her mouth. He can feel her pleasing breath carry past his lips, and looks down at hers. "Why?" she asks as they silently stare at one another.

He cuddles closer. Just then, a door creaks open.

"Dad, Mom," Jake and Jenny enter from an adjacent room and groggily make their presence known. Deliberately, they too lay on the bed.

"Was all this just a nightmare?" Jenny asks while placing her head on her mom's shoulder.

"No dear, I'm afraid not," Sheryl replies, using a comforting tone.

The brother crawls nearer as well. "Anyway, I'm glad you and dad still love each other," Jake expels while yawning, squeezing his body between his nestled parents forcing them to make room for the tired boy, who closes his eyes upon resting. "If that can happen?" he continues, "anything is possible."

Sheryl thinks about her kids and gets teary-eyed. She caresses Jenny's head—running her fingers through her daughter's hair and glances at hubby, offering a content grin. The kids drift to a quiet nap.

Forty-Three

The pleasing sound of Junkanoo melody plays, engulfing all areas of an Island tavern both inside and out. Locals and visitors alike merrily stroll and dance to it with drinks in hand. Lit tobacco products are being enjoyed everywhere, but an invigorating breeze carries the smoke away nicely leaving only a sweet scent behind. Servers greet patrons with smiles and kindness—food consumed. The sun is beginning to fade but partying and grooving to the music is alive and universal, everyone is happy—except Sheryl, who at the bar, is having trouble finishing her fruity beverage. At a festive Bahamian saloon a drinks sits in front of her. She sulks at the umbrella in a tall half-filled glass while slowly turning it, one-quarter inch at a time. Condensation drips down the side and collects on the napkin beneath, which is livelier than she is.

"Nut-ting like the sound of Calypso to get the soul into the right frame of mind, hey man," a cheery and optimistic man on the other side greets her with an enthusiastic native tongue.

"I'm a woman," Sheryl snips.

"Yes, I can certainly see dat," he smiles and wipes away the pool of water under her glass, and provides a fresh dry paper. "If da men looked like you I would be gay," he jokes.

She tries to be annoyed with him, but can't as he really is charming. She gives a delayed chuckle.

"Lighten up," he continues. "It could be worse. Could you imagine being one of those poor people caught up in that sinkhole calamity last week?"

Suddenly she slides her drink away and abruptly gets up.

"Yeah, I can envision that in ways you'll never comprehend," she spews and walks away.

"What did I say?" the startled bartender mumbles as he watches her depart.

Moments later, Sheryl enters her hotel room.

"Where have you been?" Richard harps in a pestering tone. "The President is about deliver a speech."

"I was hoping to miss it," she mocks. "But I don't feel any better being down there either."

"I spoke with Callahan," he says. "Everyone is waiting to hear what he has to say. They're all in their own rooms—we're not gathering as a group."

"I'm shocked," she lends attitude and then sits to watch.

The TV is on.

The President, shown in the Oval office sitting behind his desk rests his interlocked hands atop it. He stares directly into the camera.

"It is not easy for me to speak this evening to the people of this great nation, as we have lost so many within it," he begins with a solemn approach. "But I have no choice but to try and comfort the grieving millions whom are still suffering from this unthinkable tragedy. For starters, I want all of you to know...I will not stop until responsible parties receive due justice. I will not falter until they are behind bars."

Richard scoffs. "Jail...he's going to put them in prison. What a joke." Aloud he bursts as the President continues in an assertive and convincing tone.

"No one in this country should walk in fear, and you won't have to as long as I sit in this seat. I am gathering with my intelligence community and I will get the details of this egregious, unwarranted and heinous atrocity—a massacre on a profound scale. I want to know how this type of attack could get past the observatory skills of so many agencies. The same ones my administration depends on."

Already, at this early point in the speech Callahan, the lieutenant Governor and all the rest that were part of discussions preceding the disaster are shaking their heads about that outlandish statement. They know he knew, but they continue listening.

"Our surveillance structure and intrinsic abilities are designed to protect our citizens," The President explains. "Under my watch, I will not tolerate activity that punctures such holes into a system that I know can be executed without fail," with great poise, he delivers. "You deserve nothing less from your Commander-in-Chief so...at this time I am appointing an impartial board of moderators to investigate. I will find the flaws and fix them."

"You look in the mirror. There's the problem," Callahan mumbles from his room.

"My record speaks for itself," the President carries on, "and it's an aggressive one of protecting, abolishing extreme factions and harmonizing with necessary republics, unions and foreign nations to accomplish those safety oriented goals." He speaks of his believed prior undertakings with arrogant connotation.

"And terrorists...any mention of those guys," Sheryl hisses.

Then the President's tone becomes reproachful. "If I had known about this looming threat, I would have told this nation immediately and without delay. Transparency, among other things saves lives too. I would have stopped at nothing to thwart this threat."

"Oh my God, did he just say that?" Sheryl whines. "That's a blatant lie."

"I would have done everything in my power to give each of those that perished every available minute they had coming to them, but I simply didn't know. I did not have the information needed to make that call. Simply put, no one informed me…and for good reason. This violent and determined strike caught everyone by surprise."

"This just keeps getting better," Richard scoffs.

Callahan is perturbed too, coming unglued from his seat.

Everyone that witnessed the FBI disclose the merits of this forthcoming tragedy are at a loss for words.

As for the rest of the viewers in the Nation, they are watching with growing American resolve. Mesmerized faces everywhere glued to television sets, hinged on each word he utters. The President is increasing their morale and posture at a rate never seen.

"But this is not the time for that conversation," the President decides. "Right now we need to mourn and remember those we lost. Let us not forget the men, women and children of numerous nationalities…from of all walks of life— decent people that were taken too quickly from this world…and for no reason. We must remember their personalities, their dreams, their accomplishments and the feelings they instilled within us, 'the survivors'. Let us not forget the pride that built this nation or the spirit in which drives us to continue—to fight. No country before us can claim the nature of survival that America can. The challenges that our ancestors have overcome is nothing less than amazing—all whilst staring into the face of horrific adversity every step of the way. We have triumphed in wars and stood tall through every catastrophic event. It has never been easy but we Americans never gave up, and we are not going to stop now. Our achievements are not over—not even close. American dignity will only grow stronger. I promise you."

"Oh, this guy is good," Sheryl releases a liberating sigh while maintaining an insincere smile. "Who believes this crap?"

"You do," Richard replies.

"Well, I don't anymore," she adamantly assures.

Then the President stands, using influential hand gestures and body language to drive his philosophical crusade home—into the hearts of people falling all over themselves, his words penetrate. Citizens everywhere lift fists in support of the greatest President ever. "You get em," they shout in unison as their confidence in him grows.

"I suggest that the American spirit will emerge stronger than ever, to unite us all once again," he raises his voice to epitomize his meaning. "We will carry on with the same vigor and passion that our predecessors had, with the identical honor and integrity that they displayed. Our lineage will continue…I guarantee it," he delivers his opinion with great emotion. "I urge everyone to remember the freedoms that our peoples fought for, and how so many of them died trying to secure it. I say that we are the only populace who has brawled, scrapped and battled for such beliefs—not only for ourselves but also for so many helpless souls abroad. We promote and inspire goodness—we do that— not always getting it right but we persist until we discover a way to obtain that healthier place. We are inventers of successful methods—prospering and helping others to do the same—not just for a select few because of birthrights, financial stability or popularity. This isn't a country comprised of immaturity, irrational or puerility behavior. We promote freedom—encourage and praise it."

People in the streets are chanting his name as he delivers the words they want to hear.

"We are a nation of hope and have been since our inception," he continues more calmly. "I challenge you to remind me of another country that has executed more good deeds or made a greater sacrifice than ours—just to bring mere liberty and peace to so many and I offer up...none will ever do so in the future either."

Sitting down he continues dramatic dialogue. "Consider this, those of you listening to me right now. You did not concoct that feeling, that belief, the ultimate human right of independence. Like me, you were born into this sovereignty, but we continue to honor it by remembering the past and confessing that we will not lose sight of it—no matter where life takes us. Why do we recall history, with a passionate touch? Because it pushes us, more than anything else does. We will not stop moving onward—not as a nation, not as a country, not as a group or as an individual either. We will not give into tyranny, or to the growing criticisms that we are no longer the greatest country on earth...and I am telling you today...we are all that.

You don't need me to tell you this. In your heart, you already know it—no matter where you came from...I know you understand that this land means opportunity. The greater majority of you must believe in that...and the rest of you sense it as well. I feel you do. America means hope and freedom. It always has and that is why so many peoples want to settle here. Until this very day they do—they still will.

This land offers the greatest gift God gave to any nation and that my friends is true freedom. But let me take the time to say this," he changes to a scolding tone. "You are welcomed to raise your voice and hand against me—right here today if you like. I will not send an army after you, I will pray for you. You can shout at me—curse my name but again, that is permissible. If anyone wants to hate and mock the spirit bonding our peoples together, or labor to tear down the walls separating us from evil...then you have the God given right to do so. Better yet, I say you can," he hesitates while inhaling to make himself just a bit more prominent. Then he looks deep into the camera.

"You can spew any rhetoric you want. Try to rip apart the very fabric sheltering and protecting you from cruel regimes and the elements of despair which their methods foster," he smirks. "You can squander your time despising and loathing the factions urgently functioning and performing in unison to protect your liberties—that is your choice. And I promise I will protect your freedom to do that," he sighs. "But, I urge that you direct your anger elsewhere," he smiles. "Incomplete, unrefined and embryonic rampages excitedly and aimlessly fired at me will drag you further into misery. Ill-advised thoughts will destroy your autonomy," he relaxes. "I know you don't want that."

"As for the rest of us, we will fight and struggle for you anyway. I only ask one thing. While we concerned and involved peoples are holding hands, wrestling for this great country, praying in our groups or by ourselves— sacrificing our pride, blood, sweat and tears for this land...please let us do it. Sit back and watch if want—we will stand for you. Hide if you are fearful—that's okay...we are not. Run away if you must, we will not. Move out if you have to but we will stay and correct this terrible deed. If you need help acquiring mental fortitude...ask and I will be sure you receive it. But above all, let's stop this country from bleeding," he rests to take a breath.

Again, people around the country continue to bellow supportive gestures, or cry as if at the feet of Jesus himself—viewing a greatness never seen.

The President changes tone yet again to reflect the right mood for his words. "Today, we also must recognize those yet to be born...they will need to acquire the same feelings we have regarding this country. We have to get back on our feet," he bolsters. "And remembering gives us the power to do just that. It will not make us weaker. That's why today, I am giving this new body of water a name—following true Indian tradition."
"If you didn't know, most of the lakes, streams, rivers, ponds and land formations were first named by either the Seminole, Osceola, Miccosukee, Choctaw or Muscogee tribes...and there are others I didn't mention. America followed suit, naming many of our cities using their language. So today, I will do the same naming it...'Una Istokpoga', known as the Lake of Remembrance. From this day forward it will mean, 'Remember the many that died here,' because I say, 'We will not let their memory pass in vein. Today we remember, so tomorrow we can prevent further destruction. Remember, our people died there.' God bless their souls and ours," he concludes the address and the transmission ends.
Commentators reappear and Richard shuts the TV off.

Back at the Whitehouse, the President walks out of the Oval office taking to the hall. An advisor passes him saying, "ninety percent approval sir. Masses are in the streets, all backing you."
From afar, his wife gives him a thumbs up and smiles brilliantly.
Promptly, he enters a private room and closes the door. The Vice-President, who along with a few others, was eagerly waiting for him. They embrace, release and give each other a feisty high five while uttering an animated, "oh yeah."
"In the palm of my hands," the President energetically articulates, and confidently struts across the room to pour a drink, something strong on the

rocks. While mingling with the small group, he lights up a cigarette and receives great praise.

"That was the best speech you have ever given," the VP, mouths in complimentary fashion.

"It was good—that was great," others respond.

After a few minutes of celebration, the President brings order to the room.

"I need the FBI department head in my office, pronto," he directs to one man. He leaves to take action.

"Get me the CIA," to another he directs, "and Homeland," to a final one— they each leave.

"What's the next step?" The VP inquires.

The President turns to him and responds in haughty character.

"Destroy every document...what else? Convince everyone to keep their mouths shut and the ones who won't well..." he stops talking.

Then, after a disturbing delay, he pierces at the VP. "And then I get Florida's economy flowing."

"How does that happen? I understand the shredding part, but turning this disaster into...?" he questions the President's intent.

The President laughs. "You see there...you don't have vision Jo. Let me explain. First, seaports and harbors will pop up at key areas along...none other than 'Lake Una Istokpoga,' government built of course, and thereby controlled as such. Can you say more municipal jobs?"

"How's that possible?"

"Well, the land around it will be up for grabs, considered worthless for right now so we won't have to jump that high to secure it. We'll just push everyone else out of the way—anyone who contends for it. It is contaminated soil after all. But then we could also throw so much regulation at it that the only entity who can do anything with it is...uh...oh yeah us, the government," he laughs with a sincere zest.

"We do make the protocols," the Vice-President maintains. "And all of our constituents will be on board."

"Now you're thinking," the President points with a 'that-a-boy' gesture. Then he puffs his cigarette, putting it out in a nearby dish to swallow the rest of his whiskey and continues with his visionary perspective. "Direct access to the ocean—protected by land on all sides and space to grow. You can't beat that," he points a finger. "A new airport will be built right there...and agencies we haven't thought of yet will be implemented, and there will be a bridge required to cross—that alone will be a job creating wonder—imagine the potential."

The President gleams placing hands on hip. "That's just the start but eventually, people will thank me in mass numbers, future Presidents will regard me, and even the government will get a new and improved persona—because of me." He pours another drink.

"Sir," the VP asks while gradually turning the doorknob about to leave, seeming a bit confused or possibly lost in sober contemplation.

"Yeah, number two," he confidently responds as he chugs the new drink.

"It sounds like you were almost, I don't know...anticipating this whole thing."

The President just looks at him and says, "that'll be all."

Forty-Four

In a dimly lit room of an undisclosed location, a man quietly speaks. Only his silhouette shows against drawn shades, an outside light breaches the narrow slits enough to highlight his image. He is concerned, speaking into a phone with great secrecy, made obvious by his clutch—holding it close to his body, as if hiding the fact he is on the phone at all. He paces to the left and lifts a slat up, just a nip, to pierce outside. Cautiously, he shifts to the right edge of the window—peeking, as if expecting an unwanted guest. His movements are stealthy, just in case someone is trying to spot him. Confident there is no one watching, he crouches to assume a sneaky posture below the sill—his back sliding against the wall.

Out of sight, he lets his voice rise to put more passion into his words.
"Just remind them what happens to leakers," he advises with stern strike. "They won't be perceived as heroes—on the wrong side of the fence for that distinction. It will never happen. Tell them they are in danger," he stops to listen, and then shakes his head. "I can't make that promise," he utters with complete assurance. "Now remember…we never had this conversation and we won't have another. Do you understand?" he hangs up and looks above the windowsill, remaining vigilant.

Elsewhere, at the same moment, a man puts a receiver on its base and keeps his hand atop it, longer than normal as if lost in thought. Then he taps it a couple times with a middle finger. Simultaneously, another individual somewhere else slides a pair of headphones off his ears while sitting in front of a computer, surrounded by recorders and surveillance equipment. He begins typing a message, embodied with excerpts from the conversation that he just spied on— sends it off when done. At yet another location, someone else does the same— an NSA coffee mug sits beside the keyboard.

Alone in the white house the President sits behind the desk in the Oval Office. The facility and grounds inside and out are quiet, only the Protective Service personnel maintain active position, more than usual but that has been the case for years. He is relaxed in the Presidential chair with his chin resting on the back of his interlocked fingers, elbows propped, whilst staring at the headquarter phone. Suddenly, there is a call, but it was not on that phone. He reaches into his sweater pocket, removes a cheap cell phone, and merely listens. He covers it with an unusual gadget and says, "You know what to do," (His voice altered by the device). Then, he hangs up and stares with a cagy smirk, which becomes more exuberant very quickly. He takes a refreshing breath, removes a clean white handkerchief from his breast pocket, and begins to wipe the phone, leisurely but deliberately removing any fingerprints from it, both inside and out.

Later that week, a news report disclosed that an FBI operative gone rogue was dead from an apparent suicide hanging after killing another within his own department—two informants murdered as well. Authorities believe he had complete knowledge of the recent terrorist attack, but did nothing about it. Police say he may have been involved with the plot. Homeland is investigating—starting with the best lead they have—his prepaid cell phone found on him at the time of his demise—the list of its contacts being investigated.

Both Sheryl and Richard were watching TV when the story hit the airwaves. They were completely stunned, left staring at each other with utter loss. They merely clench each other's hand for comfort.

The End

SINK

About the Author

Photo by 'Jim McMahon'

Most people would agree that I have not accomplished much or risen to the pinnacle of prominence. Certainly, I have not become independently wealthy, traveled the world, experienced Hollywood fame, been the limelight of notoriety, held a career in the public eye, or attained a high paying profession. Rarely, have I been the center of attention, influenced groups of people or impressed my way up the corporate ladder, and never have I been the cornerstone of popularity or moved the masses with my vision. Illustrious people have not touted my worth nor celebrated my life. However, I have tried to make every day count to achieve objectives within my reach, including the groundwork for my children's future. I have plenty, in spite of what the populace believes is necessary for a grand life, and I am extremely gratified with one particular success. More importantly, she is proud of me. I have spent nearly all of my adult life with a woman who makes me whole and keeps my spirits unbroken. I have confidently walked in the ray of her appeal since we met and our marriage is the one triumph I have never questioned. Of course, we have had difficulty and trials of emotion along the way, but my heart fills with such joy merely being a spectacle in her life, there just is not enough room for those unhealthy memories. With her, I am significant, honorable and at the heart of her indisputable love and devotion, and no source of income or fame could make me feel more of a man. I am satisfied and content—will one day pass into the heavens knowing I have done well. In fact, I have flourished, fortunate to find my better half. Though I have not been a role model for Christianity, God placed her in my life anyway and I have repeatedly thanked him for that.

I seldom prayed aloud, but somehow He knew what I needed and delivered me an enduring companion—three pleasant and worthy sons thereafter. It is true that most of the plans, hopes, and dreams I made in my youth are vastly different from what actually transpired, strangely, they ended up being rewarding, meaningful, and what I wanted after all. To the world, we are a regular family but to my wife and me we are exceptional. No doubt, God feels the same. Yet I have one unfinished desire—put my imagination on paper for the world to see. I believe everyone has a story to tell…many would like to live through the words.